DISTRESSED

DAVID EVANS

**ORCHARD
VIEW
PUBLICATIONS**

ISBN-13: 978 1 9996 106 6 1

ABOUT THE AUTHOR

Born and brought up in and around Edinburgh, David Evans graduated from Manchester University and had a successful career as a professional in the construction industry before turning to crime … fiction that is and writing thereof.

DISTRESSED is the second novel in The Tendring Series set around north Essex in the late 1970s. The first, *DISPOSAL,* was published in 2018.

His Internationally Best Selling Wakefield Series is also available and consists of:
TROPHIES, the first in the series
TORMENT, the second, was shortlisted in 2013 for the CWA Debut Dagger Award.
TALISMAN is the third
TAINTED is book four
All are available in ebook and paperback formats.

Find out more by visiting David's website at
www.davidevanswriter.co.uk
or follow him on Facebook at
www.facebook.com/davidevanswriter
and Twitter @DavidEwriter

DAVID EVANS

ACKNOWLEDGMENTS

I have been privileged to meet some amazing people, without whose help, encouragement, support and above all friendship got me through some occasions when it would have been easier to walk away and do something else with my time.

First and foremost, I have to say a huge thank-you to Sally Spedding who was the first in the publishing industry to take my writing seriously. I owe her a great debt for all her continued support and encouragement.

I am also fortunate to have a great little band of writing friends and I would like to thank Sarah Wagstaff, Jan Beresford, Julie-Ann Corrigan, Manda Hughes, Glynis Smy and Peter Best, all of whom are talented writers in their own right and have made some significant contributions.

I am deeply grateful for the input of Colin Steele, ex-Detective Superintendent of the Essex Murder Squad and Steve Eastwood, ex-DCI of the City of London Police who began his career in Clacton. Also Tom Harper, ex-Principal Crime Scene Coordinator for the Kent & Essex Serious Crime Directorate. Both have given their time and guidance generously. Any residual errors here, are all mine.

Finally, a huge thank-you to the various bloggers and readers who have supported both of my crime series over the past few years. Without readers, there would be no reason to write.

*For all the writers who have inspired me
but are sadly no longer with us.*

DISTRESSED

David Evans

1

Monday 7ᵗʰ March 1977

Something was wrong; seriously wrong. Betty's rings on the doorbell had been ignored three times. Struggling to bend down to letterbox level, she pushed it open.

"Sharon! Is everything okay?" she shouted.

With no response, she straightened up and stepped to the side of the front door to peer through the living room window, hands cupped over her eyes against the glass. The curtains were drawn but there was a slight gap. Inside, a lit lamp provided some illumination. Squinting one way then the other, she spotted the upturned coffee table. She had a bad feeling about this.

Betty had known Sharon for four years, ever since the younger woman had come to work for Baldwin's. Betty had worked there since the war, part of the furniture some of her work colleagues joked. As it was, she had been kept on past retirement age. For some reason, she felt protective instincts towards Sharon, something maternal perhaps. She'd admired her spirit. And despite enjoying life to the full, Sharon was a reliable work colleague. And so, when she'd failed to turn up for work that morning, Betty decided to call round in her lunch break to see if her friend was okay.

This really wasn't right; it was one in the afternoon; the curtains should be open and the lights off.

She walked to the side of the terraced house and opened the wrought iron gate guarding the passageway between her friend's house and the identical property next door. A cat meowed as she walked forward. She paused and looked down at the animal before walking down the passage to the rear of the house. The cat followed, brushing itself around her ankles.

9

Making her way around the dustbin that stood by the side of the back door, she paused. No, she didn't like the look of this one bit. The half-glazed door wasn't quite shut. It was as though someone had made a hurried exit and hadn't checked that the lock had caught. She pushed on it gently. It swung open. Suddenly the cat shot off towards the next door garden, making Betty jump.

Moving forward to the kitchen doorway, she called out once more. "Sharon? Sharon, are you in there?"

Silence.

"Are you okay?"

She took a step inside onto the linoleum floor. There were plates and mugs in the sink and a tap dripped into the washing up bowl. On the wall a clock slowly ticked, out of sync with the tap. Everything else was quiet.

"Sharon?" Betty repeated. "Can I come in?"

Again, no response.

She slipped past the empty cooker and the humming fridge and made for the hall door. Nervously placing her hand on the handle, she listened. Finally, she pushed the door open. All was quiet; too quiet.

One stride more and she could see through the open doorway into the living room. She stood still and took in the details. An easy chair faced towards a television sitting on a unit, a cigarette lighter lying on the chair arm. Another step and she peered behind the door. A lamp on a low table by the side of the settee was still lit but the coffee table in front of the hearth was tipped over, two wine glasses lying on the carpet and a discarded red slingback alongside.

She returned to the hall and paused at the foot of the stairs. The shoe's partner lay on the first step. "Sharon! Are you up there?"

Again, no reply.

Slowly, one step at a time, she made her way up the stairs. Half way up a loud creak made her stop. Her breathing was faster now; too fast for a woman of her age, she thought. She moved her foot and the step creaked again. With a deep breath, she composed herself and continued her climb.

At the top of the stairs, directly in front, the bathroom door was ajar. She headed for that but before she reached it, something caught her eye through the crack between the bedroom door and its frame off to her left.

Changing course, she nervously stepped into the bedroom and gasped. Lying on the unmade bed behind the door was the twisted form of her friend. Dirty blonde hair half covered her face but Betty was in no doubt Sharon was dead. The eyes were open, staring at a point on the ceiling and the skin was white. Her black dress had been pulled up to her waist revealing the naked pubic triangle.

Betty shuddered. Her hand went to her mouth. "Oh God, Sharon," she said softly, "What's happened to you?"

Slowly she leaned forward, gripped the bottom of Sharon's dress and gently pulled it back down to give her friend some dignity. Tears fell down her cheeks as she turned and hurried her way back down the stairs.

2

"Cyril, with me," Detective Chief Inspector Martin Sanderson shouted through the open door of the CID office. He disappeared from view, heading for the stairs.

Detective Sergeant Cyril Claydon was already on his feet, dragging his jacket from the back of his chair. He'd decided to accept the move into CID following an adventure last year that saw him become embroiled in murder investigations, an airplane accident as well as a life-threatening situation for himself on the Harwich to Hook Of Holland ferry. Up until that point he'd been looking forward to a quiet retirement after twenty-five years' service. Fifty years old and still fit, he considered the prospect of working his allotment and walking his dog no longer held appeal on their own, and so he had decided to extend his career for another five years.

DC Bill Walker looked up from studying an open file on his desk and across at his colleague. Cyril shrugged and, picking his coat off the stand, followed his boss.

"What's up?" Cyril asked as he tried to catch up with his DCI on the way down the staircase.

"I'll explain as we go," Sanderson said over his shoulder, hurrying on and bustling his way out through the double doors of Clacton's Jackson Road Police Station and into the fresh sea air.

Martin Sanderson had eased his six foot three inch frame into the driver's seat of the Rover by the time Cyril had opened the passenger door. Sanderson was, as always, smartly dressed in a suit and crisp white shirt and tie. Cyril would describe him as a clothes-horse. At forty-seven, he still had a full head of hair which was now sprinkled salt and pepper. Turning first one way then the other to check all was clear, he reversed the car from the space. Cyril, sitting alongside him, clipped his seat belt in position. It was a habit he'd adopted since all new cars had them fitted and was borne out of his RAF service.

Finally under way, Sanderson explained, "A woman's body has been found in the upstairs bedroom of her house."

"Suspicious?"

The DCI turned to look at Cyril and raised an eyebrow, as if to say, would he be in such a rush if it wasn't? "Found by a work colleague when she didn't turn up for work this morning," he added.

It was only a ten minute drive to the property on a road tucked away on the far side of Clacton railway station. A patrol car was sitting outside a group of four terraced houses on a quiet street. As they pulled up, Cyril recognised PC Sam Woodbridge stepping out from the driver's seat of the marked car. Another young constable appeared from the passenger side.

Sam Woodbridge was twenty-five and enjoying his role with the police. Cyril had worked with Sam when he was in uniform. He liked the lad and thought him intelligent with plenty of promise. His quick thinking had saved Cyril from an awkward situation last year and had been one of the reasons he'd continued with his police career.

"Sir. Skip," Woodbridge said in greeting to the CID men.

"Hello Sam," Cyril replied.

Woodbridge indicated the other officer. "And this is PC Hayes. Ken is a probationer at the moment," he explained.

"You got this one then?" Cyril said, buttoning up his coat.

"What *have* we got, constable?" Sanderson was keen to make progress.

Woodbridge opened his notebook. "Sharon Williams didn't turn up for work this morning. That was unusual, so her work colleague, a Mrs Betty Hunt ..." He turned and waved an arm towards the elderly lady sitting in the patrol car. "She came here to check about thirty minutes ago. When she couldn't get an answer, she tried round the back and found the door unsecured. She entered and discovered Miss Williams' body in an upstairs bedroom."

"Thanks … PC Woodbridge, is it?"

"Yes sir."

"Have you checked inside yourself?" Sanderson nodded to the house.

"I did. With gloves on," he added quickly. "And it's as she reported."

"Well thanks for that. Can you sit with Mrs Hunt for now; we'll need to speak to her shortly. And PC Hayes, if you'd make sure no one else enters the property."

Sanderson led the way down the passage between the houses and round to the back door. Cyril followed.

The door was wide open following Betty's hurried exit. Sanderson had a quick look at the door and frame. "No signs of a forced entry," he said, stepping inside.

Through the kitchen to the hall, Cyril followed his boss and looked in the living room whilst Sanderson headed straight upstairs.

Cyril stroked his thin moustache and took in the scene; the coffee table on its side, the wine glasses on the carpet and the lit lamp on the low table behind the door. Signs of a disturbance at least. The two-seater settee had depressions where people would normally sit but there was something else that caught his eye. Part tucked down the side of the arm was something lacy; underwear, if he wasn't mistaken.

"Cyril! Up here!" came shouts from Sanderson.

Cyril left the room and climbed the stairs to the small landing and joined the DCI in the bedroom.

"This, I assume, is Sharon Williams," Sanderson said, looking sadly at the body sprawled on the bed.

Cyril slowly studied the corpse, then turned away, hands in his pockets.

Sanderson followed him out of the room. "I'll radio in for forensics and get the full team down here," he said. "Cyril, can you get an initial statement from the old girl?"

Thankfully, Sam Woodbridge's patrol vehicle was a marked Ford Escort, an improvement on the Austin Mini he'd had before. Betty sat in the rear front passenger seat dabbing her eyes with a tissue. Being a two-door model, made it impractical to have her climb into the back. Cyril walked round the car, opened the offside door and sat in beside her.

"I'm Detective Sergeant Claydon," he began. "I'm really sorry about your friend, Mrs Hunt."

"Betty, call me Betty," she said. "Everybody does."

He looked at the woman again and thought she looked familiar. "Betty, you don't know a lady by the name of Doris Appleby, do you?"

She stopped her activities with the tissue and looked at him. "Doris, yes. She's my friend."

"I thought so. I'm Cyril Claydon. Doris is my next door neighbour."

She brightened up. "Oh, you're Cyril? She talks about you a lot. I thought your name was familiar." A forlorn expression returned. "I'm sorry about your wife. Doris told me."

"Thanks," Cyril said quickly, then flipped open his notebook, not wishing to engage in a conversation about his late wife, Maureen. Within the past few months he had begun to get over the loss of his wife three years ago to cancer. "So what can you tell me about Sharon?" he asked.

The tissue returned to her nose as she spoke. "I've known Sharon for … ooh, about four years, ever since she came to work at Baldwin Engineering." She looked up at Cyril. "Oh God, they'll need to know what's happened. And they'll be wondering where I am."

"Don't worry, Betty. We'll sort all that." Cyril smiled at her. "So, you'd known Sharon quite well?"

"Yes. She works in the office. I think she was trying to make a fresh start up here. She told me she'd worked for an insurance company in Southend. She was married at one point. But she'd divorced Ray after she discovered he was unfaithful."

Cyril was writing notes. "What sort of divorce was that? I mean, was it all amicable?"

"I think it was a little bit difficult in the beginning. That's why she moved to Clacton; I think she wanted to put a bit of distance between them."

"Had this Ray ever visited her here, do you know?"

"Once, I think. A couple of years ago but Sharon told me he'd moved on with his life. I'm sure she said he'd found someone else down in Southend, and not the woman she'd caught him with either." She gave a scornful look.

Cyril paused with his notes and looked at her. "So is he Ray Williams, or …"

"Williams is Sharon's maiden name. Her married name was Hadleigh, she once told me."

Sanderson approached the driver's door and Cyril wound down the window. He introduced his boss. "Betty is giving me some useful background information, sir," he explained. "She and Miss Williams work at Baldwin Engineering."

Sanderson leaned in. "Thank you, Betty. Anything you can tell us, however insignificant you might think it is, could be valuable." Sanderson's attention was taken by the arrival of two white vans. "Excuse me," he said, "I need to deal with this. The doctor should be here anytime soon as well." He straightened up and walked off to speak to the forensics officers.

Cyril wound up the window and continued the conversation. "Who is Sharon's boss at Baldwin's? Who would I need to speak with?"

"Well, Mrs Whitaker is the office manager and Mr Baldwin runs the company, so either or both of them." Betty became agitated. "But I'll need to get back. I was only on my lunch break and that ended twenty minutes ago."

"Don't concern yourself with that, Betty." Cyril put a hand on her arm. "I don't think you should return today. We'll inform your bosses and I'll get PC Woodbridge to give you a lift home."

"It's just ... well I don't like ... I mean, I've never had a day sick in my life. I don't want Mr Baldwin to think..." Betty flustered.

"I'll explain," Cyril interrupted. "Now, just a few more questions for now ...when was the last time you saw Sharon?"

"Friday, when we left work. That would be just after five."

"And did she say anything about plans for the weekend?"

"Not really."

"And was Sharon close friends with anyone, do you know? Any man friend or a girl friend at work or outside of work?"

Betty furrowed her brows in thought. "There's Karyn. That's Karyn with a Y," she said mockingly. "She often goes on nights out with her."

"You don't approve of this Karyn?"

"I don't know her, only what Sharon tells me, what they get up to."

Cyril paused in his note-taking and looked over at Betty. "And does she work at Baldwin's?"

"No, I think she works for a travel agent in town. I can't think which one."

"Can you remember a surname?"

Another frown of concentration before her eyes widened. "Brown, I think."

"Well, thanks, Betty. You've been most helpful."

"Oh, there is one more thing I need to tell you," Betty said. "I had to do it, I'm sorry."

Cyril was puzzled. "What is it?"

"When I walked into the bedroom, Sharon was ..." Betty pulled a fresh tissue from her handbag. "She was ... exposed, if you know what I mean."

"I think so. So what did you do?"

"I just folded her dress back down so she was covered. A bit of dignity, if you follow?"

Cyril nodded. "But you didn't touch anything else?"

Betty thought for a second. "Well, only the door handles when I walked in and then when I looked in the living room. But I didn't touch anything else. It was weird but I just knew something wasn't right."

"Thanks for telling me that. We'll probably have to take your fingerprints, just for elimination. We'll be in touch to sort that out. And like I said, I'll get young Sam there to drop you off and we'll be in touch."

When Cyril caught up with Sanderson, the duty doctor was about to leave.

"I would give an initial estimate of between twenty-four and forty-eight hours," the doctor was saying. "But the pathologist will be able to tell you more when he gets her back to the mortuary."

"Okay thanks, doctor," Sanderson said, but his expression revealed his frustration.

As the doctor was talking, Cyril was filling his pipe with tobacco before lighting up. "So not really any further forwards then," he said. "We don't know if she died Friday night Saturday morning or Saturday night, Sunday morning."

"Exactly. Look, I've got Walker and Miller coming down with some uniforms. They can start some house to house. See if that throws up any sightings of her over the weekend. In the meantime, let's get ourselves over to Baldwin's and see what they can tell us."

"What about the DI, sir?" Cyril wondered, referring to Detective Inspector John Barton.

"Dick's on annual leave until Wednesday, but I'll see if I can get in touch." Sanderson used Barton's nickname. It had been an obvious choice after the radio series of the nineteen-fifties. "You're right, we'll need all hands for this one," he said.

3

John Barton became aware of his splitting headache just before he struggled to open one eye. Closing it again, he decided he'd have another five minutes. The headache had other ideas. Turning over onto his back he finally managed to open both eyes. The ceiling grew closer for a minute, spun slightly then moved back to its proper place. He pushed himself up on one elbow and looked over at the clock. Gone eleven.

At least he was in his own bed, he thought. Moving his arm across the mattress, he confirmed that he was actually on his own. But was he last night? He couldn't remember. Where had he been? He remembered a couple of pints in the Madena first of all, then onto a few more before a club. But which one?

Time for a pee. He sat up and swung his legs over the side of the bed. A wave of wooziness swept over him. He waited until it passed then made his way to the bathroom. Relieving himself he caught his reflection in the mirror. Depression seized him. Thirty-seventh birthday coming up, he looked and felt like ten years further on. He ran his hand up his forehead and over his scalp. Mousy brown hair, but was it thinning? He turned round and sat on the toilet seat, rubbing his eyes. Through the open door he could see the small hallway of his one bedroom flat. Had he really made such a mess of his life? Career-wise, things were going okay. As a Detective Inspector based at Clacton Police Station, he had the full support of his boss, DCI Sanderson. Some of his team thought he was a bit abrasive, he knew that. He smiled at the memory of telling his DS, Cyril Claydon, last year that most people thought he was an obnoxious arrogant twat. Cyril hadn't argued. Through circumstances, Cyril had been foisted on him. He baulked at that at first but, over time, he'd grown to like and respect the man. Definitely old school but he had some valuable qualities. He also hoped Cyril saw some qualities in him.

His personal life was a different matter. Divorced nearly two years now; his fault; he always had the straying gene. Finally, Alison had had enough. And now, where was he? Renting some crappy flat in Clacton, getting pissed up and pulling any old tart back for a bunk-up. There's got to be more to life than this? But how many times had he resolved to do something about it? The last time was probably about six months ago, just after the warehouse incident. He'd even cleaned up the place properly. But that didn't last long, a couple of weeks at most before the lure of a few beers and a female body became too strong.

"Christ," he said out loud to himself and slapped his face with both hands. "Come on, shape up."

He stood and removed a packet of aspirin from the medicine cupboard then made his way to the kitchen. Putting the kettle on, he checked the cupboard for a mug; the last clean one. He put in a tea bag. And then the thought hit him; opening the fridge; no milk.

"Bugger," he muttered.

Settling for a black coffee, he wandered back through to the bedroom. Picking up the packet of Peter Stuyvesant from the bedside table, he pulled the last one free and lit up. Screwing up the empty packet, he lay back down on the bed and made mental notes of all the things he needed to do. A laundrette visit was top of the list. He must be running out of clean clothes by now. He took a swig of his coffee. And milk, he must get some milk. He'd make a list later. In the meantime, he'd close his eyes; give the aspirin time to work.

The insistent ring of the phone brought him back to consciousness.

4

The premises of The Baldwin Engineering Company occupied a large plot on an industrial estate that had once been railway property near the station. Evidence of its core business could be seen in the yard next to the offices; steel columns and beams and other pieces of fabricated metalwork, like some giant Meccano set, lay on the concrete slab; other parts were being loaded onto a flatbed lorry.

Within five minutes, Cyril and Sanderson were seated in Peter Baldwin's office opposite the man himself who told them he had taken over the running of the company from his father five years before. Baldwin looked to be in his early fifties with short dark hair surrounding a bald pate and wearing rimless glasses. Also sitting round the table was Carol Whitaker, a short, plump woman in her late forties with shoulder length dark permed hair who was introduced as his office manager.

They waited until a young woman had brought in a tray of tea and departed before Sanderson spoke.

"I'm sorry to have to bring you tragic news," he began, "but we believe one of your employees, Sharon Williams has been found dead this morning."

Mrs Whitaker brought a hand up to her mouth. "Oh God. How? I mean, if you're here, was it an accident?"

"We don't think so but we'll know more following a post-mortem," Sanderson replied.

Baldwin removed his glasses and rubbed his eyes. "This is awful," he said before replacing them. "You'll need to see her personnel file, no doubt?"

"That would be useful, Mr Baldwin. We will need to ascertain the next of kin."

"Of course. Carol here can arrange that for you." Baldwin indicated the woman sitting with them.

Mrs Whitaker stood as if to comply but Sanderson raised a hand to stop her. "In the meantime," he went on, "I'd be obliged if you kept this conversation to yourselves for now, until we can establish the facts."

"There is one other thing," Cyril put in, "Mrs Hunt, Betty …"

"Yes, she was here this morning," Mrs Whitaker resumed her seat. "But I haven't …"

"It was Mrs Hunt who discovered Miss Williams," Cyril said.

The woman put both hands to her mouth this time, a shocked expression on her face.

"And, as you can imagine, she was quite upset," Cyril continued, "so we've arranged for her to be taken home. She was at pains for me to let you know."

"That must have been terrible for her. I did wonder why she hadn't come back after lunch. She is usually very reliable," Mrs Whitaker said.

"I gather Mrs Hunt was a friend of Sharon's," Sanderson joined in.

"They are close at work, in a mother daughter sort of way."

"Did Miss Williams have any other close friends here, do you know?"

The office manager frowned. "Not especially close. She enjoyed her work and was popular with the others, joined in the banter, that sort of thing. But I think, apart from Betty, her friends were outside of work."

"Any men friends you ever heard her mention?"

Carol Whitaker coloured slightly and looked down into her lap.

"Mrs Whitaker?" Sanderson persisted.

"Well, no …" She finally looked up. "It's just overheard snippets of conversation I hear from time to time."

"Go on."

"I don't think Sharon had any man friend in particular, it's just … well, let's say, I think she enjoyed life to the full." Carol Whitaker seemed to gain inner strength. "And since her divorce, who can blame her."

"What exactly are you saying, Mrs Whitaker?"

"Only that she often used to frequent the nightlife in town. I've heard her tell Betty that she'd had ... encounters sometimes."

"With men, you mean?"

"Look I don't want to imply ..."

This time Sanderson held up an apologetic hand. "That's okay, Mrs Whitaker. We're only trying to build a picture. Now, did she ever mention names of any friends outside of this place?"

"She's mentioned one or two over the years but the only one I can remember now is someone called Karyn. I think she went on nights out with her fairly often."

Sanderson looked to Cyril then back to the office manager. "Well thanks for that." He stood up. "Now if you could let me have Miss Williams' file, we'll let you get on." He looked to Peter Baldwin. "I'll get it back to you as soon as we can."

Baldwin, who had remained silent for most of the meeting shook his head and waved his hand. "No problem, Chief Inspector, only when you've done with it. I'm sure Carol has a copy of the important information we'll need elsewhere."

Back at the car, Cyril asked to be dropped off in town as Sanderson drove back to the station.

"I may as well make a start on locating Karyn Brown," he said.

5

After several fruitless attempts, Cyril finally found the small independent travel agent on Pier Avenue where Karyn Brown worked. He noticed the name on her badge, spelt in the distinctive fashion, as she approached him when he entered the shop.

"Can I help you sir?" she asked. "The summer brochures are all here now." She waved an arm in the direction of a bank of shelves along one wall.

"Thanks, but I'm not here for holidays, Karyn," Cyril said, discretely showing her his warrant card.

A puzzled look on her face developed into a worried one. "Is everything okay?" she asked.

Fortunately, in the late afternoon, the shop was empty.

"Do you know a Sharon Williams?"

"Sharon? Yes, of course. Why? What's happened?"

"Shall we sit down?" Cyril indicated seats at a nearby desk. "I'm afraid I have some bad news."

The shop sign had been turned to 'Closed' and Karyn sat dabbing her eyes with a paper tissue as Cyril gave her the briefest of details about her friend.

"So what happened to her?" she asked through sobs.

"We're still investigating the circumstances," Cyril responded. "But you were close friends?"

Karyn looked up at him. "But we were only together on Saturday night. We'd go out at weekends, have a few drinks, meet people. We're both divorced and we enjoy our freedom." She sniffed and wiped her nose. "I mean 'enjoyed' ourselves." Her face contorted again. "We won't be doing that again now, will we?" She collapsed into heavy weeping.

Cyril stood and walked to the back of the shop. Looking behind a screen he spotted a sink, kettle and a fridge. "I think we could do with a drink," he said.

"I'm sorry I have to ask these questions, Karyn," Cyril said as they sat at the desk a few minutes later, she with a black coffee with three sugars, he with a white tea. "You said you last saw Sharon on Saturday night?"

"That's right. We'd been in town around a couple of pubs and finally hit Mama's Nightclub in Rosemary Road." She wiped her eyes, discarded one tissue in a bin and drew a fresh one from the pack in her handbag. "Maybe about twelve."

"And how long did you stay there?"

"Well ..." The woman hesitated and looked away.

"Something wrong?"

"I ... I didn't stay. I went off with someone. Sharon ... she was still there talking to some bloke." She sipped her coffee. "I think she'd seen him before. I think he'd bought her a drink. I thought ..."

"So when you left the club, Sharon was still there."

"Yes."

"And what time was that?"

"I dunno, maybe about one." Suddenly she became defensive. "Look, that's what we'd do. Sometimes we'd leave at different times with different people. It was no big deal."

Cyril swigged his tea. "I'm not saying it is," Cyril said quietly. "I'm not judging, I'm just trying to establish facts."

She subsided and hunched over the desk. "Sorry," she said. "I didn't mean ..."

"That's okay, Karyn." Cyril paused to let the woman compose herself. "Now, do you think you'd recognise this man again?"

She shrugged. "Possibly."

"What I'd like you to do, if it's alright with you, is for you to come across to the station and give us a formal statement. Then we can get a description of this man, possibly show you some photographs and see if you recognise him."

She nodded. "When? Do you want me to do that now?"

"Well, yes, if that's okay. What about the shop?"

"I can lock up early. It's not as if they've been battering down the door as it is. Besides, I don't think I could face anyone right now." She stood. "I'll just tidy myself up and get my things. I must look a right mess."

"Take your time."

6

Sanderson picked up the telephone, dialled a number and waited. Eventually, after seven rings, it was answered.

"Barton," came the irritated reply.

"Dick, I know it's your day off but I need you into the station if you can manage it. As soon as you can."

"Why, what's up?"

"We've got a murder investigation."

"Give me half an hour." The line went dead.

Sanderson flipped open Sharon Williams' personnel file and took in the basic details. Born in Billericay on 27th July 1924, which would make her fifty-two. Address given as where she was discovered. Marital status: divorced. She'd commenced employment at Baldwin's on 1st February 1972.

He was interrupted by the phone ringing. "Sanderson," he answered.

Five minutes later, he was studying the brief notes he'd scribbled during his call from the mortuary. From an initial study, the cause of death was likely to be strangulation; the full PM was scheduled for nine the following morning.

A knock on his office door caused him to look up and see DC Ben Miller looking at him through the glass, a stony expression on his face. Sanderson beckoned him in.

Miller stepped in and closed the door behind him. "Sir, I think we have a problem," he said.

"How so, Ben?"

From an envelope he'd brought with him, Miller carefully retrieved a leather wallet, handling it with his handkerchief, laid it on the desk and opened it.

Sanderson leaned forward and looked at it closely, brows furrowed. "Where did you get this?" he asked.

"Retrieved from the side of the settee in Sharon Williams' sitting room, sir."

"Shit," Sanderson said quietly before looking up at the DC. "Who else knows about this?"

"I was there when one of the forensics boys found it. I told him to keep quiet until I'd seen you."

Sanderson stood, walked to the window, turned and leaned against the sill, looking grim. "Well we can't keep this under wraps. It'll need to be logged officially and checked for prints."

"Do we know where the DI is, sir?" Miller asked.

"On his way in now. I'll talk to him but, in the meantime, this is just between the two of us … and your forensics colleague."

* * *

Barton skipped up the three steps and into Jackson Road Police Station.

"Thought you were on days off, Dick?" The desk sergeant grinned.

"Can't do without me, Frank, you know how it is," he quipped as he swept in through the double doors and up the stairs. After months of boring shoplifting, casual assaults and a few burglary cases, Barton was excited at the prospect of something he could get his teeth into. Not since the events on the Harwich ferry and the Colchester warehouse incident last year had he been involved in anything remotely interesting. He only hoped this wasn't an open and shut case. But there was something he had to check on first.

In the CID office, the only officer present was Miller, sitting at his desk sifting through some papers. Barton breezed past. "We've got something decent, I hear?" he commented, opening his office door.

Miller looked up. "Have you seen the DCI, sir?"

Barton was shuffling some files on his desk. "Just need to find something first, Ben," he said through the open door. He began frantically opening and closing drawers in his desk. "Shit," he said. Next, he checked the two filing cabinets against the side wall.

The phone on his desk rang and he snatched it up.

"Barton." A brief pause then, "Straight away."

Miller watched his DI storm out through the CID office and disappear into the corridor.

"Ah, Dick. Come in. Sit down," Sanderson greeted in response to Barton's knock. "And close the door," he instructed.

Barton nervously did as bid and sat in the seat opposite the DCI. He fidgeted slightly. "So what have we got, sir?" he asked.

"In a minute, Dick. There's something I want to talk to you about first."

Barton was unnerved by the serious look on his boss's face. "Is there something wrong?"

"Can you show me your warrant card?"

Barton felt the colour rise in his cheeks. "Ah well … you see …" he struggled, then, "Have you found it?"

"So you've discovered it's missing?"

"Only when I put on my jacket to come in here now, sir. I thought I might have left it in the office. I was looking for it when you called."

Sanderson opened a drawer and carefully pulled out the envelope Miller had brought in less than half an hour before. He slid Barton's warrant card wallet out onto the desk.

"Oh, you've found it, that's great." Barton went to pick it up.

Sanderson quickly covered it with the envelope. "Hold on, Dick. Do you know where this was found?"

Barton looked puzzled. "No. Somewhere in the station I presume?"

Sanderson carefully replaced the wallet in the envelope and put it back in his drawer.

"What's going on?" Barton asked.

Sanderson pulled out Sharon Williams' personnel file from the drawer, opened it and turned her photo towards the DI. "Do you recognise this woman?"

Barton looked closely at the black and white image. "I don't think so," he said slowly. "Who is she?"

"This is our murder victim. Sharon Williams, found dead by a work colleague at lunch-time today."

Barton still looked puzzled. "Do we know how she died?"

"Initial findings suggest she was strangled, but ..." Sanderson paused and leaned forward on his desk. "The thing is John, we have a problem."

The DCI's use of his proper name rather than his nickname wasn't lost on Barton. "What's going on, sir?" he asked.

Sanderson looked straight at Barton. "Can you explain why your warrant card was found in the home of our murder victim earlier today?"

The colour visibly drained from Barton's cheeks. "Jesus ... you couldn't have ... it's impossible. Christ, I have no idea."

"You'll need to come up with something a bit more convincing than that."

"But I don't understand."

Sanderson let out an exasperated lungful of air. "I called you in because I needed you to get involved in this case, only I can't let you anywhere near that now."

"But ..."

"You're on leave anyway until Wednesday."

"You can't think I had anything to do with this, surely?"

"Doesn't matter what I think, John." Sanderson stood up, walked to the window and looked out. "Christ, how could you let yourself be compromised in this way?"

Barton shook his head.

Sanderson turned round to face the DI. "Where were you between Saturday night and Sunday morning anyway?"

"I …" Barton puffed out his cheeks. "I had a few drinks around town. I can't remember exactly where."

"Well you better bloody had. And be able to prove it too."

"Come on Martin, how long have we known one another?"

"That's not going to cut it. But you've been drinking again though, haven't you?"

"Shit. This is a set up. I don't know the victim. I've never met her," Barton pleaded.

"John, go home," Sanderson instructed. "And think about where you were over the weekend."

"You're suspending me?"

"No. But you need to report to me tomorrow morning at eight. I'd imagine C and D will have someone down here to interview you."

There, the dreaded initials had been mentioned. C and D; Complaints and Discipline. "You're bloody hanging me out to dry!"

"No I'm bloody well not. But you need to give me something to work with here. Now don't make things any worse. Say nothing to anyone and John … stay out of trouble."

Barton held Sanderson's gaze for a few moments then stood, snatched the door handle and stormed out.

7

Karyn Brown closed the last of the 'mug shot' books that Cyril had patiently shown her. They were sitting in the ground floor interview room, empty drinks cups on the table. She'd spent the best part of forty minutes giving her statement, details of the pubs they'd visited, culminating in Mama's Nightclub, before going through the likely suspects that Cyril thought might possibly have been the one seen talking to Sharon.

"I'm sorry," she said, "but there's no one that jumps out at me."

"Okay, Miss Brown," Cyril responded. "At least we have your description. And you say you think you'd seen this man before?"

Her expression formed a frown. "I'm sure I had. Maybe some time ago though."

"Well never mind for now. We have your statement, which is important. And if you remember something later, you can always call in or telephone."

She gave a weak smile. "Thank you."

"You never know," Cyril said, as he stood up. "You might wake at three in the morning with where you remember seeing the man."

Karyn also got to her feet and shrugged on her coat. "I'll probably just have nightmares now," she said in a feeble attempt to make light.

Cyril opened the door and they headed out into the corridor. They'd taken a couple of steps towards the reception area when Karyn gasped, took a sharp intake of breath and held it. At the same time, she brought both hands to her mouth, a shocked expression on her face.

DI Barton had just stormed down the stairs and bustled his way out through the door towards the exit, oblivious to anyone.

Cathy Rogers appeared at that moment from the secretary's room, coat on, ready to go home. When she noticed Barton, she stopped in her tracks. "Oh, I'm sorry," she said to herself in a quiet voice. "No, don't mention it. Oh, you haven't." She caught sight of Cyril with Karyn and smiled at him before observing Karyn's face.

Cyril spotted Cathy and returned her smile before realising Karyn was standing still. "Is something wrong, Miss Brown?" he asked.

She let out her breath. "That's him," she said.

"What do you mean?"

"That man who rushed down the stairs. That was the man who was talking to Sharon in the club on Saturday night."

Cyril was puzzled. "Are you sure?"

"Positive. I remember he tried to chat me up last year. That's when I'd seen him before."

Cathy approached them. "Is everything okay?" she asked Cyril.

"I'm not sure Cathy," he replied.

At that point, Sam Woodbridge came in through the door, looking back towards the exit. "What's up with the DI?" he asked Cyril.

"Ah, Sam," Cyril said, "Can you do me a favour? Could you just sit with Miss Brown in the interview room for a few minutes? I just need to speak to DCI Sanderson."

Woodbridge gently led Karyn back into the room she'd only just left.

Cyril turned to Cathy. "Sorry, love. I'll see you later, hopefully."

"Has something happened?" she asked.

He nodded.

"Don't forget you're coming to me for your tea tonight. And giving Simon a hand with his maths homework."

Simon was Cathy's fifteen-year-old son. Since Cyril had become friends with Cathy, he'd spent a bit of time with the lad and they'd seemed to get along well.

"I won't," Cyril said and made for the stairs.

8

Cyril could see DCI Sanderson through the half-glazed door to his office sitting at his desk, telephone in hand. Sanderson spotted him and held up a hand to stop him. Cyril nervously waited until he saw him replace the handset.

Sanderson looked up and beckoned him in.

Cyril entered and closed the door. "This might be a bit awkward, sir," he began. "It's about DI Barton."

"Ah. Sit down a minute, Cyril." Sanderson indicated the chair opposite his desk. "You've heard then?"

Cyril was confused. "Well, I … er … Heard?" His brows furrowed as he sat. "It's only just happened."

It was Sanderson's turn to look puzzled. "What are you talking about?"

"I could ask you the same thing, sir."

"You go first," Sanderson said.

Cyril related his discussions with Karyn Brown, the fact he now had her statement and how she'd reviewed the mugshot albums. He paused, bracing himself to tell the next part of the story. "And then, when I was escorting her back to the exit, the DI came storming down the stairs," he went on.

Sanderson leaned forward on his desk. It was as if he knew what was coming.

"He didn't see us; too wrapped up in his own situation, I think. But Karyn was sure."

"Go on, Cyril."

A deep breath before Cyril next spoke. "She identified him as the man she last saw talking to our victim about one am on Sunday morning."

Sanderson let out a big sigh, leaned back in his chair and rubbed his face with both hands. "Christ," he said softly.

"There's more," Cyril said. "She claims that he'd tried to chat her up last year."

Sanderson stood up and began to pace the room, pausing at the window to look down onto the street. "Stupid, stupid man," he said almost under his breath. He turned and faced his DS. "Okay, I have to take you into my confidence now."

Again, Cyril was baffled but said nothing.

Sanderson walked back to the desk, sat down and opened the drawer to produce Barton's warrant card. "This," he said, "was found down the side of the sofa in Sharon Williams' living room."

"Hell's bells," Cyril muttered, then quickly added, "Sorry, sir."

"I know. It doesn't look good."

Cyril hung his head for a second. "So what has DI Barton said? About the warrant card, I mean, I'm assuming that's why we saw him storm off?"

Sanderson nodded. "He can't explain it. And when I showed him the photo of Sharon Williams he said he didn't recognise her. He claims not to be able to remember where he was on Saturday night." Sanderson rolled his eyes. "The usual story, he went out for a few drinks but couldn't remember much about where or what happened later."

"I thought he'd settled down. I knew he was a bit wild last year but I thought …"

"Well, truth be told, I didn't realise things were as bad," Sanderson acknowledged.

"So what are you going to do, sir? I mean, at the very least it's Complaints and Discipline."

Sanderson puffed out his cheeks. "Well *it was,* with only the warrant card find. Now, with her friend's testimony …"

"Do you know, I can't believe he'd be involved," Cyril said.

"Where is this Karyn … Brown is it?"

"Yes, sir. I asked Sam Woodbridge to look after her in the downstairs interview room while I came and spoke to you."

Sanderson stood up. "I best have a word," he said, grabbed his suit jacket from the back of his chair and made for the door. "Come with me," he added.

*   *   *

Barton fumbled in his coat pocket as he strode along the street, feeling for a packet of cigarettes that wasn't there. "Bollocks," he muttered to himself and changed course for the newsagents on the corner.

He asked the shop assistant for twenty Peter Stuyvesant, but his attention was drawn to the front page of the Evening Gazette on the counter. The headlines blazed out:

WOMAN FOUND MURDERED IN CLACTON

He paid for his cigarettes and a copy of the paper, left the shop and immediately lit up. Opening out the Gazette, he read the article. It lacked any detail, merely talking of the police activity on a quiet road near Clacton town centre with reports of a woman found dead. There was no mention of a name and certainly no photograph of the alleged victim. Sharon Williams, that's who Sanderson said it was. Sharon; who was she and why had his warrant card been found at the scene? It made no sense to him. He drew hard on his cigarette, folded the newspaper into his coat pocket and strode off.

As he walked, his mind tried to sift the events of the weekend. When was the last time he'd had his warrant card? He could remember a few pubs in town. Normally, he'd get himself into a club after that. That was when he'd flash the warrant. No way would he pay to get into those places. But last night was Sunday and that was a bit of a blank, never mind the night before.

He opened the door to his flat and walked into the hallway. Closing the front door behind him, he leaned against it and closed his eyes. The silence seemed to close in on him. *Christ,* he thought, and not for the first time, *what a mess.*

He pushed himself upright off the door and walked into the kitchen. He'd have to sort himself out. How many times had he told himself that lately? But this was a new low. What if it transpired that he did know this Sharon woman? Had he gone back to her place? Or had some thieving little pickpocket nabbed his card from his pocket?

Tea. He needed a drink. *Sod it,* he thought, remembering that there was no milk earlier and he'd forgotten when he was in the shop. He would; he'd get some milk. He wouldn't go out to the pub. He had to use this as a wake-up call. Resigned, he left the flat to go back to the shop around the corner.

*   *   *

In the interview room, Sanderson gently led Karyn through some questions as Cyril sat at his side. He had to be sure. This was a serious situation. Finally, he placed a black and white photograph of Barton on the table.

"Karyn," he said, "Was this the man you saw talking to Sharon, the last time you saw her?"

She nodded and looked as if she was about to burst into tears. "Yes," she answered.

"And you're absolutely sure?"

"Of course." Her expression hardened. "I remembered him from before."

"Before?"

"He tried to chat me up …" She thought for a second. "It must have been last August, September time. It was still the good weather at the end of the summer anyway."

"So there's no mistake?"

"No. In fact, it's coming back to me now, Sharon ended up in his flat. She told me afterwards. A bit embarrassing, apparently. He couldn't remember her name the next morning."

Sanderson looked to Cyril then back to Karyn, leaning forward onto the table. "So, just to be clear, you're saying that, not only was this man the last person you saw talking to Miss Williams in the early hours of Sunday morning but that they had previously met?"

"Yes."

"And not only that, she'd spent the night with him?"

Karyn merely shrugged.

Sanderson leaned back. Cyril could see the concern etched on his face. "Well, thank you Miss Brown," he said, gathering up the photo and rising to his feet.

"It's Ms," Karyn said.

"Of course. Now DS Claydon here will take a formal statement from you."

Sanderson left Cyril to the task in hand and left the room.

When Cyril had written the statement and received Karyn's approval and signature he asked if she would like someone to drive her home.

"It's okay," she said. "I'll walk from here."

He escorted her back to the reception area then climbed the stairs to Sanderson's office.

He found the DCI sitting at his desk. He looked up when he saw Cyril approach and beckoned him in.

He sounded exasperated. "Bloody Hell Cyril, what's the daft sod done?"

Cyril slowly settled into the chair opposite the DCI. "Well, let's not get carried away just yet, sir. I admit, at the moment, it doesn't look good but there could be some other factors at play here we don't know about yet."

Sanderson considered Cyril for a moment. "Do you always see the good side of everyone?"

Cyril shrugged.

"Only a few months ago, I'd have put money on you jumping at the opportunity to bury John. You hated his methods and attitudes, didn't you?"

"I think 'hated' is probably too strong a word. He still is an awkward sod at times. But I don't think he's capable of anything like attacking this woman, let alone murder."

"You can't be sure though, Cyril. When he's had so much to drink he can't remember where he's been or what he's done ..." Sanderson left the sentence unfinished. "I know you might feel you owe him for saving you on that ferry last year, but God knows, you returned the favour in the warehouse, didn't you?"

"He might be a rough diamond, but he has some good points."

Sanderson stood. "Well, however you want to view it, we need to talk to him. And sooner rather than later. Come on, Cyril," he said and made for the door.

9

Cyril stood beside Sanderson as the DCI rang the bell to Barton's flat and waited. After a few seconds, he repeated the action, then rattled on the door.

At that moment, the man himself appeared on the pathway. "Hello, sir," he said. "Cyril. This must be really serious for both of you to turn up at my door. Tea?" He held up the carton of milk.

Barton unlocked the door and led them into the kitchen. He filled the kettle and switched it on, indicating for Sanderson and Cyril to sit at the drop-leaf table.

This was the first time Cyril had been in Barton's flat. It depressed him. For a man of thirty-six, it wasn't much to show, despite his obvious difficulties with divorce. But he held down a good job. Surely he should be doing better for himself?

Barton took the orders and made drinks for them before sitting opposite his colleagues at the table.

Finally, Sanderson spoke. "What's going on, Dick?" he mused. "We've known each other for what? Seven, eight years?"

Barton nodded. "1970," he said.

"A lot has changed in that time." Sanderson sighed. "You were married to Alison then."

"That didn't work out, as you well know." Barton sat up stiffly on the chair. "But what's that got to do with you turning up like this?"

Sanderson looked grim. "Other information has come to light … since we last spoke at the station," he said.

Barton was indignant. "Information? What other information?"

Sanderson turned to Cyril and indicated the brown envelope he'd brought with him. Cyril handed it over.

"Earlier on this afternoon, John, you said you didn't recognise this woman." Sanderson pulled Sharon Williams' photograph from the envelope and handed it to Barton. "Take a good look. Are you sure?"

Barton studied the black and white image.

"It's probably about four years old," Cyril added, remembering that they'd received this from Baldwin's and it was probably taken when she joined them.

"Maybe," Barton said after a few seconds. "I might have seen her." He handed it back to his boss.

Sanderson looked at the image again, placed it on the table and looked up at Barton. "The thing is, we have a witness who says she saw you talking to this woman around one in the morning on Sunday."

"Who?"

"That's not important right now," Sanderson replied. "The thing is, it's a credible witness."

Barton looked alarmed.

"And what's more," the DCI continued, "you were seen with her on a previous occasion. Last year, September time."

"Here, let me see her again." Barton leaned forward and picked up the photo once more.

Sanderson studied him closely.

"I do remember now," Barton said. "Not this weekend, but I remember we … we ended up together …" He screwed up his face in thought, then looked at Cyril. "It was that weekend when I arranged for you to stay at the holiday park. Remember? When you kept an eye on the Robinsons."

Cyril nodded. "That would have been early September, yes."

Sanderson looked from Cyril to Barton and back again. "Christ," he said. "So you did know this woman. And not only was your warrant card found in her house along with her corpse, as far as we know, you've been identified as the last person she was seen with." He leaned back on the chair and rubbed his face with both hands. "What a fucking mess."

Cyril was startled. This was the first time he'd heard the DCI use such language.

Barton shook his head. "I honestly don't remember seeing her on Saturday night. I don't remember too much about that night anyway."

"Or many other nights from what I've heard," Sanderson added. "You need to sort yourself out, John. And you need to do it quickly. You'll also need to account for your movements over the weekend. If not for me, C & D will want to know tomorrow."

The DCI stood, his drink on the table untouched. "Like I said earlier, be in my office at eight, John." He glanced down at Cyril. "Do you want a lift back to the station?"

Cyril indicated the huddled figure opposite. "It's okay," he said. "I'll walk back."

Once Sanderson had closed the door behind him, Barton raised his head. "You don't have to stay, Cyril. I'll be fine."

"Will you? What'll you do tonight? Out for more beers, Can't remember how you get home."

"What's it to you? You're not my dad."

Cyril shook his head and gave a wry smile. "What was it you first said to me last year ... you considered yourself to be arrogant and obnoxious."

"What I actually said was that I knew you thought I was an arrogant obnoxious twat."

"And I think you followed it up by proclaiming loudly that you were not bent. I believed you then and I believe you now. You can still be obnoxious and arrogant but I don't believe you were capable of harming that woman. So ... we need to get to the bottom of this and to do that you'll need to help me."

Barton seemed deflated. "This is all bollocks, Cyril. I've been set up here."

"Pack a bag and let's get back to the station, pick up my car and you can stay at my place tonight. I'm not having you wallowing in self-pity."

"I'm not!" Barton exclaimed. "Besides what will the lovely Cathy say?"

Mention of Cathy Rogers reminded Cyril that he was supposed to be going round to her place tonight. He'd promised to help her boy, Simon, with his homework. "Don't worry about that," he said. "It'll be alright."

10

Cyril replaced the handset after an awkward conversation with Cathy. He walked back from the hallway of his neat semi-detached house and re-joined Barton in the kitchen.

"Everything okay?" Barton asked.

"I'll have a bit of making up to do, but it's fine."

"You should have gone, I'd have been okay. I'll bet her lad was disappointed."

Cyril switched off the oven, opened the door and pulled the fish suppers from where they'd been keeping warm. "I'll see him tomorrow." He placed the newspaper-wrapped meals onto warm plates on the table. "Best fish and chips for miles," Cyril said. "I don't know exactly how Big Pete does it, but he does."

When they'd arrived at Cyril's house about an hour earlier, Cyril had gone next door to see his neighbour, Doris. She had a key to his place and liked to look after Charlie, Cyril's elderly Golden Labrador. She'd told him briefly that she'd had her friend Betty call round to see her that afternoon. Betty had been in a distressed state.

Cyril and Barton had walked down to the chip shop, taking Charlie with them for his evening walk at the same time. Charlie loved the company but wasn't able to walk as much as he used to.

With the old dog slumbering gently in his bed on the kitchen floor, the pair washed down their food with mugs of tea then moved to Cyril's sitting room.

As Barton went into the room, his attention was caught by the photograph of Cyril in his RAF uniform and four medals on the sideboard. "This you?" he asked.

"A lifetime ago."

"You know you shouldn't leave your medals lying around."

"I forgot to put them away the other night when I was looking for something else." He picked them up, looked at them for a moment then tidied them into a cardboard box. "No one's going to steal them, John. They're fairly ordinary. They normally live in here." He opened one of the doors to the sideboard and placed the box inside before sitting down in one of the comfortable easy chairs.

"Why are you doing this, Cyril?" Barton asked as he settled himself into the other chair opposite.

Cyril picked up his pipe and began to fill it with his favourite tobacco, packing it tightly. "I told you before, John, I don't believe you had anything to do with this woman's murder." He struck a match and lit up. "For God's sake, don't make me eat those words."

Barton looked across at Cyril who disappeared momentarily in clouds of smoke. He finally caught his eye then burst out laughing.

Cyril smiled. "You saved me on that ferry. I know I could have died if you hadn't made the effort," he said.

Barton pulled a packet of cigarettes from his pocket. "But then, you saved me when that man pulled a gun on me."

"And cutting through all that," Cyril said, waving a hand through the smoke as if to enforce the point, "you're one of us." He stood up and walked to a cabinet in the corner of the room. Opening a door, he pulled out a bottle of single malt Scotch whisky and two tumblers. "Now," he said, "if we're going to get anywhere tonight, we need to start reviewing your weekend." He held up the bottle. "And this will help."

Barton's expression brightened. "You little beauty," he said.

Cyril poured a measure into each of the two glasses, passed one to Barton then sat back down opposite the DI. "So what's troubling you, John?" he asked.

"Apart from being suspected of murdering this woman?"

Cyril shook his head. "I mean what's behind your behaviour? Are you that lonely?"

Barton held Cyril's gaze for a moment then looked away. "Too early in the evening for that," he replied.

Cyril nodded. "Fair enough. So tell me what happened on Saturday night?"

Barton took a deep draw on his cigarette and expelled a cloud of smoke. "I remember starting off in the Madena next door." Conveniently, there was a pub situated immediately adjacent to the police station. Most police and many ne'r-do-wells drank there.

"What time was that?"

"I don't know, maybe half seven. Then on to the Osborne. I think from there I might have called in at Imperial but … was that Friday? No, definitely there on Saturday." Barton pulled on his cigarette.

"Was that a typical Saturday night for you?"

"Hey, don't get all judgemental on me."

Cyril held up a hand. "I'm not John." He sucked on his pipe but it had gone out, so he put it down on the large ashtray on the coffee table in front of him. "So after the Imperial?"

"Well I might have called in elsewhere but I must have made my way eventually to Mama's Nightclub in Rosemary Road. Frank usually lets me in. Always good for a free drink in there." Barton sipped some of his whisky.

"Would that have been around eleven?"

"Yeah."

"And then what?"

"No idea. Next thing I remember was waking up in bed. My own. Alone." Barton leaned forward and forcefully stubbed out his cigarette in the ashtray as if to reinforce the point.

"And you can't remember anything after you got to the club?

Barton shook his head.

"And Frank would remember you?"

"Frank Reid, yes. He should do. We've helped him out a few times when he's had a spot of bother." Barton drained his glass.

"I know Frank Reid," Cyril said. "We've had cause to visit the place on many a night. He'll be my first port of call tomorrow then." Cyril poured another small measure in the DI's tumbler and added a dash to his own. "And we'll make this the last for tonight. You'll need to be on the ball tomorrow when you speak to C and D."

11
Tuesday 8ᵗʰ March 1977

Cyril shrugged off his overcoat and hung it up on the coat stand by the door to the CID office. Fog had rolled in off the North Sea overnight adding to the depressed air of the town as he'd driven in. The long hot summer of the previous year was only a distant memory now.

He'd brought Barton with him, making sure he was smartly turned out. The DI had gone off for his eight o'clock appointment with DCI Sanderson as instructed. C and D would give him a hard time, he was sure. The least Barton could do was turn up on time and looking tidy.

"Morning sarge," Bill Walker greeted from his desk in the middle of the office.

"Sarge," Ben Miller echoed.

"Morning lads," Cyril said, making his way to his own desk. He checked the couple of notes that had been left in his tray, one of them advising that Sharon Williams' post-mortem was scheduled for 11:00am at Lexden Hospital in Colchester. The others were of a minor nature, so he screwed them up and threw them in the bin. He looked across at the two DCs at their desks. Ben Miller was thirty-two and married. His smouldering cigarette lay in the ashtray by the side of his typewriter. He hardly looked the picture of health, seriously overweight with a florid complexion. He also tended to have a lazy streak about him which Cyril disliked. Transferring his attention to the younger of the two, Bill Walker was studying paperwork in a file on his desk. Cyril thought Walker had much more about him. He'd been impressed by the work he'd put in last year when they were trying to identify a badly decomposed body. His tenacity produced results when the enquiry needed it the most.

"Bill, you got much on this morning?" Cyril asked.

"Not a great deal, sarge." Walker looked up from the file he had open on his desk. "Just checking through this paperwork before those two burglars come up before the magistrates tomorrow. Why?"

Cyril checked his watch. "Maybe in about an hour I'd like you to come with me this morning."

"The DI not in this morning, sarge?" Miller had the beginnings of a smirk on his face.

Cyril stood and fixed Miller with a frosty stare. "He's got a meeting first thing," he replied.

Miller took the hint and switched his attention onto his one-fingered typing.

Cyril found it difficult to concentrate, his thoughts bouncing around like a pinball. He hoped Barton was staying calm in his interview. The last thing he needed was a huge blow up. Firstly, Cyril didn't believe Barton was responsible for what happened to Sharon Williams; he stood by his assessment from yesterday. That accepted, two questions surfaced; first, who would want to attempt to involve Barton in the murder, and second, why? He felt sure the why would lead to the who. The obvious place to look would be the DI's past cases. Was there some wronged soul hidden away in there? Was it some form of revenge? There again, with Barton's behaviour in recent years, he couldn't rule out some aggrieved husband or boyfriend. Still, committing murder and attempting to lay the blame at someone else's door was an extreme measure to take to avenge someone you felt had done you wrong. But was it also possible someone had found the warrant card and had a bit of malice in mind?

Glancing at his watch, he decided to take a break, he'd have time before setting off for Colchester. A tea downstairs and the possibility of seeing Cathy sounded good. As he stood, Miller looked across at him. "Not just yet, Bill," Cyril answered the questioning expression.

About to take the stairs, the door to Sanderson's office opened and a tall, heavily-built man with a pock-marked face strode out. He didn't look happy. In his wake, a shorter, younger, weasely-looking man followed, carrying a briefcase. They rushed past Cyril and down the stairs without a backward glance.

Cyril stepped forward to the open door and knocked.

"Come in," Sanderson beckoned. "And shut the door behind you."

Barton sat unmoving in the seat opposite the DCI.

"How did it go?" Cyril asked.

Barton looked ashen. "Suspended," he said, balling his fists. Cyril could feel the anger radiating from the man.

Sanderson leaned forward on his desk. "They had no choice, given what was presented to them."

Barton suddenly stood. "But I didn't *do* anything!" he protested.

"Dick, sit down," Sanderson instructed. "We need to get to the bottom of this."

"That's right … *we* need to get it sorted," Barton said, pacing the room. "How can I do that if …"

Cyril put a hand on Barton's shoulder. "Sit down, John," he said. "We need to formulate a plan of action."

Barton held Cyril's stare for a second then slowly sat back down.

"What we talked about last night, we need to solidify that." Cyril took a seat next to the DI. "You need to think clearly what your movements were on Saturday evening. You told me you ended up at Mama's Nightclub. Bill and I will go down there later and speak to Frank Reid. See what he can tell us."

"I'll come with you," Barton said.

"No you bloody well won't," Sanderson responded. "You're going nowhere near this enquiry until we get you out of the frame."

"So I'm supposed to sit around and do nothing?"

"Not exactly," Sanderson said. "I want you to go through your past cases and see if there's anyone or anything in them that might provide justification, in some twisted way, for somebody trying to do this to you."

Barton's shoulders dropped.

"You never know," Sanderson went on, "we might get lucky with some rogue prints off your warrant card."

"And one other avenue to explore," Cyril said. "There might also be some angry husband or boyfriend out there."

Barton shook his head, resigned to the task in hand.

"Oh, there is one more thing," Sanderson said, relaxing back in his chair. "You worked with Jack Tinker, didn't you?"

Barton looked up. "He was my DI when I first joined CID."

"My predecessor as DCI. You might want to visit him. He suffered a stroke last week and he's recovering in Clacton Hospital. I'm not sure what state he's in but he might appreciate a visit from an ex-colleague."

Cyril was surprised to hear that news but mention of Sanderson's predecessor provoked another thought. "He had a bit of a reputation, if I'm not mistaken," he said. "Cut a few corners in his day. You might want to have a close look at any cases the pair of you were involved with."

"What, you think I'm tarred with the same brush?" Barton was indignant.

"Just a thought, John," Sanderson said. "In the meantime, I'll have to ask you not to enter CID until we can clear you from this enquiry."

Barton stood, slipped on his coat and left the room, saying nothing more.

"He's taking it hard, Cyril," Sanderson said.

"Not surprised. I would too, especially if I knew I had nothing to do with it."

"What do you think? Could he have had any involvement in this?"

"He may be many things," Cyril answered sternly, "possibly a bit naïve, but I don't believe he was involved, sir."

"Hmm, well I suppose you're right," Sanderson reluctantly agreed. "Anyway, what are your plans for today? We need to coordinate this enquiry."

Cyril told him of the PM and his planned visit to the manager of the nightclub where Barton ended up on Saturday night. "I thought I'd take young Walker with me," he concluded.

"Good idea. Meanwhile Miller can come with me. I'm going to Southend to speak to Ray Hadleigh, Sharon Williams' ex-husband. See what he's got to say for himself. Why don't we convene back here at four and see what we've learnt?"

Cyril nodded. "Sir," he said.

12

Tony Riley loved this part of the process, working on his own, free from any distractions. Yesterday, in his excavator he'd stripped the site, removing all the top soil, weeds, bushes and undergrowth that had accumulated over the past five years or so since the old house had been demolished. The site of that had been developed a couple of years ago to incorporate two four-bedroomed detached houses. Now it was the turn of the garden to give way to three more similar properties. By afternoon, he'd formed a spoil heap in one corner, ready for collection later in the week.

Sandy, the engineer, had turned up in the afternoon too, and marked out the lines for the new structures' foundations. Before he left last night, he'd changed the bucket, ready to dig the trenches for the footings.

Today was another dry day, perfect for the work, and by ten o'clock, he'd completed the excavations for the first house. Time for breakfast. He walked to his car, parked on the old driveway, and collected his flask of coffee and bacon butties wrapped in greaseproof paper. Donna had made them this morning before he left; just how he liked them, drizzled with brown sauce. Another pack of sandwiches, cheese and tomato if he wasn't mistaken, lay on the passenger seat ready for lunchtime. A quick cigarette to finish and he was ready to go again.

About a dozen scoops in on the second house's footings, he spotted something. Killing the engine, he stepped down from the cab of the JCB and jumped into the trench. A couple of feet down, his bucket had exposed a briefcase. Grabbing a nearby shovel he began to work the case free from the earth. Finally, it came loose. Scraping the soil from the catches, he tried to open them but they wouldn't give. Taking up the shovel again, he forced the locks. Slowly, he opened the case and stepped back. Inside, in a number of plastic wrapped bundles, appeared to be banknotes of various denominations. He looked all round, expecting some camera crew to be filming his reactions, as if it were a staged TV show. Nothing. Nobody. The only signs of life had been the postman driving up to the two properties next door with the morning delivery about half an hour ago.

Bending down, he lifted one of the packages and pulled on the plastic, releasing a selection of Bank of England notes. He sat down on the edge of the trench and studied what he held in his hands. The green one-pound notes looked current but the blue five-pound notes were of an older design. He wasn't sure about the brown ten-pound notes as he didn't handle them that often. Glancing over at the case, he could see in the exposed row below the familiar colour of red ten-shilling notes. These hadn't been in use since 1970, not long after the 50p coin had been introduced the year before in the first stages of decimalisation.

How the Hell had this happened? Was it something that had been buried by a previous owner in the garden of the old house? Or something more sinister? Whatever the reason, he made a snap decision to put the notes back in the plastic and close the briefcase. With another careful look round the site, he stood up, carried the case back to his car and placed it in the boot.

Married to Donna with two children, a married daughter who now lived in Colchester and a teenage son still at school, he thought this was too good an opportunity to miss. He earned a good wage, but there were always unexpected expenses that cropped up. And then, he hadn't been able to take his family on a decent holiday for a number of years, not since paying for his daughter's wedding two years ago. There must be several thousand pounds in there and he could think of so much he could do with this windfall. But first, stay calm and get back to work.

The rest of the day passed slowly. Lunchtime came and went. He chewed his sandwiches with no real enthusiasm. Resisting the temptation to look in the car boot again, he smoked three cigarettes in quick succession. During the afternoon, every so often, he'd glance at his car, expecting a rush of activity; police or worse.

Finally, just after three o'clock, all the foundation excavations were completed. A few minutes later, Sandy arrived to check the work. When the car first appeared, Riley's heart rate shot up, until he recognised the engineer's Ford Escort. He locked up the excavator and went to join him. All seemed to be in order but Sandy seemed keen to chat. Eventually, the conversation wound round to football as Sandy leaned against Riley's car boot. He hoped his face didn't give away too much concern.

"I reckon it's Liverpool's title, Tony," Sandy said.

"I'm more interested in seeing Colchester get promoted," Riley countered.

"Should do. Who have you got this week?"

"Away at Darlington. It's not a done deal, there's Swansea, Bradford and Barnsley all in the hunt." Riley shifted from one foot to the other.

Sandy appeared to take the hint, shoving himself off the car boot. "Right, I'll let you knock off home," he said, before walking over to his own car. "I'll be over again in the morning. I think there should be some reinforcement due for delivery tomorrow too. See you."

Riley let out a breath before opening his car door and climbing in. He watched the Escort drive away before starting his own car. Again, another look round before putting the car in gear and driving off.

13

Ex-Detective Inspector Jack Tinker was trapped; as trapped as many he'd put away. They all deserved it; maybe not for what they'd actually been sent down for, but they definitely deserved it. They might well have been stitched up, but sometimes justice had to be given a helping hand.

Tinker was trapped in his own body. The stroke had certainly been a cruel twist. Two years into his retirement and the blackness swept over him; that and a painful headache. He could remember some of the morning it happened. Breakfast as usual, bacon, egg, beans, mushrooms, two sausages and two slices of toast. Perfect antidote to the heavy session the night before. But if the truth be told, he didn't remember too much of the previous evening, much less how he'd driven home. It wasn't unusual for him to drive home in that state. It was a recognised perk of the job that uniform would look after CID when they wanted to have a night out. Only that should have ceased when he retired. However, he'd still felt confident he was untouchable. But all that seemed to be consigned to history now.

He was trying to work out how long he'd been here. How long had the total blackness lasted? How much time had elapsed since that last breakfast? He was aware of varying degrees of blackness and worked out that represented the difference between his being awake and asleep. It was Thursday when he met up with his retired colleagues, he did remember that; so he must have been in this hospital bed since Friday morning.

The frustration was the worst aspect. Thoughts going round in his head, but no means to express them. He could hear what was being said, every word. And he understood, only too well. He knew exactly the position he was in. He'd seen his uncle suffer the same fate twenty years ago. He'd lasted about a week before another one took him. Was that what was waiting for him? Another stroke?

He tried to move an arm, but nothing seemed to work. He even thought he was moving a finger but that wasn't happening either. He'd wait until he'd hear a nurse or a doctor come into the room and make a concerted effort but all to no avail. If there had been movement, he was sure someone would have noticed. He even tried to speak, but his mouth wouldn't move and no sound could be heard. He thought he was opening his eyes, but that hadn't worked. So here he was, in varying degrees of blackness with only his own thoughts for company.

The doctors spoke positively. They thought they could improve his speech and movement eventually, but he'd need rest. They guessed rather than knew he could hear; the last sense to go, he heard a doctor tell his wife.

His wife had come in every day since it happened. He didn't deserve that, not after the way he'd treated her through the years. All those broken promises. Home for dinner but preferring a boozy session in the pub with colleagues instead. Holidays cancelled because of some ongoing investigation. Weekends ruined trying to force a confession from some piece of dross so they could fetch them before the magistrates on the Monday morning. No, he didn't deserve the support of Julia, but he was glad of it just the same.

"Hello, Jack darling," he heard her say. "How is everything today? I brought you a paper."

A paper, what the hell's the use of a paper, his thoughts replied.

"I know you always like to read one," she continued, "and I know you can't at the moment, so I thought I'd read it to you. That way, you'll be on top of things when you get better."

Oh God, he thought, *after all I've done, she's still thinking of me.*

"Ooh, look, someone's been murdered in Clacton," she read.

Tinker felt a tinge of excitement. This would have been the news he'd have looked forward to at one time when he was still in the job. *Who?* he asked himself. As was usual, no sound actually came from him.

"It's some woman," Julia went on. "It says here, she was discovered in the bedroom of her home on Monday. Police are not releasing any further information until next-of-kin have been informed."

He could hear her ruffling the pages.

"Oh, she lived in one of those roads at the back of the railway station."

She flicked through more pages, picking out various snippets, including Jack's horoscope. "The moon in your sign is retrograde, it says here," she read. "This gives you a feeling of disappointment, but this won't last as you'll soon be on a journey."

Well the first part's right, he thought. *What a load of old bollocks. Like I've got a real future lying here with no way of communicating.*

Lastly, she came to the back pages. "God, look at this," she said. "Sunderland beat West Ham on Saturday, six-nil."

Bloody Hell, I'm glad I didn't see that on Match of the Day.

"Sorry, Jack," she said, "I know West Ham are your team."

Six-nil. Just as well I didn't have a ticket. Not only couldn't I have gone but even if I did, I'd have had to witness a drubbing too.

"Look, I'll leave you to rest now but I'll be back later." She squeezed his hand and carried on, "And Neil will be coming with me. He's travelling down from Manchester."

Neil! Mention of their son shook him. *Oh God, he'll be devastated.*

Her lips touched his.

"Bye, love," she said.

For the first time since Julia had come into the room, he could detect the emotion cracking her voice.

A moment later, he heard the door close and, despite his inactivity, exhaustion suddenly consumed him.

14

"Interesting findings there, sarge," Bill Walker said.

"Certainly was," Cyril agreed. He was driving the CID pool car back to Clacton after attending Sharon Williams' PM. He was impressed by the way Walker had handled himself, considering that was only his second post-mortem.

"So, asphyxiation and no sexual assault," Walker went on.

"And Forensics reckon she was attacked in the sitting room."

"You said that's where you found her knickers, down the side of the settee."

Cyril looked sharply across at the young DC.

"And where they found the DI's warrant card," Walker continued. "Ben told me."

"I'll bet he enjoyed that conversation."

"He's not as bad as you think, sarge."

Cyril rolled his eyes before continuing, "She was then dragged upstairs by someone putting their arms under her armpits and dragging her backwards, hence the positioning of the shoes." Cyril stopped at a road junction, checked both ways then drove on. "High levels of alcohol in her bloodstream too, so she would have been … well, pliable, shall we say." Cyril glanced at Walker. "Let that be a lesson for you young man," he said. "Never drink so much you might not be in control."

"I never do," the young DC replied, indignant. "For one thing, I can't afford it."

Cyril broke into a broad grin. "Anyway, I've got a lot of time for Tom, he's a very experienced scientific officer," he went on.

"The Forensics guy?"

"I've known him for twenty years."

"What about that hair they found under her fingernails? You reckon that's significant?" Walker asked.

"Put it this way," Cyril considered, "it's possible it had lodged there during the attack."

"How long did he reckon before he'd have some results?"

"Tom will do his best." Cyril said. "I'm sure he'll be able to give us a colour and if there's any other distinguishing feature, like hair treatment in a day or so. And don't forget he reckons there are some fibres he found on the back of her dress that could have come from her attacker's clothing when he dragged her upstairs."

"Plus, of course, the fingerprints on the wine glasses," Walker added.

"Well, just the one, as the victim's prints have been identified on one of the glasses," Cyril said. "The prints on the other glass will be the key."

Cyril drew to a halt on Rosemary Road. The doors to Mama's Nightclub were ajar as a drinks delivery was being made when Cyril and Bill Walker approached. A man in his twenties came out carrying empty crates.

"Is Frank in?" Cyril asked.

The man merely nodded his head towards the open door.

Cyril and Walker made their way inside and up a wide staircase to the first floor. Through a set of double doors, they stepped onto the main dance floor. The area was empty. A stage at the other end with turntables for the resident disc jockey to delight the punters with the latest records stood silent. To one side, a bar took up half the length. At the side of the stage was a door and Cyril headed for that. As he turned the handle and pushed open the door, he heard a man's voice from up another staircase beyond.

"Look, I know what I'm doing," the male voice said. "I've been doing it longer than you've been involved."

Cyril looked to Walker and put his finger to his lips.

Walker closed the door as quietly as he could as Cyril slowly took the stairs.

"No, we can't increase it any more, they'll notice," the man went on.

Cyril's step creaked the wooden staircase and the man upstairs paused his conversation.

"Look, got to go, we'll speak later," the voice hurriedly said, before the sound of a handset being replaced in its cradle ended the telephone call.

The sounds of a chair scraping the floor indicated to Cyril there was no point trying to remain undetected. "Mr Reid," he called out as he took the last few steps onto the landing and stood by the open door to an office.

Frank Reid, a short man with slicked back hair, walked towards the door. "Can I help you?" Recognition spread over his face. "It's Sergeant Claydon, if I'm not mistaken."

Walker had appeared at Cyril's shoulder.

"Detective Sergeant Claydon," Cyril confirmed and produced his warrant card. "And this is Detective Constable Walker."

"CID now. What can I do for you?" Reid asked as he walked back round the desk and sat down behind it. "Take a seat," he offered, indicating a couple of rickety wooden chairs that looked as though they'd been rescued from some church hall.

"We'll stand thanks." Not least to maintain some sort of psychological advantage over you, Cyril thought.

"Saturday night," Cyril began, producing a photo from his inside coat pocket. "Did you see this man in the club?" He placed it on the desk.

Reid glanced down. "That's Inspector Barton," he said. "What's he been up to?"

"Was he here?"

"Saturday, you say?"

"That's right."

"Yes he was here. Bloody nuisance, as usual," Reid answered.

Cyril walked over to a small dusty window and looked out onto a rear yard then turned to face the man. "Why do you say that?"

Reid screwed up his face slightly. "Come on, Mr Claydon, how well do you know him? He comes in here a lot, usually at the end of the night and bums some free drinks, tries it on with the women, gets lucky sometimes and leaves."

"Did he get lucky on Saturday?"

Reid frowned. "Not sure. He was chatting up some blonde bird. She's in here quite regularly with her dark-haired mate."

Cyril approached the desk again and pulled another photo from his pocket. "How about this woman? Have you seen her before?"

Reid took hold of the picture. "That's her. That's the woman Dick was chatting up."

Cyril glanced at Walker. This wasn't the answer he'd wanted to hear, but it did confirm what Karyn Brown had told him. He thought of something else. "When he turned up on Saturday, did he show his warrant card to get in?"

Reid smirked. "He'd no need to do that, we all know him."

"And did he 'get lucky' with this woman?"

Reid leaned back and scratched his nose. "Not sure. I wasn't watching him all night." He leaned forward. "But I tell you who might have done … Billy the barman. He usually spots most things."

"And is Billy in?" Cyril asked.

"Nah. Not till seven."

"Do you know where he lives?"

Reid looked at Cyril suspiciously. "Yes," he answered slowly. "Look, Mr Claydon, what's going on here? CID don't usually come round asking all sorts of … unless …" His face lit up. "She wasn't the woman found dead yesterday?"

"Just an address please, Mr Reid."

The man pulled out a pad from a desk drawer and scribbled on it before ripping off the top sheet and handing it across.

"Thanks for your help," Cyril said and made for the door. He paused and turned back to Reid. "Oh, by the way," he said. "I think you're right. I wouldn't water down the drinks any more than you already do."

15

"Any improvement?" a voice Tinker recognised as being one of the senior doctors asked.

Probably not, he thought, *but I have had some good rest.*

"Just checking now," a younger voice answered.

Suddenly, in spite of the constant blackness, a bright light was shone into first one eye, then the other.

Christ, that was painful. He tried to screw up his face but nothing seemed to move.

"Much the same," the younger voice offered.

The older man sighed. "Well, just keep monitoring him. You never know, it might all suddenly change."

"His wife comes in regularly and talks to him."

"That's good. Now, did you say we've had two more admitted since the weekend?" The older doctor's voice faded away slightly, as if he'd walked to the doorway.

"That's right," the younger man said before Tinker heard the door close behind the two medics and the room fell silent again.

Christ, he said to himself, and not for the first time, *is this all I have to look forward to? Regular checks but no improvement. I must have been some bad bastard in a previous life. Not so much this one. I've always considered myself to be a proud upholder of the law. Okay, so sometimes that needed a helping hand, but I haven't done anything wrong. It wasn't as though anybody died. Well not that I can remember anyway.*

I wonder what day it is? What time is it? I'll see if I can work it out when Julia comes in. In the meantime ... I feel tired.

*   *   *

The two doctors left the room and made their way down the corridor to the next ward. They didn't spot the young man busying himself in the sluice. That's how he liked it; invisible, not drawing attention to himself.

Satisfied they'd gone, he unfolded the white coat and put it on. From the pocket he produced a stethoscope and hung that round his neck. The props had been easy to get hold of, his job helped.

He felt the left-hand coat pocket; the comforting shape of the vials, that and the syringe. His thoughts drifted to his mother. Three months since she'd passed. The vials were hers, part of her survival kit. Only she didn't survive. But now, he'd make good use of them. Oh, yes, he'd make sure they found a useful purpose.

Snapping himself back to the job in hand, he paused a moment, checking no one was approaching from up the corridor. One good aspect of having a private room, he thought, for him anyway   no needless exposure in a busy ward.

He approached the door, placed his hand on the handle and looked through the vision panel. Apart from his target, the room was empty. Good. Opening the door, he looked down at the pathetic figure lying in the bed. He should have felt sympathy towards him, but he didn't. This bastard deserved more than what he'd suffered, and he was determined to make sure he got all that was coming. He watched the man for a few seconds. No movement, no reaction. Satisfied, he closed the door behind him.

Something was different. He could feel it. Whoever it was who had just come into the room, it didn't feel right.

"There you are," a young male voice said. "Not feeling too clever these days, I hear."

Who the fuck are you? Tinker thought. Only this time, he could hear himself grunt. He should have been pleased with that, progress in his condition. But he was more concerned with who his visitor was. He didn't get a good feeling. This wasn't a familiar voice from the medical staff.

"What's that you say, Jack?" There was a hollow chuckle. "Of course you can't say anything now. Not even 'sorry'. Not that you would."

Tinker could sense the man walk around the bed to the other side.

"Because I don't believe you'd regret anything. Not you." The voice grew louder in his left ear, although the man was talking quieter. "You wouldn't show any remorse, even if you were physically capable."

Tinker could feel his heart rate increase. *Who was this bastard who'd wandered into his room? What did he want? He obviously knew who* he *was – he was using his name. And where were the medical staff? Unless …*

"You've been a bad boy in the past, Jack," the stranger said, taking on a mocking tone. "You probably thought you were evening things up a bit, the scales of justice perhaps, in your twisted view."

There was a pause before he was aware of the stranger leaning in to speak to him again. "The thing is, Jack, you've shat on a lot of people over the years."

What are you going on about? Big effort now … come on body.

The man mentioned a name and Tinker tried to recall it, making another attempt to move. A face came to him. *Yes,* he remembered, *a record as long as your arm. Must be nearly eight years ago, aggravated robbery on the Post Office in Dovercourt. Nasty,* he recalled. *Postmaster and his wife tied up and threatened by two masked men who broke in to their flat above the premises. One had made him open the safe whilst the other guarded the wife. A couple in their sixties, scared to death. In fact, the woman had a heart attack and died two months later.*

Tinker managed another grunt.

"That's good you do remember him," the young man went on. "It wouldn't have surprised me if you'd stitched up so many, you couldn't recall them all."

He heard him sit in the chair by the side of his bed.

"But your actions didn't just affect him. There was his family too. But you would never consider that, would you? For you, just getting a collar, sending someone down … was that what drove you? A better clean-up rate? The chance of gaining promotion?"

He heard a scuffling sound, something being pulled from a pocket perhaps?

"What you never considered … not for one moment … is how your actions affected his health."

He definitely had the right face to the name, that was his MO. No believable alibi for the time in question. Well his missus said he was at home with her, but then they always do, don't they? He wouldn't admit it, but everyone knew he was part of it. Just needed a helping hand, that's all. A little twist of the evidence. His partner-in-crime never grassed, that's what they were like, the scum he'd had to deal with. Not even the promise of a word to the judge could get names to be named. After all, who would they believe? The whole of CID, or some scumbag's missus?

The stranger interrupted his thoughts. "Did you know he died? I'll bet you don't give a shit, even if you did know. That wasn't the end of the chain of events started by your actions." The stranger sighed. "But I'm not going to waste my time telling you all of that, Jack. You wouldn't be interested."

There was another pause in this man's diatribe. He was sure he was doing something, but couldn't detect what. *Christ this was so frustrating. He wouldn't dare talk to me like this if I was on my feet.*

Finally the man spoke again. "The one bit of good news is, I heard what had happened to you. What is it they call it? Karma; what goes round comes round. Only, there's no guarantee you won't recover. Bad bastards like you always seem to survive. So that's why I'm going to help you on your way, Jack. Then you can say hello to all the people you've helped depart this earth. But no, maybe not. You might be going to the other place."

He gave a quiet laugh then Tinker heard a tapping noise.

What in the hell …

"There we are, Jack, don't want to give you an embolism now do we?"

Embolism? No, what's he … Tinker felt the bedsheet move away from his left leg.

"Soon have you on your way,"

Hey, what's this toerag up to? What's he doing? He's just stuck something in my leg. Here, what's …?

"Feeling better?" the man asked.

Another one. This isn't right. He could feel the bedclothes being rearranged.

I feel a bit woozy. God, it's suddenly got warm in here. I'm sweating. And … wait, what's this trembling I'm feeling?

Footsteps moved towards the door, a slight pause then he heard the door open and close.

My heart, I can hear it pounding in my chest, faster and faster. What's he done? Help. Somebody help me.

16

Cyril parked the car in the police station's car park and made his way inside. Walker had already gone on ahead. He glanced at his watch and decided he could afford the luxury of a few minutes to catch up with Cathy before Sanderson's review at four.

When he entered the secretaries' office, Cathy was on her own behind her typewriter. She glanced up briefly before returning her attention to her work, without a word.

Cyril reached into his trouser pocket and pulled out his white handkerchief and waved it in front of him.

The movement caught her eye. "You daft sod," she said, unable to stop a smile appearing on her face.

"Am I forgiven?" he asked putting the white flag away again.

She stopped typing and looked serious. "It's not me you need to apologise to. Simon is struggling with his algebra and geometry."

Cyril took a couple of steps towards her desk. "When's his test?"

"Tomorrow."

"Tell him I'll be round tonight."

"Not babysitting then?"

"I think Dick can look after himself now he's had his meeting."

"How did it go?"

Cyril checked his watch. "I'll talk to you tonight. I've got to be in the briefing in five minutes. See you later?"

"Don't let him down again."

He turned at the door. "I won't. See you later."

Upstairs in CID, Miller was at his desk.

"Useful trip to Southend?" Cyril asked him.

He opened his mouth to respond but Sanderson appeared in the doorway. "Ah, you're back, Cyril," he said.

"Sir."

"Right," the DCI addressed the detectives. "Let's review where we are."

Cyril summarised the findings from the post mortem; the victim had been strangled and there were no signs of sexual assault. He repeated the results of the blood alcohol tests. He also spoke of the initial forensics discoveries; the theory she was attacked in the sitting room and dragged backwards upstairs; identification of the victim's prints on one of the wine glasses and the bottle plus a so-far unidentified set on the other glass.

Sam Woodbridge appeared at the door with a folder in his hand. "Sorry to interrupt sir," he began. "The Inspector asked me to come up and bring these reports."

"Come and join us," Sanderson invited. "I'm assuming those are the door-to-door enquiries?"

Woodbridge walked towards the group. "Yes sir."

"Anything of any significance, PC Woodbridge?"

The constable shuffled through several sheaves of paper before pulling one out. "An elderly gent who lives opposite says he was awoken by the sounds of car doors closing about 2:30 am on Sunday morning. By the time he got to the window and looked out, he could see no one, only a car parked outside Ms Williams' house. He visited the bathroom before going back to bed."

"Was he able to identify this car?" Cyril asked.

Woodbridge shook his head. "Only that he'd not seen it before. Possibly a Cortina. But when he got up for another pee at four, it had gone."

Sanderson and Cyril exchanged glances.

"He suffers from his prostate," Woodbridge quickly explained.

"Thanks … Sam, is it?" Sanderson said.

"Yes sir."

"Well, seeing as you were involved in this from the beginning, so to speak, I'd like you to join us on this enquiry for the time being." Sanderson said. "I think we can do with an extra pair of hands at the moment. I'll have a word with your Inspector and square that. In the meantime, anything you hear in here will not be repeated anywhere else in the station. Do you understand?"

"Sir," Woodbridge acknowledged, before looking to Cyril who gave him a slight nod.

Sanderson then reported his visit to interview Ray Hadleigh, Sharon Williams' ex-husband. It seemed he had an alibi for the night of Saturday, spending the evening in a pub with friends and his new woman. Sanderson and Miller had also spoken to the woman who confirmed they were together all night and the landlord of the pub gave a statement that the pair were in company until they left at closing time.

"So we can take him out of the frame, then," Cyril said.

"Uncomfortable as it may seem," Sanderson went on, "at the moment, the only name in the frame, as you put it, is our illustrious friend."

Cyril sighed heavily and looked at the assembled officers. "Well I can't believe John had anything to do with it. I'll admit it doesn't look good, but … Look, I know I've only known him a relatively short while, but I like to think I'm a good judge of character."

"You were visiting the nightclub, weren't you?" Sanderson interrupted.

"That's right, sir. Bill and I spoke to Frank Reid, the manager. John was definitely there on Saturday night." Cyril paused.

"And?" Sanderson prompted.

"He saw him speaking to our victim."

"Did they leave together?"

"He couldn't say. I need to speak to the barman. I've got the address and I was going round there after we finish here."

Sanderson puffed out his cheeks. "Okay, do that Cyril. In the meantime, we need to look at any old cases Dick worked on to see if anyone might possibly want some form of revenge." He held up his hand. "Extreme, I know but, for what it's worth as well, I can't believe he'd do anything like this." The DCI looked towards Miller. "Okay Ben, make a start reviewing DI Barton's old cases. And let's see what that throws up. And use Sam here as well, if that helps." He clapped his hands. "Right, go to it."

As he left the room, the expression on Miller's face revealed exactly the level of disdain he felt at the task he'd been asked to perform.

17

Barton walked past the young man in the corridor as he made his way to where he'd been directed. He stopped outside the door and looked through the vision panel. There was a shape under the bedclothes with an oxygen mask over the face and a tube in the back of the right hand lying flat on the bed. He slowly opened the door and stepped inside. Two paces in and he could recognise his ex-superior, despite the equipment.

"Hello, boss," Barton said. "It's me, Dick, your old DC, Dick Barton."

There was no response from the man lying before him.

"Mind if I sit down?" Barton sat on the padded chair by the side of the bed. "I heard you got yourself into a bit of trouble," he went on. "I thought I'd come and see how you were." He looked up at the stand next to the bed with the upturned bottle of clear fluid, drip, drip, dripping into a bulb then into a tube feeding into the back of Tinker's hand.

"I'm assuming you can hear me … only I need to talk to you." He looked for a sign, anything that would confirm his ex-DCI knew he was there. He detected nothing. No movement of his hands, fingers, or even eyelids to show he was aware of his presence. The breathing seemed non-existent, no discernible rise and fall of the chest.

Ignoring the lack of response, Barton began hesitantly, "The thing is … something happened to me this weekend … and I wondered if you could help me." For the next five minutes, Barton gave an account of all that had befallen him over the past few days, culminating in his meeting with C & D this morning. "Big bastard by the name of Brookes did the interviewing. I'm sure I knew him from

Chelmsford once when I was up there for a course about five years ago. In fact, that's what they used to call him, Barry *Bastard* Brookes," he concluded, all the while looking for any sign of recognition from his old boss.

He stood up and rubbed his face, before slowly pacing the room. "The thing is, Boss, I was wondering if there was anyone you could think of from any past cases who would be capable of some sort of revenge? I know it's extreme, but some of the sods we've had to deal with … well, you know what I'm saying. And don't forget, there were a few we put away who … let's say might not have been innocent but they could have been of the charges we brought against them."

Barton was back facing the man in the bed. There were no signs that Tinker had heard a word. He'd resigned himself to not getting any assistance from his old boss but he felt better having talked out loud about the problems he was facing.

"Okay, Jack," Barton said, "I'll let you get some rest now. I'll pop back and see you soon. Take care."

Uncomfortable at seeing the man in that condition, Barton hurried from the room.

As he strode down the corridor, he recognised Jack's wife walking towards him in the company of a much younger man.

Julia Tinker had met Barton a few times when he worked with her husband.

"Dick," she greeted. "Have you been to see Jack?"

He nodded. "I hate to see him like that. Have the doctors said how long things might take?"

"No. I don't think they know." She turned to the man alongside her. "This is Neil, by the way," she said then back to face Barton. "Neil, this is Dick, I mean John … he was Dad's DS before he retired."

Neil offered a hand and Barton shook it. "Good to meet you," the young man said.

"You too, Neil, although I wish it was in different circumstances." Barton stood for a second, awkward at facing Jack's family at such a difficult time. "I'll come back again, but I best let you get on," he said.

They parted and he made his way downstairs.

Barton was exiting the main doors to the hospital by the time Julia Tinker let out a plaintive cry from her husband's hospital room.

* * *

Cyril walked up the path to the scruffy semi-detached house and knocked on the door, Walker close behind.

A dog barked inside in response. A woman's voice shouted a command and the dog was silent. After the sound of a door closing, the front door slowly opened.

A short woman with grey hair pulled her cardigan tighter around her as she looked at the pair on her doorstep. "Yes?" she asked in a guarded fashion.

Cyril pulled out his identification. "Mrs Small? We'd like to have a quick word with Billy if he's in."

A voice from inside shouted out, "Who is it, Mum?" before a much younger man appeared in the hallway.

"Billy Small, is it? I'm DS Claydon and this is DC Walker," Cyril said. "We'd like a quick word about events at Mama's Nightclub on Saturday night. Frank Reid tells me you were working the bar."

The man looked puzzled. "Yeah, sure. Come in." He looked to the woman. "It's okay Mum, nothing to worry about."

By contrast to his mother as well as his surname, Billy stood at just over six feet tall and broadly-built with it. Dressed in a vest and trousers, he led the two detectives into the front room.

"What can I do for you?" he asked then looked over Cyril's shoulder to where his mother lurked in the room doorway.

Cyril turned towards her. "It's alright, Mrs Small, we only want to ask Billy whether he noticed anything of interest at the club on Saturday night."

The woman gave a grunt before disappearing into the kitchen.

Cyril refocused his attention on the barman, pulling an envelope from his pocket to show a photograph to him. "Do you recognise this man?"

Billy took hold of it and broke into a smirk. "He's one of your lot," he said, handing the picture back. "That's Dick. And yes, he was in on Saturday, a bit pissed. Usual tactics. In after the pubs close and bum a few free drinks, check out what talent is in and try his luck."

"What about this woman?" Cyril asked, showing the man another photograph.

"That's her. She was there too. Dick was chatting to her. Don't think he got very far though."

"Why do you say that?"

"He left before she did." He rubbed his chin in thought. "Maybe around half one."

"And what about the woman?"

"I think she was there for another half hour or so, then she must have gone."

"Did you see her leave with anyone?"

"To be honest, she was there one minute - I served a couple of punters - and the next time I looked to where she'd been, she'd gone, if you follow."

"So you didn't see her leave with anyone?" Cyril persisted.

He shrugged and shook his head.

"But definitely not with Mr Barton?"

"Not unless they'd arranged to meet outside." Another smirk before his expression became serious. "Hey, that's not the woman who was found dead yesterday is it?"

"Just routine enquiries, Mr Small."

"And you think Dick Barton might be involved?"

"Not at all. We're just trying to establish some facts." Cyril returned the photos to his pocket. "Now, you said you'd served a couple of 'other punters'. Any chance you could remember any of them?"

The man puffed out his cheeks and gave the question some thought. Eventually, he reeled off three names. "I think they were in the club when she left," he concluded.

Cyril made notes before asking, "Oh, one last thing, can you remember what Mr Barton was wearing when you saw him?"

The barman looked puzzled. "Wearing? Usual open necked shirt, jacket and trousers. Nothing fancy. Why?"

"Well thanks for your time," Cyril said, leading the way to the front door.

As they walked back to the car, Cyril repeated the names Small had just given them. "First thing, Bill," he said, "I'd like you to track them down and arrange for someone to interview them."

*   *   *

"I'm very sorry, Mrs Tinker," the doctor said. "I'm afraid your husband might have had a second stroke. We were always fearful this could happen." He was the senior clinician who had visited Tinker earlier that afternoon.

Neil Tinker hugged his mother close as she sobbed into his chest. They'd come into the room some ten minutes before. It was when Julia had taken hold of her husband's hand, she instinctively knew something was wrong. A shout down the corridor had brought the doctor and his junior back to the room. They quickly confirmed that Jack Tinker had indeed slipped away.

"Would you like some time with him?" the senior medic continued.

Julia was unable to answer but Neil nodded and mouthed a thank-you.

The two doctors stepped outside into the corridor.

"He was stable when you examined him, was he not?" the senior man asked his colleague.

"Yes," the junior doctor responded. "There was no change in his vitals." He looked to the other man. "You think this shouldn't have happened?"

"I don't know. Maybe not so soon. I just have a feeling about this."

"What do you want to do about the paperwork? I mean, there's not normally a reason to conduct a PM in circumstances like these."

"I'd like a closer look when the family leaves and the nursing staff prepare the body," he said.

"Oh, Jack," Julia sobbed. "What am I going to do now?" she asked the lifeless body, taking hold of Jack's hand.

"I'm sorry I didn't get here in time, Dad," Neil offered. "But I know you're still here. I know you can still hear us."

Those comments prompted a full out-burst of crying from Julia.

Neil managed to comfort his mother and they were able to say some things they wished they'd been able to say earlier. Julia wanted to have five minutes alone with Jack, so Neil went out into the corridor and waited.

Once Julia appeared, they walked down to the office to let the medical staff know they had said their goodbyes for now. Reassured they could visit once Jack Tinker had been moved to the mortuary, the paperwork had to be dealt with.

18

Cyril opened his front door and was instantly attacked by the smells of curry wafting through the house. Charlie came waddling up the hallway to greet him.

He bent down to make a fuss of the dog. "What's all this about, lad," he said quietly. Louder, he shouted, "Hello?"

"Ah, you're back," Barton replied before appearing in the kitchen doorway. "I rang the station and they told me you'd gone off with Walker to speak to Billy the barman from Mama's."

Cyril shook his head. "And I'll bet it was that lazy sod Miller who told you."

Barton ignored the comment. "Anyway, I thought I'd nip out and get us a takeaway. I hope you like curry?"

Cyril made his way to the kitchen. "Not my favourite, I must admit, but thanks." He looked down at the dog bowl.

"I fed Charlie and took him round the block, so he's happy. And Doris next door was happy too that she didn't have to do it."

Cyril ruffled the dog's neck. "Thanks," he said. "You know, I think that was the final sign that made me sure you had nothing to do with what happened to Miss Williams. Charlie would have sensed it. He likes you."

"I've always been good with dogs."

"Doris might need a bit more work though," Cyril commented.

Barton took the takeaway trays from the oven where they were keeping warm, placed them on mats and sat down by one of the places he'd set at Cyril's kitchen table. "Tuck in," he said.

As Cyril scooped food onto a plate, Barton spoke again. "If it's okay with you, I'll head back to the flat tomorrow. I appreciate the hospitality, but I'll be alright. This is all a bit of a shock."

"Do what you want, John," Cyril responded. "But you're welcome to stay longer if you like."

"Thanks, but I need to get back."

Between mouthfuls, Cyril asked, "Can you remember what you were wearing on Saturday night?"

Barton paused, fork halfway to his mouth. "Ordinary jacket and trousers and shirt, why?"

"Might be an idea for me to come round first thing and bag them up," Cyril said.

"You reckon that'll prove me guilty," Barton flared.

"On the contrary, I think it might help to prove your innocence."

Barton took a breath and seemed to calm.

"And one other thing, would you mind if I took a sample of your hair?"

"Hair? Is there something else I should know?"

"Again, I think it would help your case," Cyril stated.

Barton nodded. "Okay," he said and resumed his meal.

After a minute or two, Cyril spoke again. "How did you get on this afternoon? How was Jack Tinker?"

"Not good," Barton said. "There was no reaction from him. It was as though he was dead already. I came away thinking that would probably be the last time I see him."

"Strokes are awful," Cyril said. "The trouble is, he'll probably have another that finally finishes him off. I wonder if he had high blood pressure. He certainly enjoyed boozy nights out."

"I've been on a few with him. You're right, he was certainly hard to keep up with. All those celebrations of closing cases."

"Talking of which, and his … reputation, have you thought about anyone who might want to stitch you up, bearing in mind you worked with him closely for a few years?"

"There are one or two, but I'd need to access some of the records to refresh my memory."

"If you give me some names, I'll see what I can do. But you know you can't come back to the station at the moment."

"All I'd need to do is sit in a room and flick through them. That wouldn't be too much to ask, would it?"

"I'll talk to Mr Sanderson first thing."

"Anyway, how did you get on today? Did you speak to Reid?"

"You know I can't discuss the case … not while you're suspended."

Barton stood up and walked to the window. "Christ, this is doing my head in, Cyril. I had nothing to do with this. I've no idea how my warrant card managed to find its way to this woman's settee. Someone must have lifted it from me and planted it there."

"All I can say is that you didn't leave Mama's with the victim."

"You know that?"

"According to witnesses. Anyway," he said, spooning another forkful of Chicken Korma into his mouth, "This is okay you know." He checked his watch. "But I need to get a breeze on. I promised I'd get to Cathy's tonight to help young Simon."

Barton grinned. "You take as long as you like, Cyril."

19

"Good day, love?" Donna called from the kitchen, as Tony Riley came in through the front door of the semi-detached house they'd bought fifteen years ago.

"Yeah," he responded, taking off his work boots.

For the whole drive home, he'd struggled with what he should do regarding the briefcase in the boot. Should he keep it, or hand it in? Well, that ship had sailed, he considered. He could hardly do that now he'd taken it away from the site. But maybe he could return it tomorrow? No, he decided he could do a lot with it. Besides, it looked to be all used notes – untraceable, surely? But his prime turmoil was over whether he should tell Donna. That was his biggest struggle. They told each other everything and holding back on this didn't seem right. It didn't sit well, but, there again, if she didn't know, she couldn't be blamed if things didn't go to plan. Plan, ha! What was that? He didn't have one. For the time being, he'd leave the money in the car then maybe after dark take it round the back, in through the garden gate and store it in the shed. And so he'd come to that conclusion just as he arrived home.

"Get all those footings done?"

Riley walked into the kitchen and kissed the top of Donna's head as she bent over the sink peeling potatoes. "I'd have been home sooner but Sandy wanted to gas." Putting his arms around his wife's waist he hugged her.

"Hey, what's all this for?" She put down the peeler and turned to face him. "Not been up to anything you shouldn't? Not a guilty conscience?"

He kept his face straight. "Shouldn't need an excuse to give my little woman a hug, should I?"

She raised her eyebrows and smiled. "Get yourself out of those work clothes. Tim's in his room, supposedly doing homework."

"I'll check on him," he said, walking to the hallway. "What's on the menu tonight?"

"Sausage and mash, okay?"

The three of them, Tony, Donna and son, Tim, were seated at the table, enjoying their meal.

"I was thinking today … you know how you do, alone in the cab, digging out, and thoughts just bouncing around …" Riley began.

Donna put down her knife and fork. "What hair-brained scheme are you thinking up now, Tony Riley?"

"No, I just got to thinking … when was the last time we had a decent holiday?"

"I suppose it must have been three years ago. Melanie's wedding put paid to anything since."

"Camping in Dorset hardly counts," Tim added.

They both looked at him. "You enjoyed it though, didn't you?" Riley said.

"Hardly sunny Majorca though, was it. All my mates have holidays in the sun now."

Donna smiled. "I must admit, we had more wet days than sunny, but we took in a lot of trips. You enjoyed the day out we had on that steam railway. At least you said you did at the time."

"I suppose," Tim said. "But that's not the same …"

"Anyway," Riley interrupted, "I was thinking, perhaps we could do a Spanish holiday this summer."

"Ooh, come into some money then?" Donna said.

Riley felt himself colour. "No … well, it's just I thought we maybe ought to this year. I'll be getting a bonus for this job, and I just thought …"

"We'll see," said Donna. "You never know, I might be lucky at bingo tonight."

Later that evening, with his wife out at the bingo hall and his lad round at his school mates, Tony carried the briefcase from the car boot to the back of the house and into the garden shed. Darkness had fallen and he felt more confident that he wouldn't be spotted. Once inside, he lit the storm lamp suspended from a rafter and opened the case once again. This time, he carefully removed each plastic-wrapped package. There were sixteen of them in two rows, just like a chocolate box with two levels.

Twenty minutes later, after having sorted and counted twice, he leaned back, shocked. He'd counted £47,328.00, some brand new notes but most well used. Before he re-packed the briefcase, he took five one-pound notes and put them in his wallet. Tomorrow, he'd use some to buy his cigarettes, just to test the water. They looked genuine, they felt genuine, but tomorrow, he'd discover if they truly were. Old Frank at the newsagent's checked every one in that new machine of his. That would be the acid test.

Briefcase carefully hidden behind boxes of garden implements and compost bags, he turned off the storm lamp, locked the shed door and walked back inside the house. If this worked, he could enjoy some of life's rich pleasures, but he had to be careful. He remembered all those TV programmes; The Sweeney, Z Cars and Softly Softly; and every time there was a major robbery, the thieves were always caught because they all had the need to splash the cash. All the cops needed to do was use their snouts and wait to see who was flush. That was the way of it. But he wouldn't make that mistake. Just feed it in slowly and nobody would know any different.

20
Wednesday 9th March 1977

When Cyril arrived in the CID room first thing that morning, he found Bill Walker and Sam Woodbridge poring over notes at Walker's desk.

Walker looked up. "Ah sarge, we've got contact details for two of the three names from last night. Sam and me are going to follow those up this morning."

"That's good," Cyril responded.

"We'll keep trying for the third," Woodbridge added.

Cyril shrugged off his coat and studied the few messages on his desk. "Is the DCI in?" he asked.

"Saw him ten minutes ago," Walker replied.

As he approached Sanderson's open door, he overheard the tail end of a telephone conversation.

"Are you sure?" his boss was saying.

Cyril could see the surprised expression on his face.

"Okay, I'll be right over," Sanderson said, replacing the receiver.

Sanderson looked up to see Cyril standing in the doorway. "Ah the very man," he said, rising to his feet. "With me," he added, grabbing his coat from behind the door, rushing past him and heading for the stairs.

Cyril dashed back to his desk, grabbed his coat then set off in pursuit, prompting puzzled looks from Walker and Woodbridge.

Downstairs, Cyril caught up with his DCI. Instead of turning towards the car park, Sanderson led the way down the street.

"Where are we headed, sir?" Cyril asked.

"Almost as quick to walk, and I need the exercise," Sanderson responded.

"To where?"

"The hospital. One of the doctors has discovered something suspicious he wants to show us."

"Just to keep you up to speed, sir," Cyril said, "I've just been round to John's flat and retrieved the clothes he was wearing on Saturday night. They're in the car. I'll send them off to the lab when we get back."

"That's good," Sanderson said. "Hopefully, they won't match the fibres from the back of the victim's dress."

"I'm sure they won't. I took a hair sample too," Cyril continued. "I mentioned forensics found one under the victim's fingernail."

"Let me know when we get some results," the DCI said.

"I wondered if we could arrange for John to sit in, say, the downstairs interview room and review some case notes? See if anything prompts his memory."

"I'll have a think about that."

"So what are we going to look at?" Cyril asked.

"Jack Tinker," Sanderson replied. "He's dead."

The rest of the way was covered in silence, Cyril deciding Sanderson would explain more when he was ready.

On arrival, they headed down to the small mortuary where they were met by a man in a white coat bearing the name badge of Dr Aldridge. Sanderson introduced himself and Cyril and the doctor did likewise before leading them into another room.

Inside, the doctor nodded to an attendant who opened one of the chiller doors and slid out a shroud covered tray.

"I'm sorry if this might be upsetting," Dr Aldridge began. "I know he was one of your colleagues."

Cyril looked from the doctor to Sanderson, wondering what was coming.

Dr Aldridge lifted the left hand side of the shroud to reveal the leg of Jack Tinker. "I was puzzled at the sudden deterioration in Mr Tinker's condition yesterday afternoon, so when the family left, I decided to check the body."

"And?" Sanderson asked.

"And, I found these." Aldridge indicated two small marks towards the top of the thigh with a slight discolouration surrounding them. "These are puncture marks with initial bruising. I've spoken to the medical team and nobody had cause to inject Mr Tinker here. In fact, the only point where we had cannulated him was on the back of his right hand."

"So what are you saying doctor? Someone injected something into Jack?"

The doctor nodded. "I've taken blood samples and I'm waiting for the results. Depending on what that shows, I'll be recommending a full post mortem. Normally in cases like these where the victim has suffered a stroke and succumbed, we wouldn't deem it necessary but ..."

"So how long before these results come through?" Sanderson persisted.

Aldridge gave a quick check of his watch. "I'm expecting them any time now."

"Any guesses?" Sanderson pushed.

Before he could get a response, a green clad porter knocked on the door and opened it a crack. He held up a folded piece of paper.

Dr Aldridge walked over, thanked the man and took the paper from him. Unfolding it, he read and slowly nodded.

"Well?" Sanderson sounded frustrated.

"It's as I thought," Aldridge said. "Insulin levels through the roof."

"And that isn't something that would occur naturally in cases like this?"

"Oh no." Aldridge looked straight at Sanderson. "In my professional opinion, your ex-colleague was injected deliberately with insulin. I'd like to authorise the carrying out of a full PM to determine that for sure."

"You said you were puzzled at Mr Tinker's deterioration yesterday. Can you tell me about the last time you examined him?" Sanderson gave a slight nod to

Cyril who had produced his notebook ready to take details.

"A junior colleague and myself performed an examination of the patient … I mean, Mr Tinker, at around 4:15 yesterday afternoon. There was no change in his condition but he was stable. We left to continue our rounds and about half an hour later we were alerted by the family who had come to visit him."

"And those family members were?"

"His wife and son. Apparently, his lad had travelled down from Manchester."

"Have they any indication of your suspicions?"

"No. I couldn't do that to them until I had some evidence." He held up the sheet of paper. "Now I have of course it's a different matter."

"I'd like a copy of that please," Sanderson said. "Until we conclude our investigations, we will be treating this as a suspicious death. For now, I'd like you to keep this matter to yourself. We will need to speak to your junior colleague and the other nursing staff who attended Mr Tinker, if you could give me their names?"

"Of course. If you'd follow me to the office, I can tell you all you need to know."

*   *   *

"This is going to be difficult," Cyril said. "Julia Tinker will be in pieces."

"Not something I'm looking forward to I'll admit," Sanderson responded.

The two were travelling to Jack Tinker's house, Sanderson driving the Rover.

"How well did you know Jack?" the DCI went on.

"I didn't have an awful lot to do with him over the last years he was at the station. I was in uniform when he retired."

Sanderson gave a nod. "Dick Barton was probably closest to him, being his bag man for a good few years. I wonder if he knows?"

Cyril was silent for a moment, reflecting on last night's conversation with the man. "He went to see him yesterday," he finally said.

Sanderson glanced over but said nothing.

"Thinking about it now in the light of events, it was odd what he said."

"How do you mean?"

"I asked him how Mr Tinker was and he said, 'not good'. Then he went on to say that it was as if he was dead already and that it might be the last time he sees him. Prophetic really."

Cyril saw a concerned expression pass over Sanderson's face, but it quickly disappeared as he pulled into the side of the road outside Tinker's large detached house.

Some early blossom was budding from two large trees that flanked either side of the path as they made their way alongside a border teeming with flowering daffodils.

Their knock on the door was answered by a tall man in his thirties bearing a striking resemblance to the ex-Detective Inspector. No need for a paternity test, Cyril thought.

"Hello Neil," Sanderson greeted. "Dreadful news, I understand."

"Mr Sanderson." Neil held out a hand.

Sanderson shook hands then introduced Cyril.

"Ah, yes, Mr Claydon, I remember the name." Neil opened the door wider. "Come in, come in. Mum'll be pleased to see you."

Neil led them down the hallway and into a large lounge which looked onto the rear garden. "I'll just get Mum. Would you like some tea … or something stronger?"

Both detectives held up a palm, refusing the offer. "We're fine," Sanderson said.

"Please, make yourselves at home."

Neil left the room.

Cyril sat down on the edge of a plush sofa whilst Sanderson walked over to the stereogram where a couple of framed photos of Jack Tinker in full police uniform stood. Above, on a shelved unit, there were a number of photos of Jack and Julia at various functions and a couple depicting Neil and a woman he assumed was his wife along with two small children.

When the door opened, Sanderson turned and walked towards the woman who'd entered alongside her son. "Julia," he said with outstretched arms. "I'm so sorry to hear what's happened." He embraced her lightly then took a pace back.

Cyril stood. "Mrs Tinker," he said, holding out a hand.

She took hold of it lightly. "Please call me Julia, Mr Claydon," she said.

"It's Cyril," he said with a smile.

She turned back to face Sanderson. "To be honest, Martin, after his first stroke on Friday I suppose I'd tried to prepare myself for the worst, although I was hoping he might regain consciousness. I hoped I'd be able to talk to him one more time." Her eyes were red and puffy and she dabbed a damp handkerchief to them as she spoke.

"It must have been a terrible shock when it happened," Sanderson said. "The stroke, I mean."

"Please, won't you sit down," Julia indicated the plush three-seater settee that Cyril had just risen from. "It's kind of you to call. Would you like some tea ... or something stronger?" She looked from Sanderson to Cyril and back.

"I've already ..." Neil began.

"We're fine, Julia, honest," Sanderson responded, easing himself on the offered seat, Cyril following suit.

The woman sat down on a matching easy chair by the side of the fireplace, Neil hovering just behind.

"I'm sorry I didn't get the chance to visit," the DCI went on. "We're in the middle of something."

Julia nodded. "The murder. I read about it in the paper. In fact I read it out to Jack only on Monday."

Sanderson smiled. "Yes, Jack would have enjoyed that."

"To be honest, it was nice of Mr Barton to call in to see Jack," Julia said.

Sanderson leaned forward. "When did he visit?"

"He was leaving as we arrived yesterday." She looked to a spot on the wall above the mantelpiece. "In fact that was just before ..."

Sanderson and Cyril exchanged glances. "Julia, did you see anyone else in the vicinity of Jack's room."

Her attention refocussed on the DCI. "No." Her head gave a brief shake, then she looked up at Neil.

"No," he said. "We said hello to Mr Barton then went in to see Dad. After that, it was only when we called the doctors did we see anyone else."

"Is there something wrong, Mr Sanderson?" Julia looked concerned.

Sanderson put up a hand. "No, nothing at all, I was just wondering how much attention patients like Jack get in their private room." He looked over to Cyril and began to rise. "Well, we best get off and let you get on. You've no doubt got things to arrange. And please," he continued, "if there's anything, anything at all we can help with, just let me know."

"Best get those clothes and hair sample off to the lab when we get back," Sanderson said as they drove back to the station.

"Didn't really tell us an awful lot, sir," Cyril replied. "We already knew that John was probably the last one to visit Mr Tinker."

"No." The DCI considered. "We will need to talk to him about his visit. Christ this just gets better and better." Sanderson sounded exasperated.

"But we'll also need to speak to the rest of the medical staff too," Cyril reminded him.

"Best get Miller and Walker on that. And young Woodbridge."

"So we're definitely treating this as suspicious?" Cyril asked.

"I think it's more than that, don't you?" Sanderson glanced at Cyril as he drew the Rover to a halt in the station car park.

21

With nothing else to do, Barton had made an effort to tidy up the flat. It depressed him that at the age of thirty-six, he was virtually back to square one. He knew it was all his own fault. Alison had put up with his behaviour for long enough before she finally snapped and walked out. That was three years ago; the final divorce coming through about a year after that. He smiled at the memory of the female constable he'd bedded just before she departed, then quickly wiped it from his face as he considered all that had flowed from that incident. There again, that wasn't the only occasion. Time and again, he'd succumbed to temptation. In a fit of rare openness, he remembered telling Cyril last year that he'd married a great pair of tits but just couldn't help himself from test driving other models. In the past, that recollection would have caused him to chuckle. Not now. Now, he wondered what he could do to turn himself around. He certainly wasn't in a great place at the moment, that was for sure.

The conversation with Cyril last night was something he'd really enjoyed. It had done him a power of good just chatting things through. He remembered how anti he'd been when he discovered the sergeant was about to be foisted on him last year; and that's the verb he used to describe what happened. 'Winco' they'd all called him, because of his war-time RAF service. Cyril had got all uppity when he tried to use that sobriquet; spoke about respect for those who served. He was quite right, of course. Strange how he now had the greatest respect for him too.

He sat down at the kitchen table with one of the drop-leaves up, covered with a plastic tablecloth. In front of him was a notepad and pencil. As Cyril had suggested, it was time to make some notes if he was ever going to get himself out of this mess. He thought back over the past ten years to those cases he'd been involved with where those charged and sentenced may have felt hard done by. If you asked most offenders if they'd been sent down wrongly, a high proportion would say yes. As they say, the jails are full of innocent people. But realistically, only a handful had grounds to complain.

After some time, he looked at the notepad and stared at the four names and main charges he'd written down. He'd need to check their current status; some may still be inside, although that might not preclude some associate of the offender working on their friend's behalf. He scratched his temple, scarcely believing that someone sent down for the offences he'd noted would resort to murdering someone just for revenge. To try and stitch up an officer for that seemed incredible.

The ring on the flat's doorbell interrupted his thoughts. He stood and walked to the door.

"Twice in one week," Barton quipped when he saw Sanderson and Cyril standing outside.

"We need another chat, John," Sanderson said. "Do you mind if we come in?"

Barton opened the door wide and the two men entered.

"Tidied up, I see," Sanderson remarked as he walked into the kitchen and turned to face the DI.

"Got to do something with my time, sir." he said. "That and trying to list out who might want to stitch me up." He indicated the pad lying on the table. "It would be easier if I could have access to the files though."

Sanderson ignored the comments. "I understand you visited Jack yesterday."

"That's right." Barton turned to Cyril. "I told you last night."

Cyril only nodded.

"How was he when you left?" Sanderson asked.

"Well, he was unresponsive. I talked a bit about what had gone on with me, hoping for some reaction, but … hold on … what's going on? Has something happened?"

"Jack's dead, John." Cyril said, sitting in a chair by the kitchen table.

"Oh bloody hell." Barton shook his head, obvious concern on his face. He sat down at the table opposite Cyril. "Julia will be in bits. She came in as I was leaving; her and Neil."

"We've just come from there," Cyril said. "But at least, Neil's with her."

Sanderson remained standing. "What I'd like to know, John, is exactly what happened when you visited the hospital yesterday," he said.

Barton turned to look at the DCI. "Hold on, what are you saying? Is there something suspicious about Jack's death? I thought he'd had a stroke."

"He had … only that might not be the cause of death."

"What do you mean?"

"We're awaiting the post-mortem results before we can be definite, but we're treating his death as suspicious," Sanderson stated. "So anything you can remember about yesterday, could be important."

Barton looked tense, but slowly he began to relax. "I just walked in, asked at reception where I could find him, saw the signs for the ward, went upstairs and made my way along the corridor until I came to his room door."

"Did you see anyone else?" Cyril asked.

"No … well, only some young bloke … I thought he was a doctor … well he had a white coat." Barton screwed up his face in thought. "I say that, but he wasn't actually wearing it, he was carrying it." He snapped his fingers. "And he was carrying a stethoscope, so he was probably just finishing a shift."

"That's good," Sanderson said.

Cyril thought for a second. "This young guy," he said, "Was he coming from the direction of Jack Tinker's room, or had he approached it from the other side."

"Well, I'd come up the stairs and turned into the corridor and he was coming towards me but … no, he'd already passed Jack's room, so he was coming from that direction."

"Can you describe him?" Sanderson pressed.

Barton blew out a breath of air. "To be honest, I didn't pay much attention. I was thinking about what I might find with Jack."

"You said he was a young guy, so you must have noticed something. Height, build …"

"He was a bit shorter than me, maybe around five foot nine or ten, slim build."

"That's good," Cyril encouraged.

"Oh, and he was wearing a light coloured tee shirt I think and dark trousers," Barton added.

Sanderson seemed to soften. "Thanks, John. We are here to help you, you know."

Cyril turned the pad on the table round so he could read what Barton had written. "Okay, let's see what you've remembered about any potential suspects who might want to stitch you up," he said.

Over the course of the next fifteen minutes, Barton went through the four names he'd written down and the possible reasons for inclusion.

Finally, Sanderson addressed Cyril. "Tomorrow then, you pull the records for these four and see what comes to light."

Cyril nodded, then added thoughtfully, "Of course it might not be anybody connected with John in the past … it could just be some opportunist who picked up John's warrant card somehow and wanted to create mischief."

22

"Evening Cyril. How did you enjoy your curry last night?" Doris had that twinkle in her eye that belied her seventy-six years.

"It was different, that's for sure."

He wasn't surprised to find his next-door neighbour in his kitchen when he arrived home. She had a key to his house as he had for hers. "He's a troubled soul," she said.

"Brought a lot on himself."

She looked down at Charlie slobbering over his food bowl. She'd come in to feed him when she noticed Cyril hadn't yet arrived home. "Maybe so, but I've known someone like him before. And before you ask, I don't mean my Howard."

The mention of Doris's late husband surprised Cyril. He had died in 1945, way before he and Doris were neighbours but she always spoke of him in loving terms.

"He has a drink problem, doesn't he?" she went on. "He can't settle down and before you know it, it all implodes."

"Did he open up to you then, Doris?"

"Didn't need to say it in as many words."

The old labrador finished his food, lapped up some water noisily then burped.

"Manners, Charlie," Cyril said.

Doris stroked the dog's head. "Is he in some trouble? At work, I mean."

Cyril filled the kettle and switched it on. "You could say that. It would help if he could remember certain things. Tea?" he asked.

"Go on then," his neighbour responded, sitting on one of the kitchen chairs, while Charlie waddled over to his bed and slumped down. "Are you open to suggestions?" Doris asked.

"Anything might help. Why? What do you have in mind?"

"You know my friend, Betty?" she began slowly. "Of course you do. She had that shock this week. Well, we decided to go out last night and see a show."

"You're not suggesting he needs some distraction and I take him out to see some production on stage?"

She laughed. "Not exactly. What we saw was a hypnotist. The Great Lorenzo, he called himself. He's on at the Westcliff Theatre all week."

The kettle clicked off and he put tea bags in mugs and poured water in. "Like I said, there's no way I'm suggesting he sees a show."

"You're missing the point, Cyril. If this hypnotist is in town all week, you're a policeman, go and see him away from the stage. Get him to try and …"

"But all that's just a trick. Smoke and mirrors."

"If it was some sort of mind-reading act, I might agree – the Thirty-Nine steps sort of thing. Oh I did love that film. Robert Donat was lovely." Her gaze drifted off with a broad smile on her face. "My Howard looked a bit like him, you know."

"I took Maureen to see the later one with Kenneth More." Cyril removed the tea bags and added milk for them, placing a mug in front of Doris.

"Anyway," she said, keen to refocus the conversation. "This Lorenzo character put people under and had them doing all sorts of daft things; eating an onion and telling them it was an apple."

"I can't see that helping John." Cyril took a sip of his tea.

"But he could put him under and take him back to the times when he can't remember."

Cyril began to think his neighbour had a point.

"Did you see that program on the telly last year?" she continued. "The Bloxham Tapes."

He shook his head.

"Fascinating," she said, her face lighting up in interest. "Some expert hypnotist, Bloxham his name was, would take people back not only to their youngest recollections but beyond that, before they were born to other lives."

"No," he responded, incredulity sounding in his voice.

"I know what you think, it was all fabrication. But one woman was taken back to being a Jew in York around 1200, I think, and how she took refuge in the crypt of a church before she died. Only thing was, this church wasn't known to have a crypt. Only later did they find one."

After Doris had returned home, Cyril roused Charlie from his slumbers to take him round the block before finally turning in. She had a point, he thought. It might be a useful idea to help Barton remember. It wouldn't be admissible as evidence, but it might throw something up that could help them both.

23
Thursday 10th March 1977

Cyril was nursing a mug of tea in the canteen when Cathy came in, looked over and smiled at him. She gesticulated towards the counter where various items of food were displayed but Cyril raised a hand and shook his head.

With a cup of coffee and a bacon roll, she walked over to his table and sat down opposite.

"How did Simon get on with his exam yesterday," he asked.

"Went well, he said. Told me to say thanks." She took a bite of her roll before continuing, "Apparently your explanations for geometry seemed easier than how he'd been taught."

Cyril smiled. "That's great. I remember being taught like that when I was in the RAF. One of the lads who was a navigator …" His thoughts drifted off to a time and a friend long gone. "He was only a few years older than Simon."

Cathy caught the pain in his expression and put a hand on his. "I know there were so many," she said, "but at least his knowledge has been put to good use again."

Cyril looked down at their hands on the table. "Just hope Simon uses it well now too." He drained his mug then continued, "Actually, you can do me a favour, Cathy."

"What's that?"

He passed her a piece of paper with the four names Barton had listed. "Could you pull the files for these miscreants for me?"

She looked at the list. "Sure. How quickly do you want them?"

He stood to leave. "As soon as you can, please. I'll see you later." With a smile, he turned and left the canteen.

Miller and Walker were sifting through paperwork on their respective desks when Cyril walked into the CID room. Woodbridge had based himself at a spare desk next to Cyril's.

"Morning, sarge," Walker greeted.

"Sarge," Miller joined in.

"Skip." Woodbridge gave the greeting for his ex-uniformed sergeant.

"Morning, lads," Cyril said. "How did you get on yesterday at the hospital?"

"Just going through each other's statements now," Walker answered.

"We think we've covered most of the staff. Nothing much seems to have surfaced but we thought we'd swap statements to see if anything flags up with something we might have heard from our own interviews," Miller said, flicking ash from his cigarette into the nearly full ashtray on his desk.

"Good idea," Cyril said, wondering whose idea that actually was. He sat down at his desk and read through the few messages left for him before another thought crossed his mind. "Is there any mention from any of the hospital staff about a young man seen carrying a white hospital coat and stethoscope?"

"Can't recall anyone mentioning that," Walker said.

"Nothing here," Woodbridge added.

Miller shook his head. "Is it important?"

"Not sure, Ben. Just something somebody mentioned yesterday." Cyril thought a moment. "Can one of you get back down there and speak again to the staff, specifically mentioning this character?"

Miller looked to Woodbridge who responded, "I can do that, skip."

"Thanks, Sam." Cyril then looked to Walker. "Any further forward with those three names that barman gave us?"

Walker lifted a sheet of paper from his desk and passed it to Cyril. Sam and I spoke to two of them, these two men here. Nothing out of the ordinary. Both remember the DI being in but not exactly when he left. One remembered the woman finishing her drink and leaving about twenty minutes or so after Mr Barton, they think on her own."

"What about the third name; this other man, Stevie?"

"Not sure, sarge. It meant nothing to the two blokes. Maybe Small got it wrong; made a mistake," Woodbridge answered.

"Alright, I'll pursue that. In the meantime, did anything interesting come to light when you went through Barton's old cases?" Cyril stood and walked towards the DC's desk.

"Only got part way into that when we got called to the hospital interviews," Miller said, "but I've got a couple of names here, sarge." He rummaged on the mess on his desk before pulling a scruffy piece of paper from underneath some others and holding it out.

Cyril took hold of it and nodded. "These two have surfaced already and I've requested the files." He handed the note back. "Keep on it though."

*   *   *

Barton zipped his jacket up to the neck as far as it would go. A scarf wrapped inside offered more protection against the cold wind whipping sideways off the sea. He decided he needed to blow away some of the fug that seemed to have hung around him since waking up last Monday morning. And what better way than a walk down the full length of Clacton pier.

Through the middle of the slot machine arcade and in between the waltzers and ghost train rides, he emerged into the open air just in time to feel the forty-five degree rain stinging his face. Normally, he'd turn back, but today he needed to prove to himself he could make it to the very end, come what may. Past the lifeboat station, he walked around the café at the end and past the moorings where on occasion a tourist boat would dock in the summer months. It was empty now, save for a few fishermen sitting out in waterproofs casting their lines into the North Sea. He was always amazed that, despite the weather, there would always be one or two indulging in their hobby.

Walking back, the aroma of an all-day breakfast proved too much and he was lured into the café on a promise of warmth and a large plateful of food. There was no one in the café when he entered, not many brave souls making it to the end of the pier. He ordered his breakfast and sat at a table towards the back and began to sift through the events of the past few days.

Sunday morning when he woke, his only thoughts were that he was in his own bed and on his own. He'd had a few uncomfortable experiences in the past where he'd been shocked and surprised at who he'd spent the night with. Normally, he would remember. He'd also woken up in one or two strange beds too. Trevor on security down at the Butlin's holiday camp would often oblige with a spare chalet if he got lucky with one of the holidaymakers, or even one of the pretty waitresses, but that was only in the season. No, Cyril and Sanderson were right, he had to remember something about his movements on Saturday night. Somebody must have picked his pocket for the warrant card; or he might have pulled it out accidentally, although he didn't think that likely. And another thing, how did he get back from Mama's? Not far to walk, but somebody must have seen him.

His food arrived, brought out by the only waitress on duty, a pretty girl of about nineteen with her hair plaited on top of her head, protected by a cap. She placed the plate on the table and a mug of tea alongside without a word. He began to eat.

Part way through his meal, a familiar face appeared in the doorway, spotted him then immediately turned round to leave.

"Spider!" Barton shouted to the man's back.

The back winced, froze for a split second then turned back to re-enter the café.

Barton pointed to the chair opposite. "Sit," he commanded.

The man closed the door and made his way to the table, glancing quickly round at the empty interior. "Mr Barton, I never saw you there," he said as he lowered himself into the chair. Spider was a character Barton had known for years, nicknamed as such because of a tattoo he had on his upper right arm, put there as the result of a bet, apparently.

"Of course you didn't. There were that many people in here blocking your view."

"Honest."

"You wouldn't know the meaning of the word."

The man gave a pained expression.

"Anyway, what brings you in here?" Barton asked.

"Thought I'd get a hot drink for me and my mate out there." Spider thumbed through the window in the general direction of the end of the pier. "He likes fishing."

"In this weather? I'd rather watch paint dry."

"Me too, Mr Barton, but he likes my company."

"No accounting for taste." Barton took a sip of his tea.

Spider looked put out. "No need for that," he said. The man studied Barton for a second before he spoke again. "But I could ask you the same question. Why are you sitting in a café on the end of Clacton pier? Not working this murder case then? Maybe not in charge but I would have thought you'd be alongside Mr Sanderson, you being like bum chums." The grin quickly evaporated from his face when he saw Barton's expression.

"How long have we known each other, Spider?" the detective asked.

"I don't know, maybe ten years."

"And didn't I help your brother get a suspended when it looked like he was going down big-time? Turned his life around since then, hasn't he?"

"Yeah, okay, but what about old Frankie Pearson? You tucked him up good and proper."

Frankie Pearson. Of course, there was another name that would have been added to the list, except he'd passed on a few years ago. "But that wasn't me, Spider. I had nothing to do with that. Not that the old sod didn't deserve it."

The man nodded. "True. He had gotten away with loads up till then. I suppose you'll blame Tinker for that one."

"Jack had to do what was necessary."

"So much for a fair justice system."

Barton held up his fork. "I'm not saying I agree with how he did it, but even you must admit you lot play the system, use every means possible to deny responsibility for what you do. Jack was just evening things up a bit."

"Don't go tarring me with the same brush, Mr Barton. I've kept my nose clean for the past seven years."

Barton held his gaze. "Sure," he said and resumed eating. After a moment, he began again, "While we're on the subject, have you heard about Jack?"

"Why, what's he done now? I thought he'd retired," Spider responded.

"He had. Only a bit more permanently now. He died yesterday."

"I'll put the word out for you. I'm sure the boys will want to send flowers."

Again, Barton cast a sceptical glance at the man, before deciding to press for more. "Thinking about what you said just now, Spider … is there anyone else who might hold a grudge against me? Strictest confidence, of course."

Spider looked puzzled. "Is someone out to get you, then?"

Barton mopped the last of his bread around his plate. "Just interested, that's all," he said, before stuffing the bread in his mouth.

The man gave the question some thought, then reeled off five more names to Barton. As he lowered his voice for the last, the waitress appeared to collect Barton's empty plate. Spider looked up at her. "Can I have two teas to take out, please?" he asked, then to Barton, "My mate will think I've sodded off home."

The waitress sighed and returned to the counter to prepare the order.

"Thanks, Spider," Barton said. "Don't forget, this conversation was in strictest confidence. Appreciate it."

"What conversation?" Spider said, rising and making his way to the counter.

*   *   *

Cyril rubbed his face with both hands and sat back in his chair. For the past two hours he'd been reading through the files Cathy had pulled from the records that he'd requested. He'd worked his way through each case, checked on the current whereabouts of the various individuals and come to the conclusion that the source of anyone wanting to set Barton up was unlikely to be there. Two were still inside, one had died and the other seemed too old and wasn't even living in Essex any more. He badly needed a break but was coming to the conclusion that it might just have been someone who had found or stolen Barton's warrant card and used it to create mischief when he murdered Sharon Williams.

The phone's ringing interrupted his thoughts.

"Claydon," he answered before listening to Tom from the lab reporting on the findings from the crime scene.

"So no matches on our records then?" Cyril finally said, then nodded at the answer. "And definitely not DI Barton's?" Another pause before he thanked him and put the phone down.

Cyril felt relieved. Fingerprints on the wine glasses found in the lounge of Sharon Williams' house had produced no matches. Tom was checking the Essex files before moving on to the Met's. Anything further afield would take time, if ever. Cyril thought it would be a welcome day when all fingerprint information could be gathered together in one place to allow for a comprehensive search. Sharon's prints were obviously identified on one glass but so far, nothing from the other one. The only bit of good news was that Barton's did not appear anywhere in the property.

The more bizarre he thought Doris's suggestion was, the more he came to see the advantages of pursuing it. After all, he was getting nowhere by conventional methods. Finally, he folded the last file shut on his desk and picked up the phone.

His call was answered on the fifth ring.

"Barton," came the sharp reply.

"John, listen, I have an idea," Cyril said. "What are you doing at the moment?"

24

The Great Lorenzo opened the door of the dressing room and stared at the two figures who had interrupted him. "I don't do autographs," he said in irritable well-spoken tones.

"We're not after autographs," Cyril responded. "We need your help."

"If you want a private session, you'll have to book an appointment."

"Told you this was a waste of time, Cyril," Barton said and turned to walk away.

"Just hold on, John." Exasperated, Cyril produced his warrant card. "As I said, Mr err ... Lorenzo? We need your help."

The man looked sheepish. "It's Bradshaw. Roy Bradshaw," he replied, his accent slipping, sounding distinctively northern now. "You best come in."

Cyril and Barton stepped into the small dressing room. On one wall, surrounded by lights, was a mirror. On the shelf below, a selection of stage make-up as well as a half-empty bottle of Bell's whisky.

A thin smile on his face, Cyril couldn't help himself. "Lorenzo?" he asked. "An old family name, no doubt."

"Actually, on my mother's side," the man replied. "I didn't think the name Bradshaw had any stage presence.

"Anyway, how can I help?" Bradshaw moved the bottle onto the floor behind a suitcase.

"My colleague here is struggling to remember some important details and I'd like you to help him."

The man glanced at his watch. "If I can," he said. "But bear in mind I'll need to prepare before my show, so I can give you half-an-hour at the moment. If you think you'd need longer, we could arrange a later time."

"Let's just see how we go, shall we?"

Bradshaw looked at Barton for a second then pulled the only two chairs in the room from under the make-up shelf and turned them to face each other, side on to the mirror. "Sit down here, please," he said, indicating one.

Cyril and Barton shuffled round to make way.

Barton looked unconvinced as he sat down "Are you sure about this, Cyril?" he asked.

"It'll be fine," he responded taking out his notebook and pencil. "Just relax."

"Sound advice," Bradshaw said, as he sat in the other seat facing Barton and prepared to begin the hypnosis.

"I don't know what all the fuss was about," Barton moaned as the pair walked back into town. "I couldn't remember a thing."

Cyril smiled. "Oh yes you did, John," he said, tapping the inside pocket of his coat where his notebook was.

"When?" Barton persisted. "I sat down on that chair, he talked a bit of bollocks and the next thing he said was, I could go."

"You really can't remember anything else about the last half hour?"

"Why? What did I say?"

"I'll give it to you, John. You're persistent, I'll say that," Cyril said.

Barton looked puzzled.

"I'm surprised any of your chat up lines ever work."

Barton took hold of Cyril's arm, stopping their walk. "Look, if any of this gets out, I'll make sure your days in CID are hell."

Cyril faced the DI, annoyance in his tone. "I'm trying to help you here. It wasn't me who placed your warrant card at the scene of a murder. And I wasn't the last person to see another victim alive. Now just go with me for now."

Barton held Cyril's gaze for a second. "Okay, I'm sorry," he said. "I'm just wound up over all of this."

"I know you are, but losing your cool won't help."

Barton took out a cigarette and lit up, as they walked on. "Not seen your pipe for a while, Cyril. You given up?"

"Good idea, John," he responded and took his pipe and tobacco pouch from his coat pocket. As he packed the bowl, he asked, "Any thoughts on who might want to stitch you up?"

"Oddly enough, I can think of six names."

25
Friday 11ᵗʰ March 1977

First thing the following morning, Cyril trawled back through the files Cathy had brought up to him yesterday and satisfied himself that the answer he was looking for was not there. Three of the six names Barton had given him last night were the subject of the files on his desk and counted amongst the four he'd reviewed yesterday. That left three more names. He'd nip down later, when Cathy would be in, and ask her to retrieve their files from the Records Department for him.

He studied the notes he'd taken when Barton was under the hypnotic spell of the Great Lorenzo last night. Thanks to that exercise he now had the route the DI had followed last Saturday, starting in The Madena next door. A smile came to his face as he recalled some of the more humorous memories. He had to give it to Dick, he couldn't imagine using some of his techniques with women. Different generation, he supposed.

DCI Sanderson walked in to the CID office, interrupting Cyril's train of thought.

"Are we getting anywhere, Cyril?" he asked.

"John's come up with six names he thought may hold some form of grudge against him," Cyril responded. He tapped the files on his desk. "I've checked three of them, but I don't think they'd be capable of anything like this. I've got another three to check, and when the secretaries come in I'll request those files too."

Sanderson leaned against the unoccupied desk of DC Walker. "I know you said the prints on the wine glasses at the scene were no match to Dick, the warrant card had been wiped clean and there were no other fingerprints belonging to him found at the property ..." Cyril nodded. "But what about that hair under the fingernail?"

"I'm still waiting for forensics to report." Cyril responded. "I'll chase that up. One set of prints on one of the glasses belonged to Sharon Williams but the other set, Tom's still searching for a match."

Sanderson rubbed his chin. "What about John's movements on Saturday night, Sunday morning?"

Cyril tapped his teeth with a pencil in an attempt to stop a smile appearing on his face. The last thing he wanted was to open himself to ridicule because he'd taken Barton to be hypnotised. "I think we know where he went on Saturday evening and how his night progressed. I'll be checking the various establishments later this morning."

"Right, well keep me informed. We're going to need a break soon," Sanderson said as he left the room.

Before he did anything else, Cyril picked up the phone and dialled the number for the Forensics Lab. His long-time contact, Tom, told him what he'd expected. The fibres from Barton's clothes were no match for those found on Sharon's and the hair retrieved from below her finger nail was a much fairer colour than Barton's brown. He had exhausted the fingerprint database from the Essex files and was about to move on to the Met's. But so far no match for the prints on the other glass. He thanked the man and put the phone down.

Cyril then turned to a fresh sheet of paper on his pad and began to write. From what he'd learned from Barton's initial memory of the events of Saturday night, he'd started off in The Madena, next door to the police station. It was unlikely he would show his warrant card there, after all, half of the clientele would be police. He'd make a start there and try and build some form of timetable as to where the DI was and at what time. He knew he'd left Mama's nightclub around 1:30 on Sunday morning, the rest he'd have to piece together with the aid of the notes he'd made of Barton's hypnosis.

A possible break came later that morning after Cathy had retrieved the three outstanding files from Records. Cyril was sifting through them when he came across the name of Clifford Mitchell Hammond, born 1915, now aged sixty-two and convicted of aggravated robbery in 1969 for his part in the Dovercourt Post Office robbery. Some £50,000 had been stolen but never recovered. He had a current address in the town and thought it worth a call at the very least. Sanderson agreed and the pair set off to speak to the man.

* * *

"Shit," DCI Barry *'Bastard'* Brookes muttered as he thrust down the telephone receiver on his desk.

"Bad news, boss?" his weasely-looking DS side-kick asked.

They were in his office in the small Complaints and Discipline Department in the Essex Police Headquarters in Chelmsford.

"Fingerprints from that Clacton murder scene … they don't match Barton's. In fact there's no forensic evidence he was ever in the victim's house."

"So that's it, then. We close it down?"

"No, that's not fucking it!" Brookes spat. "We keep digging."

His DS shrugged.

"And to top it all," Brookes went on, "That bent bastard Tinker upped and died this week too. A stroke, apparently."

"Not a good week, then boss."

Brookes gave his DS a withering look.

* * *

"Oh Christ, what have you come to stitch me up with now?" The heavily lined features of Cliff Hammond screwed into an expression of disgust at the two men on his doorstep.

114

"We'd like a word, Mr Hammond," DCI Sanderson said.

"Do I need a solicitor?"

Sanderson ignored the question. "Can we come in?"

Hammond sighed and opened the door wide.

Sanderson and Cyril stepped into the hallway of the semi-detached house and waited while the front door was closed. They were in a quiet street on the Peter Bruff estate in Clacton, named after the Victorian engineer who'd founded the resort in the 19th Century. Cyril had studied the file on the Dovercourt job. Hammond had been sentenced to eight years in 1969 for his part in the robbery. He'd been released last year having served six years. His convicted accomplice, Walter Mason, had died in Chelmsford Prison three years ago, before he could complete his sentence.

Hammond led the two men into the front room and bade them sit on a comfortable but aged sofa. The man himself sat in an armchair by the side of the fireplace. The open fire was dead, ashes needing to be cleaned out before it could be lit again.

"What do you want?" Hammond asked, a suspicious expression on his face. He looked from one detective to the other.

"I'm DCI Sanderson and this is DS Claydon," Sanderson began.

"I know you," Hammond addressed the DCI, "But we haven't met," he said to Cyril.

"Can you tell us where you were last Saturday night and Sunday morning?" Sanderson asked.

Hammond's eyes narrowed. "Why? Like I said at the door, what are trying to stitch me up with?"

"Look Mr Hammond," Cyril responded, "we're only trying to eliminate you from our enquiries. If you can tell us, it would be much appreciated."

"What happened Saturday night, Sunday morning? Some robbery, was it?"

Sanderson bristled. "We could do this down at the station if you prefer," he said.

Hammond paused a moment as he considered his answer. "If you must know, we went to the club, Mary and me," he finally said.

"And which club would that be?" Sanderson asked.

"Comrades Club on Old Road. You can check if you like. They'll tell you we were there all night. They had a turn on. Not bad too."

"So what time did you leave?"

"Just gone eleven and we were back here by half past."

"And Mary … she can confirm that?"

"Mrs Hammond, yes if she needs to."

"And you were home here for the rest of the night?" Sanderson persisted.

"We're both over sixty Mr Sanderson, we're not likely to venture out clubbing or whatever it is the young 'uns do nowadays."

"Where is Mary, Mr Hammond?" Cyril asked.

"Shopping. She shouldn't be too long."

Sanderson glanced to Cyril and he took his cue. "Mr Hammond … Cliff," he began.

Hammond looked at Cyril and gave a slight nod.

"Can you tell me about what happened back in 1969?"

"You know what happened. I got sent down for eight years."

"You and Walter Mason for an aggravated burglary on the post office in Dovercourt," Cyril expanded for him.

"So why ask?"

"You know Walter Mason died in prison."

Another imperceptible movement of the head.

Cyril pressed on, "Walter Mason always maintained his innocence."

Hammond shook his head. "Pha!"

Cyril sat forward on the sofa. "You never gave evidence against him, nor he against you … and I get that, thieves' honour and all that."

Hammond didn't respond.

"You pleaded guilty, but he didn't. After all this time, and bearing in mind Walter's no longer with us … did the two of you carry out that job?"

Hammond looked to the window and seemed to be watching something from a different time and place. Eventually, he turned and looked back to Cyril. "Six years I served for that. I did my time. But I never got a penny from it."

"I've looked through the files, Cliff," Cyril went on. "The Post Office estimated something like fifty thousand pounds was stolen."

"That's as maybe, but I never benefitted from any of it."

"But Mason was with you, right?"

Another slight nod.

"So was Mason responsible for hiding the money?"

Hammond looked down at the carpet and let out a deep sigh. "He said he'd hide it for us … until the heat died down." He looked up at Cyril. "But it never did. I was arrested soon after and Walter a day or so later. Like you say, I never did grass him up. I wouldn't. But I also never found out what he did with the money."

"He wasn't involved," Cyril said, making his way back to Sanderson's Rover.

"No, you're right," he said. "Mrs Hammond confirmed his story."

"Not best pleased to see us, though. Don't blame her either."

Sanderson said nothing more and unlocked the car parked on the street outside Hammond's house.

"Do you believe him about the post office job? Not benefitting from any of the cash?" Cyril asked as he closed the car door.

"I can't see any evidence of it, can you? Still living in a council house, not looking particularly flush. No, I think he was telling the truth there."

Cyril nodded. "I agree." He clipped his seat belt then asked, "I'm assuming you'll want me to call in at the Comrades Club to check their story?"

"Waste of time," Sanderson said, "but it'll cover all the bases."

After a few minutes driving, he asked what Cyril had planned next.

Cyril glanced at his watch. "I thought I'd trace John's route on Saturday night," he said.

"Through all of Clacton's dens of iniquity, no doubt," Sanderson remarked.

"I thought I'd try and establish where and when he last showed his warrant. Someone got hold of it; either lifted it from his pocket or picked it up if he dropped it somewhere."

26

"Afternoon, Larry." Cyril walked into The Madena just after one that afternoon, pipe puffing away.

"Mr Claydon?" The barman looked up from reading the Sun. "We don't often see you in here."

"Always busy," he said.

"What can I get you? On the house, of course."

"No, nothing for me, Larry, thanks. I wanted to pick your brains."

"Sounds interesting."

"Can you cast your mind back to last Saturday?"

Larry folded the newspaper closed. "If I can. The days just seem to blend into one another," he said, a nervous grin appearing.

"You know DI Barton?"

The man laughed. "Dick? What's he done now?"

"Nothing. I was just wondering if you can remember him being in that evening?"

The barman looked up to the ceiling for a moment, as if for some divine inspiration. "Last Saturday?" He snapped his fingers. "Yep. In just after half seven, had two pints and then was off."

"On the house?"

Larry made a face as if to say, stupid question. Many a copper used their status for free drinks. It was a wonder pubs like The Madena stayed in business. On the other hand, when they were celebrating some success, the money and the drinks would flow.

"So what time would he have left here?"

"Maybe just after eight."

"And he wouldn't have shown his warrant card either," Cyril asked, half-heartedly.

"Dick? No."

119

Cyril thanked him and left, amused at one or two early drinkers he recognised with criminal records who were avoiding his glances.

Next up, he made his way to The Osborne Hotel on Rosemary Road. Along the route, he checked his watch; no more than five minutes for the walk. Inside, similar questions of the barman produced blank answers. He wasn't working last Saturday, the manager would probably know as he was behind the bar but he wasn't around at the moment.

Next, a few doors along, about 30 yards, Cyril walked into The Imperial Hotel. The young girl serving behind the bar only worked lunchtimes through the week. Different staff worked nights, especially on the weekend.

After leaving, Cyril decided it was a waste of time trying to walk round the rest of Barton's route. The best idea he thought would be to conduct the exercise tomorrow night, a week after the memories he wanted to jog. While he was out in the town, he walked up to the Comrades Club to check on Cliff Hammond's alibi for Saturday night. Unsurprisingly, that was confirmed by a couple of the stewards there; another task completed. Resigned, he set off back to the police station on Jackson Road.

As he took the steps up to the main entrance, Sam Woodbridge was leaving. An idea came to Cyril.

"Ah, Sam," he said. "What are you up to tomorrow?"

"It's my weekend off, skip." Woodbridge replied. "I was going to Portman Road. We've got Bristol City at home."

"I was thinking more of the evening?"

"Well …"

"Sorry, Sam, you're probably taking some nice young girl out on the town."

"Actually, no. I was only going out with a few mates, that's all. Why are you asking?"

"Just a thought …"

A few minutes later, plans had been made.

27

Tony Riley had had no problems spending the one-pound notes over the previous couple of days, sundry purchases of cigarettes, newspapers and such. He'd even risked using one of the ten-pound notes to fill up the tank of his car yesterday with no comeback. His confidence was growing. Tomorrow, he considered calling into his bank to see if they would exchange some of the withdrawn five-pound notes. He was working on a story about finding them in an old wallet he'd forgotten about.

On site today, his main job was loading the spoil from the site strip and excavations onto the tipper trucks arriving to take it off site. The groundwork team had already poured the concrete for the foundations of one of the houses, and work was well underway preparing for the first pour on the second this afternoon.

Half of the spoil had been removed by the time he stopped the engine and climbed down from the cab to walk to his car. The drizzly rain that had begun yesterday afternoon had persisted overnight and appeared to be getting heavier. On the basis of that, he sat in his car to enjoy his bacon butties and coffee. As he ate, his thoughts drifted to summer holidays. The conversations he'd had with Donna since Monday, encouraged him to think about calling in to some travel agents in the morning too. Cracking open the window, he lit a cigarette and allowed himself a broad smile. Yes, things were looking up.

The passenger door opened and Richard, the site manager clambered in, startling him. "Weather's not getting any better," he said.

"Might have to cancel this afternoon's concrete," Riley responded.

"Just when things were going well," Richard said. "Knew it was too good." He pulled a cigarette from a packet in his shirt pocket and lit up. "You up for a bit of overtime tomorrow, Tony?" he asked, opening his window a touch.

"Er ... tomorrow? I was ..." Riley stumbled.

"Just the morning. Forecast's better. Should be dry and I can switch today's pour until then."

"But you won't need me for any digging out, though?"

Richard took a draw on his cigarette and blew out smoke. "Ah, no. Maybe not," he said. "How long do you think it might take?"

Riley let out a sigh of relief. The last thing he wanted was to have his plans for a Saturday morning visit to the bank and travel agent scuppered. "Should get most of them dug out on Monday. That'll only leave the septic tanks to be done, but I would have thought you could do them a lot later. You won't want bloody big holes open for long."

The site manager turned over his options. "No, you're right, Tony. Just get the rest of the muck-away wagons loaded and you can piss off for the rest of the day." Richard opened the door. "See you Monday," he said and climbed out.

28
Saturday 12th March 1977

"Appreciate this, Sam," Cyril said as he drove into Clacton at just after 7:00pm on Saturday night.

Woodbridge had agreed to Cyril's plan and turned up straight from the game. He'd bemoaned a poor performance by Ipswich against Bristol City, despite a 1-0 win. Cyril provided some fish and chips from Big Pete's to set them up for an evening's work.

"No problem, skip," Woodbridge replied as he sat in the passenger seat alongside his sergeant.

"Listen Sam, for tonight, call me Cyril will you. This isn't strictly official but it sort of is, if you know what I mean."

"Sure."

Cyril indicated a folder he'd brought with him which he'd put on the rear seats. "Have a look in there. I've listed down the route that DI Barton took last Saturday night."

Woodbridge leaned behind, opened the folder and began to study the notes.

"Also there are the photos of DI Barton and Sharon Williams and the route that she and Karyn Brown took before they ended up in Mama's. Interesting that they all visited the Railway Hotel at some point but not, as far as I know, at the same time."

Once he'd read through, Woodbridge looked over to Cyril. "So why me?" he asked. "Why not take the DI with you tonight?"

"Well, for one thing, I'm not sure if he would be a help or a hindrance in this instance. And for a second, he's gone off for the weekend; visiting relatives apparently."

Cyril pulled the car into the police station car park and got out, Woodbridge following suit.

"You said you'd spoken to Larry in The Madena yesterday," Woodbridge stated.

"That's right, but I thought we might concentrate on some of the punters. Did they see John last week? Did they notice anything unusual? But we'll try to keep it low key and conversational." Cyril put on his jacket and locked the car. "Come on."

They headed next door to the pub.

Larry behind the bar gave the pair a nod as they walked in but there was no point in talking to him again. For now, they would concentrate on the drinkers who were in. A few officers out of uniform and winding down after a shift were there as well as a few more salubrious characters. Cyril and Woodbridge began talking to them, seeing what they could remember about the events of a week ago.

One was typical of many. "Oh aye," he said. "Dick was in last Saturday. Had a couple and then went on his way." No, he hadn't seen him talking to anyone in particular and, no, he couldn't remember anyone suspicious in the bar at the time.

Cyril and Woodbridge moved on to The Osborne, Barton's next port of call.

By the time they'd reached the Railway Hotel over the road from Clacton railway station, they were feeling disconsolate. Barton had been seen in The Osborne, The Imperial and The Marine but there was nothing conspicuous about his visits. He'd spoken to one or two people he knew and chatted to a couple of women with no success. One fact to emerge was that he had shown his warrant in The Marine in an attempt to get free drinks. The landlord had reluctantly given him one pint.

The barman at The Railway recognised Barton's photograph. He knew he was 'job' but, although Barton had tried the warrant trick, he'd refused to co-operate and Barton had to pay for his drink. According to the barman, Barton had obviously had a few before he'd reached his pub. The clientele was much the same as was in tonight, he told Cyril.

When Cyril had showed him Sharon Williams photo, he remembered her being in the previous Saturday, along with a dark-haired friend. They'd been in on previous occasions and had had a couple of drinks before moving on. Interestingly, they'd been and gone by a good hour before Barton had come in.

"So was there anyone in particular showing an interest in the two women?" Cyril asked.

"They were quite attractive, especially the younger one," the barman responded before breaking off to serve a customer. When he returned, he carried on, "Come to think of it, there was a young bloke … maybe late twenties, longish fair hair. He was trying his luck for a bit."

"Had you seen him before?"

"No. But now I come to think of it, I got the impression he'd begun to bug the women. You can tell with body language when you've been in this game as long as I have. I think that made them finish their drinks and move on."

"Did this man follow them?"

"No. In fact he had another pint after that."

Cyril thought for a moment. "Was he still here when Barton came in?"

"You know, I think he was." The man indicated a drinker sitting on a stool at the far end of the bar. "He was in last Saturday," he said, "In fact he's always in. Ask him if he noticed anything. He used to be a journalist for one of the big dailies, so he might be able to tell you more."

Cyril approached the man sitting hunched over his drink at the bar. "Mind if I have a word?" he said.

"Police," the man responded, hardly raising his eyes from his drink.

"That's right. I understand you were in here last Saturday."

"In most nights," the man said, eventually shuffling round on the stool to look at Cyril. He shook a finger at him. "I know you," he went on. "I thought you were uniform."

"CID now. What I'd like to ask is if you remember anyone unusual in last week." Cyril indicated the barman. "Apparently there was some young guy in pestering two women, a blond in her early fifties and her younger dark-haired friend."

The man scratched his ear. "I remember. Young lad, in his twenties maybe. He'd got no chance. Pissed them off a bit though. Finally, they left. I thought he might have followed but he didn't."

"Did you see this guy come in?" Cyril showed him Barton's photo.

The now familiar smirk appeared. "Dick, yeah he was in too. Came in after the two women had left, quite a bit after, maybe an hour."

"Did you notice any … interaction between this young lad and … Dick?"

"Interaction? They didn't talk to one another, if that's what you mean. In fact, Dick sat down over there." The man indicated a table where two men and a woman were sitting near a window. "And the guy was standing over there." He nodded towards the fruit machine. "But …" The man scratched his ear again, obviously a mechanism for thought, then spoke, "Thinking about it, he did seem to be looking across at Dick from time to time. And when he left, he took his pint and sat down where your colleague had been sitting."

"If we need to speak to you again, Mr er…"

"Marshall, Duncan Marshall. Here, you can have a card." He opened his wallet and pulled out a business card. Producing a pen from the top pocket of his jacket, he wrote more information on it. "That's my address, but you'll probably get hold of me here."

Cyril took the card as the man turned back to his beer. "Thanks," he said.

On into Mama's, Cyril felt distinctly out of place. What was it they called it now? Disco. It was certainly a far cry from the dances he used to attend during and just after the war. It was at one of those he met his beloved Maureen. Despite the noise, his mind went back to that Saturday evening nearly thirty years ago now. Before he could dwell on it, Woodbridge nudged him and nodded to two young women dressed in hot pants dancing round their handbags.

Cyril leaned in towards his young colleague's ear. "I hope you're not suggesting we try our luck there," he said, loud enough to be heard above the music.

Woodbridge turned to him with a look of amazement on his face before he caught Cyril's grin.

Cyril leaned in again. "Glam rock has grown on me," he continued. "Come on, I want a word with our Mr Small." He led the way towards the bar leaving Woodbridge to follow looking puzzled.

After a few minutes, Billy Small spotted Cyril and came across.

"Mr Small," Cyril began, "when we last spoke, you gave us the names of three people who were in here last Saturday."

"That's right."

"We managed to track down and speak to two of them, but the last one, this Stevie bloke …"

A smile wrapped itself around the barman's face. "That's because Stevie's not a fella, she's a bird. Stephanie, but she prefers Stevie."

"She wouldn't happen to be …"

"Over there." The barman indicated some seats on the far side of the dance floor. "She's the one in the red dress with that group."

Cyril followed Small's gaze to a number of people sitting at a table with drinks. "Thanks," he said and made his way over, Woodbridge close behind.

Cyril drew some strange looks from the men who were seated in the group.

"Alright Grandad?" one of them said.

Cyril said nothing and, not looking at the source of the remark, held his warrant card close to the man's face.

"Stevie, is it?" he asked, his attention fully on the woman.

"I'll get the drinks in," the man who had spoken said, rising to his feet and making a hurried exit from the table.

"Do you mind if I join you?" Cyril hesitated then sat in the seat next to Stevie vacated by the smart mouth. Woodbridge remained standing at his shoulder.

"What do you want?" she asked, looking annoyed.

"I understand you were here last Saturday," he began.

She looked wary. "Yes."

He turned to Woodbridge who passed the envelope to him. "Did you see this man last week?" he asked, producing Barton's picture.

She smirked. "Yeah, he was in. Pissed as usual. Looking for a cheap bunk up, if he could."

"Did you see him leave?"

She gave the question a bit of thought before confirming she had.

"On his own?"

"Yes. He'd tried chatting up a few before he left but got nowhere."

Cyril pulled the other photo from the envelope. "What about this woman?"

Again, her face told him she recognised her. "She was in here too, along with her mate; a dark-haired younger woman, but her friend had left earlier. He'd tried his luck with this one too," she said prodding her finger at Sharon Williams' photo.

"But she turned him down?"

"Oh yes. In fact, I think he'd gone well before she did."

"One last thing, if you don't mind," Cyril continued, "did you notice anyone in here last week that was a bit unusual, out of the ordinary? Anyone pestering this woman?"

She took a sip of her drink and looked to her friend sitting next to her. "Was it last week that weird guy was in here?" she asked her.

Her friend nodded and said something that Cyril couldn't hear. Stevie turned back to him. "Thought so, it was last Saturday when there was some guy who was trying to chat us up. I saw him trying it on with her as well."

"Can you describe him?"

Stevie looked to her friend as if for assistance. Her friend leaned in closer and said a few words. Finally, she answered, "He was probably late twenties, longish fair hair, slim, maybe about his height." She indicated Woodbridge standing behind Cyril. "Cheesecloth shirt and light coloured trousers."

"Had you seen him before?"

Again another exchange of glances with her friend. "We don't think so."

"Did this man leave with this woman?" Cyril indicated the photo.

"No. I think she left on her own and he'd gone just a bit before her."

"So, to be clear, this younger man left after the man in the picture but before the woman?"

Stevie nodded. "Yep."

"That's a great help," Cyril said. "Now, if you don't mind, can you give me your full name and address and where you work? I'll need a formal statement from you."

She wrote the details on a blank sheet of Cyril's notebook. "Would it be possible for you to come into Clacton police station on Monday? I'd like you to have a look at some photos … see if you can identify this individual. Your friend too?"

Again the two women exchanged a few words before Stevie confirmed she could nip in during her lunch break.

Cyril thanked her then took his leave.

29
Monday 14ᵗʰ March 1977

The female cashier worked through her regular Monday morning task of processing the deposits from the night safe that had been posted over the weekend. By half-past-nine, she came to the envelope left by the travel agent's just a few doors down. Opening it, she removed the covering deposit slip and the usual mix of cheques and banknotes. This week, she thought, there seemed to be a greater percentage of notes than cheques.

One of her fascinations since she had begun working at the bank as a fifteen-year-old some twenty years ago now, was banknotes. She'd seen a fair few incarnations and had a great knowledge of when the various types had been introduced and withdrawn. It was probably her early dealings with white five-pound notes that had sown the seeds. They'd disappeared back in 1961 but she still had the odd customer present one to exchange, lost and forgotten in a drawer or jacket pocket, or discovered when an ageing relative had passed on. They could still be processed.

She was counting out the cash from the travel agent when something unusual struck her. Amongst them was a wad of ten-pound notes which felt new but old at the same time. She looked at the numbers and saw they were consecutive. The design was of the previous one, still legal tender, but a newer note with Florence Nightingale on the reverse had been introduced about eighteen months before. Also, when cash sums of this size were presented, the use of the twenty-pound note would be more usual. These had been reintroduced in 1970 after a gap in this denomination since the war. No, something began to flash on her radar; three hundred and eighty pounds worth of older design but fresh feeling ten-pound notes with consecutive numbering; this warranted further investigation.

*   *   *

Cyril was sitting at his desk, puffing on his pipe and pondering over the findings of the morning briefing. Sanderson led the order with a review of the investigation into the suspicious death of ex-DCI Jack Tinker. Walker and Miller reported that, when they had revisited Clacton Hospital, a couple of people, one a receptionist, had reported sightings of a man maybe late-twenties, possibly thirty in the unit around the time Tinker died. The descriptions were vague; medium height and build, possibly fair hair, dressed in a tee shirt.

He and Sam Woodbridge had spoken of the results of their exploits on Saturday night. Generally, they'd confirmed Barton's movements, the last time he'd produced his warrant in the Station Hotel, that Sharon and Karyn had also visited the pub but at different times from him and they wouldn't have come across each other until they were all in Mama's.

There was no forensic evidence to put Barton at the murder scene, the fingerprints and the hair below the victim's nails were no match, and that was borne out by all their enquiries which showed Barton had left the night club alone a good half hour or so before the victim. The fingerprints on the second glass found at the scene were still being reviewed against the databases, but it was going to be a slow process. There was also the possibility that they weren't on any records. Cyril also mentioned the younger man who had been seen in the club talking to the victim shortly before she left. He also reported the Station Hotel's barman and customer who'd seen a young man pestering Karyn and the victim earlier in the evening. He'd speak to Karyn again and try to get a description. Meanwhile, Stephanie and her friend from the nightclub should come in at lunchtime to give a statement and look through some mug shots. As far as the Williams' murder enquiry was concerned, could these two sightings be of the same man? But thinking beyond that, could it also be the same man spotted in the hospital corridor?

The phone rang, snapping him out of his deliberations.

"Got a strange one here, Cyril," the desk sergeant announced, *"The manager of the Williams & Glyn's Bank on Station Road would like to speak to someone about some banknotes."*

Glad to have some relief from the boredom of the paperwork piled on his desk, Cyril perked up. "Stick him through," he said.

"He's not actually on the line. He just wondered if someone could call in to the branch and see him."

"Did he now?" Cyril responded with a hint of sarcasm in his tone. He cast a glance to the window, saw some watery sun attempting to break through the cloud cover and decided a walk and a smoke of his pipe might just be the thing he needed. "Alright then, leave it with me," he finally said.

Arthur Savage, manager of the Clacton branch of the Williams & Glyn's Bank on Station Road, welcomed Cyril into his office and bade him sit in the chair opposite his large mahogany desk. Savage appeared to be in his early sixties with thin dark hair rimming a bald pate, reminding Cyril of Friar Tuck. The expansive stomach only added to that image. Black thick-rimmed glasses adorned his clean-shaven face and his dark suit looked to be well-worn.

"So how can I help you, Mr Savage?" Cyril asked, settling himself into the chair.

Without any further preamble, Savage opened the top drawer of his desk, produced a brown envelope and held it open for Cyril to see, inside which were a bundle of ten-pound notes.

"We discovered these notes amongst a deposit made by a local travel agent over the weekend," he began. "There are thirty-eight of them. What brought them to our attention was the fact that they were of an older design, although still currently legal tender, but they appear to be in mint condition." He paused for a moment and Cyril wondered if it was for dramatic effect. "We've handled them as little as possible, as I thought you may want to conduct some tests on them," he added.

Cyril nodded slowly, doubtful that anything useful could be gained from forensic analysis, despite the manager's optimism. "Very commendable," he said, "But what makes you think they might be of interest to us? Are they good forgeries?"

Savage opened another drawer and pulled out a sheet of paper. "We have regular memos sent round to all the branches detailing serial numbers of notes stolen during various raids on any variety of premises," he said. Turning the sheet around so Cyril could read it, he passed a well-manicured finger down the list to rest above an entry which startled Cyril. "If you look at the numbers on the notes, you'll find they correspond with that," Savage added.

*   *   *

Barton had driven back from his sister's home in Hertfordshire that morning. It was a last minute decision on Friday to go and see her. He felt he needed some links with his past, some family ties and she was his only living relative; her and the kids.

"So what brings you over?" she'd asked, with no edge to the question.

All the while he was going through the divorce, not once had she been judgemental. She was two years older than him and had been married for twelve years now. Everything he'd witnessed displayed a happy marriage. Her husband was an easy-going individual and he and Barton got on well enough. The two children seemed well-balanced and they'd been, if not exactly excited, then at least interested in seeing their uncle John.

He kept mention of the past week's events quiet and only said he wanted a quick break from work and to catch up with what was going on in her life. He thought she'd bought that line but, in the end, he knew she was shrewd enough to guess there was something else, just below the surface. However, she never pried into his affairs and she knew that if he wanted to discuss anything with her, he'd tell her in his own time. She'd adopted the same tactics when his divorce was pending and, eventually, he'd told her everything, admitting how he'd screwed up big time. She said that it had been a shame as she'd really liked Alison. They'd got on well and she thought she would be good for John. But, in the end, there's only so much humiliation someone can take. When she'd voiced that view to her brother, he'd broken down. For the first time since they were children she'd seen him in tears.

This visit though, was all about re-connecting and maintaining his relationship with his sister and her family. At least, that was what he'd told her.

As he'd driven back to Clacton, he'd felt refreshed, having enjoyed the weekend. He'd had nothing to drink too, and hadn't missed it. It had made him miss the opportunity he'd destroyed with Alison to start a family. But it also made him determined to change his ways. Cyril had tried to tell him that last year. For a while, he'd settled down before the black mists had descended again and he'd adopted the habits of drinking and seeking out any woman for a quick bunk-up. Mostly severely disappointing.

Thoughts of Cyril brought him back to wondering what he'd been up to over the weekend. He felt sure he wouldn't be sitting idly in his house doing nothing on the cases he was involved in, both with implications for himself.

Parking up outside his flat, he looked over to the building. This afternoon, he'd study his financial position and see what could be done to improve his situation. All that, of course, would depend on his being reinstated. He'd give Cyril a call later to find out the latest news.

30

Cyril returned to the station and breezed up the stairs to the CID office and sat down at his desk. He placed the envelope full of notes on one side then sifted through the files he'd left on the desk. He had to sign a receipt for the cash before the manager allowed him to take the package with him. Pulling out the file he wanted, he opened it and began to read and make notes. There was no doubt about it, they did match. Grabbing the file, the notes he'd made and the envelope, he strode out towards Sanderson's office.

Cyril knocked on his boss's door and was immediately waved in.

"Interesting development, sir," Cyril began, before placing the envelope on the DCI's desk and explaining his visit to the Williams & Glyn's bank.

Sanderson listened until he'd finished, his eyes widening.

"Are you sure?" Sanderson finally asked.

"I've checked with the file." He opened the folder he'd brought with him at the appropriate page and placed it on the DCI's desk facing him.

Sanderson leaned forward, picked up the file and read the section in question before taking hold of the envelope and looking inside at the money.

"Right," Sanderson said. "I'll get these off to the lab and see if they can tell us anything about who might have handled this lot, but I doubt we'll get much after all this time. Meantime, you and I will head down to the travel agent's."

As luck would have it, the travel agent involved was the same one Karyn Brown worked for. When Cyril and

Sanderson walked in, she was dealing with an elderly lady with a pile of brochures on her desk.

Karyn looked up, recognised Cyril and an immediate expectant expression appeared on her face. Hurriedly making excuses to her customer, she rose from her desk and approached the detectives.

"Have you some news?" she asked in low tones. "Have you found out who killed Sharon?"

"We're still investigating, Miss Brown," Cyril said.

Her expression changed to one of disappointment.

"We'd like to talk to you about another matter," Cyril went on. "In private, if we could."

Now concern was etched on Karyn's face. "I'll just finish dealing with this lady, if that's okay?" she said and returned to her desk.

The elderly lady was finally hurried out the door with an armful of brochures and the promise that Karyn could sort out whatever the lady decided when she'd discussed the options with her husband. The sign was turned to *CLOSED* and Karyn sat down at her desk with Cyril and Sanderson seated opposite.

"So how can I help?" she asked.

"Can we ask you which bank the company uses?" Cyril began, Sanderson happy for him to lead the questioning.

"Yes, we have a business account with Williams & Glyn's, just down the street."

"Over the weekend, we assume you took some cash payments which were then deposited in the night safe."

"That's right, from holidays booked on Saturday. That's the busiest day of the week for us, especially at this time of year."

"Do you remember who might have paid for their holiday with ten-pound notes, three hundred and eighty pounds worth?"

"I do," Karyn responded immediately, standing up and opening a filing cabinet behind her. She flicked through a few folders before pulling one out and returning to her desk. "Is there something wrong? Are the notes fake? They looked okay to me."

As Cyril opened the file and noted down the details, Sanderson spoke for the first time.

"No, no, nothing like that. We'd just like to speak to whoever gave you those notes," he said.

"So do I cancel the booking?" Karyn looked puzzled. "I'd have to explain to head office and it'll take a bit of palaver to sort it," she said.

"We'll be in touch and let you know if you need to do anything further, Miss Brown," Cyril said. "But in the meantime, I'd like to ask you about your movements on the Saturday night you were out with Miss Williams."

She looked confused. "You've got my statement."

"I know, and that's great, but I'd like you to think back to when you were in The Railway Hotel."

Karyn's brows furrowed.

"I understand you were pestered by some man?" Cyril continued.

"Oh him? That's right. Just some young bloke trying it on. We told him to piss off. Sorry." She looked abashed.

"Don't worry," Cyril assured her. "Had you seen him before?"

"No, I don't think so."

"Or later that night? In Mama's perhaps?"

"Do you think he had something to do with Sharon's murder?"

"We're just following a variety of leads," Sanderson added.

She gave the question some thought before replying, "I don't think so. At least I don't remember seeing him again."

"Do you think you could come into the station again and give us a description and look at some photos?" Cyril asked.

Instinctively, she looked at her watch. "I can call in when we close, about half five, if that's okay?"

"Perfect. Thanks."

Both men stood.

"Thanks again for your help," Sanderson added, as they both left the shop.

"Do you think you have something with this young bloke spotted in The Railway and at Mama's? You think they're one and the same?" Sanderson asked as they walked back towards Jackson Road.

Cyril puffed on his pipe. "Too early to say but I need to follow it up."

"Have you heard from Dick?"

"Gone off for the weekend to see his sister, he told me. Last minute decision, apparently."

Sanderson was pensive for a few seconds. "We need to get him back in. I can't keep him suspended given the forensics findings. Obviously not on the Williams' case," he added quickly. "But we could use him looking into Jack Tinker's demise."

By now they were back at the station. As they climbed the steps and entered the building, Cyril recognised the young woman, Stevie, he'd spoken to in Mama's on Saturday night.

She stood up. "I've got half-an-hour," she said making a point of looking at her watch. "Unfortunately my friend works in London, so it's not easy for her to come in. But she won't be able to tell you anything more than me."

Cyril apologised to Sanderson before leading the woman to a room on the ground floor. "Can I get you anything?" he asked. "Tea, coffee?"

She shook her head. "I haven't got time. Can we just get this done."

"Sure."

Cyril and Stevie sat down and he proceeded to write out her statement. Once done, she signed the statement and seemed keen to leave.

"Before you go," Cyril said, "I'd like to show you some photos and see if you can identify the man you encountered."

She nervously looked at her watch once again. "I do need to get back to work," she said. "But if it helps, I can come back in when I finish, maybe around half five?"

"That would be great. Thanks."

Cyril escorted her out and hurried up to the CID office. He had a phone call to make.

31

"Are you sure this is where he's working?" Sanderson asked as he drove the Rover out of town.

"That's what his wife told me," Cyril responded.

"And you didn't give anything away as to why you wanted to speak to him?"

"When I asked if he was around, she told me he was at work. I asked her where and she said it was this building site, so when she asked what it was about, I told her there was a job I was doing. I'd never mentioned I was police. In fact I didn't give a name."

Sanderson glanced over and smiled. "So no chance she'd try and contact him and tip him off?"

"I said I was out that way later and maybe call by."

They travelled through Thorpe-le-Soken and took the road through Stones Green arriving at the cross roads in Wix. Ahead, they could see work progressing on the new by-pass.

"Not before bloody time," Sanderson remarked. "Main route to the port of Harwich with all that traffic and it still comes through places like this."

"It's a fair set up they've got there." Cyril indicated the site compound with numerous temporary cabins.

Sanderson chuckled as he waited for a gap in the traffic to turn right. "Bloody Dick nearly wiped us out on this road last year when we were hurrying to the passenger port when you were on that ferry. Christ, we were so close to some big wagon coming the other way."

Cyril didn't need reminding of his time trapped in a refrigerated van on board but remembered Barton telling him about the incident. "Good job you didn't come to grief," he said. "I wouldn't be sitting here now."

Sanderson finally managed to pull out and turn right behind a van. "Down here, you reckon?"

"About half a mile further on, take a turning to the right."

*   *   *

Tony Riley was busily engaged digging out a drain run from one of the houses towards the road where a connection with the main sewerage pipe would eventually be made. As he swung the bucket of the JCB round to deposit another load of earth onto the side, he saw the dark Rover pull up on the street. His pulse quickened and his stomach lurched. He'd seen enough to recognise plain clothes officers when he saw them. He watched as a tall, smartly dressed man in a dark grey overcoat stepped from the driver's door whilst a shorter, older man with a thin moustache appeared from the passenger side. He took a deep breath to calm himself. It wouldn't be anything to do with him. After all, how would they know his secret? No, he told himself, it must be about something completely different.

He swung the bucket back to the trench and pulled another load from the ground, all the while glancing over to the new arrivals and following their progress.

The site manager appeared about five minutes later, waving his arms to him and pulling his hand across his throat in a sign to stop operations. When the engine noise died, the manager approached. "Tony, there are a couple of detectives here to see you," he said, indicating the two visitors waiting patiently on the edge of all the activity. "What have you been up to?" he went on, a wry smile appearing on his face.

"Nothing," Riley responded, making an effort to keep all emotion from his face as he jumped down from the cab.

A few minutes later, Riley was sitting in the rear seat of the Rover, Cyril alongside. Sanderson took up position in the driver's seat, half-turned towards the man.

"How's the job going?" Sanderson began, in a chatty manner.

"Fine," Riley replied. "We've only just started here last week."

"No problems at the moment? I know how these things go; construction work's notorious for throwing up unexpected glitches …"

"Look, what's all this about?"

"Pay well, does it?" Sanderson continued, ignoring the man's question.

"Can't complain."

"You get paid cash … or cheque …?" Sanderson picked a speck of fluff from his trousers as he spoke. "Or maybe even directly into your bank account?"

Riley looked out of the window and saw one or two of his work colleagues casting furtive glances towards the car, a few quick words exchanged between them. "Er, cash normally," he eventually responded.

Sanderson nodded. "So it would have been cash you received in your pay packet that you used to pay for your family holiday on Saturday morning then?"

Shit, Riley thought, so that's it. Bloody cash at the travel agents. He looked down to his lap and nervously played with his hands. "Yer, that's right. I'd saved up over the past few months."

"All ten pound notes, of the older design?"

"If you say so."

"And all consecutively numbered."

"Really?"

"So if we start questioning your employer's payroll people, they'll confirm that over the 'past few months' they just happened to pay you in ten pound notes … over the course of some weeks … and they just happened to be from the same batch? You know, with consecutive numbers?"

"I don't know." Riley gave a shrug. "Maybe."

Cyril spoke for the first time. "Come on, Tony, where did you really get the money?"

Another shrug, but Riley felt his resistance crumbling. His mind buzzed around, trying to decide his best course of action.

"We can only help you if you help us, you know," the DCI said before an awkward silence followed. "Well I think we should continue this back at the station," he said then turned in preparation to start the car.

"I knew it was too good to be true," Riley eventually said.

Sanderson paused and turned back to face him. "How do you mean?"

"I found it," the digger driver said.

Sanderson let out a deep breath. "You'll have to do better than that."

Riley looked up at Sanderson, turned to Cyril then back to the DCI. "It's true, I tell you," he pleaded. "I dug it up. Here, last Tuesday."

Sanderson and Cyril exchanged looks.

"Let's hear him out, sir," Cyril said. "Anyone with you when you dug it up?"

"No. I was on my own. It was the first day. I'd stripped the site then begun on the foundations."

"Whereabouts?"

Riley pointed through the window. "Over there, towards the back of the second house we're building. I was digging out the footings and the bucket exposed it."

"What, paper money just lying in the ground?"

"No, it was in an old briefcase. I opened it up. Well, I had to break the catches. It was all covered in soil. Inside there were sixteen packages, all wrapped in plastic, all different notes."

"And you still have this briefcase?"

"It's in my shed at home."

"Have you still got the money? Apart from the £380 you used to buy your holiday with?"

Riley nodded. "Apart from a couple of quid I used just to see if it was genuine." The man looked to Sanderson. "Does this mean I won't be having a holiday this year?"

"Not the two weeks in Majorca you were planning with the family," Sanderson remarked, "but you might be spending time at Her Majesty's Pleasure."

*   *   *

"Got his statement?" Sanderson asked as Cyril entered his office.

"Yes sir. Not much more than he already told us."

The DCI indicated for Cyril to take a seat.

"You know, I can't help feeling sorry for him. He finds a load of cash, seemingly untraceable, but the first thing he does with it catches him out."

"On the other side of the coin," Sanderson countered, "you have to bear in mind where it originated. Two elderly people were frightened to death, one arguably literally, in its acquisition."

"But how did it end up there?" Cyril pondered.

Sanderson sprang forward in his seat, arms on the desk. "We need to look back through the files of the case. You've already pulled them from Records, yes?"

"On my desk."

"Good. Go back through everything and make yourself familiar with every last detail and start digging afresh. Use young Woodbridge too. He seems a smart lad. In the meantime, I'll try and get hold of Dick. He can start involving himself with the enquiry into Jack Tinker's death."

Cyril told Sanderson what Stevie had said in her statement and that she was returning after work to go through the mug shots and, if need be, try and produce some sort of identikit resemblance of the man she'd seen talking to Sharon Williams. He also had Karyn coming in to do the same.

*   *   *

"Hello, Dick. How are you?"

Barton spun round to seek the source of the familiar female voice. "Marnie," he said, as he spotted the slightly overweight woman in her fifties, sitting in the driver's seat of the Mark 3 Ford Cortina that served her as a taxi.

"Not working today?" she asked, looking down at his jeans and trainers. "Unless you're under cover."

"Sort of," he said. "Mind if I sit in?"

"Help yourself. Things are a bit quiet, and there're four ahead," she said, referring to the taxis in front of her on the rank by the railway station.

Barton walked round to the passenger side and sat in the front seat alongside her. "How's Fred these days?"

"Frustrated. I struggle to get him to take things easy, but you blokes …" Marnie was talking about her husband who used to drive the taxi. After decades of sitting in cars with little exercise, he'd had a heart attack five years ago whilst about to set off with a fare. It was probably only the fact that his passenger at the time was a doctor that saved him. "Anyway," she went on, "You're looking a lot better than the last time I saw you."

He pulled out a packet of cigarettes and offered Marnie one. "Oh, when was that?" he asked.

She took a cigarette. "Thanks. Early hours of Sunday morning. You looked like you'd had a good night."

He lit both cigarettes then exhaled through the open window. "Why didn't you stop and give me a lift?"

"One, I already had a fare – on my way to Holland." She was referring to Holland on Sea, a few miles away rather than some international journey. "And two, I like to keep my car clean."

"You'd have been safe, Marnie. I never part with anything." He laughed at his own remark.

She took a drag and studied Barton for a second. "I'd have thought you'd be hard at work trying to find out who murdered that woman they found over the back there." She waved a hand in the general direction of Sharon Williams' house.

"How do you know I'm not?"

She nodded. "True. I hear she was last seen at Mama's?"

"The taxi jungle drums beating loud," Barton remarked. "Did you know her?"

"I think she might have been in the back once or twice. But not on Saturday night. She might have been safer if she had."

"So what's the word?"

"A bit of a mystery," Marnie said. "Nobody we know picked her up or saw her outside the club. There again, it was a busy night with a few of the lads taking the night off." She paused and appeared to be in thought.

"Something else?"

"Might be something or nothing …"

"Go on," Barton encouraged.

"A few of us have seen an individual hanging around the club on a few occasions, outside, offering lifts to one or two women."

"Can you describe him?"

"Late twenties, slim, medium height with longish fair hair. Oh, and drives a Ford Cortina, like this one."

"So you've seen him getting in the car?"

"Not me, but one of the others mentioned it."

"With a woman?"

"Not sure. Might be worth asking around though."

Barton opened the door and dropped his stub in the gutter. "Thanks, Marnie," he said, as he stood up. Leaning back in through the door, he added, "Say hello to Fred for me. See you." He closed the door and walked away.

32

Cyril walked down the hallway to answer the ring on the doorbell.

"Hello Cyril," Barton greeted.

"John, how was the weekend?" Cyril asked then hurriedly held the door wide. "Come in, come in," he said before leading the way into the lounge.

"I'm not disturbing anything am I? Not spending time with the delightful Cathy?"

"No, not tonight."

Charlie waddled up the hall, tail wagging to greet the visitor. Barton made a fuss of him before following Cyril into the room.

"Can I get you anything?" Cyril asked.

"Tea would be good, but only if you're having one," Barton responded.

Ten minutes later, the two men were seated opposite one another, mugs of tea on the hearth.

"So a good weekend?" Cyril repeated.

"It was good to see Linda and the kids, yeah. I hadn't seen my sister in ages." Barton pulled out his cigarettes, prompting Cyril to do the same with his pipe. "So what have I missed?" the DI asked.

"Has Sanderson called you?"

"Not heard anything. Why?" Barton lit a cigarette.

"As I understand it, they found no forensic evidence to connect you with Sharon Williams' house."

"That's because I was never there."

"So he wants you to come back in." Cyril lit his pipe in harmony. "Sounds like he's planning to lift your suspension. Best give him a call though. You can do it from here."

"Thanks, I will in a bit. But, in the meantime, what developments have I missed?"

Cyril told him of his expedition with Sam Woodbridge on Saturday night retracing Barton's footsteps the previous weekend and the discovery of several witnesses who saw him in various pubs before finally leaving Mama's in the early hours of Sunday, well before Sharon Williams did.

"Tell me, John," Cyril said, an amused expression on his face, "Do you really try chat-up lines like, 'That's a gorgeous dress you're wearing. Why don't you hang it up on my bedroom floor?'"

Barton looked embarrassed. "Who told you that?"

Cyril laughed heartily. "You did."

"Me? When?"

"Courtesy of The Great Lorenzo."

Barton's expression grew fierce. "Cyril, you mention one word of this ..."

"Relax. You know that whatever you've ever told me in strictest confidence remains just that."

Barton visibly eased back into his chair, took a drag on his cigarette and smiled. "So what did you find out?"

Cyril put his pipe down in an ashtray on the hearth before answering. "Well, the last time you flashed your warrant card was in The Railway. Do you remember being in there?"

"Vaguely. As I recall, the miserable bastard charged me for my pint."

"That's right, he did. Oddly enough, Sharon Williams and her friend were in there on Saturday too."

Barton leaned forward and stubbed out his cigarette in the ashtray. "I don't remember seeing them."

"No, they'd gone by the time you arrived. Do you also know a chap by the name of Duncan Marshall?"

Barton thought for a second. "Older bloke, a bit miserable. Used to be a Fleet Street hack?"

"That's him. Well he saw you in there on Saturday. He also saw another man who seems to crop up elsewhere, that's if it's the same one of course. Do you remember seeing some young guy, late twenties maybe, longish fair hair, cheesecloth shirt and light coloured trousers?"

Barton shook his head. "Can't say. That could describe any number of young lads out on the town at the weekend. Is he relevant?"

"Not sure but we've had Sharon Williams' friend and another witness come in today to try and identify this guy. Not on any mugshot in the files, but Sam was trying to get some Identikit image worked up. You never know, it may ring a bell with you."

Barton frowned.

"Something wrong?" Cyril asked.

"It's just something I heard earlier today," he said before relating Marnie, the taxi driver's tale.

"We'll need to follow that up," Cyril said, seemingly concentrating on something else.

"What is it?" Barton queried.

"The description of this young fella, a bit generic, I know, but it couldn't be the same man you saw in the hospital corridor coming from the direction of Jack Tinker's room?"

Barton rubbed his face and looked to the ceiling as he considered the question. "As you say, Cyril, the description could match any one of dozens of blokes that age but … it might be. But that's a hell of a leap."

"I know."

The two men were silent for a minute or two before Barton spoke. "Is there something else that makes you think they could be linked?"

It was Cyril's turn to rub his face. "I'm not sure. We've been looking into some of the old cases that you or Jack Tinker worked on, either together or separately …"

"And?"

"An interesting coincidence today."

Barton leaned forward in his seat. "Now you've piqued my curiosity."

"You were involved to some extent on the Dovercourt Post Office robbery back in '69, weren't you?"

Barton nodded. "With Jack leading it, yes."

Cyril proceeded to relate the story of how he'd been alerted to some of the stolen banknotes turning up in a bank in Clacton and the tale of Tony Riley's discovery in a former garden out at Wix.

When he'd finished, Barton was visibly shocked. "Don't suppose you have any of that single malt left?"

When Cyril had poured them two measures, Barton went on, "I don't remember anybody by the name of Tony Riley coming up in the original investigation."

"There's no reason to think he was involved. Just happened to think he'd found a pot of gold and planned to spend it. I suppose it was his bad fortune that he used notes which, thanks to a sharp-eyed bank teller, were spotted immediately."

"And Wix? I can't think that any of our enquiries linked to there either," Barton puzzled.

"Early days on this one," Cyril said. "Why don't you give the DCI a call and he'll tell you what he wants you to do."

33
Tuesday 15th March 1977

The briefcase had been taken to the lab late the previous afternoon and was being examined for prints and any other clues it might offer. DCI Sanderson had called the briefing for eight that morning and Cyril, Bill Walker and Ben Miller were at their respective desks as Sanderson walked in.

"Gentlemen," he greeted. "A bit thin on the ground but DI Barton will be joining us in a few minutes."

"He's back then?" Miller asked.

"That's right, Ben, the suspension has been lifted in light of all the evidence. It still means we have to find out who placed the DI's warrant card at the scene of a murder, and no doubt the murderer will be one and the same. However, John won't be involved in that case."

The DCI turned his attention to Walker. "What news from the lab, Bill?"

Walker lifted a sheet of paper from his desk and read from it. "Some prints from the case, sir. They're running some checks on them now. One or two from the bags the money was in and numerous on the notes. They've counted them up and it comes to £46,871.00."

"Right, do we know the amount taken on the post office raid?"

Cyril was shuffling through the original file notes. "I've got that here," he said. "£47,328.00 was what the Post Office had worked out at the time."

Barton walked in at that moment. "That's right," he said, "Nearly fifty grand."

"Welcome back, John," Sanderson greeted. "I think it best you get yourself up to speed with this discovery. I want you involved with this as you were on the original investigation. Something you spot now might make connections with what you found out back in '69."

"Cyril told me all about it last night and, as far as I remember, there was no connection with Wix at the time."

"Well you and Cyril keep digging, no pun intended." Miller and Walker smiled but said nothing. "Also, I need you to lead the investigations into Jack Tinker's death. The team will put you in the picture." His attention swept around the room. "Right, I need to be going. I've got a meeting in Chelmsford in an hour. Anything breaks, let me know." With that, he strode from the room seconds before Sam Woodbridge appeared.

"Morning Sam," Cyril greeted. "Any joy with those Identikits?"

Woodbridge held up a couple of sheets with an artist's drawing of a face, prompting Miller then Walker to burst out laughing.

"Christ," Miller said. "Is that it? That's the best those witnesses could do?"

Woodbridge looked put out. "*Those witnesses* have jobs to go to and they've been in twice to look through the mug shots. They've tried their best."

Barton smiled at the young lad. "Don't worry about the Flower Pot Men, Sam, you just stick with it." He turned to the two DCs. "Who's got the witness statements from the hospital?" He was keen to scrutinise all the available information on Jack Tinker's death.

"Here, boss," Walker said, holding out two files.

Barton took hold of them and headed for his office. "I'll have a look through them. No interruptions for a bit, okay?" With that, he closed the door behind him.

"Bit of a find yesterday, Skip," Sam Woodbridge commented as he approached Cyril's desk.

"Can't believe it, Sam." Cyril leaned back in his seat before pulling out his pipe and tobacco. "Riley reckons he dug it up on some new building site out at Wix."

"Wix?"

Cyril stuffed tobacco in his pipe as he spoke. "That's right. He's a digger driver who was just starting works for some new houses and his bucket pulled up a briefcase."

"Whereabouts in Wix?"

"Just out on the Oakley Road." Cyril lit up and puffed out some aromatic smoke.

"Can you show me on a map?"

"What's your interest, Sam?"

"Let's have a look. It might not be relevant but I'll tell you in a minute."

Cyril opened a drawer on his desk and pulled out an ordnance survey map of the area. Woodbridge made his way behind Cyril to look over his shoulder. Opening the map out, Cyril's finger scanned Wix before settling on an area on the left hand side of Oakley Road. "Here," he said. "That building and area around it is what's being redeveloped."

"Jees," Woodbridge reacted.

"You know it?"

"You see this here." Woodbridge pointed at an area on the opposite side of the road with a couple of buildings on it. "That was my Gran and Grandad's place. I used to go there a lot when I was growing up."

Cyril turned to look at him. "So do you remember who lived here?"

"It was old Mr and Mrs Goodlove. I think he was a gardener. Used to chat to my Grandad from time to time. Have a quiet smoke together, that sort of thing."

"What happened to them?"

"Mr Goodlove died when I was about … ooh, twelve, I guess, and Mrs Goodlove stayed there on her own, I believe. My Grandad passed in 1969 and Gran two years later, so I'm not sure when Mrs Goodlove moved away or died."

Cyril was pensive, studying the map. "What else can you tell me about the Goodloves? Any relatives?"

It was Woodbridge's turn to trawl his thoughts. "I remember they had a grandson … Billy, he was called. I remember going over there, playing football with him and his dad." He scratched his head. "There was something … I seem to recall my Mum and Dad not being too happy with Grandad taking me over there. I think it was something about Billy's dad."

"Can you remember his name?"

"Tell you what, I'll call my dad. He'll remember."

"That would be handy, Sam. Can you do that and let me know?"

"Sure." Sam walked off to make the phone call.

34

John Reginald Tinker
After a short illness at Clacton District Hospital
8th March 1977
Much missed husband, father and grandfather
Further announcement will be made in respect of funeral
details

A grin slowly formed on his face as he read the notice in the Deaths section of the Gazette. He circled the announcement with a blue Biro. So, the old bastard had succumbed. He knew the dose was enough but it felt good to have the confirmation.

Picking up the tumbler with a good measure of whisky in, he raised it to the ceiling. "Cheers," he said before taking a gulp.

But the grin changed. It had been over a week since he'd died. Why the delay in announcement? He read the notice again; no funeral arrangements either. Was that because there was a problem with the cause of death? Had they found something unusual? If they looked closely enough, he knew they would. He was hoping it would be just waved through as a deterioration in his condition, another stroke. No need for a PM. But this didn't sound as though that was the case. Or maybe the family just needed time to arrange things. There were bound to be a good number of his colleagues still around who'd want to come and pay their respects.

Folding up the evening paper, he put it down on the table. That was when he noticed the main story on the front page. He'd been so intent on checking the

155

announcements, he hadn't paid much attention before. He took it up again and read the article.

Clacton Murder Appeal
Investigations are still ongoing into the murder of 52-year-old Sharon Williams who was found dead at her home in Clacton on Monday. Police are anxious to speak to anyone who saw Miss Williams on Saturday night into the early hours of Sunday morning. They are especially keen to speak to a man seen speaking to her and described as being in his early twenties, of slim build with long fair hair ...

He stood and began to pace the small front room that he'd known all his life. When his mum died, he just stayed on. Paid the rent on time, just keeping his head down. But now, things had just blown up. Had he thought things through? Not really, he just wanted to exact revenge. And what if they tried to tie him into this case?

Calm down, he told himself. Nobody knew anything about what he'd done, let alone why. And anyway, he was on duty twenty miles away when it was done.

Talking of which, he glanced at his watch, time to get ready if he was going to be on time for his late shift.

35

"That was interesting," Sam said as he approached Cyril.

"What was, Sam?"

"Just got hold of my dad and I asked him about Mr and Mrs Goodlove's relatives. He reckoned their daughter, Valerie, married a guy by the name of Walter Mason, a bit of a ..."

"Hang on, did you say Walter Mason?" Cyril interrupted him.

"That's right. Why?"

Cyril smiled. "Because Walter Mason was convicted along with Cliff Hammond for his part in the Dovercourt robbery."

"Bloody hell."

"Language, young Sam," Cyril joked. "Now, come with me and we'll go and see Inspector Barton. He'll be interested in that snippet, especially as Mason always protested his innocence."

Cyril knocked on Barton's door and was waved in. "There's something you might be interested in," Cyril began as Woodbridge followed him into the office. "Sam here has some information which may be pertinent to our enquiries."

Woodbridge recounted what he'd told Cyril earlier and what his father had just said.

When he'd finished, Barton stood and walked to the window before turning to face both men and leaned against the sill. "So your dad was unhappy for you to play with this lad because he knew Walter Mason was a *bit of a rogue*, as he judged?"

"That's right, sir. But he didn't tell me that at the time, only that he didn't want me to be mixing with them."

Barton was thoughtful for a moment. "This Billy, Walter's son, he'd be about your age?"

"A couple of years older," Woodbridge replied. "But we got along together. Like I say, we used to kick a ball about in his grandad's garden, down the side where it was all grass." Woodbridge smiled at the memory. "We didn't dare wander into the rose garden or the vegetable patch."

"So he'd now be, what … twenty-seven or twenty-eight?"

Woodbridge nodded. "Around that."

There was a knock on the door and Miller's head appeared. "Sorry to interrupt," he said, "but I thought you should know…"

"Yes, Ben," Barton said.

"Prints from some of the plastic bags have given us a match. They belong to Walter Mason."

A broad grin appeared on Barton's face as he walked back to his desk. "So the bastard was involved, despite all his claims he was innocent. Jack was right."

"And, if proof were needed," Cyril said, "it confirms the money *was* that stolen from the post office raid."

"And we now have the connection with where it was found," Barton added. He sat down. "Good work," he said.

Miller left the office and Woodbridge and Cyril were about to follow suit when Barton spoke again. "Mason's wife … Valerie, she tried to give Walter an alibi for the night of the robbery. I think it might be timely to pay her another visit."

36

Their knocks on the door went unanswered. The house on the quiet street in the Hythe Hill district of Colchester appeared neat and tidy with net curtains at the window. Barton tried to peer in.

"Do we know if she still lives here?" Cyril asked.

Barton turned to Cyril looking annoyed. "I know, I should have checked."

"I could try the Electoral Role," Woodbridge suggested. He had accompanied Barton and Cyril to the address they had for Valerie Mason.

"Yes you should have," Barton snapped. "Waste of time. Let's go."

Cyril, who had been looking up and down the street, held up a hand. "Hold on a minute," he said, before walking across the street to a house opposite and knocking on the door.

After a few seconds, the door opened a crack and an elderly woman peered around the edge.

"Yes?" she said.

"Sorry to bother you, Mrs …" Cyril spoke in a quiet compassionate tone.

"Jarvis," the woman replied. "Mrs Jarvis."

"I was just wondering Mrs Jarvis, if you could help me out."

Guardedly, she responded, "If I can."

"The house over the road … can you tell me a bit about who lives there?"

"It's just young Billy there now. Hey, you're not from the council are you?" Concern edged into the old lady's voice.

"No, Mrs Jarvis. We're looking into a possible bequest," Cyril lied.

"Bequest? You mean you're solicitors?"

"I'm sorry Mrs Jarvis but, as I'm sure you'll understand, I'm not at liberty to say."

She considered a moment. "Well, as I said, there's only Billy living there now. That's Billy Mason. His mother Valerie passed three months ago and his dad … oh, must have been three years ago now."

Cyril nodded, appreciating the lady's careful omission of any detail surrounding Walter Mason's death. "Mrs Mason, Valerie Mason, you said?"

"That's right. She was a nice woman. Used to help me out. Sad really …" The old lady looked wistful. "Not in good health. Diabetic for years."

"Diabetic? That's not good," Cyril said.

"But like I said, she died. Just before Christmas, it was."

"That must have been awful for her son."

"Oh it was," she agreed.

"But Billy doesn't seem to be in," Cyril continued. "Do you know if he has a job?"

"Oh, yes. He works at the hospital."

"Essex County?"

"That's right. He's a porter there. He left about an hour ago, so he must be on a late shift."

"You've been a great help Mrs Jarvis," Cyril said, about to turn away before adding, "Oh, one other thing, do you know what car Billy drives?"

"It's a small blue one. But I couldn't tell you what it is; I'm not up on cars."

Cyril gave her a smile. "Thanks again," he said and returned to his colleagues who had been watching his progress as they stood by the car.

"Can we go now?" Barton said sarcastically.

"I think so, but not back to the station. Thanks to a twitching curtain, I now know where Billy Mason is." Cyril opened the passenger door and climbed in. "And some other interesting info too," he added.

Barton turned left off the Lexden Road and into the car park of Essex County Hospital. The grand Georgian building, brick-built with a small stone port cochere and the word HOSPITAL inscribed in the stone lintel above the columns was an impressive sight. Cyril and Barton were not particularly concerned with the architectural appeal of the place however, and quickly made their way inside, Woodbridge having been left in charge of the car.

On route to the hospital, Cyril had told the others what he'd found out from Mrs Jarvis across the road.

"Christ!" Barton exclaimed. "So Billy would have access to his mother's insulin?"

"I think that's a fair guess," Cyril confirmed.

Barton looked in the driving mirror at Woodbridge who was sitting in the back. "Have you any idea what this Billy looks like, Sam?"

"Not seen him since he was about ten or eleven maybe."

"What did he look like then?"

"He was quite a tall lad with fair hair, but everybody changes from how they appeared at that age, don't they?"

"We'll see," Barton said, hands gripping the steering wheel tighter.

"You don't think he knew what his father had done, do you?" Cyril asked. "Burying the money in his in-laws' garden?"

"I intend to find out," Barton replied. "Anyway, good work with the neighbour," he grudgingly added.

"Never underestimate the knowledge of a curtain twitcher."

At the reception desk, Barton asked the man behind the counter where he could find the porters. The man gave him some directions before Barton led the way down one of the corridors. Along the way, he passed a porter wheeling a patient in a chair. He asked him where he could find Billy Mason and was told he was in the office downstairs.

Next floor down where Cyril knew the mortuary was located, the men made their way to a room at the rear of the building. As they approached, they could hear a conversation then a burst of laughter, as if someone had just told a joke. As they approached, a stocky man in his fifties emerged and walked towards them, a broad grin on his face which evaporated when he saw the two detectives approach.

"We're looking for Billy Mason," Barton asked.

"He's in the office," the porter said before hurrying away.

Barton gave Cyril a quick glance. "I'll bet he's on our records," he said beneath his breath before stopping at the open door.

A man in his late twenties with shoulder-length fair hair was sitting at a table reading a *Titbits* magazine.

"Interesting reading," Barton said.

The young man looked up at the two men standing in the doorway. "Who are you?" he said.

Barton took a step into the room which was set out as a small kitchen area for the porters, a kettle, toaster, mugs and a small sink behind the man. A small fridge was below a worktop on which a breadboard and some cutlery stood. "Are you Billy Mason?" Barton asked.

The man was guarded now. "Who wants to know?"

From behind Barton, Cyril held up his warrant card. "DS Claydon," he said. "And this is DI Barton."

The man's eyes narrowed. "Barton?" he said, fixing his gaze on the DI.

Barton nodded but said nothing, just standing with his hands in his coat pockets.

Mason folded the magazine and laid it on the table. "What do you want?"

"We were sorry to hear about your mother," Cyril said.

Mason still looked to Barton as he gave a slight nod.

"What happened?"

Reluctantly it seemed, Mason turned his attention to Cyril standing at Barton's shoulder. "Complications due to diabetes. She'd suffered from that for a long time."

"Not helped by your father's behaviour," Barton said.

Cyril could see anger rise in the young man as he stood up.

"Not helped by your fucking behaviour," he snarled.

Barton turned to look at Cyril. "Not a very helpful attitude," he said. "I think we ought to continue this conversation back at the station."

The speed of the man's movements caught the detectives by surprise. Mason picked up a bread knife from the worktop, lunged at Barton and grabbed him around the neck and held the knife to his throat. Barton could do nothing, hindered by the fact that he'd had both hands in his pockets.

"I'm going fucking nowhere," Mason said. "Especially not to be stitched up by you."

Cyril held up both hands in surrender. "Hold on, Billy," he said. "You don't want to be doing this. Put the knife down before this gets really out of hand."

"This bastard was one of the two who stitched up my dad," Mason said. "Sent down for something he didn't do. Died in prison. Did you know that?"

"Billy, please," Cyril begged. "There are things you need to know."

"More lies? No. Move back, away from the door."

Cyril took a pace backwards as Mason pushed Barton forward towards the door.

Cyril could see the knife was pressing against Barton's throat as he stepped back again.

Another prod and Barton was almost out in the corridor.

"Look," Cyril said, "You're only making things worse. Drop the knife, Billy. Give it up and we can talk properly."

"Billy," came a voice from down the corridor behind Cyril. "Billy, it's me, Sam. Remember? Sam Woodbridge. We used to play at your grandad's place, remember?"

Barton felt Mason's grip loosen a touch.

"Sam? Sam from over the road? What are you doing here?"

"I'm with the police now, Billy," Sam said as he approached the scenario behind Cyril. "These men will help you. You don't need to threaten anybody."

Mason's grip tightened again. "This one's not here to help me. He's probably going to stitch me up, just like he did my dad eight years ago."

"That's not how it was," Barton struggled to say. "We've uncovered new evidence … literally."

"A bit late if it's going to prove dad's innocence."

"Billy, despite what he told you and despite what you believe," Cyril said, "your dad *was* involved. Why do you think we've come to see you? We wanted to break the news to you in person."

"You're lying. It's another plant."

"No Billy," Sam joined in. "The proceeds from the raid were dug up in your grandad's garden."

"In the garden? No."

"It's true. That's why we're here."

"Doesn't mean Dad had anything to do with it?"

"Just think about it," Sam pleaded. "Put the knife down and let Mr Barton go and we can sort this all out."

"He's right," Cyril said.

Slowly, Barton could feel the tension drain away from Mason's grip. Finally, he put his hand up and took the knife from the lad's hand. As soon as he did, Barton spun him round and held his arm up his back. "Cuffs Cyril," he ordered.

Reluctantly, Cyril pulled a pair of handcuffs from his coat pocket and gave them to Barton.

"Bastard!" Mason yelled as the cuffs clicked shut on his wrists behind his back.

37
Wednesday 16th March 1977

Barton was in Sanderson's office reporting on the previous day's events at Essex County Hospital.

"So, do you recognise this character, Billy Mason?" Sanderson asked.

"It's possible he could be the bloke I saw in the corridor near Jack's room. I didn't pay too much attention, I was thinking about what I might find with Jack. But he'd certainly have had the opportunity to borrow a stethoscope to make himself look inconspicuous."

"And you think he knew you?"

"I'm not sure about that but he knew my name when we introduced ourselves yesterday and he linked me with Jack and his father's conviction."

A knock on the DCI's office door interrupted the conversation and Sanderson waved Woodbridge in.

"Sam, I heard you did well talking Mason down from the situation yesterday."

"Just as well he ignored my orders to stay with the car," Barton said.

Woodbridge smiled, becoming used to Barton's comments. "Just to let you know, sir, we have the search warrant for Mason's house and DS Claydon and DC Walker are on their way to meet the forensics officers there."

"Good," Sanderson said, still focused on Woodbridge. "In the meantime you and I will conduct the first interview with Mason."

Barton looked put out. " But sir ..."

"You're a bit too close, Dick," Sanderson explained. "Besides, Sam here has a bit of a connection with him which could be of use. I'll probably need you later in the process."

Barton shook his head resignedly.

"In the meantime," Sanderson continued, "get some photos of Mason copied, put them in one of the mugshot books and see what our witnesses from the Hospital make of it. Take Miller with you; he interviewed some of them."

*   *   *

When Cyril, and Walker drew to a halt in the car outside the Mason house, they saw the forensics van already waiting for them. As he got out of the driver's side, Cyril saw the curtains move in the house across the road where Mrs Jarvis lived. He'd call on her again later. Meantime, he had Billy's keys to allow the officers to enter.

As the forensic team began upstairs, Cyril walked into the small sitting room. Immediately his attention was drawn to the copy of the previous evening's Gazette lying on the coffee table, folded to reveal the front page's main story of ongoing investigations into Sharon Williams' murder and the prominent appeal to speak to a man whose description could match that of Billy Mason's.

Opening the newspaper out, he flicked through the various pages until he came to the announcements page. There he saw the notice of Jack Tinker's death circled in blue ink. He folded it back up and put it into an envelope.

"Sir! Up here!" he heard Walker's voice from upstairs.

He made his way up to the bathroom at the top of the stairs. The medicine cabinet on the wall stood open, one of the forensics officers and Walker standing to one side. On the top shelf were a number of vials and some hypodermic needles as well as various packets of clinical wipes.

"Labels made out to Valerie Mason," Walker said.

"Insulin," Cyril read. "Bag them up and get them analysed."

Cyril left the bathroom and walked along towards a bedroom where another forensics man was searching through a wardrobe. "Anything?" he asked.

"Not yet," the man replied, pushing shirts on hangers to one side and raking through socks and underwear on the floor of the wardrobe. "Do you want me to bag all of this?"

"Yes," Cyril responded. "We need to compare any fibres against what we found at the Sharon Williams' crime scene."

Cyril then bent down to look below the bed. He reached in and pulled out a small suitcase. Carefully, he flicked the catches and opened it. Inside were newspaper cuttings. He lifted the top few out and read. All seemed to refer to Walter Mason's arrest and trial for aggravated robbery. But underneath, separate from those clippings were some media cuttings related to ex-DCI Jack Tinker; a couple of cases he'd brought to court before finally, notices of his retirement.

To Cyril, Billy Mason seemed obsessed with his father's conviction and Jack Tinker.

Before they left, Cyril again called across the road to speak to Mrs Jarvis. He asked her a couple of questions and thanked her for the answers she gave, glad there appeared to be nothing wrong with her memory.

*   *   *

Billy Mason was seated at the table in Interview Room 1 on the ground floor of Jackson Road Police Station in Clacton, somewhat subdued after a night spent in police custody. When Sanderson and Woodbridge entered, Mason briefly looked up then dropped his eyes back to the table as they sat down opposite him.

"Mr Mason … Billy," Sanderson began, "not a particularly clever move yesterday, attacking one of my officers."

Mason snorted but said nothing.

"The reason we wanted to speak to you was to inform you of recent developments which affect your late father's conviction."

Mason looked up at Sanderson then to Woodbridge. "You said you'd made a find at Grandad's place."

Woodbridge nodded but Sanderson responded. "That's correct. I don't know if you know but the plot where your grandparents' house stood is being redeveloped."

"It was rented when Grandad worked as a gardener for the Health Authority in Colchester. He was one of a team looking after the gardens of Severalls Hospital. You know, that psychiatric unit set in extensive grounds on the north side of the town," Mason clarified.

"I'm aware of Severalls," Sanderson said and pressed on. "I understand the house was demolished a few years ago and a couple of houses built on the plot. This latest work is redeveloping the garden area. That's where the find was made."

"So how does this connect to Dad?"

Sanderson leaned forward. "Look, I know you've always been convinced that your father was innocent, because that's probably what he told you and your mother, but one of the workmen dug up a briefcase in the middle of the plot which contained money we believe was stolen in the post office robbery. Plus, your father had a connection with the location."

Mason sat up. "But how do you know the money was from the robbery?"

"The serial numbers of some of the notes corresponded to those on Post Office records."

Mason sagged.

Sanderson continued, "And your father's fingerprints were found on the packets that contained some of the notes."

Mason bristled. "Is that in the same way you found his prints on a cigarette packet mysteriously discovered in the postmaster's house."

"I understand your scepticism but the briefcase had been in the ground since the robbery took place."

Mason took a deep breath. "Look, Dad told me he never smoked on a job. It was unprofessional he said."

Sanderson glanced at Woodridge who spoke next. "Billy, did your Dad say anything in particular that convinced you he wasn't involved in the robbery?"

Mason looked intently at Woodbridge. "You met him," he said. "What did you make of him?"

"I remember him with you and your mum visiting over the road, but I was only fourteen or fifteen when I last saw him," Woodbridge said. After a second, he continued, "What I do remember was that my Dad wasn't keen on me going over when your dad was there." He held up a hand. "He never told me why, he only said he didn't want me to be there, that's all."

Mason looked disappointed. "I know he wasn't always honest. God knows he had a bit of a track record. But Mum always said he was with her the night of the robbery so he couldn't have been involved. I always thought that as he was known for what he'd done previously, it would be easy for you lot to stitch him up. He always believed evidence was planted."

A knock on the door interrupted proceedings and a uniformed officer entered and handed a folded piece of paper to Sanderson before leaving.

The DCI opened it up, read the contents then folded it in half again.

"Can you tell me where you were last Tuesday, that's the 8th March between two and four in the afternoon?"

"Last Tuesday?" Mason considered. "I was on a late shift at the hospital. Started at twelve and finished at eight."

"So, if we checked, someone there would confirm that?"

"Ask Ray. He's the supervisor. He has the work schedules. He'll tell you."

Sanderson got to his feet. "Okay Billy, that's it for now. The constable will escort you back to the cells."

Mason was shocked. "What? I thought I could go home."

"You assaulted a police officer and engaged in threatening behaviour, Mr Mason. We also need time to check your story for last Tuesday."

*   *   *

When Sanderson and Woodbridge entered the CID room, Cyril and Walker had returned from Colchester.

"Thanks for the note about what you discovered at his house, Cyril," Sanderson said. "Mason reckons he was on duty last Tuesday on a late shift. Says his supervisor will confirm. Can you and Sam get back over there and check it out."

Cyril raised his eyebrows in surprise. Sam must have made a good impression on the DCI, that was the first time he'd referred to him by his Christian name. "Sure," he said.

Just then, Barton and Miller turned up.

"How did it go?" Sanderson asked.

"The receptionist recognised him. Picked him out from the mugshot book."

Sanderson grinned. "Great."

"I'll arrange for an identity parade," Barton continued. "Let's see him wriggle out of that."

38

For the second time in twenty-four hours Cyril and Sam Woodbridge walked down the basement corridor of Essex County Hospital towards the porters' den. When they reached the open door they saw two younger men drinking tea from mugs and an older man sitting at the table reading the sports pages of that day's *Daily Mirror.*

"We're looking for Ray, the supervisor?" Cyril announced.

The older man looked up from reading about tonight's League Cup Final replay at Hillsborough. "I'm Ray," he said, removing his reading glasses. "What can I do for you?"

The other two porters finished their drinks and made a hurried exit. "We'll get back up to the wards," one said.

"Ray, I'm Detective Sergeant Claydon and this is Detective Constable Woodbridge." Cyril displayed his warrant card.

"Is this about Billy Mason? I heard what happened yesterday."

Cyril ignored the man's search for information. "How long has Mr Mason worked here?"

The man scratched his head. "Ooh, must be three years now."

"And how would you describe him? His work, I mean."

Ray nodded. "He's okay, fairly conscientious, reliable."

"He tells us he was on a late shift here last Tuesday. I wonder if you could confirm that?"

The supervisor turned behind him and pulled a box file from the worktop and opened it on the table in front of him. Glasses back on, he flicked through some sheets. Identifying the one he wanted, he tracked a finger down until he stopped at a name. "Here we are, Tuesday 8th

March, Billy was on a late shift, starting at twelve and finishing at eight."

"So he was definitely here?"

"Of course. I wouldn't have entered the details if he was absent. What's recorded here means he'll be paid for that shift this month."

Cyril wondered how efficient the system was as he studied the man for a moment. "Okay," he said, "Do you mind if I have a copy of that sheet?"

"Well, I'm …"

"They'll have a photocopier in the secretaries' office upstairs, surely?"

The man sighed and stood up. "Give me a minute," he said and left the room.

"What do you reckon, Skip?" Woodbridge asked.

"He seemed sure, Sam. It would certainly give Mason an alibi for the afternoon when Jack Tinker was attacked. At the moment, we just collect as much evidence as we can."

Ten minutes later, the supervisor returned with a photocopy of the porters' timesheet.

"How is Billy?" Ray asked. "Will he be returning to work?"

Cyril gave the stock answer. "He's still helping us with our enquiries." As he left, he folded up the sheet and put it in his pocket, adding, "Thanks for this."

They were making their way to the main entrance when one of the young porters who had been drinking tea in the office approached. "You police?" he asked.

"That's right," Cyril said.

"Will Billy be back soon?"

"We can't say."

"Only I've been covering his shift this morning." The man hesitated.

"Is there something else?" Woodbridge asked.

"Did Ray help you?"

"How well do you know Mr Mason," Cyril asked.

"We've worked together here for a year or so."

Woodbridge changed focus. "Were you on shift last Tuesday?"

"Tuesday?" The man gave the question consideration. "Well …"

"Look Mr er…" Cyril said.

"White, Frank White."

"Well, Mr White, if there's anything you want to tell us, it'll be treated in the strictest confidence."

White led the way outside and produced a cigarette packet and a lighter. The detectives declined his offer of a cigarette before he put one in his mouth and lit up. Eventually, he spoke. "The thing is … Billy disappeared not long after he came on shift. I should know, I had to cover for him."

"Was he away for the rest of the shift?" Cyril asked.

"Oh no, he was only gone for a couple of hours or so."

"But wouldn't the supervisor have noticed."

He snorted. "Huh, he was otherwise engaged."

"How do you mean?"

White drew on his cigarette and nodded in the direction of the building on the opposite side of the main road.

Cyril and Woodbridge followed the man's gaze. "The Hospital Arms?" Cyril queried.

"Regular as clockwork," White said, exhaling smoke. "Two o'clock onwards."

"Until closing at three," Cyril said.

White rolled his eyes. "Yeah and the rest."

"After hours?"

"Sort of." He gave a chuckle. "On Tuesdays, he spends a bit of time with the barmaid after she clears the other drinkers from the bar. Bit of a flirty piece."

Cyril and Woodbridge exchanged glances.

"Mr White," Cyril said. "Just to be clear, are you saying Mr Mason was not here last Tuesday afternoon?"

"Well, I don't want to drop anybody in it, but he kind of did it to me."

"So how long had he disappeared for? You said a couple of hours or so."

"Obviously he clocked in at twelve, but I didn't see him after that until about half four."

Woodbridge looked thoughtful. "And he couldn't have been anywhere to do with his job?" he asked. "Looking after a patient in some remote department or a transfer to another hospital?"

"No. His little blue Escort was gone from the car park. I noticed that when I came out for a smoke about half two, and again an hour later."

Cyril stiffened. "Mr White, we will need a statement from you detailing what you've just told us."

White dropped his cigarette butt onto the ground and trod on it. "Sure," he said. "Anyway, I'd best get back."

39

The receptionist from Clacton Hospital offered to come into Jackson Road Police Station when she'd finished her shift that afternoon. A handful of volunteers of similar age to Billy Mason had also arrived to make the line-up. Unfortunately, they were one short when Cyril and Sam returned.

"Ah, Sam," Sanderson said. "Did you go to the hospital to take statements from any of the staff when Jack Tinker died?"

"Some, yes sir." Woodbridge replied. "I went there the second time and spoke to some of the nursing staff."

"What about the receptionist?"

Woodbridge shook his head. "No, never saw her. Ben conducted her interview, I think," he said

"Would she have seen you?" Sanderson asked.

"I don't think so."

"Good. Get yourself in there. We're one short for the parade."

Woodbridge was shocked. "What?"

"Go on," Sanderson encouraged. "Get yourself ready."

After Woodbridge had left to prepare himself, Sanderson remarked to Cyril, "We're buggered if she picks him out."

Mason lined up as number three and Woodbridge two away at number five when the men positioned themselves in the parade room. The receptionist was a formidable woman in her fifties with grey hair in a tight bun. Sanderson felt confident she would be a good witness. He'd briefed her to look closely at the men, take her time and let them know if she could identify anyone as the person she'd seen in the hospital on the day in question.

Led in by a uniformed sergeant, she walked slowly up the line pausing at each man and staring hard at their faces. After studying each one, she walked back to look again at number 3. Finally she left the room and spoke to Sanderson.

"Number three," she said. "He was the one I saw that day."

"And how sure are you?" Sanderson asked.

"As I can be," she affirmed.

"Thanks for that," he said. "The sergeant will escort you out."

Mason was taken to the interview room whilst the rest of the line-up left the station.

Sanderson called Barton, Cyril and Woodbridge into his office.

"Shut the door, Sam," he said when they were assembled. "Take a seat."

"I tell you, she scared the pants off me, when she stared up at me," Woodbridge commented. "I thought she was going to pick me out."

"So did I," Cyril said, a broad smile on his face.

"Anyway," Sanderson said, "What did you find out at the hospital?"

Cyril outlined their discussions with the porters' supervisor then explained the comments made by Frank White.

Sanderson rubbed his chin. "So Mason has no alibi at all for the time that someone matching his description was seen in the corridors of Clacton Hospital when he was also identified as having been there by the receptionist," he stated. After a moment's thought, he continued addressing Cyril, "Right, I want you and Sam to take the mugshot book with Mason's photo and check with the witnesses from the Railway Hotel and Mama's. If he's also our mysterious character seen talking to Sharon Williams, then we're into a whole new ball game."

"What about me?" Barton queried.

"It's time you and I questioned Billy Mason. But remember, keep it calm," Sanderson said.

This time, Mason had requested the presence of the duty solicitor and so it was an hour or so later before Sanderson, carrying a brown folder, walked into the interview room along with Barton to conduct the next stage of the process.

The two detectives sat down opposite Mason with the bespectacled, balding solicitor alongside his client.

"Mr Mason," Sanderson began, "we've had the opportunity to check your story that you were on duty at Essex County Hospital last Tuesday, the 8th." He paused a second. "Before we proceed, do you wish to add to your previous statement?"

"I don't think so. I already told you I was on a late shift that day," Mason said.

"You are aware, are you not, of the reason we're interested in certain incidents which occurred on Tuesday 8th March?"

"No."

"We're investigating the events surrounding the death of ex-Detective Chief Inspector Jack Tinker at Clacton Hospital on that day," Sanderson stated.

Mason grunted. "So the bastard's dead, is he?"

"Oh, I think you already know that."

"How do you make that out?"

"You read the notice in the paper," Sanderson said. "Marked in blue ink in the one we found on the coffee table in your front room."

Mason looked alarmed. "You've been in my house! You've no right …"

"We obtained a search warrant, Mr Mason. We have every right."

Mason shook his head and looked down to the floor.

"But the fact that you had yesterday's newspaper wasn't the main purpose of our search."

The man looked up at Sanderson. "I don't follow."

"We found a substantial number of insulin vials and hypodermic needles in your bathroom cupboard."

"Not surprising. My mother was diabetic for years."

Sanderson paused a second. "When did your mother pass, Mr Mason?"

"December 21st."

"I would have thought you'd have disposed of her medication by now, especially with you working in the hospital." Sanderson glanced over to Barton sitting beside him. "Wouldn't you say DI Barton?"

"That would be the responsible thing to do, sir," Barton said.

Mason snorted but made no response.

Sanderson took up the questioning once again. "Our enquiries have revealed that you actually left the hospital not long after you clocked in and you weren't seen again until around half-past four."

Mason tried his best puzzled look. "I was there," he insisted. "Ray, the supervisor should have confirmed that."

Sanderson nodded and pulled a sheet of paper from the folder he'd put down on the table in front of him. "That's certainly what the paperwork says here, I'll grant you," he said. "However, as I'm sure you're aware, the supervisor has a, shall we say, habit he likes to indulge in on a Tuesday afternoon in the Hospital Arms."

"What do you mean?"

"You drive a dark blue Ford Fiesta, Mr Mason?"

"You know I do, seeing as you seized it from the hospital car park yesterday."

"And you normally park in that car park when you're at work?"

"That's right."

"What would you say if I told you we have a witness who will testify that you disappeared from your shift for at least a couple of hours on that day? And that your car had gone from the car park also."

The solicitor interjected. "I think I'd like to speak to my client in private, if you don't mind?"

Sanderson looked to Barton then back to Mason. "I think you need to consider your position, Mr Mason," he said, rising to his feet.

Barton followed suit and the pair left the room.

It was fifteen minutes later when Sanderson and Barton resumed the interview.

"Okay, Mr Mason," the DCI began, "would you like to tell us where you actually were last Tuesday afternoon?"

Mason braced himself. "Your precious Chief Inspector Tinker was as bent as arseholes. He couldn't find the evidence to prove my Dad's involvement in the Dovercourt Post Office job, so he planted it, as you very well know, DI Barton," he stated.

Barton gave a slight cough but remained silent.

Mason continued, "I heard he'd had a stroke. So I decided I would try and visit him."

"Take him grapes, was it?" Barton said.

Sanderson gave Barton a stern glance.

"Something like that. The bastard stitched my Dad up, got him sent down and hastened my Mum's demise. I wanted to ask him if he realised what he'd done and try and find out why."

"And did you get any answers?" Sanderson asked.

"No. There wasn't a glimmer."

"And pumping him full of your mother's insulin would help would it?"

"He was dying anyway."

"But you just wanted to make sure?"

"I thought it might help him on his way."

"So you're admitting injecting Mr Tinker with insulin?"

Mason nodded.

"Whilst he lay incapable in bed?" Barton added.

Sanderson put a hand on Barton's arm. "Just to be absolutely clear," he continued, "you are admitting injecting Mr Tinker with insulin?"

"Yes."

40

It was later that afternoon when Cyril, a large book tucked under his arm, and Sam Woodbridge were making their way back to the station having spoken to Karyn Brown at the travel agents and Duncan Marshall, the retired journalist they'd tracked down in the lounge bar of the Railway Hotel.

"I didn't think it could be him," Woodbridge said.

"There is a similarity though," Cyril responded. "In the descriptions, I mean."

The pair were silent for a while before Woodbridge spoke again, obviously troubled. "Do you think the DI capable of planting evidence, skip?" he asked.

Cyril stopped walking and looked intently at the DC. "Whoah. What made you ask that, Sam?"

"It's something that Billy said."

"In the interview?"

Woodbridge nodded. "He accused Mr Barton ... and Mr Tinker of having planted incriminating evidence at the scene of the post office robbery."

Cyril shook his head and continued walking, Woodbridge dropping into step beside him. "I can't believe John would do such a thing ... Mr Tinker on the other hand ..."

The two walked on for another few minutes. "Is there something troubling you, Sam," Cyril wondered.

"It's just I got the impression that Billy believed his father had been stitched up back then. I know subsequently we've discovered the money which proves he was involved but at the time, according to Billy, the only evidence was a cigarette packet found in the postmaster's flat with his father's fingerprints on it."

"People can be careless," Cyril offered.

"But he said his father wasn't. In fact he said his father never smoked on a job."

They were back in Jackson Road by then. "Never mind that for now, Sam," Cyril said. "We need to report our findings to the DCI."

When they entered the CID Room, Cyril checked his desk for messages. There was nothing that couldn't wait. "Come on," he said to Woodbridge, "let's find the DCI."

When they approached Sanderson's office, they found Barton there too.

"Ah, Cyril, how did you get on?" Sanderson asked.

Over the next few minutes, Cyril appraised Sanderson and Barton of their discussions with two of the witnesses and their view that Billy Mason was not the man seen on the night Sharon Williams was murdered. "And one other thing, of course," Cyril concluded, "his car is a Fiesta which couldn't be confused with a Cortina which is the vehicle the neighbour across the street saw parked outside her house in the early hours. It's much smaller."

Sanderson nodded.

"And that ties in with the fact that Mason's neighbour remembered his car parked outside his house on the same night," Cyril concluded, relating his latest conversation with the ever vigilant Mrs Jarvis.

Unusually, it was Cyril's suggestion to go for a pint. They were in the Medina early doors and it was fairly quiet. Barton sensed Cyril had something on his mind, so he waited patiently until the drinks were brought back to the table in the quiet corner they'd chosen.

After filling his pipe, packing it and lighting up, Cyril spoke. "So Billy Mason has been charged with the murder of Mr Tinker," he stated.

Barton took a mouthful of his beer before producing a packet of Rothmans cigarettes from his pocket. "We had no choice," he said. "The lad admitted it."

Cyril waited until the DI had lit his cigarette before he continued. "Was there ever anything you felt uneasy about in your dealings with Walter Mason all those years ago, John?"

Barton was guarded. "What are you getting at Cyril?"

"Sam told me some of what Billy said in the first interview, the one he was in with Mr Sanderson."

"Specifically ...?"

Cyril sipped his beer then said, "Billy was convinced his father wasn't involved in the Dovercourt job." He held up his pipe to prevent Barton interrupting him. "I know we now know that he was. The discovery of the proceeds and the forensic evidence there makes it irrefutable but ..."

"You're asking what evidence we had to convict in the first instance?"

"According to Sam, Billy stated that it was a cigarette packet found at the scene with his father's prints on it. Yet, his father never smoked on a job. At least that's what he'd told him. Unprofessional in Walter's view, apparently." Cyril puffed his pipe and waited for Barton to respond.

For the first time in years, Barton thought back to that interview; really thought about it. It was the second interview he and Tinker had conducted with Walter Mason in the very room that he'd just listened to his son, Billy, describe more recent events.

It had been two days after the post office raid. This time, DI Tinker, as he was then, had seemed less aggressive. Barton was used to his hard tactics in interviewing suspects. Tinker wasn't averse to physical violence against them if he thought he could extract information. Sometimes some burly uniforms would be sent in. Mostly, their presence would be enough to loosen a tongue.

But this interview was different. Tinker was almost friendly towards the man.

"Walter," Tinker had begun, "we all know you were involved with Cliff Hammond at Dovercourt two nights ago."

Mason had shaken his head. "I was at home with Valerie," he replied. "I told you that already."

"So how come your prints were found in Hammond's car? The one used to drive the pair of you away from the scene."

"Didn't say I don't know him. He's given me a lift a few times. Bound to have touched things in there." Mason had looked at the cigarette packet lying on the table.

Tinker nodded. "Help yourself Walter."

Barton remembered being mildly surprised at that. Normally when you knew suspects smoked, it was the obvious tactic to deny them access. Then go further, light up yourself and blow smoke over them. Nine times out of ten, a short while later, they'd tell you all you wanted to know with the promise of a fag.

Mason had picked up the packet and shaken out what was the last one. Instinctively, he'd screwed the packet up.

Barton was surprised to see Tinker leaning over the table to light it for him rather than grab him by his shirt lapels. Perhaps this was a different way the DI thought he'd get Mason to come clean.

The man inhaled deeply and blew out smoke. "Like I say, Mr Tinker, I was at home all night with the wife. Ask her."

"We already have and I don't believe a word of it."

Mason had shrugged.

Tinker let the man enjoy the rest of his cigarette before it was stubbed out in the metal ashtray on the table.

Tinker had watched him then turned to Barton. "Take Mr Mason back to the cells, would you? I think he needs to consider his situation a bit longer."

Mason had looked disappointed but stood and followed Barton out, leaving Tinker alone in the interview room.

Later that same day, Tinker and Barton had re-visited the postmaster's flat, still a crime scene, although the forensics officers had completed their work.

Barton remembered being sent into the kitchen, supposedly to check that there was nothing that had been missed that might provide evidence of the two suspects' presence. When Barton had returned to the sitting room, Tinker was standing looking out of the window, hands deep in his pockets.

"Nothing, sir," Barton had said.

"Oh well, Dick, just have one last sweep round here then we'll get back."

That was when Barton had discovered the discarded cigarette packet beneath one of the easy chairs by the side of the fireplace.

"Hang on," Barton had said. "What's this?"

Tinker joined him quickly, down on his haunches. "Don't touch it," he'd said. "Bag it and get it off to the lab."

That proved to be a vital piece of evidence; Mason's prints were found on the packet. Only now, thinking back, did Barton realise what his boss had done. It had only been the packet. No cigarette butts had been discovered.

He knew that wasn't the only occasion over the years that Tinker had bent the rules. "Sometimes you've got to play the bastards at their own game," he'd said. And, "Needs must."

But the one aspect that annoyed Barton was that Tinker had manipulated him to legitimise those tactics in some way.

"I think I was used, Cyril," Barton finally said, a despondent look on his face.

"Are you saying Mr Tinker acted … unprofessionally in some way?"

"Totally." Barton stubbed out the cigarette in the ashtray on the table. "But I'm only just beginning to realise how badly," he concluded, downing the rest of his pint.

It was about seven o'clock when Cyril put the key in the lock of his front door; a bit later than he expected to be but it was a useful conversation with Barton in the pub. His mind was exploring what he could have for his evening meal. Perhaps a visit to Big Pete's would be in order for some fish and chips. It was getting a bit late to cook something, after all.

He walked into the kitchen and found Charlie lying in his basket. Doris had obviously called in as there was a full bowl of his biscuits next to the water bowl. Charlie barely looked up at his master and Cyril could tell he was not himself.

"What's up old lad," Cyril said to the dog. "Are you not hungry?"

Charlie gave a couple of short wags of his tail but remained in the same position.

Cyril walked over to the hook by the pantry door and took down Charlie's lead. That action would normally prompt Charlie to his feet then a shake of himself in readiness for his evening walk. "Fancy a stroll down to Big Pete's?" he said. But this time the dog ignored him.

He put the lead back on the hook and went over to his companion. He knelt down and stroked his big head in a shared moment of love. That moment was short-lived, interrupted by a ring of the doorbell. He answered to find Doris on the step.

"How is he?" she asked.

"Come in, Doris," he beckoned, standing aside to let his neighbour in.

"I saw you come home," she said, walking into the kitchen.

"He's not good." Cyril looked at Charlie once again.

Doris noticed the dog bowl. "He's not touched his food. He wasn't interested when I put it down about five o'clock."

Cyril tried to brighten up. "Maybe it's just an upset stomach."

Doris looked up at him. "Or maybe he's just getting old."

"I'll see what he's like in the morning and ring the vet."

"Have you eaten?" she asked.

"I was going to get something from Pete's but Charlie wasn't interested in that."

"Tell you what, you go and get yourself something and I'll stay with Charlie."

"Are you sure?"

"I love the big pudding just as much as you do, Cyril," she said, struggling to raise a smile.

41
Thursday 17th March 1977

St Patrick's Day was bright and sunny. A cold wind whipped in off the North Sea but that only affected the few brave souls who were walking along the sea front as Cyril drove to the station. His mind was on Charlie. The old dog still hadn't eaten. The temptation of a few bits from Cyril's fish supper the previous night wasn't enough to coax him. In fact the only time he'd risen to his feet was to make the slow walk out into the back garden for a pee.

Doris said she'd stay with him today. She was the best neighbour he could wish for. She'd been a good friend to Maureen too. When she was so ill, she stayed with her and talked or just read a book beside her when she was sleeping. It meant Cyril could carry on working without the constant worry of thinking his wife was on her own.

First thing he'd do when he got to the station would be to call the vet and arrange a time to take Charlie in. He knew his colleagues would all be busy formalising the paperwork for Billy Mason's murder charge; and then there was still the person responsible for Sharon Williams' death to find too.

The vet's appointment was made for midday and by his calculation Cyril would have time to secure the formal statement from Mrs Jarvis, the neighbour who lived over the road from Billy Mason before he'd have to get home and collect Charlie.

About to put on his coat, the phone rang on his desk.

"Hello," he greeted.

"Cyril, it's Doris," came the familiar voice of his neighbour. *"I think you'd better come home."* Her tone of voice was serious.

He could feel the colour drain from his cheeks and the pricking in his throat. He turned away from the others in the room to face the wall. "Is it bad?" he struggled to ask.

"He's gone. I'm so sorry." The upset in her voice was clear and he knew she would shed tears too.

There was a pause before he spoke again. "I'll be back as soon as I can." He gave a sigh. "And Doris ... thanks," he added before putting the phone down gently and walking from the room.

He'd experienced death many times, too many when he was just a young man in the war. He'd lost young colleagues, some not even out of their teens. He lost his dear wife, Maureen, nearly four years ago now, and that was something he still hadn't recovered from totally, probably never would. But this, the loss of his good friend and companion who had been there with unconditional love through all the heartache of his wife's illness and passing, well ... this was staggering. He found himself in the toilet, tears flowing like a waterfall.

*   *   *

"Okay, let's review where we are," Sanderson announced as he entered the CID Room.

Woodbridge, Miller, Walker, Barton and a handful of other detectives drafted in from another team assembled round the DCI.

"Where's Cyril?" he asked.

"I think he's gone to collect a statement from Billy's neighbour," Woodbridge answered. Despite the murder charge, Sam still used the man's first name by which he'd always known him.

"Okay, well someone brief him on this. Now," he said, pacing the floor and looking up occasionally, "well done with finding Jack's killer. I say that because Mason has been charged with murder. What we need to do is get all the paperwork in place so his brief, whoever that might be, can't wriggle him out of that. So I'll need all those witness statements tied up tight." Sanderson stopped and looked round at the gathered faces.

Mumbled affirmative responses came from the group.

"But that still leaves the killer of Sharon Williams at large," he went on. "We know Mason wasn't responsible for that. So what have we got?" Sanderson proceeded to outline all the salient points so far uncovered regarding the victim's movements on the night she was last seen and all the information gathered from the various witnesses. After a few minutes, he began to summarise. "At the moment, we have a description of a man in his twenties, looking a bit like this." He pointed to an identikit image pinned to a board on the wall. "Now I know it's a little bit sketchy but at the very least we need to identify this individual, if only for elimination."

"We also think he drives a Ford Cortina, sir," Woodbridge added. "It was a car of that size that Sharon Williams' neighbour saw parked outside her house on the night in question."

"We've also yet to identify those fingerprints on one of those wine glasses in the victim's front room," Sanderson said. "Who was following that up?"

"I believe Sergeant Claydon was, sir," Woodbridge responded.

"I think we need to speak to the town's taxi drivers," Barton added.

"But there are no reports of Sharon getting into a cab," Sanderson responded.

"No, but I have heard that some of the cabbies have seen a bloke similar to this description around town offering women a lift in a Cortina."

"This is becoming a recurrent feature. We need to find out more about this car," Sanderson said. "If we can get a registration, even partial, that would be something to work with at the very least."

"What about getting the local press involved?" Barton suggested. "Only in specific areas, like getting the public's help for this guy in the Cortina?"

"We'll give it a day or two more and see what happens," Sanderson responded. "These press blokes can be double-edged swords."

"I do know Alan on the Gazette quite well. Usually, if I give him copy to use, he sticks with it," Barton said.

Sanderson nodded. "I hear what you say, Dick but hold fire a bit longer, then we'll discuss."

Over the course of the next few minutes, the DCI outlined the various actions he wanted his officers to take before the briefing came to an end.

*   *   *

It was gone three that afternoon when Barton rang Cyril's doorbell. He was surprised when Doris answered.

"Come through," she said. "He's in the garden."

Barton was puzzled. He knew Cyril had left the station that morning. Sam Woodbridge had surmised that he was off to Colchester to collect a witness statement. Later in the morning, when Cathy had come into the CID room with some typing, she'd asked Barton if Cyril was alright. According to her, he'd seemed upset when he'd left the station but she hadn't had the opportunity to speak to him.

When Cyril hadn't reappeared after lunch, his concern had grown.

Barton made his way through the kitchen and out the back door into the garden. Cyril was by a tree near the rear fence, spade in hand, filling in a hole in the lawn.

"I didn't think you were on gardening leave, Cyril," he said, light-heartedly.

When Cyril turned to face him, he could see how upset he was.

"What's happened?"

"It's Charlie," Cyril struggled to say.

"Oh no, not the poor old lad."

"He liked you."

"I liked him. When?"

"This morning. Doris was with him. I'm so glad. They shouldn't be on their own for their last moments, should they? Well, that's what I think, anyway."

"And this was his favourite spot?" Barton asked.

Cyril nodded. "He often lay in the shade of the flowering cherry we'd planted when we moved in 27 years ago."

Barton put a hand on Cyril's shoulder. "I'm really sorry, mate," he said. "I know how much you loved that dog."

"Would you like a cup of tea, Mr Barton?" Doris asked from the back door.

"Go on," Cyril said. "I've only got the turf to put back here and I'll be in."

Barton walked back to the house. "That's very kind," he said to the lady.

"He's taken it hard," she said as she poured him a cup from the pot she'd made.

"But you saw as much of the dog as Cyril did." Barton put a spoon of sugar in his drink and stirred it.

"I did. But when you get to my age, death is a part of life."

Barton gave a short laugh. "You have a great way with words," he said.

She glanced out through the kitchen window. "Look, Cyril's coming back in, so I'll leave you two alone. Tell him to call round if he wants to later."

Doris closed the front door as Cyril came in through the back.

"There's tea in the pot," Barton said. "She's a grand old stick, isn't she?"

"Best neighbour I could have," Cyril said as he sat down at the kitchen table opposite Barton. "Anyway, what have I missed?"

Barton proceeded to outline the relevant points, mentioning the search for the wine glass fingerprint match.

"Last time I spoke to Tom, he was pursuing the Met's database, but that could take some time," Cyril said.

Barton then related his suggestion for contacts with the press.

"Is that Alan Watson, you mean?" Cyril asked.

"That's him," Barton confirmed.

"I know him quite well too. You're right, for a reporter, he's pretty straight up."

"Although Martin didn't say no, he wants more time to consider that."

42
Friday 18th March 1977

When Barton climbed the stairs to the CID Room that morning, DCI Sanderson was waiting to intercept him. His expression was serious.

"A word, John," he said.

Use of his Christian name put Barton on his guard. "What's up?" he asked.

Sanderson lowered his voice. "I've got DCI Brookes and his lapdog in my office. He wants to talk to you again."

"Christ what does that bastard want now? He certainly lives up to his nickname." Barton shook his head in disbelief. "I've been cleared of any involvement in Sharon Williams' murder."

"I know. Apparently, he wants to talk to you about the investigation into the Dovercourt raid."

"Fuck me! That was eight years ago."

"Just calm down, John. He'll only try and bait you. Come on," he said, turning away to his office. "I'll be in there with you, so just take things easy."

"Easy for you to say," Barton remarked as he followed him towards his office.

Brookes and his oppo stood up from the chairs they'd been occupying in Sanderson's office when the DCI and Barton walked in.

"DI Barton," Brookes greeted, a supercilious smile on his face and holding out a hand. "Thanks for agreeing to this interview."

Barton looked at Brookes' hand for a second before grudgingly, briefly taking hold. "As far as I'm aware, this is an informal chat, not an interview." He glanced at Sanderson.

"That's my understanding DCI Brookes," Sanderson said. "And I'll sit in on this one, if you don't mind."

Brookes pock-marked face grew dark.

"Please, sit down," Sanderson invited.

Slowly, the big DCI sat down in the chair, his weasel companion following suit.

"You know DS Chapple," Sanderson said to Barton, indicating Brookes' bag man.

"We met last time," Barton said, taking a seat at the side of Sanderson's desk, half facing Brookes and Chapple.

"I'd like to talk to you about your actions during the investigations into the post office raid in Dovercourt in 1969," Brookes began.

"My actions?" Barton asked, guardedly. "What about them?"

Brookes shuffled through some papers in a manila folder he'd brought with him then looked across at Barton. "According to the files, the conviction of Walter Mason was secured primarily due to the discovery of a cigarette packet found at the scene with his fingerprints on it," he stated.

"Yes." Barton was making a great effort to remain calm.

"I understand this was found by you?"

"As I recall, that's correct."

"After there had already been a forensic search of the postmaster's house."

Barton shrugged. "I don't recall."

Brookes smirked. "Of course you don't."

"Is there a point to this DCI Brookes?" Sanderson asked.

"We believe there may have been some … tampering of evidence in this case and we're duty bound to investigate."

In flat level tones, Barton responded, "I'm not aware of anything like that."

"You weren't aware of any practices by DCI Tinker that you didn't agree with … didn't feel comfortable with?"

"No."

"So anything your boss did, you were quite happy to go along with?"

Barton leaned forward in his seat. "Are you trying to put words in my mouth, DCI Brookes? I said I was not aware of anything untoward. You're making a big leap to imply I knew of anything and was compliant in that."

"And were you?"

Despite his advice to Barton, Sanderson had grown frustrated. "The case is over eight years old and we have just uncovered fresh evidence of Walter Mason's guilt. Mason himself is dead. The senior investigating officer in the case has recently passed away. What the Hell are you trying to achieve with this witch hunt?"

The atmosphere in the room suddenly became claustrophobic.

Sanderson pressed on in a calm voice, "I would have thought you'd have had more urgent matters to take up your time."

Brookes face coloured.

Internally, Barton felt gratitude to his boss for his support.

"We have to investigate these matters," Brookes finally said.

Sanderson stood up. "There is nothing *to* investigate. Walter Mason - and Cliff Hammond for that matter - were found guilty of a crime they committed together and evidence we've uncovered in the past week makes that irrefutable." He walked to the door. "So, if you don't mind, we're in the middle of a live murder investigation ..." Sanderson opened the door.

Reluctantly, Brookes got to his feet and, with a scornful glance towards Barton, left the office with DS Chapple following close behind.

Sanderson closed the door behind them and turned to face his DI.

"What prompted that?" Barton asked.

"A bloody fishing trip, that's what that was," he said. "You did well, Dick."

Back to my nickname, Barton thought, so all must be well. "He must have really hated Jack," Barton said.

Sanderson walked back round his desk and sat down. "They must have had history."

"You did well too, sir, if you don't mind me saying."

Sanderson scowled. "Wasting our bloody time."

A broad smile appeared on Barton's face as he spoke, "To paraphrase something someone once said in the canteen, 'he might have been a bent bastard but he was *our* bent bastard.'"

"Was Jack bent?"

"Well he might have bent the rules a bit but, let's face it, they all did in those days."

Sanderson raised his eyebrows. "Just be careful, Dick. Brookes is obviously out to sully Tinker's name for whatever reason and, by definition, he sees you as an extension of him, so you're in his sights as well."

*   *   *

Cyril was locking the car after parking up when he spotted Brookes and Chapple scurrying out through the main doors and climbing into their vehicle. The engine started and Brookes drove hurriedly away.

When he walked up the steps and into the entrance, George, the desk sergeant who had stayed on past his retirement, looked up at him. "What's Bastard Brookes and Weasel doing back here again, Cyril?" he asked.

"They're C and D, aren't they?" Cyril replied, knowing full well they were the two Complaints and Discipline officers he had seen a couple of weeks ago having interviewed Barton.

"They've been up with the DCI," George said. "I think they wanted to see Dick too."

"You seem to know a lot already," Cyril remarked.

"Bloody creeps. I wouldn't trust that bugger Brookes further than I could throw him. And that's not very far at my age."

"You know him, George?"

The sergeant pulled a face. "Oh yes. He started off here, you know. Didn't you ever come across him?"

"Must have been before my time," Cyril said.

"Lucky you. He left under a cloud. In fact it was old Jack who got rid."

"Mr Tinker?"

"That's right. I say got rid but he actually had him transferred away to Harlow, I think it was," George recalled, then as an afterthought, "After that incident."

"Incident?"

"Oh, you wouldn't know if you came here later."

Cyril leaned on the desk. "Any chance of enlightening me?"

Cyril was removing his coat when Barton came through the room towards his office.

"Everything okay?" Cyril enquired.

Barton indicated his office, so Cyril followed.

"Just had that twat Brookes back in again," Barton said once the door was closed.

Cyril indicated surprise. "I thought that had all gone away, no evidence."

"Like Martin said, it was a bloody fishing trip." Barton sat down heavily in his chair. "It's a vendetta, against me it seems. But he's also trying to dig up old dirt on Jack."

"Tinker?" Cyril was intrigued, especially following his conversation with the desk sergeant. "What good will that do, the man's gone. And he hasn't even had a funeral yet."

Barton invited Cyril to take a seat then proceeded to give him an outline of the conversation that had taken place in Sanderson's office earlier.

"I tell you, Cyril, it's as though he has a fixation with old Jack." Barton leaned forward on his desk, head resting in his hands. "I wish I could find some dirt on the bastard."

"Well, I might just be able to help you there," Cyril said as he got to his feet and made for the door.

"How?"

"Must get on," Cyril said. "Statements to check."

Cathy walked in to the canteen and scanned the tables. Cyril raised a hand and she made her way over to join him, breaking into a broad grin. "To what do I owe the honour of an invite to the canteen?" she asked.

"Ah, well you see, there's no such thing as a free lunch."

"So do I buy my own?" she asked, half turning away.

Cyril stood. "Sit down Cath, I'll get it. What do you want?"

Once he'd returned to the table with their meals and cutlery, Cyril sat down opposite her.

"I was really sorry to hear about Charlie," Cathy said. "I did try and call you last night but you didn't answer."

"Sorry Cathy, I just felt I wanted time to reflect. I mean I knew the day was coming, he was a good age but, like all these things, they hit you hard when they do happen."

"I quite understand."

"One thing though," Cyril said, "I was so glad that Doris was with him. I tell you, I don't know what I'd have done over these past few years without her as a neighbour."

They were quiet for a few minutes as they ate before Cathy asked the question that had intrigued her. "Go on then, Cyril, what's this about?"

He put down his knife and fork on the plate. "How long have you worked here, Cathy?" he asked.

She finished chewing a chip. "Ooh, it must be nearly twenty years now. Why?"

"Do you remember a young CID officer here, maybe fifteen years or so back, by the name of Brookes, Barry Brookes?"

Cathy hardly gave the question a moment's thought. "Oh yes I remember the big creepy sod."

"Why do you say that?"

"Well, he was always hanging around the typing pool, leaning over some of the girls' shoulders, looking down their blouses, that sort of thing."

"Did he ever bother you?"

"I always tried to avoid him. But there was one young girl who seemed to attract more than her fair share …"

Cyril took a drink of his tea. "That wasn't someone by the name of Shirley Miles, was it?"

"Shirley, yes, little Shirley." Cathy waved her fork around. "Sorry. Thinking about it now, I don't think she stayed too long."

Cyril nodded. "And this would be around the same time that Brookes left?"

"I suppose so."

"I don't suppose you know where this Shirley might be now?"

Cathy looked intent. "Why? Is it important?"

"It could be."

She continued eating her meal. "I've no idea," she said between mouthfuls. "She was only with us a few months, I think. She was young, maybe late teens, twentyish. She could be anywhere."

"What about employment records? Could you have a look and see if there's an address?"

"Well … maybe. I could have a look. But that would only be where she was fifteen years ago. She's probably married and living elsewhere now."

"But it would be a start."

"Okay. Leave it with me," she said, putting her knife and fork down on her empty plate. "I'll let you know what I can find out."

"Thanks," he said, a wide smile on his face.

She stood up. "See you later tonight?" she suggested. "Simon's staying over at his mates. His friend's dad is taking them to Colchester tomorrow for the football."

"Come over to me. I'll cook us some tea." Cyril had a wide smile on his face as he watched her leave the canteen.

*　　*　　*

All afternoon, armed with the poor quality Identikit image produced by the various witnesses, Barton trawled through the army of taxi drivers pulling up at the railway station rank asking about the mysterious man offering young women lifts at night. He'd drawn a blank so far and was beginning to wonder whether Marnie had got her facts wrong when one of the younger drivers confirmed that he'd spotted a car cruising Rosemary Road late one night when it stopped next to a woman walking on her own. This had been about three or four weeks ago and he remembered this because he felt annoyed that someone might be robbing him of a fare. He'd pulled to a stop behind this car and the woman had looked towards him. She obviously spotted the cab sign on his roof, because she walked away from this other car, approached him and got in. The other car had quickly driven off.

"Did the woman say she'd been cajoled in any way to get in to this car?" Barton asked.

"She said he'd asked if she needed a lift home as he could take her," the driver replied as he flicked ash from his cigarette onto the road.

"I don't suppose you can remember where you dropped her off?"

The taxi man thought for a minute. "Nah, not exactly, sorry. She got out on Frinton Road in Holland but she walked away after that so she could have gone anywhere down the side streets."

"What about the car, can you remember anything about it?"

"It was a Cortina, a new one as I recall. 'R' registration and possibly a 1.6. Oh, and blue."

"And the driver?" Barton pressed.

The taxi driver shook his head. "No. I only just saw the shape of his head through the back window with my headlights." He took a last drag on his cigarette, flicked the butt onto the street then exhaled loudly. "Could have been fair haired, I'm not too sure. Longish, so maybe a youngish guy, but who knows."

"You don't know if any of your colleagues has had a similar experience with this driver trying to nick a fare?"

"I think I heard one of the older blokes mention he'd had something similar happen to him a week or two back, but only snippets of an overheard conversation. To be honest, I wasn't really paying any attention."

Barton thanked the man and moved on to the next driver.

After another fruitless half hour or so, Barton tried the cab rank in town. This time, he heard from another driver, possibly the one the younger cabbie referred to, who had spotted a similar car and driver one Friday night about a fortnight ago. On this occasion, the woman hadn't got into the car and one of his colleagues had picked her up.

*   *   *

"This is really nice, Cyril," Cathy said after the first mouthful. "You're not a bad cook on the quiet."

"Thanks very much," he said with a hint of irony. "I learnt a lot in the RAF. But when Maureen became ill, I had to take up a lot of the responsibility."

Cyril had relied on his tried and trusted ability to do a mean chilli con carne.

"You haven't spoken much about her," Cathy probed. "I'd like to know more."

"Not that much to tell, really. We were married for twenty-four years. She developed cancer and, after two years fighting it, she passed, nearly four years ago now."

"But you were happy together?"

He didn't answer straight away, thoughts straying to time spent with Maureen, conversations had, confidences shared. He looked up at Cathy then replied, "Yes, of course. She was my best friend."

Cathy was quiet for a little time as they continued eating. Eventually, Cyril spoke. "Did you get anywhere finding out about Shirley Miles?"

"Ah, now then," Cathy began. "I managed to find her address from her personnel file along with a phone number."

"That's good."

"So, I called the number."

"Oh, how did you approach that?"

"She doesn't live there now. But her parents still do. I told them I was trying to track Shirley down for a reunion."

"And they believed you?"

"Of course. Anyway, she's married now, name of Crabtree, and lives in Great Bentley. I've got her phone number and address." She rummaged in her handbag and pulled out a slip of paper.

"Very good, I'm impressed."

"Be even more impressed." She beamed at him. "We're going to call in tomorrow and have a chat."

"We? How have you managed that?"

"Her husband will be out with their boys, so she'll be in on her own."

"What exactly did you say to her?"

"Well, she remembered me from Jackson Road, and I said someone would like to talk to her about her time there."

"How did she take that?"

"She seemed reluctant at first but I said I would be there too. Eventually she agreed to tomorrow afternoon when her husband's taking the boys to rugby practice."

43

He was alerted by the shouting; a female voice, young woman maybe. At first, it wasn't clear where it was coming from. The words were incomprehensible. But as he approached the corner, it grew louder, more insistent.

"Get off me, you …" the woman was shouting, the next few words were cut off.

He looked down the side street but couldn't make out any figures. But it was definitely down there, he was sure.

"You bastard! Get … fuck …" the female voice came again.

All the time the sounds of scuffling could be heard.

After another second or two with the sounds of a struggle, there came a loud yell. "Aargh!" This time a male voice, closely followed by footsteps, running, high heels clacking down the street.

Now he saw the silhouette shape of a young woman running towards him.

He held up his hands. "Hey, is everything alright?" he asked.

"And you can fuck off an' all," the woman said rushing past him, evading all attempts for him to speak to her. He watched her totter down the High Street before he heard the sound of a car door slam, the engine firing up, revving hard, then screeching out from behind a building. The car approached the junction at speed before drawing to a sharp stop. The driver looked straight at him, then beyond to check for traffic. Another glance from the angry face and he turned left and accelerated away quickly in the opposite direction to the woman.

He turned back to check on the woman's progress but she had disappeared from view.

He hoped all was well but made a mental note of the car; a blue Cortina, R registration, or was it P? No definitely R, quite a new one. And the driver, yes he'd remember him.

He pulled out his cigarette packet, nudged one out and lit it. Enough excitement for one night, he resumed his journey for home.

But his thoughts kept returning to what he'd witnessed. Was it just a squabble between girlfriend and boyfriend? Didn't sound like that. Was it something more sinister? If it was, why didn't she respond positively to his offer of assistance? Probably didn't want to have to deal with another man at that time. All the way home, he was torn as to what to do. What could he do? Report it to the police? Report what? Unless the woman makes a complaint …

He flicked his cigarette end into the gutter and stuffed both hands in his coat pocket.

What was he thinking about? Even if something had happened, he could hardly report it. His missus would discover he'd been out on the town when she was expecting him to be at home all evening. Staying overnight at her mother's, gave him the opportunity to have a good night out, like he used to with his mates before he got married. Might even pull something, he'd thought in a moment of lunacy on his way round town. The trouble was, things always moved on. None of his old mates were out. Most of the people out and about were years younger than him. Talk about a fish out of water. But he'd enjoyed the experience though, hadn't he? Well, maybe not; especially the incident he'd witnessed on the way home. And so his thoughts had turned full circle as he opened the gate, walked up the short path to his front door and put his key in the lock. He suddenly felt very tired … and alone. Roll on tomorrow when his wife returned.

44
Saturday 19th March 1977

"So what happened then, Chelle?"

This was the first time Kate had spoken to her friend since they'd been out in Harwich the night before. They were sitting in the pub they normally met up in, chosen because it was equidistant from where they both lived, plus they did some good food. But not today, today was only the chance for a hair of the dog.

"Urgh, it was horrible, Katie." Michelle made a face. "To be honest, it was a bit frightening too. But he picked on the wrong one with me."

Kate stubbed out her cigarette in the ashtray on their table. "How do you mean?"

"I was going to walk home and this creep came up to me ..."

"Which creep?"

"I dunno ... some bloke. No that's not true. I think we'd seen him earlier in the Diva." The Diva, a disco in the town they both liked to visit. "You remember, he tried chatting us up. Slim guy with longish fair hair."

"I can't think. There were a few tried it on."

"And you'd had a few by then too."

"And you hadn't? Anyway, go on." Kate encouraged, taking a sip of her tonic water. Normally she'd have a gin in it but today, she was feeling a little delicate.

"He asks, did I want a lift and I said, no, I'm fine. Besides, I couldn't see a car."

"He said he was parked just round the corner on one of those side streets. I must admit, I was feeling pretty knackered by then, so ..."

Kate looked aghast. "Oh, you didn't, did you?"

"Well I thought he looked alright. I still had over half a mile to go and there were no taxis."

"Jesus, how many times have we said?" Kate opened her packet of Embassy and offering one to her friend.

Michelle took a cigarette and lit both hers and her friend's with her lighter. "I know. But I thought it would be okay," she said, blowing out smoke. "We went down the street about fifty yards. He had his car parked behind a building. It was really dark and I suddenly thought, hang on a minute, Chelle. This is stupid. I know I'd had a few drinks, but I suppose it sobered me up a bit. I just had an uneasy feeling. When I told him I'd changed my mind, but thanks for the offer, he grabbed me and tried to bundle me into the car."

Kate put her hand to her mouth, a look of alarm on her face.

Michelle pressed on, nervously tapping the ash from her cigarette. "We struggled. He'd grabbed hold of both my arms here." She indicated above the elbows. "He had the passenger door open and got me half in. I was shouting at him, hoping someone would hear. And then, as we twisted around, I managed to face him and raise my knee into his bollocks as hard as I could. He cried out and his grip went slack. That's when I ran … well I say ran … I was in these bloody heels if you remember."

"And did anyone hear you?"

She smiled now, glad to have some of her pent-up tension relieved, as well as at the memory of the next part of her story. "At the top of the street, on the main road, there was another bloke, older, perhaps in his thirties. As I came up to the corner, he asked me if everything was alright."

"And what did you say?"

"I told him he could fuck off as well." She laughed at this. "I suppose I was feeling pretty bold by then. I know he was probably only offering to help but I thought I'd just get away. The last thing I wanted was to have to explain and be pestered by someone else."

"So he would have seen all this?"

"I don't know what he might have seen, it was a really dark street, but he would have heard the commotion. Anyway, I doubled back and ducked down an alley and waited. The last thing I wanted was for the creep to come after me in his car. I heard it drive off fast in the opposite direction. So I waited a few minutes and set off for home."

"Can you remember any details?" Kate asked. "Do you think you'd recognise him again?"

Michelle answered slowly, "I … I think so."

"And what about the car? What make was it, colour, interior, anything like that?"

"Bloody Hell, Kate, are you looking for a job in the police?"

Kate smiled. "Comes from sitting with my dad watching *Z Cars* and *Softly Softly*. And this new one *The Sweeney* … have you seen it?"

Michelle shook her head.

"Now that Dennis Waterman … I wouldn't resist him getting me into a car." She saw the look on her friend's face. "Sorry. Getting carried away. But what about the car?"

"It was bigger than an Escort, that I can say, because my dad drives one of them. No idea of the colour, it was too dark to see. But it was new. When he opened the door I got that lovely whiff of new car. You know the one, sort of plasticky scented smell. And the seats were brown."

"Chelle, you need to report this. This was an attempted abduction. You could have been raped … or worse."

Those comments hit home. Michelle knew her friend was right and she finally crumbled into a sea of sobs.

Kate passed a handkerchief across and waited for Michelle to recover.

Finally, Michelle wiped her eyes dry and gave the hankie back to her friend. "I know. I've been thinking about it all night."

Kate studied Michelle. "He might have done it before," she said. "He'll probably do it again. And some poor sod might not be as lucky as you."

Michelle stood up. "Right. Let's do it before I lose my nerve."

45

Great Bentley has the second largest village green in England. Cyril and Cathy took the road through the middle of it where, on one side, a game of football was in progress. On the other, the cricket pitch was fenced off; it would be a few more weeks before any activity would take place there. Turning left, then left again before they came to the railway station, they found the small street of semi-detached houses where Shirley's address was located.

Cyril paused before getting out. "You know what to do?"

Cathy gave him a look as if to say, we've been through this enough times. "Introduce you and let you take the lead," she said.

He smiled at her. "Good. Let's see what she has to say."

Their ring on the doorbell was answered by a small dainty woman in her late thirties.

"Shirley," Cathy said. "I'd know you anywhere. It must be fifteen years ago now."

"Sixteen," Shirley replied. "And you look much the same as I remember too, Cathy. Come in," she beckoned.

Cyril followed Cathy into the hallway.

"This is Cyril Claydon. I don't know if you remember him, he's a DS now at Clacton."

Shirley shook her head. "No sorry." She led the way into the front room. "Look, come through to the lounge. Would you like some tea?"

"That would be nice thanks," Cyril said.

As Shirley made them tea in the kitchen, Cyril looked around the room whilst Cathy sat on the three-seater settee facing a gas fire in the hearth. "Two good looking boys," he said, studying a photograph of Shirley's sons in school uniform.

After a few minutes, Shirley returned with cups, saucers, sugar and milk and a teapot on a tray and set it down on a coffee table. Once the woman had organised their drinks, offered biscuits and fussed around, she sat in an armchair by the side of the fireplace. Cyril joined Cathy on the settee.

Shirley looked across at Cyril. "Cathy tells me I might be able to help you somehow, Mr Claydon," she said.

"Cyril, please," he responded. "First of all, thanks for agreeing to see us. And you're quite right, you might be able to help me. If any of what I ask is uncomfortable for you, I quite understand and I'll leave things where they stand."

"Now you have me intrigued."

Cyril sipped his tea as he formulated his next statement. "I understand you worked with us at Jackson Road Police Station sixteen years ago."

The woman's expression grew dark and she nodded.

"During that time, did you come across an officer by the name of Barry Brookes?"

She made a face. "He was horrible."

"Did something take place when you worked there?"

She glanced over to Cathy.

"It's okay, Shirley," Cathy said. "Cyril only wants to know what happened. We think it could help another situation."

She looked alarmed. "You mean he's done it again?"

"Not as far as I know," Cyril said. "But I would like to hear directly what you can tell me from all those years ago."

She put down her cup and composed herself. "He was always a bit of a creep." She looked at Cathy. "You must have known that?" Back to Cyril. "He always stood close to you when he was telling you what he wanted you to do; closer than he needed to. He'd hover over your shoulder, trying to see down your blouse or dress." Again, her attention switched to Cathy. "You must have experienced that?"

Cathy nodded but said nothing, not wanting to interrupt the flow.

Shirley carried on, "Well one lunchtime, there was only me in the typing room. I was trying to finish a report when he came in. I'm sure he knew everyone else was out. After a bit of chat, you know, a bit of innuendo, he asks about some folders and writing pads. He needed some fresh supplies, he said. I told him they were where they always were; in the stationery cupboard." Again she looked to Cathy for confirmation. "You know that walk-in room at the back of the office. He went in and after a few seconds, he said he couldn't find any pads. Stupid, I know, but I got up, left what I was doing and walked into the cupboard. He shuffled around so he was between me and the door and he pulled it to. That's when he began to touch me." She shivered, looked out of the window and paused for a few seconds.

Cathy looked over at Cyril and silently mouthed, "I never knew."

Cyril moved a hand in acknowledgement. "What happened then, Shirley?" he prompted.

"I was really frightened. 'Come on,' he was saying, 'you know you want it.' I had a blouse and skirt on that day. He touched my breasts through my blouse then grabbed my bum. Sorry," she said, apologising for her turn of phrase, as if that was as bad as the incident she was describing. "The next thing, he was trying to lift my skirt. 'Get off. Get off me,' I was shouting." She stopped and pulled a handkerchief from her sleeve and wiped her eyes. "Sorry," she repeated.

"That's okay," Cyril said, gently. "You're doing really well." He exchanged glances with Cathy before going on, "So what happened next?"

Shirley wiped her nose then continued, "The next thing I remember was the door opening and Mr Tinker, DI Tinker, appeared. He shouted at Mr Brookes. What did he think he was doing, or something like that? Then he grabbed him by the shoulders and sort of threw him out."

"So Jack Tinker witnessed this?"

"Yes. He asked me if I was alright then led me out of the cupboard. Brookes had disappeared by this time. In fact, it was a report for Mr Tinker I was typing when all this happened. I always liked Mr Tinker. He was kind to me. A bit like my dad really."

Cyril felt sick. He'd known one or two individuals like Brookes, from his time in the RAF and in the police, but not a serving officer. "Did you make a complaint?" he asked.

"We're talking 1961 here," Cathy said. "Women were almost expected to endure that sort of behaviour."

Again, Cyril moved his hand to Cathy. "Shirley?" he persisted.

"No," she said. "Mr Tinker said he'd sort it and I suppose he did to a certain extent."

"How do you mean?"

"Well, Barry Brookes was transferred to Harlow a few weeks later. But then I got a new job in Colchester, more money, and I took it. Glad to be away."

Cyril drained his tea. "Thanks for being so open with me, Shirley. I realise that wasn't easy."

"So has he done this sort of thing again?"

"To be honest, I don't know. But what you've told me will help someone I know, for sure."

Shirley had composed herself again. "I was really sorry to hear about Mr Tinker," she said. "I saw it in the paper this week. But there was no mention of when his funeral might be. I'd like to go and pay my respects."

"I will let you know, Shirley," Cathy said.

"Of course we will," Cyril confirmed.

As they drove away, Cathy turned to Cyril, "I had no idea," she said.

46
Sunday 20th March 1977

DCI Sanderson had called the team in to work the weekend. He felt the Sharon Williams' inquiry was stalling. The review was held at eight and a few bleary eyes looked up at him from desks, full of resentment, no doubt, at having been pulled in on the Sunday when the clocks went forward, losing an hour in bed. Ignoring the atmosphere, he asked for summaries of where the various threads were.

Barton recounted his progress with the cabbie fraternity which seemed to confirm there was some character chancing his arm offering women, perhaps the worse for wear, a lift in his car. The description, a new blue Ford Cortina, tied in with a vehicle seen parked outside Sharon Williams' house at the time she was believed to have been murdered. Although there was no description of the driver from there.

Other lines of enquiry seemed to have petered out with no additional details added to the sketchy description of the man seen talking to Sharon on the Saturday night before she died. The fingerprint enquires had also drawn a blank so far.

One aspect still taxed Cyril's mind; how did Barton's warrant card turn up at the murder scene? That fact seemed to have been forgotten about since the forensics evidence could make no connection between the DI and the scene. He believed the man. Cyril's view was that Barton had dropped his warrant as he put it back into his pocket, probably at the Railway Hotel, and it was picked up by the murderer. However, that little mystery would probably never be solved until they caught the perpetrator.

Sanderson rubbed his face with both hands in frustration. "Look," he said, "At the very least we need to identify and speak to this individual." He tapped the Identikit image on the display board. "Dick, you need to try and trace these women who were approached by the driver of that Cortina. The rest of you, we need more on this man."

"But he may not be connected with the murder," Bill Walker offered. "Perhaps we should be looking at other avenues."

Miller gave a snigger.

"That's also what I was thinking, Bill," Sanderson said. "So get out there and re-interview people, track down more potential witnesses and let's see some progress."

Sanderson clapped his hands to reinforce the point before making his way across to Cyril's desk.

"Morning, sir," Cyril greeted.

"Cyril," the DCI said, placing a piece of paper he'd brought with him on the desk. "Might be something and nothing, but this was reported in Harwich yesterday. Happened on Friday night apparently. The Inspector over there thought we might like to have a chat with this woman. He just had a little niggling feeling it might be connected with what we're looking at."

Cyril picked up the note. "You think it's relevant?" he asked, quickly scanning the report of the attempted abduction of a young woman.

"The thing that caught my eye …"

"Is the description of the car," Cyril finished for him.

"Exactly. Take young Woodbridge with you," Sanderson said. "Have a chat with him. I think it might be worth putting him in for the detective's course when this is over."

"He's a bright lad," Cyril agreed.

"And we can always do with those," Sanderson commented as he walked away.

Cyril was driving back from Harwich with Woodbridge alongside.

"I wish we could get hold of the man she ran past on the street corner on Friday night," Woodbridge said, referring to the details Michelle Harris had just reiterated to them regarding the incident at the weekend. "He must have witnessed the attack."

"He probably doesn't know it was as serious as it was. He might only have seen part of it, maybe thought it was just a lovers' tiff. Sometimes witnesses don't know what they've seen; don't appreciate the relevance. He might not even have seen the driver," Cyril considered.

"Surely that's a good reason to issue an appeal in the papers?" Woodbridge suggested.

"That might be true but it won't be our decision to make."

"Unless she herself approaches them? She did seem quite upset that she was so close to being taken."

Cyril was silent for a few seconds before he continued, "You think a lot about how we've investigated these cases, don't you Sam?"

"I suppose I do."

"You're enjoying your spell in CID?"

"Yes, although I don't know how long it'll last."

"So would you be interested if you were sent on the detectives' course?"

Woodbridge's face lit up. "Of course. That would be great."

Cyril saw the broad smile on his face.

"Where do they take place then?" Woodbridge asked.

"Well I did mine in a lovely country place called Eynsham Hall out the other side of Oxford."

"Oh, I thought it might be Hendon."

"No that's the Met. Eynsham's a lovely place. Anyway, Mr Sanderson thinks you might benefit."

"So I've impressed?"

Cyril smiled. "Let's not get carried away, Sam."

47

Ruby Clarke was nineteen years old. She was an attractive dark-haired young woman who enjoyed her job working in a department store in Colchester. She lived alone with her mother, her father having died when she was ten, in a rented bungalow in Clacton. She would never become twenty.

A night out with some friends in Colchester had been good fun but Ruby had run out of money after visiting a few pubs in the town, then a nightclub. With no money for a taxi, the trains having stopped running earlier in the evening, and not wanting to embarrass herself by borrowing from her friends, she decided to hitch a lift back. She wasn't too concerned, she'd done it a couple of times before; there was always someone travelling back to the coast.

A couple in their early thirties stopped and picked her up from the St Botolph's area and dropped her off in Elmstead Market. They were turning off onto the Harwich Road to head towards the small hamlet where they lived. The woman gave her a warning to be careful about who she got in a car with but Ruby assured her she'd be fine. As the woman turned to watch Ruby walking along the Clacton Road, she would be the last person to see her alive; except one, of course. And she'd be haunted forever that she didn't insist that her husband take the young woman all the way into Clacton.

Ruby drew her coat tighter around her neck. She could see her breath and hear the silence of the night. The temperature must have dropped to zero, so she quickened her step.

A car drove past in the opposite direction but she never looked up. Why would she? She was heading the other way. If she had paid attention, she might have noticed that a few minutes later, the same car drew alongside her.

She paused and bent down to look inside. The driver leaned across and wound down the window. She could feel the warmth escape from inside.

"Where are you off to?" the driver asked with a beaming smile.

"Clacton," she responded. "Down near the Westcliffe Theatre."

"Hop in, I'll give you a lift. It's bloody freezing out there."

She considered a moment before opening the door and climbing in to the front passenger seat. She put her bag on the floor and wound up the window as they set off, keeping the chill air out and the heat in.

*   *   *

He parked the car in the compound, locked the door and listened. All was quiet, as it should be. Walking back through the entrance, he swung the gate closed and secured it with the padlock. Next stop was the toilet block. Here he stripped down and ran the shower until it was hot. Stepping under the water, he let the jet play down on his head as he shut his eyes tight. The images came back to him and a sudden feeling of self-loathing threatened to overwhelm him. And then the guilt. It had happened again.

No amount of showering could remove the stains from his mind. He was disgusted with himself. He needed help. But how? There was no one he could turn to. It was bad enough the last time. That one struggled when he'd tried to help her into the car. All he wanted to do was give her a lift and she turned on him. He gently rubbed his groin, still feeling the pain she'd inflicted.

And now tonight. How could he explain that away? Even to himself, he struggled. Why did she have to say what she did? How did she think he'd react? He wasn't after what she thought he wanted. He only wanted to have some company. And then she insults him like that. He looked down at his hands. He held them in the same fashion he had earlier tonight; fingers touching, then thumbs, before closing them together, squeezing tighter and tighter. He didn't mean to do it, it just happened. She'd provoked him.

It was the same with that first one. She thought he was after her body too. He wasn't. He'd offered her a lift and she'd invited him in for a drink. A nice glass of wine and they were talking. And then, he discovered she'd removed her knickers. She'd stuffed them down the side of the cushions. And when he didn't react as she'd obviously wanted, she started taunting him. What else could he do?

Putting that warrant card down the other side of the settee was a masterstroke, though. He could imagine the sort of trouble that copper would be in. Serves him right. Silly bastard shouldn't have got so pissed he didn't notice that he'd slid it down the outside of his jacket pocket rather than inside. He'd seen it fall to the floor and land under the chair he was sitting on. He'd looked round at everyone else in the pub, but no one else had noticed. So when the copper left, a nonchalant stroll over to the chair he'd vacated and, leaning down, he picked it up. Initially he thought it was a small wallet with one of those new-fangled bank cards in it. It was only when he left the bar and opened it up outside did he realise what it was.

He looked again at his hands before turning the shower flow off and letting the water drip off him. A few seconds later, he grabbed a towel and started to dry himself down. After a minute or so, he stopped and caught his misted shape in the mirror. Rubbing the glass with the towel, he studied his face. Is this the face of a killer? More than that, is this the face of a serial killer? No, it wasn't like that.

He slapped himself; once, twice, then stopped.

He got dressed then walked from the toilet block over to his caravan. It wouldn't happen again. He told himself that, and repeated the message in his mind. He'd get his head down and feel better in the morning. He always did. Stepping inside his billet, he checked his watch. Not much time to sleep as he'd have to be up first thing to open up. He crawled under the covers and closed his eyes, still unable to remove the revulsion he felt for himself. He slithered into the foetal position and slowly the tears came.

48
Monday 21ˢᵗ March 1977

At five to eight on Monday morning, Dennis Bolton, sitting in the driver's seat of the car watched as his boss approached from Manningtree railway station having just come off the train from London.

Peter Fitzgerald was a tall, well-built man with dark hair, cut short. He lived in Reading and had spent the weekend with his wife and young son and daughter. His career had begun as a civil engineer, progressing to become a site manager for several road improvement schemes and now the project manager for the A120 road improvement works at Wix, about seven miles away. He lifted the boot and placed his suitcase inside before opening the passenger door and climbing in.

"Good weekend?" Bolton asked.

"Not bad," Fitzgerald responded. "Everything okay back at the ranch?"

"Quiet as the grave."

Bolton, twenty-six years old, a site engineer on the project, released the handbrake and set off to drive to the site.

The manager looked across at the dials on the driver's side. "I hope you've left me some fuel in, Dennis?"

"Filled up on Friday after I dropped you off."

"That's good. I've got to go to Cambridge this afternoon. Management meeting. It'll save me time not having to fuel up."

The next few minutes passed in silence. "Have the steel-fixers turned up?" Fitzgerald asked.

Bolton nodded. "Just before I set off."

"We've got that first bridge pier concrete pour tomorrow but we need to get the other one ready for pouring next week," the manager said, referring to the support structure for one of the two bridges they were constructing.

Bolton was silent. He had plenty on his mind since last night, the last thing he wanted to do was talk about the job.

"You sure everything's okay, Dennis?" Fitzgerald went on. "You're normally a bit more chatty than this."

Bolton struggled to smile. "No, I'm fine," he said.

For the rest of the journey, the manager ran through some of the operations they'd need to complete this week. "We're just about holding programme but we can't let it slip," he concluded.

After dropping his boss off outside the portakabin office, Bolton parked the car and walked out onto the site. He needed to be outside, unrestricted by walls, somewhere to think.

As well as disgust and self-loathing, he had an overpowering feeling of being alone. He'd experienced waves of this over the past few years, ever since his twin sister, Emma had died, but nothing as strong as he'd felt in recent months.

Emma. God he missed her. They'd both been put into care at sixteen when their parents were killed in a motorcycle accident. With no other living relatives, there was no alternative. Initially, he had handled the situation better than his sister, passing his exams and securing a place on a Civil Engineering course at Manchester University. Given the circumstances, he'd been given a full student grant. He insisted Emma had gone with him to Manchester where they shared a flat. He was worried she was struggling to cope with what had happened. Eventually, she found work in a department store as well as a variety of bar jobs in the evenings. They'd rubbed along very well for the three years he studied. By the time he'd graduated in 1972, she seemed to have become more confident and had applied for teacher training at Alsager College near Crewe to begin in September 1973. That's when tragedy struck. Within a few weeks of beginning the course she was struck down with meningitis. Unfortunately, she didn't recover and died in the October. He was devastated; still was.

*   *   *

That same morning, a worried mother walked into Clacton Police Station and approached the desk sergeant.

After she had stood for a minute or so, he looked up from the notes he was writing. "Yes, madam," he said. "Can I help you?"

"I'm worried about my daughter," she began. "She didn't come home last night."

"And how old is your daughter?"

"Nineteen."

"Young girl that age … probably met up with someone and stayed over."

"That's not like Ruby."

"And you've tried contacting her friends?" the sergeant continued.

"Of course. That's the first thing I did." She was becoming irritated. "And she hasn't turned up for work. She loves that job."

"Can you give me a description?" he asked.

The woman began to give details of her daughter which the sergeant started to write down.

"But I can do better than that," she said. "I have a photo." She passed across a 6x4 photo as she continued with the description of her daughter.

The sergeant paused writing and took hold of the picture. After a few seconds, he spoke, "If you'd like to take a seat, Mrs Clarke, I'll get a CID officer to have a word with you."

She looked alarmed. "Has something happened?"

"It's routine in a missing persons' report," he said, trying to sound as relaxed as possible. He couldn't explain it, just copper's instinct perhaps. "We always try to involve CID to speak to whoever makes the report. Just take a seat for me, will you?" The sergeant indicated the uncomfortable chairs opposite the counter.

Up in the CID room, only Sam Woodbridge was in.

"Where is everybody, Sam?" the desk sergeant asked.

"I think Bill and Ben are out conducting interviews," Woodbridge responded.

This drew a smile from the sergeant.

"What?"

"Oh nothing, just thinking of The Flowerpot Men, that's all."

"Right," Woodbridge nodded then continued, "The DI is along in Mr Sanderson's office and the skip ..." The habit of calling your sergeant 'skip' when in uniform had stuck with Woodbridge when he referred to Cyril. He broke off as the man himself appeared behind the desk sergeant.

"Everything alright, George?" Cyril asked.

"Ah, Cyril, I've got a Mrs Clarke downstairs, wants to report her daughter missing. She's nineteen, the daughter that is." The sergeant held out the photograph Mrs Clarke had given him.

"Probably stopped out with friends," Cyril said, taking hold of it and looking at the smiling face framed by dark curly hair that stared back at him. "At that age, that's what they do." He looked at Woodbridge for confirmation, who nodded.

"That's what I thought," the sergeant said, "But I just get a feeling ..."

"All right, I'll come down and have a word."

Phyllis Clarke had been shown into the front interview room and was nursing a plastic cup of tea when Cyril entered.

"Mrs Clarke," he began. "I understand your daughter failed to return home last night."

The woman wiped a paper tissue around her red eyes before speaking. "Yes. She's never done this before. She's never stayed out – not without telling me. And then it's only been with people I know – her friends."

Cyril put the photograph down on the table between them. "This is a recent picture?" he asked.

"Taken last Christmas."

"Do you mind if we keep hold of this for now?"

"Please, if it'll help."

"So when was the last time you saw Ruby?" Cyril asked.

Phyllis took a deep breath before relating the details of Ruby going out to meet some of her work colleagues in Colchester for a few drinks and possibly a disco afterwards.

"How did she travel to Colchester? Does she have a car?"

The woman shook her head. "She got the bus."

"And if she was going to be late, I mean after the last bus back, how was she planning to get home?"

"She'd take a taxi."

Cyril tried not to let his feeling of alarm show when she mentioned a taxi. Instead, he pressed on with another question. "The sergeant tells me you've tried contacting her friends and you say she hasn't turned up for work this morning."

"That's right. That's the first phone call I made when I realised she hadn't come home. She works in a department store on the High Street. She really enjoys that job. Her manager told me she hadn't appeared this morning."

"Do you know who she was out with last night? You said work colleagues, from the department store?"

"Yes." Phyllis proceeded to list the names of the friends she believed she'd gone out with, and also Ruby's manager. He would make enquiries with them concerning the night out.

Cyril concluded the interview with reassurances that in cases like Ruby's, the missing person usually turned up quickly with a believable explanation. He showed Mrs Clarke out, but he wasn't convinced by his own words to the woman, sharing the desk sergeant's concerns that something wasn't quite right.

49

It was mid-morning and heads were down, concentrating on reading or writing reports, sifting through various snippets of information coming into the CID room, when DCI Sanderson walked through and into DI Barton's office. From his expression, he didn't look pleased. After a brief exchange with Barton, Sanderson led the way back out with Barton following. In answer to Cyril's questioning look Barton silently mouthed, *'Brookes'.*

Cyril could feel his anger rise. If DCI Brookes had returned to continue his assault on Barton and Tinker's reputations, he wouldn't sit idle. He got to his feet and slowly followed Barton out onto the corridor where he watched the two men enter Sanderson's office and close the door.

Taking his pipe from one pocket and his tobacco from another, he packed the bowl and lit up. Before he'd had time for a couple of puffs, the office door opened and Barton strode out, obviously pumped up. Cyril held up a hand to his DI to stop him on his way back to his own office. "What's happened?" Cyril asked quietly.

Barton looked as if he was about to explode but took a breath and in a low voice said, "*Bastard* Brookes wants to see my notebooks from the time we interviewed Walter Mason and discovered the cigarette packet in the postmaster's flat. Reckons Mason junior has made a formal complaint. I tell you Cyril, that little shit's only trying to muddy the waters for himself."

"Well hold on," Cyril said as Barton was about to continue on his way back to his own office. "I think it's about time I had a word with DCI Brookes."

"You? But you weren't involved in anything to do with the Dovercourt raid."

"Maybe not, but …" Cyril left the sentence unfinished, gave Barton a pat on the shoulder and set off for Sanderson's office.

Knocking on the door, Cyril saw Sanderson's puzzled look through the glass panel. Not waiting for an invite, he opened the door and stepped inside. "Sorry sir," he said, "I was wondering if I might have a word with DCI Brookes."

"Cyril, I don't think …" Sanderson began.

"In private, please," Cyril interrupted. "It is important."

Brookes looked at the new arrival with a puzzled gaze, taking in Cyril's posture as he held himself almost to attention. "If …," he prompted.

"Detective Sergeant Claydon, sir," Cyril responded.

"If Detective Sergeant Claydon has something to say to me in private, then I guess I should hear it," Brookes said.

As he stood, Sanderson gave Cyril a look that seemed to say, *I hope you know what you're doing, even if I don't*, walked to the door and left his office.

"Well DS Claydon," Brookes said once the door had closed, "What is it that's so important? Do you have something fresh to raise with me, or is it something to do with why I'm here?" Before Cyril could respond, Brookes continued, "I suppose you do know the purpose of my visit, station whispers and all that."

Not invited to sit down, Cyril preferred to stand anyway. "It could be a bit of both, sir," he said.

"Carry on sergeant."

"As I understand it, you're investigating matters surrounding recently deceased ex-DCI Jack Tinker's handling of a robbery investigation in 1969."

"Not forgetting DI Barton's role too," Brookes added. "And you have some relevant information?"

"I was curious as to why you were so intent on digging around a case where the main player is no longer with us and unable to defend himself."

"I did also mention DI Barton."

Cyril nodded.

"But have you something relevant and useful to add, or are you just here to get in my way." Brookes was showing his obvious exasperation.

"I wouldn't dream of wasting your time, sir," Cyril said.

"Well, get on with it man."

Cyril took a breath and pulled himself even straighter. "I'm assuming the name Shirley Miles means something to you?" he asked.

Initially, Brookes looked confused before, it seemed, he did recognise the name, although he tried his best to conceal that. "Not really," the DCI said. "The name didn't feature in the Dovercourt case as far as I recall."

"Let me remind you then, sir," Cyril stated. "Shirley was a young woman of around twenty years of age who worked here, in this station, in the typing pool around the same time you were based here. You were based here, weren't you?"

"You obviously know I had a brief spell here, but I can't be expected to remember everyone who worked here at the time."

Cyril knew he had to tread cautiously. "Oh, I think you would remember Shirley. Petite young thing, quite attractive ..."

Colour flushed to Brookes cheeks. "Just be very careful DS Claydon." There was no mistaking the implied threat in his tone.

"I recently spoke to Miss Miles," he said, letting the point sink in. "I was wondering why you transferred to Harlow?"

"A suitable position came up," Brookes replied, almost automatically, before he became indignant. "Anyway, I don't see that as any business of yours. Remember who you're speaking to, DS Claydon."

"I'm well aware of your position, sir, which is why it might be awkward if Miss Miles decides to make a formal complaint. She could still consider that an option, despite the obvious discomfort that may give to those closest to her. But let's face it, this enquiry is prompted by a complaint made years later from the son of one of the robbers convicted of the Dovercourt raid; that perpetrator rightly convicted, as recent evidence has confirmed."

Brookes was now puce. "Are you threatening me?"

"It was DI Tinker, as he was at the time, who uncovered the incident with Miss Miles, was it not, and who was actually responsible for your transfer?"

"Pure speculation!"

"When in actual fact, you could have been facing criminal charges yourself. So, rather than embarking on some revenge attack against Mr Tinker, and by implication DI Barton, you might reflect that DI Tinker actually did you a favour and you've had a career in the police which might have been cut short before it had even begun."

Brookes was speechless.

"I'll let you consider that, sir. Much as it might upset Miss Miles now, all these years later, I'm sure she would be prepared to make a statement herself." Cyril studied the big DCI who now appeared to sit much smaller in his chair. "By the way, my colleagues don't yet know about all this. I'd like to keep it that way but … Thank you for your time, sir," Cyril concluded before leaving the office.

Outside, Sanderson and Barton were waiting in the corridor.

"What the hell have you done, Cyril?" Sanderson asked. "I hope you haven't exposed yourself to the wrath of C & D?"

In a quiet voice, Cyril said, "I did what I thought was necessary. I hope DCI Brookes will consider the matter dead."

"Just hope it's not you who's dead," Barton replied. "You could have taken your pension last year."

Before the conversation could continue, Sanderson's office door opened and Brookes bustled his way out. "Forget it," he said to Sanderson before looking at Barton. "Consider the matter dropped DI Barton." Finally, he looked at Cyril. "I hope our paths never cross," he said to him.

Cyril held his gaze. "Nor do I, sir," he said.

After a split second, Brookes turned and strode along the corridor and down the stairs.

"What in God's name did you say to him?" Barton asked.

"You don't need to know," Cyril replied. "Come on, we have some murders to solve." A broad grin spread over his face as he made his way back to the CID room, leaving his superiors astonished.

*   *   *

Later that afternoon, Cyril was sitting at his desk studying the Identikit image they'd worked up from the early stages of the investigation. None of the witnesses could help enhance it any further. He also had the photographs of the fingerprints recovered from one of the wine glasses in Sharon Williams' front room.

"Are you one and the same?" he muttered to himself. "Where are you?" Giving the fingerprints his full attention, he continued, "Are you even on any force's records?"

"What are you mumbling about, Cyril?" Barton asked, as he stood by the DS's desk.

Cyril looked up, "Oh, just thinking out loud, that's all."

Barton lowered his voice. "Listen, do I owe you one for earlier with Brookes?"

"Don't worry about it," Cyril said. "It was a pleasure. Blokes like him really get my goat."

Barton merely nodded. "Where's young Sam and Bill? I haven't seen them for quite a while?"

"Ah, sorry, I should have said … we had a missing person's report come in this morning and … I don't know." Cyril put his hand behind him to his jacket that was draped over his chair and pulled out his pipe and tobacco. "You know how you just get a feeling that something isn't right."

Barton pulled up a chair from an adjacent desk and sat down. "Go on," he said.

"A young girl, nineteen, from Clacton, out for a night in Colchester last night with other girls she works with. Well, she didn't come home." Cyril packed the pipe bowl and lit up.

"You mean out last night and didn't come home this morning?"

"Yes."

"She probably got lucky." Barton smirked.

Just when Cyril thought Barton was maturing, he reverts to form.

"Sorry," he said. "You're gut telling you that there may be something sinister?"

Cyril raised his eyebrows and exhaled. "Right," he said. "So I sent Sam and Bill over to Colchester to take statements from her workmates and her manager."

"Fair enough," Barton considered. "I think those two will be good for that." He studied Cyril again. "There's more, isn't there?"

Another puff on the pipe. "Her mother said she'd normally take a taxi back if it was after the last bus."

"You're not thinking …"

He motioned to the Identikit image and fingerprint photo on his desk. "Just want to check it out, that's all, so I asked them to speak to any cabbies over there. You never know, our friend might have tried his luck in Colchester too."

50

"Good day, love?" his wife shouted from the kitchen, as he closed the front door behind him.

The smells of a gravy dinner wafted into his nostrils. "Not bad," he responded. "Smells good." He made his way to the kitchen, came up behind his wife and put his arms around her waist.

She wriggled. "Hey, no time for that, it's ready to dish up."

"Spoilsport," he said and turned towards the dining table. A copy of the Evening Gazette lay folded to one side. He picked it up. About to turn to the back page to see what the reporter had to say about Colchester United's last performance, the front page headline caught his eye.

Attempted Abduction
A 23–year-old woman was attacked on Friday night on Main Road in Harwich as she was walking home from a night out with friends.

He caught his breath and hoped his face gave nothing away. As he was reading, his wife was busy dishing up the meal.

"I've done a beef stew tonight," she announced, putting a plate down in front of him. "I thought we could do with a wholesome meal." She glanced at her husband reading the paper then turned back to the cooker. As she dished up her own plate, she said over her shoulder, "A bit concerning that."

"What?"

She joined him at the table. "That girl," she said. "Tried to push her into a car, apparently. Not far away either."

He read a bit more.

> **Police are anxious to speak to a man who is believed to have witnessed the attack. It is thought he may have vital information.**

"Says some bloke witnessed the attack. Let's hope he does the right thing and comes forward," she commented.

He didn't reply, just put the paper down and started on his meal. Christ, he thought, I can't say anything otherwise she'll be wondering what I'd been up to. I already said I stayed in watching telly.

"Stew all right?" She interrupted his thoughts.

He nodded between mouthfuls. "Yeah, very good."

Picking up the paper again, he read on,

> **The attacker is described as in his twenties or early thirties, medium height and build with longish fair hair and driving a dark saloon car.**

She must have been more pissed than she appeared, he thought. Not much of a description. Dark saloon car – ha! It was a blue Ford Cortina, 'R' registration. And the driver was a bit younger, maybe mid-twenties.

"You seem to be fairly interested in that story," she said.

"What?" He put the paper down once more. "No, just surprised that's all. As you say, it happened not far away." He waved his fork to make the point. "You need to be careful if you're out on your own."

She laughed. "Why would anybody try and bundle me into a car?"

"There are some weird buggers about." He took another forkful of food. "I read not long back, they've had three murders up in Leeds, reckon it might be the same man. Not this one, I mean. But you do get them."

"I'll be careful. Anyway, that was the night I stayed at Mum's. If you'd gone out, you might have seen him." A mischievous look passed across her face. "Or it could even have been you."

"I watched TV. Besides, my car's ..." He suddenly realised he was about to say 'not blue' when he stopped himself. "Well, it's not a saloon. It's a hatchback. And it's white."

*   *   *

The site manager hadn't yet returned from his meeting in Cambridge and Bolton was locking up the various welfare units on the site. It had been another busy and productive day. The steel-fixers had made good progress on the second bridge pier and the carpenters would start preparing the remaining shuttering tomorrow. The officious Clerk of Works had approved the first pier for the concrete pour in the morning.

He wandered through the canteen, collecting discarded copies of The Sun, most left open at page 3, and putting them in the bin. On the wall were various calendars, some classed as glamour, others downright porn. About to turn out the lights and leave, he spotted a copy of that evening's Gazette.

Prominent, was the article about Friday night's attempted abduction. It made him catch his breath. Picking up the paper he began to read. His heart rate increased when he saw the description of the driver that the police wanted to speak to. Yes, that was vague, but it was definitely him. The car could be any thankfully, but that bloke who saw him drive off would have a better idea. He'd looked straight at him. Unless he was a bit the worse for wear, he'd be able to provide more detail.

Would he be able to identify the car? Very probably. And the police have appealed for him to come forward too.

He searched through the rest of the paper but could find no reference to the murder in Clacton from two weeks ago; and strangely, nothing on the girl from Sunday night. Surely she'd been discovered? Were they keeping it under wraps for some reason?

The feeling of despair came over him again. There must be something wrong with him; something in his make-up that forces him to do these things. He felt wretched. He'd thought about it a lot today. He was sure he wouldn't have done those things if Emma had still been here. She'd kept him balanced. If only he could have talked to her.

It might be time to make plans.

As he walked back to his accommodation, the project manager drove into the compound. The car stopped alongside him.

"Everything go okay?" Fitzgerald asked.

"Yeah, we're all set for tomorrow's pour. What about you?"

"They seem to be pleased in head office. There might be more work in the offing they said, so we just need to keep everyone sweet."

Bolton nodded. "That's good."

"Are you sure you're alright, Dennis?"

"Fine. Just a bit tired, that's all. Been a busy day."

Fitzgerald hesitated for a moment before putting the car in gear. "Okay, I'll see you in the morning."

Bolton watched as his boss drove off site and back to the bed and breakfast accommodation where he was staying. Unlike him, Fitzgerald liked a bit of comfort. 'My days of roughing it in some caravan on site are long gone,' he'd once told him. But the arrangement suited Bolton. It was an opportunity to save money and, with access to Fitzgerald's car on some weekends, an opportunity to prowl.

51

Cyril picked up the copy of the Evening Gazette off the mat from behind the door along with the mail that had been dropped through the letterbox that morning. Normally, they would be on the table in the kitchen, Doris having come in to see Charlie and feed him when Cyril hadn't come home by half-past five. She didn't need to do that anymore.

As he walked through to the kitchen he flicked through the envelopes, nothing of any interest, before scanning the front page of the newspaper. The article gave the known facts and mentioned the appeals for information that might help the enquiry. With a bit of luck, something might come of it.

He placed the paper and the correspondence onto the table before looking down at the empty basket where his dog had spent many hours over the years. His eyes became watery and he wiped a hand across his face. Come on, he told himself, you've seen so much in your life, don't get all soppy over a dog. But he couldn't help himself, and the tears began to flow.

After Maureen passed, at least he felt there was still someone in the house to greet him; some connection with the past. That had now gone. He looked up, out through the window and into the dark garden. Out there under the shade of the cherry tree, his old mate rested.

A ring on the doorbell brought his reverie to a sharp end.

Opening the door, Doris stood on the step, a casserole dish in her towel-wrapped hands.

"I saw you drive up," she said. "I thought you might like some hot pot."

He stood aside and let her walk through to the kitchen. Rubbing his face for a second time, he followed her through.

"I know you probably wouldn't cook tonight." Doris placed the dish on the hob. She turned around to face him and saw the sadness. She stepped forward and gave him a hug.

"Oh, Doris," he said. "What would I do without you?"

She pulled herself away. "You've got Cathy. She's a lovely girl."

Cyril grinned. It always amused him how women of Doris's age referred to women of Cathy's age as girls.

"When you feel it's right," she continued, "you'll know what to do."

He wiped another tear away.

"Now get that while it's still hot," she instructed. "I'll leave you to it." As she reached the door, she turned around. "And you never know, in a little while, you might fancy getting another dog."

The front door closed and Cyril lifted the lid of the dish and sniffed. Smiling, he reached into a cupboard for a bowl.

He'd call Cathy once he'd eaten this, he decided.

52
Tuesday 22nd March 1977

At just after half past seven that morning, an elderly man walking an equally elderly dog made a shocking discovery.

By nine o'clock the lane leading towards the village of Great Bentley, about six miles from Clacton and possibly four from where Ruby Clarke was dropped off in Elmstead Market, was a flurry of police activity.

Marked patrol cars blocked the lane to through traffic from each end. DI Barton squeezed the Rover past the officer standing by one of the vehicles who waved an arm in recognition of the CID officer. Cyril was sitting alongside.

"You think it might be our missing girl?" Barton asked as they drove slowly along the final few yards to the scene.

Cyril rubbed his face, "Dear God, I hope not, but I do think so."

The Rover drew to a halt behind one of the SOCO vans that were in attendance, having made quicker time from Colchester. The Scenes of Crime officers were setting up a white tent just inside the entrance to a field about fifteen yards from the side of the road and tucked behind the hedge, out of direct view. Cyril recognised the duty doctor from Clacton and nodded to him as the doctor walked away from the body.

"Sad business," the doctor said. "Young life cut short."

"No question it was foul play?" Barton asked. "Couldn't have been a road accident? It was a bit misty through the night."

"I'd say strangled, John," the doctor replied. "Just like that woman in Clacton the other week," he added as he carried on back to his car.

Cyril and Barton exchanged glances before they carefully approached the scene. Standing on the gravel by the field entrance at the roadside, they had their first view of the victim through the opening of the tent. Lying on her back with her skirt around her waist and underwear removed, Cyril looked to his DI. "That looks a similar position to Sharon Williams," he said.

Barton looked taut. "I don't think we can make quick conclusions, Cyril."

"I'm not. It's just an observation."

Before the white sheeting obscured the body as the tent was fixed in position, they saw that her head was turned towards the road with her dark curly hair obscuring her face. Inside, flashes began as the photographer recorded the scene.

A uniformed sergeant approached the pair. "We've got the gentleman who found the body, sir," he said, indicating one of the marked cars nearby. "I presume you'll want to talk to him before someone takes him and his dog home."

"Thanks sergeant," Barton acknowledged. "I'll have a word. Cyril, see if you can have a look at the victim. You've studied her photograph the mother gave you. I'll also notify Martin. The DCI needs to be down here."

Half an hour later, DCI Sanderson arrived and took in the scene, Barton and Cyril flanking him. Barton gave a brief account of his conversation with the dog walker who'd discovered the body, although more accurately it was the dog who'd found it.

"And this is a regular route for him?" Sanderson asked.

"One of them. He didn't come this way yesterday."

The DCI turned to Cyril. "Are you sure it's Ruby Clarke?"

"As sure as I can be," he replied. "From the photograph her mother gave me yesterday along with the description of what she was wearing, I'd say so."

"But no identification found on the body?"

"She had a handbag with her, we believe," Barton said. "A pink clutch bag, apparently. But no sign of it as yet. We'll get uniform to check the hedgerows and the field."

The DCI looked grim. "And initial signs are that this is similar to Sharon Williams?"

"That's what the doc said but we need to wait for the PM," Cyril said.

"Okay, not much more we can do here. Let's get back to the station and start the official enquiry," Sanderson said. "In the meantime, get uniform to go door-to-door in Great Bentley. Someone may have seen a vehicle here over the past two days. Cyril, you attend the PM whenever that might be. Having attended Sharon Williams' one, you may spot similarities. If it is the same perpetrator ..." Sanderson left the sentence unfinished, walked back to his car and drove off.

As they watched Sanderson drive away, a couple of other vehicles drew to a halt by the cordon formed by the two marked patrol vehicles Sanderson had just passed.

"Great. That's all we need," Barton said.

Cyril followed his gaze and saw a couple of men get out of the first vehicle and begin to offload camera equipment as two more emerged from the other vehicle.

"Bloody TV cameras now." Barton sighed. "I'll stay here, Cyril," he said. "One of us needs to. You get off and help the DCI set things up, though God knows we'll be up against it with the other murder case still without a break." He held out the keys to the Rover. "Uniform will give me a lift back."

Cyril took the keys. "Are you sure?" He plunged a hand deep into his coat pocket and pulled out his pipe.

"I'll contact you when they've recovered the body." Barton watched as Cyril brought his pipe to life and puffed away before he took out a packet of cigarettes from his own pocket and lit one up himself. "You interviewed the mother, and it was you who had the feeling something wasn't right. You'll be best placed to take her to make the formal ID, I think."

Cyril motioned agreement. It wasn't something he was looking forward to but he had to agree with the DI's assessment, he probably was the right man for that job. With a final look round at the scene, he made his way to the car and drove away past the television crew who were filming the scene from a distance.

53

It was just before midday when Barton contacted Cyril to say that Ruby's body had been taken away to the mortuary at Colchester hospital. At half past twelve, Cyril and Woodbridge pulled up outside the neat little bungalow on a residential street near the West Cliff Theatre where Cyril had taken Barton to see the hypnotist at what seemed like ages ago.

"Have you done any of these?" Cyril asked.

"Agony calls, you mean?" Woodbridge responded. "Only one, but that was reporting an elderly lady who'd been found dead in her flat to her son."

Cyril looked serious. "It shouldn't be like this, Sam. Parents shouldn't outlive their children. An oft-quoted saying, I know but true, nevertheless. Come on, let's do it."

Phyllis Clarke was distressed. She collapsed in agony when Cyril said the words she'd been dreading. At Cyril's indication, Woodbridge went through to the kitchen and made some tea for the woman. "Two spoons," Cyril said.

"I knew … I knew when I saw you turn up," she said between bouts of crying.

"Is there someone who could come and stay with you?" Cyril asked.

She shook her head.

"It's just been the two of us … since her dad died."

"A neighbour, perhaps?"

Again, a shake of the head. "And now it's just me."

Woodbridge returned with a mug of tea and handed it to the woman.

She looked up and gave a faint smile. "Thanks," she said.

Cyril waited a few seconds then said, "There is something we need you to do, Mrs Clarke."

She nodded. "I know. When can I see her?"

"No rush. Whenever you feel able."

She looked earnestly at Cyril. "Will you come with me?"

"Of course."

*   *   *

Cyril accompanied Phyllis Clarke to Essex County Hospital, Woodbridge having volunteered to walk the short distance back to Jackson Road. She broke down when she saw Ruby's body. Confirmation of identity made, she sat with her daughter for a little while before he drove her back to Clacton. When they arrived, her next-door neighbour appeared. Despite what she'd said earlier, Phyllis invited her in and, between sobs, told her the tragic news. The neighbour made some tea then reassured Cyril that she would stay with Phyllis for as long as necessary and see that she wouldn't be left on her own.

Back at the station, Cyril was called into Sanderson's office. Barton was already there, sitting opposite the DCI. Sanderson asked about the visit to identify Ruby. He seemed in a reflective mood and it appeared to Cyril that the DCI was taking five minutes to recharge his batteries before facing the huge task in front of them. He took the opportunity to talk about something else.

"Tony Riley, sir," Cyril said.

"What about him?" Sanderson was sitting behind his desk.

"I was just thinking …"

Barton picked up Cyril's mood. "You want us to go easy on him, don't you?" he said.

"Well, if he hadn't dug up that money, we would only be left with the cigarette packet and the nagging doubt that maybe, just maybe, Walter Mason was not involved in the Dovercourt job."

"I suppose that's true," Sanderson considered.

"And Mr Brookes would have been far more aggressive in his pursuit of you," Cyril said to Barton.

"Don't milk it, Cyril. I am grateful that you got him off my back, no matter how you managed to head him off at the pass."

"All I'm saying is that what would anyone do in that position? You dig up a small fortune, apparently untraceable, which it would have been but for the sharp eyes and keen interest of our bank clerk. He tries to spend some on a much needed holiday, which he can't now have, and we've recovered virtually all of the money that was stolen. I mean, who's to say that the overall total wasn't as we found it?"

Sanderson leaned forward. "You're saying perhaps, maybe a caution might be appropriate?"

"I think he's learned his lesson and has had to do some making up at home … and I don't see how taking away his livelihood on the building sites will do anybody any good."

Barton and Sanderson exchanged glances.

"Leave that with me, Cyril," Sanderson said.

54

Dennis Bolton had been called into the site manager's office just after lunch-time.

"I'd like you to take these reports to the engineer's offices in Colchester," Peter Fitzgerald had told him. "You know where to go?"

He'd nodded. Of course he did. "On North Hill. Been there before. Got a cracking little receptionist with big tits."

Fitzgerald had smiled at him. It was true, she was a lovely looker who gave him the horn. "That's her," he'd said, before issuing a note of caution. "But one of the engineers is going out with her, so don't embarrass yourself … or us."

As he parked the car in a parking bay on North Hill, his anticipation grew with the prospect of looking down into that lovely cleavage once again. Forget what his manager had told him, if he could persuade the lovely Dawn to come out for a drink with him one night, he was confident she'd forget all about some pimply engineer she worked with.

As it turned out, he was in for one big disappointment. The dragon on reception must have been nearer fifty, highly unattractive, and overweight with her bingo-wing arms oozing out from the sleeves of her dress. Without much interaction, he handed the envelope to her, explaining which site he was from and for whose attention it was intended. The woman never broke conversation from the telephone call she was on, merely nodded to him and placed the envelope in one of a bank of filing trays behind her.

He'd made good time into Colchester and wondered what he could do to amuse himself for half an hour or so.

He didn't want to return to the site just yet. Leaving the car where it was, he walked up North Hill to the High Street. He'd have a browse in some of the shops. Turning the corner, he spotted a newspaper seller standing behind a billboard. The headline made him stop dead in his tracks.

MURDER ENQUIRY LAUNCHED IN GREAT BENTLEY

He scrambled in his pocket for some change, bought a paper and opened it out. He stood for a second and read the opening paragraph.

> **A woman's body was discovered early today by the side of the road leading to the village of Great Bentley. The road was still closed at noon as police and forensics officers continued their work at the scene.**

Turning to page 3, the article continued to describe what little was known about the discovery. The victim's relatives were being traced, apparently. One further comment alarmed him. Police had so far refused to connect this morning's tragic finding with the reported attempted abduction of a woman in Harwich at the weekend.

Shit, he thought, the very fact they were denying this, in his mind, meant they possibly were trying to link the two incidents. He'd only tried to do the silly cow a favour. He read on. Police also refused to make any connection with the murder of Sharon Williams in Clacton three weeks ago which has still to be resolved. Folding up the paper, he hurried back to the car.

Driving back to site, he had the local radio station on. Just before he arrived in the compound, the three o'clock news bulletin came through. He listened as the top item reported on the Great Bentley murder. Apparently, the victim had been identified, although police were not releasing her name. Police were still appealing for information from anyone who was in the area in the early hours of Monday morning as well as anyone who had seen the victim attempting to take a taxi from Colchester late Sunday night or early Monday morning. A description of the victim and how she was dressed ended the news item.

He waited until the news report had finished before switching off and walking to the manager's office.

"Deliver that okay?" he was asked.

"No problem."

"Get a good look at the receptionist's tits?"

"Yeah, and her fat arms too." Fitzgerald looked surprised as Bolton went on, "Some old dragon was sitting there; old enough to be my gran."

The manager grinned. "You might have got lucky there."

He ignored the jibe. "Anyway, have you heard about the murder?"

"What murder?"

He placed the car key and the early copy of the Evening Gazette he bought in Colchester on the manager's desk. "Found her dumped in Great Bentley, apparently. That's not too far away."

The manager slowly picked up the newspaper and began to read. "No it isn't," he agreed. After a few seconds, he looked up. "Why don't you get the car washed for me." He held out the key to him. The area director's visiting tomorrow. I know it's a construction site but we can still keep things clean and tidy."

Bolton took the key and left the office as the manager continued to read the newspaper.

55

With half an hour to go before the four o'clock briefing, Detective Chief Superintendent Viney marched into Sanderson's office and closed the door.

Sanderson had been reading reports and looked up sharply at the unexpected interruption. "Sir," he said and made to stand.

Viney waved a hand instructing him to resume his seat. The DCS was a short man, around five feet eight inches with dark hair around a bald pate. He wore dark-rimmed glasses and was less than eighteen months away from his retirement at fifty-five. He continued to stand, no doubt enjoying some form of psychological height advantage over Sanderson who, at six foot three would normally tower over the man.

"This latest murder, Martin," Viney began, "do you think the team can handle it? Along with the Sharon Williams' inquiry, I mean."

"It's early days, sir, but the team is focused. We're making steady progress."

Viney walked slowly around the office in front of Sanderson's desk before pausing to look out of the window onto the carpark. Eventually he turned back to face the DCI. "Look, I'm getting pressure from HQ. They're wondering if we're up to it. I know what they're trying to do. They want to impose one of their squads to take over, thinking out here in the sticks we haven't got the ability."

Sanderson checked his watch. "Well, we have a briefing in ten minutes. You're very welcome to join us and see exactly where we are."

Viney looked down at the carpet for a moment. "You know I've only got a relatively short time left in post. I'd hate to leave on a sour note. We need to crack these."

"I think you'll find everyone is of the same opinion, sir."

At the allotted time, DCI Sanderson walked into the incident room with DCS Viney close behind. As many of the detectives as could be mustered were in attendance and the room hushed when Viney was spotted. DCI Sanderson led the review. He began to outline the known facts surrounding the murder of Ruby Clarke. Cyril confirmed that her mother had formally identified Ruby earlier that afternoon before relating the statement she'd given to him when she'd reported her daughter missing on Monday.

Barton appraised them of his morning at the scene and the initial findings of the forensics officers. The thinking was that Ruby had died somewhere between midnight on Sunday night and six o'clock on Monday morning. That was confirmed by the fact that her clothing was soaked by rain that had begun on Monday morning and had persisted for most of the day. However, they would expect further information following the post mortem that was scheduled for later that evening. Searches along the road and behind the hedges of the field failed to recover Ruby's missing handbag. Door-to-door enquires in the village were ongoing, but so far, nothing of any interest had come to light.

Woodbridge and Walker summarised the statements they'd taken from her work friends with whom she'd spent the evening on Sunday. A circuit of some town centre pubs then a nightclub and when they left, she parted from her friends to take a taxi home from a rank on the High Street.

"So," Sanderson said, "we know she left the nightclub. Do we know if she took a taxi?"

"We've not been able to find any driver who was working on Sunday night who can positively identify her," Woodbridge stated.

Sanderson looked from Woodbridge to Walker. "Can you two keep on that with the drivers." He glanced at Viney. "I'll get some officers from Colchester to work with you on that. At the same time, has anybody seen our mystery man from the Sharon Williams' inquiry?"

"Are we officially linking the two cases, sir?" Miller asked.

"At this moment in time, we're keeping an open mind on that, Ben," Sanderson said. "There might be something from the PM that leads us to do that." He turned towards Cyril. "What time is that scheduled for, Cyril?"

"7:00pm, sir."

"And you'll be there?"

Cyril nodded.

"Good. Let me know what you find out." Sanderson then addressed the whole team. "Okay gents, we have plenty to do. Priority one, we need to locate the victim's handbag. Two, we need to firm up her movements on Sunday night. Someone must have seen her as she tried to locate a taxi. Three, we still have this bastard to find." He pointed to the Identikit that had been a permanent fixture in the CID room for over a week now. "Right, let's get to it and we reconvene tomorrow morning at eight."

A general hubbub began as the meeting broke up and various officers discussed what course of action they were about to take. Cyril steeled himself for yet another visit to Essex County Hospital and the delights of the mortuary.

"Keep me informed of progress tomorrow morning, Martin." Viney said as he turned to leave. "I'll hold off the reinforcements for now."

56

Sharon was dishing up the evening meal. Robert had laid the table after he'd come in from work about half an hour earlier and the television was on in the corner of their neat lounge/dining room. Their one-year-old daughter was happily playing in the playpen on the floor. About to sit down and enjoy, Sharon's attention was grabbed by the story unfolding on the local evening news bulletin.

'Police are investigating the murder of a young woman whose body was discovered on the outskirts of the Essex village of Great Bentley early this morning,' the reporter was saying. Accompanying footage of the busy scene showed a man, obviously one of the detectives, dressed in a coat and smoking a pipe walking towards a car before driving past parked patrol cars and the cameraman.

'The woman has been named late this afternoon as Ruby Clarke, nineteen years old from Clacton,' the TV voice went on as a photograph of an attractive dark-haired girl filled the screen.

"Rob!" Sharon exclaimed, mouth open.

Robert turned and looked at the television. "Shit," he said. "That's not …"

"It is," she said before covering her mouth with her hand.

Both fully concentrating on the story, the reporter continued, *'Police are trying to piece together Ruby's last known movements from the time she left her friends in Colchester to return home to Clacton just after midnight in the early hours of Monday morning.'*

"We need to call the police," Sharon said.

'Anyone with any information should contact the police at Clacton's Jackson Road Station, the correspondent

concluded, before relating a telephone number which also appeared on the screen. The report ended and the programme moved on to the next story.

"I knew something would happen," Sharon said, clearly upset. "I just had a feeling. We should have taken her on into Clacton."

"But it was late; we had to get back for the little one. Your mother gave us earache as it was. And we had to be up for work in the morning," Robert responded.

"But we should have done the right thing." Sharon's tears flowed. "I feel responsible."

Robert approached his wife and attempted to put his arms around her. Initially, she shrugged him off, but only for a second before she dissolved into his hug, shaking uncontrollably.

*   *   *

It had played on Ronnie's mind all day; the woman who had had a lucky escape on Friday night. In the future, there may be someone else subjected to that sort of attack. Information he had might, just might, prevent that. He had a duty to report what he'd witnessed. Surely his statement would be treated in confidence? If he went to the police, surely they wouldn't need to come to see him at home? His wife would never know he'd had a night out on Friday rather than one in front of the TV as he'd told her. In the scheme of things that little white lie was irrelevant. He had to do the right thing. But there again, these things had a habit of surfacing. She'd wonder why he'd lied. And her thinking would probably be, what else might he have lied about to her? No, let's just consider this again, he told himself. Let's just see what develops. As he was contemplating all this sitting in his car outside the police station in Harwich, unbeknown to him, the local news programme was being broadcast on the television. Finally, he decided what he must do.

*   *   *

Cyril was deep in thought driving back from the hospital in Colchester. Once again, he'd witnessed the post mortem of another victim of crime. Ruby Clarke had been an attractive, vibrant teenager, on the cusp of adulthood with a job she enjoyed, only to have her future robbed by some callous individual. Cause of death was confirmed as strangulation and she had died somewhere between midnight and six on Monday morning, which is what they already suspected. She was not a virgin but there was no evidence of any recent sexual activity or assault. So just why had she been murdered? Was it another senseless attack? She had been left exposed, exactly as Sharon Williams had been, so was it some final act of humiliation?

He thought of Phyllis Clarke and how she must be feeling; her only child taken from her. The old adage that parents should never outlive their offspring returned to his mind. There again, what did he know of being a parent? He thought of his beloved Maureen once more. She always blamed herself for not being able to have children, despite his assurances that he didn't care about that and that he loved her anyway. Was she convinced? He hoped so because it was absolutely true. His pain, having to watch her battle against the cancer that eventually took her from him, was the worst he could endure. It had been nearly four years now since she'd left him. God, he missed her every day.

And then he remembered the conversation he'd had with Doris last year and his mood lightened. What was it she'd said to him, 'You've got a lot going for you. You're still young, you're a good looking man with a good job, your own house, got all your own teeth and hair.' He smiled to himself as he remembered her quip, 'Ooh d'you know if I was thirty years younger, Cyril Claydon ...' But that was a preamble to Doris relating a conversation she and Maureen had had when Doris used to sit with his wife when she was really ill so Cyril could continue to work. Maureen was so unselfish, she'd insisted he carry on. But what he recalled now was what Maureen had told Doris near the end. She'd said, 'Tell him, when the time is right, I won't mind if he found someone else. In fact, I'd love it. I couldn't bear to see him unhappy because of me.'

And that brought his thoughts to Cathy. He glanced at his watch. Half-past-eight. Not too late. He'd call in and see her before he went home. After the evening he'd spent in a sterile hospital room, he needed to end the day in pleasant company.

57
Wednesday 23rd March 1977

The next morning, as Barton walked up the steps to Jackson Road Police Station, a couple in their mid-thirties sat on the uncomfortable chairs in the reception area.

"Ah, Dick," the sergeant said, indicating the man and woman waiting, "Mr and Mrs King would like to speak to someone about the Ruby Clarke investigation."

Barton turned and studied the couple who were now sitting straight and giving him their full attention.

Robert King stood up before glancing down to his wife. "We have some important information," he said.

Barton made the instantaneous judgement that these two probably did have something important to impart. He'd become adept at telling the time-wasters from those with useful knowledge.

"Is the interview room free, George?" he asked the desk sergeant.

George nodded and Barton led them into the ground floor room.

Once they'd sat down, the Kings on one side of the table, Barton on the other, he began, "So, what can you tell me?"

The couple exchanged a quick glance before Mr King took up the story. "It's about this young woman, Ruby Clarke. It was gone midnight Sunday, early Monday morning and we were driving home from Colchester when we saw this young woman hitching a lift."

Barton opened his notebook and began to make notes. "Exactly what time and where was this, Mr King?"

Again the Kings looked at one another. "It must have been about ten past twelve," Mrs King confirmed.

"It must have been," Mr King agreed. "And it was by the Town railway station."

Barton nodded as he wrote. "So you stopped?"

"Yes. We asked her if we could help and she said she was heading for Clacton. I said we could take her as far as Elmstead Market, which is where we turn off …"

Mrs King became visibly upset. "God, I wish we'd taken her all the way," she said. "We'll never forgive ourselves."

Mr King took hold of his wife's hand as he looked at her. "But we weren't to know, Sharon. We had to get back for your mother. She was babysitting."

"I know but it's …" The rest of Mrs King's words were muffled as she held a tissue to her nose.

"So you picked her up," Barton continued, keen to refocus the conversation. "Where did you actually drop her off?"

"At the junction of the Clacton Road and Bromley Road just coming out of Elmstead Market."

"Did you see which way she went after that?"

"She got out on the left just as we turned the corner. As I pulled away I saw her cross the junction and walk on towards Clacton on the left-hand side."

"Was there any traffic around at that time? I mean did you see any other vehicle drive along towards Clacton as you pulled away?"

"No, there wasn't much traffic around at that time of night. After I saw her cross the road in the mirror, I was concentrating on driving. We were out onto an unlit road."

Barton finished writing. "Can you describe what the girl was wearing?"

Sharon King responded, "She had a pink short jacket on, midi-length black crushed velvet skirt. And black boots."

"No handbag?"

"Oh, yes, she had a pink clutch bag."

"And she definitely had that when she got out?"

"Definitely, because I reminded her to make sure she'd got everything with her. She'd put it down on the floor and almost left it behind."

Barton paused in thought, made a note then asked, "Did she say where she'd been, what she'd been doing and why she was hitching a lift?"

Sharon King replied, "She said she'd been on a night out with some of her colleagues from work. It was later than she intended to return home. She would have got the bus but the last one had gone and she'd miscalculated what she'd spent. I got the impression she was embarrassed to ask to borrow the taxi fare from them." Again Sharon became visibly upset and looked at her husband. "Oh, Robert, the silly girl. If only she had …"

Robert put a comforting arm around his wife's shoulder. "You can't blame yourself, Sharon," he said.

"Look, can you spare a little bit longer?" Barton asked. "I'll need to get an official statement from you. I'll draft out what you've just told me and we can go through it before you both sign. Is that okay?"

*   *   *

Sanderson walked into the CID Room, glanced around then approached Cyril. "Dick not in yet?" he asked.

"Not seen him this morning, sir," Cyril answered.

"You spoke to the victim of the attempted abduction in Harwich the other day, didn't you?"

"Sam and me went over on Sunday."

Sanderson looked round the room to where Woodbridge was sitting, head down, sifting through some paperwork. He brought his attention back to Cyril and placed a sheet of paper on his desk. "We might have something on that," he said. "Harwich think the bloke who witnessed the attack has come forward. Take Sam with you again and speak to him. This is where he works."

Cyril picked up the note. "Okay, he said. "We'll get off now."

"Just hold on a minute though would you?" Sanderson called for everyone's attention in the room before inviting Cyril to address them. "You attended Ruby Clarke's PM yesterday. Can you tell us what that showed?"

Cyril stood and outlined the findings from the procedure that had taken place yesterday evening, detailing the cause and estimated time of death and that no sexual activity had occurred immediately prior to her death.

"So, similar to Sharon Williams, especially when you consider the body as we saw it, skirt drawn up above the waist and underwear removed," Sanderson considered.

At that point, DI Barton appeared.

"Ah Dick, good you could join us," Sanderson said, sarcastically.

"Actually, sir, I was waylaid on the way into the building by a couple who gave Ruby Clarke a lift part of the way home in the early hours of Monday morning."

Sanderson's eyes widened. "Go on."

Barton then related the details of the interview he'd just conducted with the Kings, concluding with the confirmation that Ruby had in her possession a pink clutch bag when she got out of their car in Elmstead Market.

"So that's still missing," Sanderson stated. "We need to find that as a matter of urgency."

58

Cyril and Sam Woodbridge drove over to Harwich later that morning. The man they wanted to speak to was Ronald Thompson, or Ronnie as the Harwich-based sergeant who took his statement yesterday at Harwich Police Station told them he liked to be referred to. The company he worked for was based in the port of Parkeston Quay where the North Sea passenger ferries docked. That brought back fearful memories for Cyril. Last year he'd become trapped on one of those ferries and but for the actions of his companion today and John Barton, he might not have survived.

They located the office unit on a small industrial estate and walked into the reception area. After a few minutes, a tall man in his late thirties appeared.

"Mr Thompson?" Cyril queried.

"Ronnie, yes," the man said, holding out a hand.

"We're here about the statement you gave one of our uniformed colleagues at Harwich Police Station last night."

Thompson ushered them into a small room behind the reception desk. "Would you like a tea, coffee or anything?" he asked.

Cyril and Woodbridge declined as they all sat down at a small table in what was obviously a meeting room.

From the small leather case he'd brought with him, Cyril pulled out a folder with some papers inside. "Can you just tell us, in your own words, what you saw last Friday night, Mr Thompson?" he began.

"I appreciate you coming here rather than visiting me at home," Thompson said. "I'd rather my wife didn't know I'd been out around the town on Friday night." He caught the look of surprise on Cyril's face. "There was nothing untoward," he quickly continued. "it's just she was staying overnight at her mother's and … well, I thought I'd see what was happening … a few beers, you know how it is. Anyway, I'd told her I was in all night watching telly. A little white lie, I know but you can see how it might look to her."

"Mr Thompson, at this stage, we're only interested in the events of Friday night and what you witnessed. So if you can tell me what that was."

The man took a deep breath and exhaled before he related what he saw as he walked home from town.

When he'd finished, Cyril followed up with some questions to clarify. "What time was this?" he asked

"Must have been just before midnight."

"And you got a clear view of the car?"

"Yes. It was a Ford Cortina. A new one, 'R' registration."

Both Cyril and Woodbridge were taking notes. "And colour?" Cyril said.

"Dark, maybe a dark blue. They look a bit different under the sodium street lights, don't they?" Thompson responded.

"Now what about the driver? You said you got a good look?"

"Yes. When he stopped at the junction, he looked to his right where I was standing on the pavement. He looked beyond me to check nothing was coming before he pulled out and accelerated away."

"Can you describe him?"

"Quite young, maybe mid-twenties, longish fair hair, sideburns and slim build."

Cyril pulled a copy of the Identikit image from the folder and placed it on the table in front of the man. "Could this be him?" he asked.

The man gave a chuckle as he picked up the sheet. "Sorry," he said, "but this is pretty poor."

"But could it be?" Cyril persisted.

The man turned the sheet over, took a pencil from behind his ear and began to draw.

Cyril and Woodbridge looked at one another before watching the drawing develop.

"A bit of an artist are you, Mr Thompson?"

"Ronnie, please." The man carried on with the sketch. "I did art at school and thought I might go to college but I ended up following a different career path." With a flourish, he shaded in the last part before turning it round so the detectives could see the final product.

Again, Cyril and Woodbridge exchanged glances before Cyril studied it. "And this is a reasonable likeness?" he asked.

"As good as I can remember," Thompson confirmed.

"And have you seen this man before or since?"

He shook his head. "No, I didn't recognise him."

Cyril stood and Woodbridge followed suit. "Thanks for this Mr ... er Ronnie," Cyril said. "This is very useful. And the vehicle description too."

Thompson led the way to the door.

"If we need to speak to you again, we'll be in touch," Cyril said. Then, following the expression he caught on Thompson's face, "At this office, of course."

"Appreciate that," he said.

*   *   *

Barton spent the rest of the morning coordinating further searches by the uniformed team of the route between Elmstead Market and Great Bentley for the missing handbag. Confirmation that Ruby had it with her when she was last seen was vital. He'd also spoken to the traffic unit and asked the inspector in charge to check the officers' logs from the early hours of Monday morning in the area to see if anything of interest came to light.

Another task he set himself took him out of the station at one o'clock. For some time, he'd been concerned about his situation in the flat he'd occupied since his split and eventual divorce from his wife, Alison, nearly three years ago. Cyril and Martin Sanderson were right, he needed to sort himself out. Another reminder of how far he'd gone down the path of self-destruction had been the incident with the warrant card. God, he only hoped they'd catch the bastard so he could prove completely his total innocence. The number of times he'd descended into situations that a man in his position, a Detective Inspector with the Essex Police, shouldn't have; all those easy pick-ups, drunken nights out. No, he needed to turn things around. And that, he told himself, begins with finding some decent accommodation; somewhere not so convenient for trawling the town's pubs and clubs. As he drove away from the station, he was looking forward to viewing the two-bed semi-detached property that was up for rent about a mile from the town centre.

On the way, he passed the entrance to the Butlin's Holiday camp that was one of the major employers in the town, especially in summer, and thought of the times he'd trawled the bars in there. There was an arrangement with the security team that there were always a couple of chalets spare so that if he got lucky, he had some on-site facilities as they liked to refer to it as. He smiled at the memories before resuming a serious expression. Those were just the incidents he was trying to outgrow.

At the property, he was met by the estate agent, a short bespectacled man clutching a small case. After a brief tour of the house, he agreed the terms and confirmed he would call into the office later that afternoon to sign the paperwork and pay the necessary deposit.

The agent had departed and Barton was having a final look at the house from the pavement before getting back into his car when a blue Mini drove onto the adjacent driveway. He paused and watched as an attractive leggy blonde got out, looked across at him and smiled before letting herself into the next door house. He smiled to himself as he climbed into the driver's seat. A promising sign, he thought to himself, then drove away.

*   *   *

"Where to now, skip?" Woodbridge asked as Cyril drove away from Parkeston Quay.

"Whilst we're over here, Sam, we may as well run this sketch by the young woman he saw being attacked."

Woodbridge looked at his watch. "She's likely to be at work now," he said.

"Then that's where we're going." Cyril gave his colleague a smile. "Down in the port wasn't it?" he said, meaning the Port of Harwich this time, main area for cargo and directly across the river from the Port of Felixstowe.

Michelle Harris came down to the reception area of the transport company she worked for, a frown on her face. "Has something happened?" she asked.

"We've been contacted by a witness," Cyril began, "and we'd like to show you something." He unfolded the sheet of paper with Thompson's sketch on it and handed it to her.

He watched as tears filled her eyes.

She looked up as one escaped. "That's him," she said. "That's the bastard." She wiped her face with the back of her hand. "It's a good likeness," she confirmed.

"Thanks, Michelle," Cyril said as he folded the sheet up and put it back in his pocket. That's all we needed to know."

"You will get him?" she asked.

"We'll do our very best," Cyril assured.

59

At the four o'clock briefing, the assembled team listened as Sanderson led them through events once again.

"The revised sketch of this man," he said pointing to the sheet brought back by Cyril and Woodbridge from their interview with Ronnie Thompson, "have we shown this to the other witnesses?"

"Took a copy to Karyn Brown," Cyril responded. "And her reaction was that it was a far more accurate likeness of the man she and Sharon met on the Saturday night. I want to show it to Duncan Marshall, the retired journalist we spoke to in the Railway Hotel later."

"I'll take a copy and run it round the cabbies in town too," Barton offered.

"Good. Now where are we with the search of the roads for that handbag?" Sanderson asked.

Barton shuffled through a couple of sheets of paper in his hand. "Nothing so far, sir," he said. "Uniform are working their way along the A133 from Elmstead on both sides of the road, but there's a lot of grass verge and hedgerows to check. Then again, it could have been jettisoned after the killer dumped the body and we don't know where the killer was headed." He shuffled another sheet out from below. "And nothing untoward from the traffic logs on that night either."

Sanderson looked at the sketch pinned up on the board. "We don't even know if this fellow was involved, not for sure," he was saying, almost to himself. He faced the room. "All we can say is that he was the one who tried to force the young woman into his car on Friday night in Harwich." He paused a moment in thought. "Talking of which, anything we can do with the description of the car?"

"Not really without some clue as to the registration," Barton said. "There are thousands of Cortinas out there, even new R registration ones. The company car of choice at the moment."

"We can't even say the exact colour," Woodbridge added. "Under street lights they can look different to how they appear in daylight."

"And your witness in Harwich can't recall anything from the number plate other than it was definitely 'R' registration?"

"I'm afraid not."

*   *   *

Duncan Marshall was in his regular spot at the bar of the Railway Hotel when Cyril walked in. He turned and a look of recognition passed over his face as Cyril approached. "I'd have thought you'd have had your hands full at the moment without calling in for a pint," he said. His expression betrayed the humour he'd intended in the remark.

"This is work, Mr Marshall," Cyril replied.

"Shocking news about that young lass," Marshall remarked. "Short life cut short." He took a drink from his glass. "Let's hope it doesn't develop into what's happening up in Yorkshire," he said.

Cyril was puzzled. "What's that?"

"I think it's three now that have been murdered, in Leeds."

The penny dropped for Cyril. "Oh, yes. I've seen that in the papers."

"My contacts up there reckon it's the same bloke. Awful what he does to them."

Cyril was keen to concentrate on the reason he had sought out the man. "What I wanted to ask," he began, unfolding a piece of paper from his pocket, "Do you recognise this man?"

Marshall took hold of the copy of the sketch and looked closely. "That's him," he said. "That's the young lad who was in here that you were asking about last time. That's a damn sight better than the last effort you showed me." Marshall handed the sketch back.

"New information," Cyril said. "Thanks, Mr Marshall." He was about to leave, when Marshall spoke again.

"Oh there was something else I remembered," the retired journalist said. "That night when your mate Dick was in here …"

"Go on," Cyril encouraged.

"When he got up from his seat to leave," he indicated the one in question. "that young lad walked over and sat down. I'd forgotten when we last spoke … and it may be nothing … but I saw him bend down and reach underneath. I didn't see what it was but he put something into his jacket pocket."

Cyril nodded. "And you're sure you can't remember what it was?"

"It's not I can't remember, I didn't actually see it."

"Okay, thanks again."

60

Bolton sat at the small table at the foot of his bed in the caravan and re-read the letter he'd received from his old university mate, Barry. They'd met as they both studied for their Civil Engineering degrees, becoming firm friends and maintaining contact ever since. Barry was a regular visitor to the flat he shared with Emma. He had worried that at one point Barry might have tried his luck with her but they had just remained good friends. 'Got too much respect for you two,' Barry had once said. With Barry's reputation, he was glad of that.

This last letter, received a couple of weeks ago spoke of the amazing life his friend was having, working for an International construction company in Thailand. *'So listen, Dennis,'* the letter concluded, *'you need to get your backside out here. There's plenty of work for someone like you. I know a couple of people looking for a guy with your experience. I can introduce you. It'd be just like old times except the weather's better. And as for the talent!'*

That last comment brought a smile to his lips. He could just imagine his mate let loose amongst the fleshpots of Bangkok. He'd heard it was an amazing place. Maybe now, with everything that had gone on in recent weeks, it might be the time to do it.

The transition from school to university was something Dennis had adapted to seamlessly, despite the tragedy of becoming orphaned a few years earlier and the trauma of going into care. He was glad to be free of the ribbing he'd had from his classmates due to his surname. It had started at primary school when, nearly every time his name was read out at roll call, some smart arse would always add 'nil' to it, referring to the football team.

But thoughts of his university days brought him back to Emma. He looked round to the bed. Underneath, there was a small suitcase with the personal effects he kept after she died. They were amongst his most prized possessions. He bent down, pulled out the case and clicked the catches. Opening it, there were some photographs, her passport, a few items of makeup that he couldn't bear to discard, including her favourite perfume and some of her favourite clothes. He never felt there was anything unusual in that, he just held them and inhaled her decreasing scent from time to time, just to feel near to her. Others, who couldn't understand, would think it odd. They shared something magical. Being twins, they knew what each other was thinking, even before they knew it themselves, it seemed. When she died, it was as if part of him had gone too. This time, he studied a photograph of the two of them smiling at the camera. There was no mistaking that they were twins, identical too, they looked so much alike; same height, same slim build and with the same hairstyle which, since men had grown their hair long from the late sixties, seemed to be unisex. They were sitting on a bench outside a pub near the university in the final year of his course. Barry had taken it. He remembered the day well, hot and sunny. God he wished he could go back there one more time.

He shrugged himself free of his reverie, put the photograph back in the case and picked up Emma's passport. Like his, it still had four years to run. He opened the dark blue book and studied the details. The photo looked exactly like his own. He smiled at the image.

61
Thursday 24th March 1977

Peter Fitzgerald could have done without this; the site manager had enough work to do as it was. The phone call was from his boss. Could he get over to Harwich and speak to the Essex County Council Engineer about another section of the A120 road they wanted to improve? The meeting was to be held in the council offices there.

A glance at his watch told him there was no time for Dennis to finish cleaning the car. He'd have to set off now. After his director's visit the other day, there had been some mucky weather and he'd asked him to give it another good going over; inside this time too.

He left his office and found the young engineer wiping down the rear panels with a chamois leather.

"Looking good, Dennis," Fitzgerald said. "But you'll have to leave it for now. I've got to get over to Harwich."

"But I haven't done the inside yet," the young engineer said.

"No time. I need to be at the Council offices by four-thirty."

Instinctively, Bolton checked his watch as he handed him the key and stood aside.

The manager placed his briefcase on the back seat then slid into the driver's seat and started the engine. "I'll see you when I get back," he said, before driving through the gates and out onto the A120.

A couple of miles towards Harwich with the radio on, distracted thoughts caused him to brake heavily when he was late spotting a van turning left in front of him. As he did so, something caught his eye in the front passenger footwell. A pink object had rolled out from under the seat.

As he accelerated away again, moving up through the gears, the four o'clock news bulletin came on the radio. Up into fourth, he was glancing down to try and identify the strange article that had suddenly appeared on the floor when the newsreader stated,

> *"Police investigating the murder of a woman whose body was discovered early on Tuesday morning near the Essex village of Great Bentley are appealing for information, including the whereabouts of ..."*

By now, he was travelling at around sixty miles an hour and heard no more. He looked up too late to see an articulated lorry coming towards him on the other side of the road being overtaken by a large van.

That split second of panic shot his heart rate off the scale. The last thing he would see was the front end of the van crumpling along with the bonnet of his car. The engine block was thrust through the bulkhead. The sound was deafening; the pain excruciating; then blackness and finally, for him, silence.

The first police traffic car on the scene was met by an apocalyptic sight. The van had pushed the Cortina some way up onto the grass verge. The articulated lorry had pulled to a halt some hundred or so yards further on from the point of impact. The wagon driver, in an agitated state, was being comforted by other motorists who had stopped to offer help. That help was not needed by the van driver or by Fitzgerald. It was difficult for the experienced officers in the patrol car to recognise the two vehicles involved. The fire brigade had been called and the officers only hoped they would arrive before any fire broke out. There was nothing they could do for the two drivers and it was stupidity to risk their own lives in any attempt to free the victims.

A few minutes later the first of three ambulances arrived, closely followed by two fire engines. The firemen quickly sprayed the wreckage with foam and declared the scene safe for the paramedics to approach, who quickly realised there was nothing to be done for the drivers. Recovery by the fire brigade was the only action required.

First to be freed was the body of the van driver. Whilst that operation was carried out the traffic sergeant was taking statements from the HGV driver and the other motorists who'd had had the misfortune to witness the accident.

Two more traffic units arrived to assist as other police cars blocked the road and set up a diversion. The A120 was, after all, the main artery from the port to the rest of the country.

Finally, the fire officers managed to free the remains of the site manager from what was left of his vehicle. The constable who had accompanied the traffic sergeant in the first response vehicle oversaw the release of the body and sought a wallet from the driver's pocket. He carefully opened it up and found the driving licence. Peter Anthony Fitzgerald with an address in Reading in Berkshire was revealed. No endorsements. That would be a visit for the local constabulary, the officer thought, and one he was glad not to be making. He'd made enough 'agony visits', as they were known, in his time.

To release the body, the roof had been cut off and that allowed the traffic officer to see wedged behind the driver's seat a brief case. He reached in and, after a bit of effort, managed to lever the case free. Laying it on the grass and opening it up, he discovered various items of paperwork before spotting a small compartment with business cards. "Peter A Fitzgerald BSc (Hons) MICE Senior Engineer", the card proudly announced along with the logo and name of the company the officer recognised as being responsible for the A120 road improvement project at Wix. That, no doubt, would be their next port of call.

The sergeant joined him at that point. "What have we got?" he asked.

The constable explained about the driver's wallet and the briefcase indicating the connection to the road improvement works at Wix.

The pair then walked around the rear of the car and looked in the boot. The lid had popped open with the impact. It was clean and empty. Round to the other side, something pink caught the sergeant's eye wedged below the passenger side dashboard, just below the glovebox, which hung open. He stretched down and pulled free what appeared to be a woman's clutch bag. Opening it, he could see a packet of ten Rothman's cigarettes. He pulled that out and flipped it open to reveal three cigarettes and a disposable cigarette lighter wedged inside. He rummaged further in the bag and saw some paper tissues, a lipstick, a small make-up mirror and a small perfume bottle. It always amazed him just how much women can fit in a bag. At the bottom there was a small purse and a security pass for one of the department stores in Colchester. A young woman's face smiled up at him and below it, was the name, Ruby Clarke.

62

Bolton was making his way back to the offices from the bridge site where the carpenters had been beginning to erect shuttering to allow the concrete for the second support pier to be poured on Monday. He needed to keep a close eye on how it was being put together and make sure the reinforcement was correctly spaced. The men were also heading back to the site compound ready to depart for the day. The sight of a marked police car pulling into the compound increased his pulse rate and he picked up his pace.

Walking into the main office, he was mystified to see Sandra, the site secretary in floods of tears.

"What's going on?" he asked.

"Oh, Dennis," Sandra managed between sobs. "It's Peter. He's …"

The police officer who was standing in the room, his white-topped cap in hand, helped her out. "I'm sorry to have to tell you that Mr Fitzgerald has been killed this afternoon."

"What! But I only saw him leave about a quarter past four."

"There was a road traffic accident on the A120 about three miles away."

"God, I heard all the sirens earlier but never thought …"

"And you are, sir?"

"Dennis. Dennis Bolton. I'm an engineer on the project. Peter is … was my boss."

"Have we met before?"

Bolton's pulse rate rose. "I don't think so."

"Do you mind if I have a look round Mr Fitzgerald's office?" the officer asked Sandra.

Still visibly upset, Bolton stepped in. "It's through here," he said, leading the way into a small office behind reception.

The policeman looked around briefly, spotted a framed photograph on the desk and picked it up to examine it. "Is this Mr Fitzgerald, do you know?" he asked.

The picture showed Fitzgerald and his wife, son and daughter. "Yes," Bolton said. "That's Peter and his family."

"Do you mind if I keep this for a while? We'll return it as soon as we can."

In answer to Bolton's questioning look, the policeman responded, "It was a severe impact. We need a photograph."

Bolton put a hand to his mouth. "Oh God. I see."

"And CID will be in contact later."

"CID? Why would they …?"

"I'm afraid I can't tell you that, sir. You'll need to wait to see what they have to ask."

"Was there something wrong with the car?" Bolton couldn't help the panic rise to the surface. "I mean, why would CID be involved? That's not normal, surely?"

"I'm afraid I can't tell you any more, sir. You'll just have to be patient." The officer slipped the picture frame into his pocket and walked back to the reception area.

One of the other workmen had brought the distressed Sandra a mug of tea which she was nursing in between mopping her eyes with a paper tissue.

"We're off to the pub, Dennis, if you want to join us," the workman said.

"Thanks, but I'll see to Sandra and lock up."

The workman looked at Sandra then to Bolton. "Well, when you've finished. We'll no doubt be there for a while," he said before leaving.

It was half an hour or more before Bolton saw Sandra leave the site, watching as she drove away in her Volkswagen Polo. He quickly closed the gates and locked up. Thankfully, there was no visit from any further police and he hurried back to his caravan.

*　　*　　*

Barton picked up the phone on his desk. "DI Barton," he answered.

"Dick, I've got Traffic on the blower for you," the desk sergeant announced. "Something about that handbag you've been trying to locate."

Minutes later, Barton was on his feet shrugging himself into his overcoat and striding through the CID room. "Cyril," he said. "With me."

Not waiting for a response, Barton left the room as quickly as he'd come in. Cyril struggled to put on his jacket and coat and follow the DI downstairs.

In the car, Barton told Cyril that there had been a fatal collision on the A120 earlier.

"What's so interesting though?" Cyril asked as they set off from the station.

"Inside the wreckage of a car, they found Ruby Clarke's handbag."

Cyril's eyes opened wide. "Definitely?"

Barton concentrated on overtaking a bus for a second. "Amongst other things, it contained her security pass for the store where she worked."

"What about the driver? Is he our man?"

Barton made a face. "Too much damage to tell but he's probably too old. According to the driving licence he's forty-two and lives in Reading."

"Reading?"

"But he's the manager of that road improvement scheme in Wix, so he has connections to the area."

They were now passing through the village of Weeley. "Is that where we're going now?" Cyril asked.

"First I want to go to the scene and pick up that bag, make sure it goes to the Forensics lab as soon as possible."

Barton gave his full attention to the winding road for the next few miles, driving as fast as he could. Once on the Harwich Road, he spoke again. "By the way, I want to thank you, Cyril," he said.

"Oh, what for?"

He picked up the packet of his favourite cigarettes, Peter Stuyvesant and shook the packet one-handed then put it to his mouth and expertly removed one with his lips. "The advice you've given me. Starting from last year." Again, with one hand, he lit it. "Maybe it's taken me a while to recognise it."

"You've lost me, John."

"I'm moving out of that scruffy fleabag of a flat in town." A sharp exhalation of smoke. "Too bloody handy for the pubs and clubs. It's about time I … well, I suppose, grew up."

Cyril said nothing. He was shocked.

"I've decided to rent a two-bed semi just off St John's Road."

"Sounds like a good start."

"Might give me a chance to save for a deposit to buy."

Cyril gave a slight laugh. "Steady on. I might start to think of you as being sensible."

"And then there's the cracking blonde living next door."

Cyril shook his head. "Not that sensible then."

They slowed as traffic approached a patrol car parked across the Harwich bound side of the road. Nothing was coming in the opposite direction. The young officer was directing the vehicles in front of them down a side road to the right.

Barton wound down the window and produced his warrant card. "A nasty one, I hear," he said to the uniform.

"Yes, sir," he said. "The incident is about a mile further on."

"Thanks," Barton replied and slowly drove around the police vehicle.

The fire engines had left the scene and an ambulance was departing when Barton drew to a halt beside one of two recovery vehicles. Police photographers were capturing the location while the light still held. A traffic officer in white cap approached the two detectives as they stepped from Barton's Rover.

"DI Barton, is it?" The officer held out a hand.

"That's right," Barton responded, shaking hands. "And this is DS Claydon."

Cyril shook the offered hand also.

"Dreadful," the officer said by way of preamble. "From what we can ascertain, it was the van driver's fault. Overtaking the artic on a bend on the brow of the hill and collided head on with the poor chap in the Cortina."

Cyril stared at the wreckage on the left hand verge about thirty yards from where they stood.

"Yes that is, or should I say, was a Ford Cortina," the traffic officer said.

All three walked over to the vehicles. Barton looked into the empty boot then walked round to the passenger side and looked in. The roof section, having been cut away, lay on the grass behind.

"You made an interesting discovery, I understand?" Barton said.

"That's right. We found a handbag which I think is the one you've been looking for with regard to the body discovered in Great Bentley. I've got it safe in the car for you."

"Where exactly did you find it?"

The officer made his way round to join Barton on the passenger side. "My colleague saw it on the floorpan just below what was left of the glovebox."

Barton bent down to look more closely before standing up and studying the cab of the van which was embedded together with the front of the car. "I don't suppose it could have been thrown from the van?" he wondered, almost to himself.

The traffic officer shook his head. "No. If it had originated in the van, say on the windscreen dashboard, in my experience, it would have been thrown clear of the car altogether and I would have expected to find it behind the car."

Barton considered this opinion.

"No, I think it was probably thrown forward from under the passenger seat," the officer continued.

Barton nodded. "I think you're right," he said. "What do we know about the driver of the Cortina?"

The officer related the details they'd gleaned from his driving licence and a check on the car registration plates. The vehicle was owned by the civil engineering company currently building the new road by-passing Wix, a few miles down the A120. "One of my colleagues has gone down there to make enquiries," he concluded.

"Okay, let's have a look at the bag," Barton asked.

The traffic officer led them to the patrol vehicle where a colleague was sitting in the front passenger seat writing a report. He opened the back door and lifted a large paper evidence bag from the back seat.

Barton put on some gloves, took hold of it and peered inside. There, opened, was Ruby Clarke's pink clutch bag. He could see the cigarette packet and, rummaging with his fingers, he saw the photo ID badge from the Colchester department store. He held it open to allow Cyril to look inside.

Folding the evidence bag up once again, Barton thanked the traffic team and headed back to his car with Cyril.

63

Bolton switched on the small television set in his van and dragged the suitcase from under the bed. The national news was finishing on the TV and the opening announcements were being made for the local bulletin being broadcast from the Norwich studios. At the bottom of the case, inside a pair of socks, he pulled out a roll of bank notes and began to count. This was his immediate savings stash. He'd already counted one hundred and sixty-five pounds when he was distracted by what the news reader was saying.

'Police continue their investigation into the murder of nineteen-year-old Ruby Clarke from Clacton whose body was discovered on Tuesday morning near the village of Great Bentley in Essex.'

He turned as the photograph of the attractive girl filled the screen. A lump came to his throat and he felt tears prick. What the hell had he done? All this sadness. And then, this afternoon, Peter. What must his wife be going through now? Two young kids. The newscaster moved on:

'Police have refused to discount any connection with the unsolved murder of fifty-two-year-old Sharon Williams in nearby Clacton or the attempted abduction of a young woman in Harwich last Friday.'

Panic froze his blood as another image flashed onto the screen. This was the updated sketch that Ronnie Thompson had produced ... of him!

'And police have issued an image of a man they wish to question in connection with the incident in Harwich. Anyone with any information on any of these incidents should contact Clacton Police Station on …'

Shit! Shit! Shit!

'… or any police station. And now to other news …'

He wasn't listening to any other news. He knew he had to act. What was it that traffic policeman had said? *'CID will be in contact later.'* They must have connected Peter's car somehow. No, the time to move was now. Right now.

*   *   *

Barton and Cyril arrived back at the station after half past seven. Most of the detectives had already left but Woodbridge was working his way through some statements. He looked up when the two walked into the CID room. "Is it the missing handbag?" he asked.

Cyril looked grim. "Yes, Sam."

"The DCI was looking for you both," Woodbridge said. "I think he's still in his office."

Cyril looked to Barton. "You go and bring him up to speed. I'll check on other progress."

As Barton walked off to see Sanderson, Cyril sat down at his desk and scanned the messages left there. "Did the Gazette publish that revised sketch?" he asked.

Woodbridge held up a copy. "Along with another request for help from the public. And I think the BBC and ITV have been alerted too."

Cyril pulled his pipe and tobacco from his jacket pocket. "We took the bag to the lab personally, so we'll see what clues that might yield," he said.

Woodbridge watched as clouds of smoke obscured his sergeant's face for a few seconds. "I spoke to the cab companies in Colchester," he said. "and none had any drivers in the area of Elmstead Market and Great Bentley in the early hours of Monday. There was only one driver who took a fare to Clacton, a couple who'd been visiting friends, but he'd seen nobody on the road."

"Good work Sam. Why don't you get off home," Cyril suggested. "I get the impression tomorrow's going to be busy."

Reluctantly, Woodbridge stood and put on his coat. "Night, skip," he said.

"See you, Sam,"

Woodbridge paused at the door and looked back at Cyril who'd looked deep in thought, puffing his pipe.

After Sam had gone, Cyril stared into space for a minute or two taking in the events of the day. It had been hard. Eventually, he looked to the phone on his desk, picked up the receiver and dialled a number.

"Hello," he said when it was answered. "Do you mind if I call round? I could do with some therapy."

"Of course," Cathy said. *"I heard it's been a difficult day."*

64
Friday 25th March 1977

Cyril pulled into the Jackson Road police station car park about a quarter to eight. Cathy said she'd make her own way in as that would be too early for her nine o'clock start. The night spent together had done him a power of good after the difficult day he'd had. Today could potentially be more challenging and he drew in a lungful of fresh sea air before walking up the steps and into the building.

DCI Sanderson prepared to take the eight o'clock briefing once again. Barton was already there when Cyril walked into the CID room. Woodbridge, Walker and Miller along with all other available detectives and uniforms were engaged in various discussions.

"Right everyone," Sanderson called out, quelling the conversations and bringing the meeting to order. "Late yesterday, Ruby Clarke's missing handbag was discovered in the wreckage of a fatal RTA on the A120 near Harwich," he explained. "John, you and Cyril attended. Can give us a report?"

Barton stood and outlined their visit to the crash site and how they took possession of the bag and transferred it safely to the forensics lab in Colchester. One of the forensics officers had agreed to stay late to take possession of it.

"Have we had any results yet?"

"I'll give them a call as soon as we're finished, sir," Barton responded. "I also arranged for Thompson's fingerprints to be taken."

"Good. Thanks John," Sanderson said. "Now, to bring you all up to speed," he went on, "I had a call from Thames Valley police who had the unenviable task of breaking the news of the death of Peter Fitzgerald, the driver of the Ford Cortina, to his wife. She confirmed that he'd been with her all last weekend when the attack on Michelle Harris and the murder of Ruby Clarke occurred. She also confirmed he'd been home with her on the weekend Sharon Williams was murdered."

"So why was Ruby Clarke's handbag in the car?" Woodbridge asked.

"Good question, Sam," Barton answered. "We think it was wedged under the passenger seat and somehow shot free in the impact. That's what the traffic officers think."

"Which means we need to look at who had access to the vehicle on the relevant dates." Sanderson spoke as he paced in front of the group. "So when we've finished here, you, Cyril and Sam and myself will visit the road improvement site," he said to Barton before turning to the rest of the team. "Any leads from the TV and newspaper coverage of our friend here?" He tapped the sketch of the man they'd been trying to identify.

"Working our way through the call responses now sir," Miller said.

"Right, keep on with that and let me know if anything interesting surfaces. Thank you, gentlemen," Sanderson concluded. "You all know what you're doing. In the meantime, I'll give DCS Viney an update then we'll head out." He looked to Barton before leaving the room.

Sanderson was in the front passenger seat, Barton driving with Cyril and Woodbridge in the back when they pulled into the contractors' compound at just past nine o'clock. Two Jaguar cars were in the parking spaces next to a red Volkswagen Polo adjacent to the main cabin. Sanderson led the way. When they entered, Sandra, the site secretary looked up from her typewriter through red-rimmed eyes. "Gentlemen," she greeted.

Sanderson introduced himself and the other three detectives before asking if they could have a look in Mr Fitzgerald's office.

"I'm afraid we have two of the company's directors in there at the moment," she replied.

"Can you tell them we're here," Sanderson said.

As Sandra returned from Fitzgerald's office, a tall man in his fifties with neatly styled salt and pepper hair and dressed in a sharp suit, followed her.

"Gentlemen," he said. "Dreadfully sad business. I'm Simon Watts, Construction Director. How can I help?"

Sanderson repeated the request he'd made to Sandra, adding that he'd also like to talk to the other members of the site team.

"Come through," Watts invited, leading the way to the office. "My Commercial Director, Nick Wallace, has come with me this morning," he added.

Sanderson paused at the office door and turned to Cyril. "Can you and Sam identify the other staff working here and start interviewing?"

"Sure," Cyril said.

"John, with me please," Sanderson said, using Barton's proper name for official reasons.

As Cyril and Woodbridge turned away, Sanderson and Barton walked into Fitzgerald's office and closed the door.

With four adults in the room, there was little space to move around. Watts introduced his colleague, a shorter man with dark brylcreemed hair and rimless glasses, who had stood up from the Fitzgerald's chair behind the desk. Sanderson did the same for Barton.

"So how can we be of assistance?" Watts asked.

Sanderson began the conversation in a fairly easy manner, asking how long Peter Fitzgerald had worked for the company, how well they'd known him, enquiring into his employment history.

Between them, the directors answered the questions satisfactorily before Watts asked, "I know this has been a tragic situation but what exactly has prompted this level of interest from the police? Unless there was something more about the crash that we're missing," he added, looking at Wallace.

"What's your policy on company cars, Mr Watts? Specifically the one allocated to Mr Fitzgerald."

"It's the same for all our company car users," Watts replied.

Wallace spoke for the first time. "They're allocated to a specific member of staff," he said.

"But, presumably, other employees are insured to drive them? With permission, of course," Barton asked.

"Well, yes."

Watts had been thoughtful. "Are you saying there is an issue with Peter's car, Chief Inspector?"

Sanderson scratched his ear. "We know that Mr Fitzgerald travelled back to Reading by train when he had a weekend break. Do you know if the car would have been left here on those occasions?"

"I would expect so, but the best people to ask would be Joe Mansfield our site foreman or … er, well our assistant engineer, but he …er."

Barton detected a problem. "Is something wrong, Mr Watts?"

"It's the engineer who resides on site. Some of the lads like to use a caravan on our sites, saves on accommodation and they generally lock up last thing at night and open up first thing in the morning." Watts paused but Sanderson and Barton said nothing, waiting for the man to carry on. "Well, it seems, he's disappeared."

"How do you mean, 'disappeared'?"

"Exactly that. According to Sandra and Joe, he was here to lock up last night but by this morning he'd gone. Joe had to open up when he arrived. And when he checked the caravan, it had been cleared out of all of his things."

Barton looked to Sanderson. "What's this engineer's name?" he asked.

"Bolton. Dennis Bolton."

"And how old is he?"

Wallace lifted a sheet from the manager's desk. "He's twenty-five."

Barton had a hunch and pulled from his jacket pocket a sheet of paper which he unfolded. "Is this Dennis Bolton?" he asked, showing the directors the sketch Ronnie Thompson had produced for them.

"Hold on," Watts said. "I'll ask Sandra. She'll know."

*   *   *

Dennis Bolton looked out of the window of the cheap hotel he'd checked into last night. The view was particularly uninspiring, the brick wall of the next door property was about six feet away. He could hear the constant drone of the traffic on the nearby street interspersed with the angry sounds of car horns.

It had been after eleven o'clock when he'd arrived last night. He'd walked down to the village of Wix and called a local taxi from the callbox by the crossroads. The taxi had taken him to Manningtree railway station. During the taxi ride in brief conversation, he'd made sure he'd dropped comments to the driver regarding his planned journey to Norwich. That might give him a bit more breathing time. In actual fact, he'd caught the train to Liverpool Street. He was sure the man who sold him the ticket had paid him little attention. He'd kept his head down to reduce any chance of him being remembered.

Once out at Liverpool Street, he'd taken the tube around to Kings Cross where he knew there was a multitude on anonymous hotels. This one looked one of the cheapest he could find and, at the end of the day, it was only a place to keep his head down where he wouldn't be asked any awkward questions. From that point of view, it had served its purpose. The comings and goings from adjacent rooms throughout the night was a price worth paying for the anonymity he sought. And now, it was time to move his plans forward.

He checked his watch then the contents of his jacket pocket. Inside were a passport, a roll of notes and a building society passbook. He pulled out the passbook and opened it. The balance of £1,760.00 looked good.

First stop would be the building society but the lazy buggers never opened until half past nine. That, plus the bundle of notes he'd squirrelled away totalling £985.00, should be enough.

An hour later he was back in the room. He'd been asked a number of 'security' questions at the building society but his answers and his passport ensured he'd been able to close the account and he held the banknotes in his hand. On the way, he'd stopped to browse the morning's papers in one of the newsagents. Only the East Anglian Daily Times covered the story of Ruby Clarke's murder. The sketch of his face was small enough not to be instantly recognisable but the fact it was out there in print still worried him.

Now would be the creative part. He opened the suitcase he'd brought with him and retrieved the letter from his friend in Thailand and read it again. This was the best solution to his situation, he was sure. He'd passed a travel agent's on his way to the building society and began to make plans to call in and make a purchase. He only hoped he had enough money to allow his plan to proceed.

* * *

"Hello." Cyril approached the site secretary. "Sandra, is it?"

"That's right," she responded.

"I know this is difficult but could you give me a bit of information about who works on this site?"

She stood and pulled a sheet of paper from a file in a cabinet behind her. "These are the staff members who work for us," she said. "There are other subcontractors from time to time, steel-fixers, carpenters, those sorts of trades." She held out the paper.

Cyril took the sheet and looked at the list. "This fellow here … Joe Mansfield, the site foreman. Would he be the best one to speak to first of all about all that goes on on site?"

She looked at her watch. "Joe knows what goes on, yes. At this time, you should find him in the canteen."

Cyril thanked the woman and, along with Woodbridge, made his way to the canteen, next but one cabin down. When they approached, a group of men were just leaving the unit.

"I'm looking for Joe, the foreman," Cyril said.

One of the men indicated with his thumb. "Just about to follow us out," he said.

As Cyril walked in he saw one man sitting alone at a long table, glasses on, reading the back page of The Sun newspaper.

"Are you Joe Mansfield?" Cyril asked.

The man looked up, took his glasses off and folded up the paper. "That's right." After draining the white mug in front of him, he added, "Investigating Mr Fitzgerald's accident?"

"Sort of."

"Dreadful what happened. He was a good bloke too," Mansfield considered. "Better than most I've worked with."

Cyril nodded. "Have you got five minutes?" he asked.

"Sure."

Cyril sat down at the bench table opposite the foreman. Woodbridge did the same.

Attempting to ease into a general conversation, Cyril began, "How have things been? Making good progress?"

Mansfield was leaning forward, arms on the table in front of him. "We have been, until this morning."

"Why, what happened this morning?"

"Well that young sod."

Cyril was puzzled. "Which young sod?"

The foreman leaned back. "Dennis. The assistant engineer. He normally opens up but he seems to have taken off."

"How do you mean, 'taken off'?"

"Like I said. He lives on site. Has a caravan over the other side of the offices." He held his arms wide, emphasising the point. "Not unusual, a lot in his position do it, saves on accommodation. In return, we've got someone who, for the most part locks the site up at night and opens up in the morning. Only this morning, it was still shut when I arrived at seven. The lads were a bit restless. They like to make an early start when they can and sod off early if they get finished what they need to do. 'Job and knock' we call it."

"I'm assuming you've checked this Dennis's caravan?"

"Cleared out. Empty. All his belongings have gone."

"Has that surprised you?"

Mansfield looked stunned. "Well, yes. He's a bright lad. Been with us a few years. I know Peter thought highly of him."

"And no idea where he's gone?" Cyril persisted.

"Not a clue."

"Could you describe him, Mr Mansfield?"

"Well, he's a young lad, mid-twenties, longish fair hair, like the fashion these days. A good looking lad, I suppose."

Cyril thought for a moment then produced the revised sketch of the man they'd been trying to identify since Sharon Williams' murder. "Does this look something like Dennis Bolton?"

Mansfield glanced at the image. "That's the bloke you've been asking about in the papers, isn't it?"

Cyril nodded.

The foreman took a deep breath. "I was wondering that when I saw it in last night's Gazette," he said. "It does bear a close resemblance."

"Can we have a look in his caravan?"

Mansfield stood up. "I'll show you."

Cyril and Woodbridge followed the foreman past the main office to a caravan parked nearby.

"Do you mind?" Cyril said, indicating that he didn't want Mansfield to go into the caravan again but let the detectives enter on their own.

"No problem, it's open," the foreman said, glancing at his watch. "I need to get out on site."

Cyril thanked him as the man strode off. Pulling a handkerchief from his pocket to protect his hands, Cyril opened the door and stepped up into what had been Bolton's temporary home until yesterday. "Try not to touch anything, Sam."

They went straight into a small living area with a kitchen at the left hand end. The space was dark as the curtains were still closed. Cyril opened those at the far end and Woodbridge those over the small kitchen sink. The sink itself contained a bowl, mug, knife and fork and a spoon soaking in water. A couple of newspapers lay on the coffee table in front of the settee. Woodbridge was careful to open both cupboards by the sink with a covered hand to find a few cans and some crockery. Behind the door hung a thick jacket, obviously used for work on the site.

"Let's have a look down here," Cyril said, walking to the opposite end, past a small bathroom that appeared devoid of anything other than a spare toilet roll, and into the bedroom.

The bed lay unmade. He opened the doors of the small wardrobe. Inside, on the floor of the wardrobe an old pair of dirty trousers had been rolled up. By the bed, a pair of work boots lay, one on its side. Cyril bent down to look below the bed. Nothing. No suitcases or travel bag. "Let's find the DCI, Sam," he said. "I think we need to get forensics down here."

65

Watts asked Sandra to join them in the manager's office.

When she arrived, Watts showed her the sketch. "The detectives are wondering if this is a likeness for Dennis Bolton?" he asked.

She looked at the sheet with a puzzled expression before a look of alarm took hold. She looked to the detectives. "Is this the one I've heard about? The one in the papers?" Finally realisation dawned. "It's him," she said. "Even down to the long sideburns."

"So you've seen this sketch before?" Barton asked her.

"I didn't really take any notice."

Barton glanced at Sanderson before he continued, "Can you tell us about the last time you saw Mr Bolton?"

"Please, sit down, Sandra." Watts indicated Fitzgerald's chair.

Gingerly, she sat down, Barton and Sanderson sitting in the two chairs on the opposite side of the desk. Watts and Wallace stood behind the woman, transfixed at the way things had developed.

Finally, Sandra answered. "It was last night, after the dreadful news. The site was winding down for the day and Joe, that's the foreman, said a few of them were off to the pub in Wix. I just wanted to get off home. I don't think Dennis wanted to go either. He offered to close up as usual. I had a few things to tidy up but, to be honest, I was feeling pretty upset. I still am, really." She wiped her eyes with a paper tissue. "I just sat and cried for a while. Then, when I left about six, Dennis waved as I left and he would have locked the gates. That's the last I saw of him."

"Do you know if he had access to Mr Fitzgerald's car, Sandra?" Sanderson asked.

She half turned in an attempt to look at the directors before responding. "He would use it if he needed to. I mean, he went into Colchester on … Tuesday it was. Peter asked him to take some reports to the engineer's office there."

"What about weekends?"

Sandra coloured.

Sanderson glanced at Watts. "Don't worry about getting anyone into trouble. We just need to know the facts."

"Well, Peter, that's Mr Fitzgerald, never liked the drive home. It was an awkward cross-country route with only the last bit of it on a motorway. So he used to take the train. It was almost quicker so he'd have more time at home. I know Dennis used to drop him off at Manningtree on a Friday night and pick him up on a Monday morning."

"So Dennis had the use of Mr Fitzgerald's car on some weekends?"

"Yes."

Before the conversation could continue, there was a knock on the door and Cyril appeared. "Sorry, sir," he said, "I think you need to see this."

By the time they left the site, forensics officers were sifting through for details in Bolton's caravan and the workdesk he used in the office. Sanderson had called Miller, Walker and some other available detectives to site to begin taking statements from the site workers.

As he drove the car back to Clacton with the other three detectives, the discussion was in full swing.

"So we know he was at the site around six, six-thirty," Barton mused. "And we know he didn't join the foreman and the others in The Waggon. And he wasn't there to unlock this morning just before seven."

"He'll have scarpered last night," Cyril said. "That visit by uniform about the accident yesterday afternoon will have unnerved him. They might even have mentioned that CID would be following things up."

"And he'd have seen that image in the papers," Woodbridge added. "It was on the local TV news last night too."

"Good point," Sanderson said. "But he didn't have a car anymore, so how would he leave? It would have to be by taxi."

"Unless someone gave him a lift?"

"Didn't sound as though he had any friends as such," Barton put in.

"My money would be on a taxi," Sanderson continued. "So let's check all the possibilities when we get back to the station. Someone would have remembered picking up a fare at the site last night."

"Where do you think he'd go?" Barton wondered. "Harwich for the overnight ferry?"

"Might do," Cyril said. "Or Manningtree for the train. That's where he used to take his site manager for his trips home. London perhaps?"

"Or possibly the other way," Woodbridge suggested. "Ipswich or Norwich?"

"Let's see what his personnel file shows us," Sanderson said. "That might reveal any connections he may have with other parts of the country. I hope we don't have to wait too long for it. Watts said he'd have it driven down to us as soon as possible."

By the time Sanderson drew to a halt in the car park of Jackson Road Police Station, the four of them had discussed most of what they'd learned in the past few hours.

"Right, we all know what we're doing," Sanderson concluded. "Share everything we know with the rest of the team. I'll speak to DCS Viney and we best reconvene this afternoon. Two o'clock."

*   *   *

For the second time that day, Bolton left the seedy hotel and walked down the street to the shop he wanted. Inside his jacket, he hoped he had all the items he would need;

passports and money. By the time he returned an hour later, a few hundred pounds lighter, he had the all-important ticket for tomorrow's flight.

Along the way, he passed an old-fashioned barber shop. About to walk on by, he paused. Of course, he thought, he'd get a much better result here than trying to shave himself, so he walked in. The shop would close at six, so he made an appointment, the later the better for his purpose. He'd be sad to see the departure of his long sideburns but needs must, and they'd always grow back.

In the small room of the hotel with a few hours to kill before heading back to the barber shop, he had time to arrange the packing and refine the details of his plan.

*   *   *

At just before noon, a driver from the construction company dropped an envelope into the front desk, telling the sergeant it was urgent, for the attention of DCI Sanderson.

A few minutes later, up in his office, the DCI pored over the few sheets of paper the envelope contained. There was a copy of Bolton's degree in Civil Engineering from UMIST in Manchester in 1972. A form confirmed his personal details; date of birth, 24th April 1951; place of birth: Stoke-on-Trent and the names of his parents. Another sheet gave his previous employment details; first job in a consultant engineer's office in Manchester before joining his current employer early in 1974. Since then, it appears that he's lived a nomadic existence, moving around the country on a variety of road projects, including some sections of the M62. Interestingly, there was no current address for him. The last one in the file was a flat in Manchester. Still, he thought, worth a call to the area force and get them to check it out. The only other piece of useful information was Bolton's bank account details.

At two o'clock, the team was assembled with plenty of activity on the phones and the site statements being read through by the officers who had been to the site. DCI

Sanderson and DCS Viney entered the CID room. The two senior men exchanged looks, Sanderson with a proud expression on his face.

"Gentlemen," Sanderson announced, waiting for a hush to descend.

The last man talking, Sam Woodbridge was engaged in a telephone conversation. He lowered his voice to complete the call, eventually looking up, embarrassed. "Sorry sir," he said.

Sanderson had waited until he'd finished. "No problem, Sam. It's encouraging to see all this activity." He walked into the centre of the room. "Now, we're concentrating on finding this man," he said, pointing to the now-familiar sketch. "We believe him to be Dennis Bolton, aged twenty-five, employed as an assistant engineer on the Wix road improvement scheme. Last seen at the site last night about six-thirty." Looking round at all the team, he focused on various individuals. "Sam, you're investigating taxi firms. With no car that we know of, he must have travelled from the site somehow. Any joy?"

"Not yet, sir. I've still got a couple of firms ringing me back."

"John, you were looking into his bank account activity."

Barton had a sheet of paper in front of him. "Usual ins and outs," he replied. "Salary in every month, cash withdrawals regularly, nothing untoward. He must have an account with the Leeds Permanent Building Society though, as he's made some payments to them over the past twelve months. I have a call in to them for more details."

Woodbridge's phone rang and with Sanderson nodding to him, he picked it up and answered in quiet tones.

"What about the rest of the site team?" Sanderson continued.

"In the process of taking statements. sir," Miller contributed. "Most of us have been involved in that. Nothing much to add to what we already know. Bolton, it seemed, was given use of the manager's car when he had weekends away."

Woodbridge put the phone down and Sanderson could see the excited expression on his face. "Good news?" the DCI asked.

"Taxi company in Harwich," Woodbridge said. "They reckon one of their drivers picked someone up from Wix village centre last night. Call from a call box, apparently. Should I go and interview him?"

"Of course, Sam," Sanderson said. "Take Cyril with you and follow up what he tells you."

66

The taxi driver was waiting in the office for Cyril and Woodbridge to arrive. He stood when the two detectives walked in. "DC Woodbridge?" he asked Cyril.

Cyril smiled. "No, I'm DS Claydon. This is my colleague who spoke to you, DC Woodbridge."

The men shook hands.

"So what can you tell us?" Woodbridge asked.

"I got a call on the radio at 8:37 last night," the driver began.

"That's very accurate?"

"We keep a log," he responded. "Well, a man had rung up to book a taxi. He was at the call box in the centre of Wix and wanted to go to Manningtree railway station."

Woodbridge produced the sketch. "Is this the man?" he asked.

"That's right." The man looked closely at the image. "That's him."

Cyril joined the conversation. "Did this man say anything on the journey?"

The man looked to Cyril. "He mentioned something about catching a train to Norwich."

"Norwich?"

"Yes. You can get the train from Manningtree."

"I know." Cyril stroked his moustache. "What luggage did he have with him?"

"Just the one suitcase."

"Anything noticeable about it?"

"No, just an ordinary black suitcase."

"Did it appear heavy?" Cyril persisted. "Any labels on it?"

The driver thought a moment then slowly shook his head. "No. Nothing I noticed."

"So what time did you drop him off at the station?"

"Collected him at 8:54 and dropped him at 9:11."

Cyril smiled as he took notes. "That's great," he said. "Very useful."

As Cyril and Woodbridge turned to leave, the driver was keen to continue the conversation. "So is he the one who's done that young lass from Clacton?"

Cyril paused. "He's someone we're keen to speak to about a number of incidents. Thanks for your help."

Half an hour later, Cyril pulled the car to a halt in the station car park at Manningtree. They got out and approached the ticket office. A balding man in his forties sat behind the booth. The man didn't look up, merely grunted, "Yes?"

Cyril held his warrant card up to the screen.

The man raised his eyes, saw the open wallet then sat up straighter in his seat.

"Do you mind if we have a word?" Cyril asked.

"Sure."

"Can you tell me who was on the desk here last night at nine o'clock?"

The man screwed up his eyes. "That would be me," he said.

Cyril held up the sketch for the man to look at. "Do you remember this man buying a ticket around that time?"

"Look, I don't pay much attention to people," the man said.

Cyril rolled his eyes and glanced at Woodbridge. He could believe that.

"Okay," Cyril persisted, "But can you tell me what tickets you sold around that time last night."

The man thought for a minute then said, "Hold on." He disappeared from view before coming back with a sheet of paper. He ran his finger down a list. "Only one. At 9:15," he said.

"And?" Cyril prompted.

"Adult single to Liverpool Street," the man replied.

"Nothing to Norwich then?"

"Said so, didn't I? Only one ticket sold then."

"And you couldn't say if it was this man who bought it?"

"Like I say, I don't pay much attention to who comes here."

Neither wonder British Rail had such a poor reputation, Cyril thought. "Was there anyone else here last night? On the platforms, say?"

Again, Cyril could almost see the man's brain going through the thought processes. Finally, he answered, "Old Bert was on there."

"And is 'Old Bert' around now?" Cyril asked.

"Should be. He's on late shifts this week, same as me."

"Thanks," Cyril said, with some degree of irony.

A short grey-haired man who looked not far off retirement was standing by the ticket barriers when Cyril and Woodbridge approached.

"We're looking for Bert," Cyril said.

"That'll be me," the man replied cheerily in a soft Suffolk accent.

Cyril produced his warrant once again. "I understand you were on duty last night," he said. "The man in the ticket office told us."

Bert gave a chuckle. "Miserable ol' bugger, in't 'e?"

Cyril grinned as he showed Bert the sketch. "Have you seen this man recently?"

The man nodded. "Last night," he replied. "Got on the 9:27 to Liverpool Street."

"And you're sure about that?"

"Oh yes. That time of night, there's not a lot of passengers around."

"Did he have luggage with him?"

Bert nodded. "Black suitcase, yes."

"How did he seem? I mean, was he nervous? On edge?"

"Seemed perfectly normal to me," the ticket collector said.

"Thanks for your help, Bert."

"You're welcome," he said and raised a hand as the two detectives turned and left.

*   *   *

The good traditional wet shave left him with cheeks as smooth as a baby's bottom. He was sure the finished look would be convincing. Fortunately, his facial hair grew extremely slowly. He smiled at the memory of one lad in his university year who could shave first thing but still look as if he had four days growth by lunchtime. He was of Greek extraction, though. On the walk back, he called into a pub in a side street near his hotel. He suddenly felt hungry. They offered pub grub, so he ordered a steak pie chips and beans. He'd seen a plateful come out for someone else and was encouraged by the size of the portions. The kitchen didn't disappoint and fifteen minutes later he was tucking into his food, half way down his pint.

On a high-level shelf in the corner, a television was on silently. The regulars obviously didn't take kindly to their conversations being interrupted. As he ate and drank, he kept a watchful eye on the news bulletin that was being broadcast. The national news had finished and the local London news was on next. A second pint was ordered as he continued to check what was on the TV. Finally, the news programme ended with a look at the weather. He breathed a sigh of relief and began to relax. No intrusive image of himself and no appeal for information had appeared on screen.

He could have comfortably quaffed another pint but decided he should return for the last time to the hotel room. He needed to keep his wits about him and getting more beer under his belt wouldn't help. There would be plenty of opportunities for beers later. Now the priority was the chance for a final run through of his preparations before the big day tomorrow.

*   *   *

When Cyril and Woodbridge returned to Jackson Road, the CID room was still a hive of activity. When they walked in, Barton slammed down the phone, obviously fuming at something.

"Fucking arsehole!" he blustered, prompting the team to go quiet and turn to look at him. "Bloody Building Society manager. Who the fuck does he think he is?"

"What's up, John?" Cyril asked, trying not to break into a smile.

Barton held his head in his hands and rubbed his face. "Two hours I've been trying to speak to someone who can give me information about this little turd's account. Now this arsewipe tells me the only person who can give me the information I need isn't in until tomorrow. Aarrgh!"

Sanderson appeared at Cyril's shoulder. "How did you two get on?" he asked.

Cyril reported what the taxi driver and the station staff had told them.

"So he's in London," the DCI considered. "The question is, is he hiding out there or is he travelling on. We need to alert all airports to keep a watch."

"And we can't narrow any of this down, sir?" Cyril asked. "Not found any connection with any friends at all?"

"Seems a bit of a loner. No one on site ever heard him mention anyone."

"What about Manchester?" Woodbridge suggested. "That's where he went to uni. Maybe he still knows someone there? Could have travelled on to Euston and headed north?"

"Could be any bloody where," Sanderson admitted. "Okay, listen up," He announced. "Take the train stations, Heathrow and Gatwick airports and Victoria bus station and see what you can find out. Anyone answering Bolton's description travelling anywhere. I'll speak to DCS Viney and get something out to the nationals to see if that prompts any response. Right, let's get to it." He clapped his hands then left the room.

By eight o'clock, they'd all drawn blanks with their inquiries when Sanderson reappeared. "Okay gents," he said. "Get yourselves off home for now. We'll reconvene first thing and see if we get any response from the national newspaper appeals."

Cyril walked over to Barton's office. "How are things?" he asked.

"Could murder a pint, Cyril," he replied. "But I daren't."

"Good man. How is your move progressing?"

"Take possession on Monday, so if you're offering some assistance?" A grin broke out on Barton's face.

"I'll ask Sam if he's free. Big strong lad like that."

67
Saturday 26th March 1977

He was awake early. Some of last night's preparations were still in place. He got dressed and touched up the makeup he'd applied, plenty of concealer as a base. Flared trousers, trainers, shirt with a subtle addition below and a jacket with one of Emma's scarves around his neck completed the look. He checked his appearance in the milky mirror in the shared bathroom before returning to his room for the last time.

The foreign man on the front desk said nothing as he put his room key down on the counter and walked out with his suitcase. He'd paid cash in advance when he'd arrived, as all these establishments required. Outside in the street, he was amused that no one seemed to pay him any attention. It never ceased to amaze him how anonymous a large city like London was. He thought back to his time in Manchester. The chances were that he'd see someone he knew when he walked around those city streets.

Down into the underground, he bought a ticket for Victoria. On the bookstall he became alarmed at the display of newspapers. One or two carried the image of him on their front page. He'd be surprised if the others didn't have the story on their inside pages. Self-consciously, he lowered his head as he passed through the ticket barrier.

*   *   *

Early that morning in the CID room, Cyril took a phone call from the lab in Chelmsford where the forensics teams were based. At last they had something tangible to work with. When he put the phone down, Cyril announced that the fingerprints on the wine glass found in Sharon Williams' house were a match for those found in the site caravan belonging to Dennis Bolton. A whoop went up before the team focused on their individual tasks. The scientists were also looking into hair recovered from the sink in the caravan which they were in the process of comparing with those found under the fingernails of Sharon Williams and Ruby Clarke.

While Cyril was speaking to the lab, Woodbridge took a call from Ronnie Thompson, the author of the improved image of Bolton. *"I was watching last night's BBC Local News broadcast,"* Thompson said. *"They did a feature on that tragic accident on the A120 where the manager from the Wix road improvement scheme was killed."*

"Shocking," Woodbridge agreed.

"But the thing is," Thompson continued, *"they used some footage ...what do they call it, library pictures? Basically, they re-ran some footage from a feature they broadcast a few months ago when the scheme was just starting up."* Woodbridge was about to prompt Thompson to get to the point when the man did. *"Well, the man I saw attempting to force that girl into the car appeared,"* he said. *"The man I saw and produced the sketch of is one of the site team on that job."*

Woodbridge jolted himself straight. "It was on the BBC news, you say?"

"That's right."

"Well thanks very much, Mr Thompson, we'll get on to that straight away. That's very useful."

When Cyril had finished his call to the lab, he'd observed Woodbridge's reactions. "Got something, Sam?" he asked.

Woodbridge related the story.

"Right, get hold of the BBC up in Norwich and get them to send the film down here," Cyril instructed. "If they can identify Bolton themselves from the sketch we've already given them, see if they can do some stills of

Bolton's image. I know the sketch is good, but a photo of the man himself will be even better."

Barton waited until 9:30 on the dot before he made his call to the building society. Finally, after waiting to be transferred from pillar to post, he spoke to a manager who agreed he would track down the information he required. Whilst waiting for the return phone call, he walked from his office into the CID room.

"Any joy?" Cyril asked.

"Hopefully very soon," he said. "What about the rest of the team?"

Cyril told him about Thompson's call to Woodbridge and that the BBC were sending a copy of the film and some stills. "The papers all carried the story, though not all on page 1 but we might get something from that," he concluded. As he spoke, Woodbridge was taking a call.

"Ticket collector at Liverpool Street," Woodbridge said, after putting the phone down. "Certain he saw our man on Thursday night. Got off the 10:31 arrival, which is the train the staff at Manningtree told us he boarded."

"Right, so he definitely went to London," Barton said. "But where to after that?" Before anyone could react, his desk phone began to ring and he turned back to his office.

"DI Barton," he said, picking up a pencil to write down the expected information. A few seconds later, he was back out in the main room.

"Okay," he said. "Finally the building society has come good. Dennis Bolton has had an account with them for the past four years. On Saturday in their King's Cross branch, he closed it, withdrawing the sum of £1,760.00."

"That should cover him for a while," Miller said.

"There's one other thing," Barton continued. "He used his passport for ID."

* * *

The journey was stressful; from the moment he boarded the tube train at King's Cross. A couple of the fellow passengers were engrossed reading the morning papers and he hoped they wouldn't read the appeal at the same time as he sat opposite them. The only slight good fortune was that today was Saturday, the tubes much quieter, not the usual commuter traffic, more tourists and family day trippers who did not seem to give him a second glance.

At Victoria Coach Station, he bought a single ticket to Heathrow. Again, he kept his head down to reduce any chance of recognition. It was a pity the Jubilee Line that was under construction had yet to be opened; so near yet so far. As the coach made its way down the M4, he kept wondering if or when it might be stopped.

On arrival, he collected his case from the coach luggage hold and made his way through the departures entrance, stopping to look for the check-in desk number. He'd booked the flights through Qantas, but before making his way to the appropriate check-in and joining the queue, he wanted to check his appearance. But which toilet? He waited to see which one was least busy before finally darting into the gents and diving into a cubicle. Several times he heard the door open and footsteps come and go. Eventually, deciding there was no one else in there he opened the cubicle door and checked his face in the mirror over the sinks. It looked convincing. Just then, the door opened again. He put his head down and scampered out, sure the man who had come in was staring at his back.

He quickly made his way to the check-in desks and joined the queue. His pulse rose the closer he got to the front. Images of the check-in woman asking him to wait a moment, flashed through his mind. Next, some bloke in a smart suit would appear and ask him to accompany him. With two people in front of him, he cleared those thoughts and prepared himself to present his ticket and passport. At last it was his turn.

"Good morning," the woman behind the desk greeted.

He merely nodded and passed over his ticket and passport and waited as she studied both.

She looked up at him again. "Luggage?" she asked.

Nervously, he bent down to put his suitcase on the belt beside her desk.

"Just the one?"

He nodded, aware she was studying him.

Another look at the passport then she asked, "Any preference on seats? Smoking, non-smoking?"

He merely shook his head and waved a hand to his throat as if indicating a lost voice.

"I'll put you in non-smoking," she said and waited for the baggage receipt to print out. When it did, she stuck the receipt on his passport and printed out the boarding pass. With a final look at him, she passed over the documents. "Have a pleasant trip," she said.

He waved a hand in acknowledgement then felt relief as he heard her speak to the passenger who was behind him in the queue. He hurried away towards the next hurdle.

*   *   *

"Right," Sanderson said, "I'll get the Met to concentrate their inquiries around the King's Cross area."

Barton and Cyril had entered the DCI's office with the latest update on progress. "He could just as easily have got on a train anywhere," Barton countered.

"I know, but as this is the last known location, we need to start there."

"As someone once said, 'Follow the money'," Cyril put in.

Sanderson stood up, stretched and cracked his back. It was early afternoon and he'd been sitting at his desk for hours. "How are the team getting on talking to railway stations, bus stations and airports?" he asked.

"All on the case," Barton replied. "I sometimes think their phones are glued to their ears."

"Can't knock the enthusiasm," Cyril said.

Sanderson walked around his desk, trying to think of something, anything that might get them further forward. "No activity on his current account?"

Barton had been enquiring into Bolton's finances. "Not a lot left in it. He seemed to withdraw cash on a regular basis. Salary in every month but, as he lived on the sites, he'd got no significant outgoings. No mortgage payments or insurance policies."

"So he might have had some ready cash as well as what he withdrew from the building society?" Sanderson thought aloud.

"What about friends?" Barton wondered. "He must have had some."

"Sam suggested that someone on his degree course might still be in contact with him?" Cyril put in.

"Good idea," Sanderson said. "Can you get him to look into that?"

"No doubt he'll give it a go, but it's Saturday and trying to get hold of someone at the university might be a bit optimistic."

Sanderson looked at his watch. "Okay, let's keep at it and we'll catch up at four."

*   *   *

The process had been smoother than he'd anticipated and he was glad to be on his way, free of luggage and in possession of his boarding pass. Next step, immigration. That was his big worry. Through that and he could relax for a little, perhaps enjoy his last pint on British soil for some while. He pulled the scarf up around his neck, knowing the Adam's apple was always a giveaway. The officer in the booth seemed to study his passport longer than he thought he should. He hoped he didn't look guilty. Finally, the man in the uniform looked up at him and handed the passport back, face totally expressionless.

He breathed a sigh of relief as he strode along the corridor towards the departures lounge. A check of his watch showed he had a good two hours before take-off.

Time for something to eat and maybe a couple of pints. What the hell was he thinking? If he was to carry this off, the last thing he should do would be to sit in a bar like some … well some bloke and scoff pints of beer. No, a glass of white wine would be it. Plenty of time to down some beers when his journey was over.

Relaxing in one of the bars, he allowed himself time to consider all the tidying up he'd done. He tried to think if he'd left any clues as to his whereabouts and his plans. He'd spent last night clearing all his surplus personal possessions from the caravan. There was nothing in his office to lead anyone to where he was going. He had the letter from Barry along with his local Bangkok address in his pocket. Barry wouldn't have suggested he visit if he didn't want him to come, he was that kind of friend. He'd get a surprise, that was for sure. His qualifications should stand him in good stead and, from what Barry had said, should attract a decent salary, especially with the low cost of living. Thinking about it now, it was a wonder it had taken him so long to make the move.

But his thoughts returned to the catalyst for his decision. In fact, catalysts, plural. He was worried about his behaviour and what he'd done. He regretted the implications for the victims and their families. Would he have ever taken the decision to leave the UK if it hadn't been for Peter's accident? Oh, God, poor Peter. He was a decent bloke. He'd learned a lot from him in the time they'd worked together, and he'd given him quite a free reign with his car. But that, after all, had been what gave him the opportunity to do what he'd done. If he hadn't had access to a vehicle then … Well, no sense in wondering about that. Now, he had a new life to look forward to. And he'd change, he was determined to do that. And from what Barry said, the women out there were absolutely to die for.

The announcement came over the tannoy, snapping him back to the here and now. Passengers for his flight should proceed to the gate. This was it then. Time to go.

*   *   *

The team were assembled for the four o'clock briefing. Once again, DCS Viney accompanied DCI Sanderson. They ran through the various lines of inquiry being pursued. Apart from the spot by the ticket collector at Liverpool Street station on Thursday night, no further sightings had been reported. No further transactions had been made from Bolton's bank account and Met officers were concentrating on the myriad of cheap hotels around the King's Cross area. Bolton hadn't been spotted at any of the capitals' termini or coach stations.

Gatwick and Heathrow had been contacted, as well as the small developing holiday airport at Stansted in Essex. So far, there was no news.

"One other thing to report, sir," Cyril said. "Forensics have matched hair from the sink in Bolton's caravan with those retrieved from under the fingernails of both Sharon Williams and Ruby Clarke."

"So he's definitely our man," Viney said through gritted teeth. "We need to capture this individual as soon as we can." He punched his palm to reinforce the point. "Keep me informed, any time, day or night, Martin," he said to Sanderson before leaving the room.

Sanderson ran a hand through his hair. Cyril thought he looked strained.

"I got the Manchester lads to check out his last known address up there," he announced. "As you'd expect, it was a typical student flat in a Victorian house. Nobody currently living there could remember him. Not surprising really. The turnover must be huge." He turned towards Woodbridge. "Sam, you suggested trying to see if Bolton was still in contact with any course mates. How did you get on?"

"I rang the university but there was no one there to speak to," Woodbridge responded. "Looks like I'll have to wait until Monday to be able to speak to anyone."

Woodbridge jotted down a note on his pad.

"Well, we've just got to keep at it," Sanderson concluded. "Anybody discovers anything, let us all know." With that comment he also left the room.

*   *   *

The attractive young woman on the departure gate gave him a smile as she handed him back the passport and boarding card. He'd risked using the women's toilet near the gates to subtly touch up the make-up. He could see no signs of any stubble to his cheeks; the wet shave had been well worth the money. Just a hint of mascara, a little bit of concealer and a touch of lipstick did the trick. Down the corridor to the waiting jet, his excitement grew. Finally, he removed his jacket and sat down in his seat and fixed the seat belt. A glance of his watch told him it was about fifteen minutes to take-off and he'd be away and who knew when, if ever, he'd be back.

68
Sunday 27th March 1977

It had been an arduous journey. They'd first touched down in Frankfurt before heading on to refuel in Bahrain. Finally, after almost twenty-four hours in the seat, he arrived in Bangkok. As the plane taxied towards the arrival gate, he rubbed a hand over his chin. He could feel the sandpaper effect of stubble. From Emma's old handbag, he produced a mirror and some concealer and applied the cream. Next, a freshen up of lipstick and a fluff up of his hair. He had to carry this one off. He'd come so far, he couldn't fail now.

In the Arrivals Hall, the place was heaving. A number of flights had landed within a short period of time. Before joining one of the queues for immigration, he thought he might have a chance to prepare himself. The stewardesses on the plane had served him his meals and drinks without any questioning looks. But now, fiddling nervously with the scarf around his neck which had served him well so far, he wondered what his next move should be. A couple of his fellow travellers who looked as if they'd been through this process before stood nearby. He noticed the passports they were holding in their hands, German possibly. He approached one and gestured towards their passport, holding out his own along with his boarding pass. Feigning the lost voice again he nodded towards the queues. Fortunately, the International language of signs and gestures helped him to be understood. No, they only needed to see the passport through Immigration they told him. That crystallised his next move. He'd been uncomfortable for too long.

In one of the toilets alongside the Immigration Hall, he went into a cubicle and removed the scarf, grabbed some tissue and wiped the make-up and lipstick from his face. Next he took off his shirt to remove the bra he'd been wearing along with the socks he'd used to alter his body shape. They wouldn't be needed any longer. To complete, he left the cubicle and washed his face and hands over a sink before drying them on the roller towel. A final look at the result in the mirror and he was satisfied. Finally, he dug out his own passport from the bag he'd brought with him and walked back out into the main hall to join one of the long queues.

He was in line with a variety of nationalities from the numerous flights that had recently landed at the airport, some locals but mostly tourists. It was a slow process but, finally he was almost at the counter. With only one traveller in front of him, he took a few deep, steady breaths in an attempt to calm his nerves.

At last, it was his turn and he presented his passport to the officer.

"Mr Bolton?" the man asked, his English heavy with accent.

"That's right." He coughed and nodded.

"You here for holiday?"

Again another nod.

Finally, after a nervous wait that seemed like minutes but could only have been a few seconds, the man stamped the passport and held it out.

Bolton took it back and walked past the Immigration desks, relief flooding over him. Next stop the baggage hall to collect his suitcase. While he waited for the carousel to deliver his suitcase, he studied some of the information displayed on various boards spread around the hall. The most interesting for him was a city map. By the time the carousel started to deliver the luggage from his flight, he had a reasonable grasp of the local geography. After another long wait where he wondered if his case had ever been loaded back in Heathrow, or if it had stayed on the plane to Sydney, he spotted it making its way round.

Out through the doors, the heat hit him like a sledgehammer. It was certainly more pleasant than Essex in March. A taxi driver agreed to take him to the address he had for his friend Barry and they set off towards the busy streets of the city.

69
Monday 28th March 1977

Sunday had passed with no progress. Hopes were higher for something to emerge on Monday. The team were back in, refreshed and determined to find something that would lead to the capture of Dennis Bolton.

Woodbridge was on the phone to the course administrator at UMIST in Manchester where Bolton had studied. Two students from his year had gone on to take their Masters and PhDs. One was now a member of the teaching staff. He should be free by ten-thirty the administrator told him, and he would make sure he would call Woodbridge as soon as possible.

"Don't forget we're giving the DI a hand to move after work tonight, Sam," Cyril said as he passed by the desk on his way to his own desk. Woodbridge gave him the thumbs up. Before Cyril could sit down, Sanderson entered with Barton.

"I've just heard from the Met," Sanderson announced. "A receptionist at one of those seedy hotels near King's Cross identified our man as having checked in with them late on Thursday night and paid for a room for two nights. Paid in cash."

"So do we have any idea where he's moved to?" Cyril asked.

"They're trawling the nearby streets with the photograph the BBC sent us from that news report," Barton explained.

"We need to redouble our efforts to find out where he went when he checked out on Saturday morning," Sanderson instructed.

"The team are onto all the stations, airports and ferry ports," Barton confirmed.

"If you hear anything, anything at all, let me know straight away. I need to update the DCS." With that, Sanderson departed.

An hour or so later, Woodbridge received a call from Manchester. When he'd finished, he walked over to Cyril's desk.

"That was a guy who'd been on the same degree course as Bolton. Reckoned Bolton was a bit of a loner and lived with his twin sister," he reported. "He said they were close and they'd been orphaned a few years before when their parents were killed in a motorcycle accident. She worked in a department store and also behind a few bars when they lived there." He checked his notes. "He remembered the bloke he was closest to was Barry McGowan. They seemed to be matey all through the course. He thinks Barry was from Ireland somewhere but couldn't say exactly where. The guy I spoke to is still in contact with another man from the course and he gave me his number so I'll speak to him next."

"That's useful, Sam." Cyril got to his feet. "Let's take this to the DI and see what we can ascertain."

In Barton's office, Cyril, Woodbridge and Barton sat around his desk after Woodbridge had reiterated the conversation he'd had with Bolton's old cohort.

"Well that gives us some new avenues to explore," Barton said. "First, see if we can track down this Barry McGowan. Bolton could have picked up a train from Euston to Holyhead and got the ferry over to Dublin. He'd need his passport for that."

"What about his twin, sir?" Woodbridge suggested. "That's the first time we've heard of her."

"You're right, Sam," Cyril agreed. "We need to try and locate her. If they were as close as your Manchester contact suggests, he may well try and go to her."

"Strange how she doesn't appear as next of kin on his personnel file, though," Barton added. "Okay, so Sam, you try the Irish ports; could be Holyhead, or possibly Stranraer or even ... oh, where's that bloody place in Wales?"

"Fishguard," Cyril said.

"Yes, all of those. And Sam, there's that other course mate you've got the number of too. Cyril, see what you can find out about the sister."

"I've got an old friend who works in the PRO, Public Records Office," Cyril explained. "I'll get on to him."

*   *   *

Barry had the surprise of his life the evening before when he opened his apartment door to his old university mate. "I hope it's okay," Bolton had said.

McGowan's face was a picture of shock and surprise. "Christ! How did you get here?"

"Flew in this afternoon."

McGowan gave his friend a bug hug as he welcomed his old friend into the apartment he rented. They talked for a long time about their days in Manchester and how their careers had developed; all accompanied by plenty of Singha, the local beer.

This morning, McGowan had gone off to work leaving his keys and promising to put the word out that Bolton was in the country and looking for work. It was gone ten-thirty before Bolton woke, the flight having taken its toll.

He walked to the window and looked down on a bustling street full of strange shops and bars. Yes, he thought to himself, he was really going to enjoy this.

Barry spoke of a 'fixer', a go-between that the company he worked for uses to ease the mechanics of employment visas and other official red tape. He was assured the paperwork wouldn't be a problem for this man. There was plenty of work available for someone as well-qualified as Bolton. It might take a few days but Barry was confident he could get him a start. In the meantime, all Dennis had to do was enjoy himself and acclimatise himself to his new way of life.

*   *   *

316

"That's really interesting," Woodbridge was saying into his phone. "Thanks very much for that." A pause. "No, nothing to worry about, just general enquiries. Thanks again." He replaced the receiver and looked at his notepad for a second or two. He stood and made his way over to Cyril's desk, notebook in hand.

"I've just spoken to the other bloke that was on the degree course with Bolton," he said.

Cyril looked up and saw the frown. "Go on," he encouraged, leaning back in his seat.

"He recounted a story of an incident one night between Bolton and some girl."

"Take a seat, Sam. I get the impression this could be significant."

Woodbridge pulled up a spare chair from an adjacent desk and sat down opposite his DS. "They were at some party, Bolton, this bloke and a few others. There had been some banter previously about Bolton's ability to … well, as he put it, 'get it up'." Woodbridge paused a moment but Cyril made no comment, keen to allow him to tell the story in his own time. "Apparently, they set Bolton up with this girl who had a reputation for being … what did he say, game for a challenge and a 'bit of a goer'. Obviously, drink was involved but after a bit, Bolton and this girl sloped off to a bedroom. A little bit later, they heard a big commotion. At first they thought it was just the pair of them having a bit of a raucous time but as it went on they became concerned, so this bloke…" Woodbridge glanced at his notes. "Brian Stevens, his name is, he decided to investigate. He walked in on Bolton and the girl. Bolton seemed a bit angry and jumped up from the bed. She had her hand to her throat and was coughing. Bolton pulled up his jeans and dashed past Brian and hurried out. She was very upset and frightened. Only later did she tell him she thought he had tried to strangle her."

Cyril opened his mouth as if to say something but didn't. After a second or two, he finally did. "Did he give any reason? Did he speak to Bolton afterwards?"

"She told Brian that she thought it was her fault. She'd led him on. She put it down to the alcohol but he couldn't rise to the occasion and she'd made a gesture to him."

"What sort of gesture?"

"Like this." Woodbridge bent his forefinger and wiggled it.

"She hardly invited him to strangle her though," Cyril stated.

"Bolton apparently, said she was a tease and asking for it. She'd pissed him off but he never spoke about it again. Brian tended to avoid him after that. He always thought him a bit weird."

"And what about the girl? Did you get a name?"

"Stevens couldn't remember. Didn't know her that well. Just someone he came across for a while."

Cyril slowly nodded. "So he'd got form," he said.

*   *   *

At just after half-past-five, Cyril and Woodbridge turned up outside Barton's flat near the town centre in Clacton. Parked outside was a Ford Transit, the back doors open. The man himself was carrying a cardboard box down the path.

"Thanks gents," Barton greeted. "There's more inside."

Cyril and Woodbridge made their way indoors and each grabbed a box and followed the DI's steps to the van. Fortunately, the property was rented furnished so at least they didn't face the prospect of struggling with a bed or a wardrobe. The van was loaded fairly quickly and, Barton driving, Cyril and Woodbridge followed in Cyril's car.

"Not a lot to show for a lifetime, so far, skip," Woodbridge remarked as they pulled away from the kerb.

"No, not really," Cyril responded. "I suppose that's what happens when you've been through a divorce and you're the guilty party."

"I'd heard."

Cyril was quiet for a moment before he remarked, "I dread to think how much I have if I ever had to move."

"You might though. You and Cathy could pool resources." Woodbridge made the remarks without thinking. "Sorry, skip, none of my business," he added.

Cyril gave a chuckle. "Don't worry, Sam. I know that's what some people are thinking." He glanced over at his companion. "We're just taking things easy."

No more was said until they drew to a halt behind Barton's borrowed van outside the semi-detached house the DI had rented.

The three of them made light work unloading the van; within twenty minutes, all the boxes were inside. Barton showed Cyril and Woodbridge around his new abode.

"Furniture looks good," Cyril said.

"Yeah, not bad. It'll do while I'm here." Barton pulled out his cigarettes and lit up.

"Thinking of moving on already?"

"I think I need to buy, Cyril. Renting's just dead money."

Cyril patted his shoulder. "Glad to hear a bit of sense at last."

Before Barton could reply, the doorbell rang and he went to answer.

Standing on the step was the attractive blonde he'd seen going in next door when he came to view the place.

"Hi," she said, a big smile on her face and a covered plate in her hands. "I thought I'd just say hello to my new neighbour. You are the new neighbour, aren't you?"

"Er … well, yes I am," Barton stumbled. "Er, John, John Barton." He held out a hand then immediately withdrew it. "Sorry."

"Donna, Donna Wilkins. I brought you a cake to say welcome." She held up the plate.

"Come in. Come in," Barton said, standing aside. "I'll dig out the kettle and tea bags. You'll join us, won't you?"

"Okay," she said and stepped inside.

319

In the living room, Cyril gave a knowing glance to Woodbridge as they both overheard the conversation on the doorstep.

Donna appeared, still holding the cake, Barton just behind.

"These are my colleagues who've just come to give me a hand to move in. Cyril and Sam," he said in turn. "Donna's brought me a welcome cake. Teas all round?" Cyril and Woodbridge said they would. "Donna? How do you like it?" he asked, prompting a giggle from the visitor.

"Just milk please," she said.

Barton disappeared with the plate into the kitchen.

"So, Donna," Cyril said. "You live next door?"

"That's right. I've been there for the past four years, ever since my husband died."

"Oh, so you're widowed? I'm sorry to hear that," Cyril said. "He must have been young?"

The smile fell from her face. "He was just thirty," she said. "A brain tumour."

"That's tough."

"But I'm coping. I have my job and my parents live in Colchester, so …"

"You'll be glad to have a new neighbour?" Woodbridge asked, prompting a scowl from Cyril.

Donna didn't seem to mind. "Just good to have someone here a bit more pleasant than the last. He was a miserable old sod. Sorry, didn't mean any offence."

Woodbridge gave a chuckle as Barton entered with mugs, two in each hand. "Donna's just telling us about your predecessor," he said.

"Oh yes. I'll just fetch the cake, by the way."

"I suppose he wasn't that bad but he was probably seventy and never said a word to me in all the time he was here." She took a sip of her tea.

"Here we go," Barton said, this time carrying a tray with four plates, each with a slice of cake. "This looks delicious. Did you bake it yourself?"

"I can't lie," she said. "My mum did and I thought it would be something nice to offer you."

Barton took a bite of the sponge. "Very good," he said.

"So what do you do … John?" Donna asked.

"I'm, er, I work for the police," he replied.

"Oh, you're a policeman. Does that mean you have to wear a uniform?"

Cyril stifled a laugh and Woodbridge turned away.

"Not now," Barton said, aware of the amusement the conversation was giving his colleagues. "I'm a detective."

"I'll bet that's interesting," she said.

"It has its moments."

Cyril stood at that point having finished his cake. "Well. We'd best be off now John. Come on, Sam. And thanks for the delicious cake, Donna."

"I'd best be getting back too," the woman said, getting to her feet the same time as Woodbridge.

"Oh, okay." Barton stood up, looking slightly disappointed. "Well thanks for the help lads," he said to his colleagues. "And thanks for the welcome, Donna. Hopefully, see you again."

She smiled at him as they made their way to the front door. "Oh, I'm sure of it," she said.

As Cyril drove Sam back into town, he couldn't help remarking, "I'm sure of it too."

70
Tuesday 29th March 1977

Woodbridge was sifting through copies of flight manifests from Heathrow Airport when he suddenly stopped and looked across at Cyril.

Cyril, for his part had been studying information his friend at the Public Records Office had provided. He became aware of Woodbridge staring at him. "Something wrong, Sam?" he asked.

"I don't know, skip. I'm just looking through the lists of passengers who left on flights on Saturday …"

"Heathrow?"

"Yes. I've come across this entry here." He stood and walked over to Cyril's desk with a sheaf of paper in his hand. Placing the relevant sheet in front of Cyril, he pointed to the entry that had attracted his attention.

Cyril looked at it then up at Woodbridge. "Good God," he said, before shuffling through some pages on his desk. Picking up the sheet from his desk and the manifests Woodbridge had brought, he got to his feet. "Let's see the DI," he said, making his way to Barton's office.

Barton was sitting behind his desk, telephone to his ear and pencil poised writing notes, when Cyril and Woodbridge knocked on the door. He looked up at the pair and excitedly waved them in.

"That's great, thanks for that," he said as he ended the call and picked up the cigarette that had been smouldering in the ashtray on his desk.

"That was the Met," Barton said. "Apparently, a man answering Bolton's description bought a flight ticket in a travel agent's near the hotel he was staying."

Cyril held up a hand. "And we've got something too," he said.

"Go on then," the DI responded, sucking hard on the white stick. "What have you got?"

Cyril indicated Woodbridge go first.

"I've been checking the passenger lists for flights that left Heathrow Airport," he began. "And I came across this." He placed a sheet of paper on Barton's desk. "The 17:30 flight to Sydney."

Barton gave a smile. "He didn't piss off to Australia."

"Boarding as far as Bangkok is someone called Emma Bolton," Woodbridge stated.

"That's what the Met found out. He bought a ticket in that name. Is she a relation?" Barton queried.

"You could say that," Cyril joined in. "Dennis Bolton had a twin sister, Emma, obviously born on 27th April 1951, same as him."

"That's what it says here," Woodbridge agreed.

"Except ..." Cyril held up a finger. "Emma died of meningitis on October 16th 1973."

Woodbridge looked across at Cyril, obviously surprised at what he had just been told and silently mouthed, 'What?'

Barton leaned back, a knowing expression on his face. "He used his passport as ID in the building society ..."

"But he obviously kept his sister's and used that to travel," Cyril added.

Barton exhaled sharply. "They must have looked alike to get away with it."

"But most importantly, we have no extradition agreement with Thailand." Barton gave a sigh. "If he had travelled on to Australia, we could have had him arrested."

71
Wednesday 30th March 1977

Cyril adjusted the rear view mirror to see the state of the knot in his black tie before returning it to its original position

"It looks fine, Cyril," Cathy said.

She was sitting alongside him in a smart black coat covering a white blouse and black skirt. He'd just drawn to a halt in the car park of Colchester Crematorium a couple of miles south of the town on Mersea Road.

"I know," he said. "Only it's just …"

She looked at him. "Is this …?"

He was looking down to his lap. "Yes. This is the first funeral I've attended since … since Maureen."

She squeezed his arm.

He looked up. "Thanks," he said.

The car park was busy and he recognised a few faces from the past as well as many of his colleagues. As they stepped from the car, Cathy saw Shirley Crabtree emerge from a car two bays away. Shirley waved across and approached her.

"Thanks for letting me know," Shirley said. "I so want to pay my respects."

"No problem." Cathy gave her a big smile.

"You two go on ahead," Cyril said. "I'll be fine."

He watched the two women link arms as they made their way slowly towards the chapel. Cyril buttoned up his overcoat and locked the car before following on behind. Although it was a bright sunny day, a cold northerly wind swept across the crematorium grounds. He acknowledged a lot of old faces loitering around the entrance as they waited for the hearse to arrive. The Assistant Chief Constable looked resplendent in his full dress uniform and Cyril was pleased the man had taken the trouble to attend for the ex-DCI. He was standing next to Martin Sanderson and John Barton. Cyril joined his colleagues.

"Good turnout," Cyril commented.

"A few faces too," Barton agreed, noticing Spider lurking behind a few mourners. Surprising really, when so many known toe rags that Tinker had put away spoke in derisive terms of the man, proclaiming a stitch up, but still turning up to pay their respects. Either that or they were here to make sure he'd really gone.

The first funeral car pulled up and the three detectives acknowledged Julia, Neil and his wife as they stepped from the vehicle. Next, the hearse slowly drew to a halt and the undertaker and pall bearers appeared, preparing to remove the coffin from the back.

Over the top of the car, Cyril scanned the mourners. And then something else caught his eye. "Excuse me a minute," he whispered to Barton before making his way around the outside of the knot of people looking on.

A car had pulled to a halt in a parking bay about fifty yards away, two figures sat inside. Cyril approached and knocked on the front passenger window. The window was dropped half way. "I hope you're not going to create any drama, Mr Brookes?" he said.

"Just looking," Brookes responded.

As usual his partner in crime DS Chapple sat impassively in the driver's seat.

"These occasions are for family and friends," Cyril went on. "And you fall into neither category so I'd suggest you just go."

Brookes eyes narrowed. "Who the fuck do you think you are, DS Claydon?"

Cyril gave a sardonic smile. "I'm someone who knows what happened back in 1961. And I'm also someone who can approach the Assistant Chief Constable over there." Cyril indicated the funeral party, by now making their way into the chapel. "And I have access to your victim. You remember her?"

Brookes face looked like thunder. "I've seen what I came for," he said then turned to his DS driver. "Let's go."

Chapple started the engine and drove slowly away.

Cyril watched them depart, hoping there had been no chance of Brookes recognising Shirley. He was sure he hadn't seen the last of Brookes, but this was a situation he couldn't shy away from. He hurried back to join the others.

The service was enhanced by the warm words given by the ACC who had apparently trained with Jack Tinker. Cyril thought his sentiments genuine. Another tribute was offered by DCS Viney. Finally, after the curtains closed for the committal and the last prayers were said, Julia, Neil and his wife stood beside the vicar by the side exit and accepted the condolences of the mourners as they left.

Outside, Cyril joined the ACC, Sanderson and Barton who were standing together. DCS Viney was engaged in conversation with the family.

"So," the ACC said, "You know who was responsible but, unless he returns, you can't make an arrest?"

"That's just about it, sir," Sanderson replied.

"Bugger. All we can do is keep a watch on all the ports and airports."

"We've got that in place."

"Well, we'll wind down the enquiry on that basis then," the ACC said. "I'll just have a word with Julia before I go."

"So that's it?" Barton queried.

"Nothing else we can do, Dick," Sanderson said.

Cyril walked over to Cathy and Shirley who seemed to have moist eyes. "I'm glad I came," Shirley said. "And got the chance to say goodbye. I'll never forget what he did for me."

Cathy patted her arm. "I'm glad too," she said. "Can we give you a lift?"

"Thanks, but I've got my car here. I need to get back to work."

Cyril and Cathy said goodbye to Shirley then walked towards Cyril's car. "Where did you disappear off to just as the coffin was being brought in?" she asked.

"Just a little bit of what I thought was unfinished business. Come on, let's get back."

72
Three months later

Cyril walked into Barton's office, a mug of coffee in one hand and one of tea in the other. He placed the coffee on the DI's desk and sat in the seat opposite him. "Here you are," he said.

"Thanks, Cyril. Have a piece of cake." Barton opened a drawer and pulled out a plastic box.

"The delectable Donna again?" Cyril asked, a broad grin cracking his face.

"One of her own this time, and very good it is too." The DI picked up the packet of Peter Stuyvesant cigarettes from his desk.

Cyril lifted a piece of cake from the box and took a bite. "Not bad. You'll have to cultivate that relationship, you know."

"That's one phrase to describe it," Barton commented as he lit his cigarette. "You know she has lovely legs."

"If you say so." Cyril took a drink of his tea.

The two men were silent for a few seconds as Cyril ate the rest of his cake and Barton puffed his cigarette.

"Do you know what really sticks in my throat, Cyril," Barton finally said.

"What's that?"

The DI leaned forward. "The bastard's got away with it."

"Bolton, you mean?"

"Absolutely. It's just like Ronnie Biggs."

"The Great Train Robber?"

Barton nodded. "Living it up in Rio. No extradition arrangements." He flicked ash into the tray on his desk. "For Brazil, read Thailand." He gave a sigh. "We've issued an International Arrest Warrant but, so far, nothing."

"Have we tried to make contact with the Thai authorities?"

"No point. We can only get him if he returns or visits somewhere we *do* have an agreement."

Cyril took out his pipe, packed it and lit up as Barton sat thinking.

"So the cases are officially shelved." Barton said.

"Shelved but never closed," Cyril elaborated.

Barton looked at his watch. "Thailand is something like seven hours ahead." He took a last drag and stubbed his cigarette out in the ashtray. "I can just imagine him now, tanning himself on a beach somewhere ... or living it up in some sex bar on an evening with lots of nubile women."

"We will get him," Cyril said. "Maybe not this year or even next. But we will get him."

*   *   *

Chuachan was twenty-two. She had come to Bangkok when she was seventeen to earn money for her mother and her younger siblings, a brother and two sisters. At first, she helped out in a restaurant, but the pay was low. A girl she met introduced her to a bar owner who offered her a job hostessing. She knew the sort of work she'd be required to do, she'd been around the bars near the restaurant. It was typically foreign tourists, mostly middle-aged Americans but one or two younger men in the past couple of years. The pay was good and, if they were drunk, it was easy pickings. The money she sent back every week to her family was vital.

She had thought the Englishman would be fun. He had been, at first. They had shared a few drinks and a few laughs for an hour or so in a couple of bars in the streets below. She knew what was expected; or she thought she knew. He'd accepted her invitation to come back with her to the room she rented.

She never knew what she'd said to turn things sour but events took a dramatic turn in the early hours. The effects on her family would be devastating.

Now, in a top floor room above a bar on a side street in Bangkok's Patpong district a young woman lay on a bed. Her short dress was up around her waist and her underwear had been removed. Her sightless eyes stared at the ceiling. It would be morning before she would be discovered.

THE   END

Did you enjoy DISTRESSED?

Then please review on Amazon, Goodreads etc.

Have you read more in the series?

See the next few pages …

The Tendring Series

Book 1 DISPOSAL

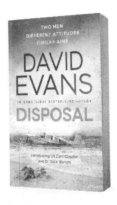

August 1976 and it seems as though the long hot summer will never end. Early morning at Clacton on the north Essex coast, a light aircraft takes off from the airstrip but struggles for height and crashes into the sea. First on the scene, Sgt Cyril Claydon pulls the pilot's body from the wreckage. But something else catches his eye. A bulky package wrapped in black plastic is on the passenger seat. Returning to investigate, he makes a grim discovery – another body. And so begins a series of events that puts him and others in danger as he is drawn into the investigation, having to work alongside DI 'Dick' Barton, a man with totally alien attitudes.
Can they work together?

Available through Amazon:

Getbook.at/Disposal

By the same author …

The Wakefield Series

Book 1   TROPHIES

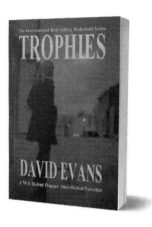

By the turn of the millennium, memories had dulled. But the discovery of a trophy case at the scene of a murder leads to the realisation that a series of attacks on women over the previous twenty years had gone unconnected. DI Colin Strong is convinced there is also a link with one other notorious unsolved crime. His best friend from schooldays, journalist Bob Souter, has returned to Yorkshire and begins to probe. Working separately and together in an awkward alliance, they seek the answers.

Available through Amazon:

Getbook.at/Trophies

Book 2 TORMENT

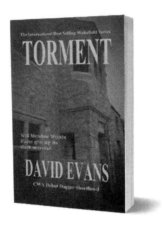

A message left in error on a young woman's answerphone is the catalyst for uncovering some dark deeds. Three young women are missing; luxury cars are being stolen; and just what did happen to two young schoolgirls, missing since the 1980's?

DI Colin Strong and journalist Bob Souter are drawn into murky and dangerous worlds

Available through Amazon:

Getbook.at/Torment

Book 3   TALISMAN

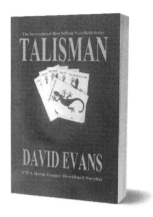

A man's body found naked and shackled to a frame in a house fire; a body lying undiscovered in a bath for over a year; massive European funding for a controversial construction project. Is there a link between the bodies and the business deal? And what exactly is the Talisman Club?
In the third instalment of the Wakefield series, DI Colin Strong and best friend, journalist Bob Souter must work together to bring the guilty to justice before time runs out.

Available through Amazon:

Getbook.at/Talisman

Book 4   TAINTED

A botched attempt to extort money has tragic consequences. An embarrassing DNA match to an unsolved rape and murder twenty years before means DI Colin Strong has to use his best diplomatic tactics.

Simultaneously, journalist Bob Souter is tasked with writing about that same case to re-focus public attention. Will the newspaper's actions help or hinder the police?

Meanwhile, Strong's team has two separate murder enquiries to run.

With their friendship under duress, will Souter and Strong be able to work together?

Available through Amazon:

Getbook.at/Tainted-DavidEvans

Printed in Great Britain
by Amazon